A PLACE CALLED
BROOKLYN

A PLACE CALLED
BROOKLYN

LIMITED EDITION

ORIGINAL MANUSCRIPT BY:
FRANK CORNACCHIULO

REVISED MANUSCRIPT AND DESIGNED BY:
JOE DEL BROCCOLO

TABLE OF CONTENTS

DEDICATION

I dedicate this book, A Place Called Brooklyn, to all our readers who, like my collaborator Joe and I, learned life-lessons in the streets of Brooklyn. We ventured out every day to face life. This socialization process helped us acquire life-long experiences still in use to this day. Experiences that were, in retrospect, those experiences that helped us to make important decisions throughout our adult life.

To my wife Frances Claire: for her support and unconditional love, throughout this endeavor. My Mother Francesca, my Father Francesco, and my sister Isabella, who instilled in me love of family and that family always comes first. I would be remiss if I didn't mention my wife Frances' parents: Anna and Pasquale Arcati, who embraced me with both love and support.

I also dedicate this book to my loving family. The Cornacchiulos': Frank & Lydia, Patrick & Tammy, Daniel & Grace & grandchildren, Patrick, Nicholas, Chloe, Frank, Alexander, Sara, Laila & Alana, Who I encourage to always embrace our family traditions.

-Frank

My dedication is one of gratefulness and love to my wife Ellen, who on her worst day made my life sunshine. To my children: Ellen, who raises me up on her strong shoulders, My parents Olympia and Anthony (Lena and Tony) who always made sure I was never as wonderful as I thought I was, my son Anthony who encouraged me to write as a writer himself and who has worked all his life to better his life and those around him, to my son Mike who by his actions defines humanity at its peak, and my departed son Joseph who like his sister teaches me that life goes on and we put one foot in front of the other.

My grandmother Frances, who as a young girl came to America with no English and a brave heart, enduring and never wavering when someone needed help. And most of all to my beautiful daughter-in-law Courtney Hyde Del Broccolo, Anthony's late wife who gave me two beautiful grandchildren; Darby Shea and Robert Courtney and last but not least, my partner Frank who has made this endeavor one of joy and pleasure.

-Joe

We were compelled to document our Brooklyn childhood experiences for our fellow Brooklynites. It doesn't matter where you're from because we are all cut from the same cloth. Perhaps the adventures and games we played in the streets had different names but it yielded the same memories.

A special salute: to Michele DePalo who introduced us and helped forge a great friendship in collaboration in the joy of this special project

-Frank Cornacchiulo & Joseph Del Broccolo

INTRODUCTION

Growing up in the 1940's and 50's in a place called Brooklyn, the center of our universe was located deep in the section called Red Hook and Bushwick. At Smith-9th, the old IND Subway is grandly elevated as the highest elevated station in both Brooklyn and the city, conforming to old regulations that allow tall-mast ships to navigate the Gowanus Canal. The metal trestles and pillars are constructed of concrete. Like that grand station, so are our memories casts in a concrete never-dying remembrance of what life was like once upon a time.

A generation of very poor children living in Brooklyn, NY post World War II lived in cold water flats. Their immigrant parents arrived here from such places as Ireland, Italy, Germany, Puerto Rico, and were mainly unskilled laborers. They struggled day-to-day to support their families with basic needs and an education with a deep God-abiding focus on hope for the future.

Out of that setting, we would like to take you by the literary hand and revisit some of the experiences that made Bushwick, and Red Hook, in our lives so memorable. Join us as we document and recall eye-witnessed accounts of some of these experiences. Join us as we view street games we played, many of these games self-taught and many others passed along from one generation to the next. Imagine these children not having electronics with perhaps the exception of a portable radio. Many living in cold-water flats or apartments, with or without an indoor toilet. This meant whoever did not have an indoor toilet, used an outhouse: a narrow shack located outside the building without plumbing!

Generally, a flat had two or three rooms, no heat, and no hot water from a sink, no bathtub, maybe a laundry sink, which could double as a bathtub. Some apartments had a coal stove for cooking food and the stove also provided heat. The children lived with their parents, grandparents and in some cases along with aunts and uncles. These children would wake up every morning, to a meager breakfast and either sent off to school or let out of their home to fend for themselves. But the rule was: they were expected to return home for dinner and be on time.

These stories are not meant to chronicle pain and suffering that a generation endured, but to document some the experiences growing up on the streets of the densely- populated Brooklyn. Their ingenuity bested boredom through street games and spontaneous adventures. Games like tag, buck/buck, hide & go seek, one and over, ring-a-leavee-o, and others that did not require a ball, rope, skates, bat, baseball cards, marbles, straws etc occupied our time. And, we can add to this mix various adventure games that involved fireworks, chalk, balloons, lumber, sticks, yo-yos, straws, also discarded items (Skates, Gallon Glass Jars, Cans, Carriages, etc.) that could be recycled into a game or new object. These stories feature 'Pepino' a nine-year-old Italian American kid, who lives with his mother, father and teenage sister in the Red Hook neighborhood of Brooklyn New York during a summer right after World War II, and told through his eyes.

Francesco & Friends Taking a Break

If you lived in Red Hook after the war, the families and particularly the single men who lived in the area were primarily blue collar day laborers and dock workers also known as longshoremen. It is here that I started my street education that served me all my life.

Chapter 1

A Place Called Brooklyn-Red Hook Stories

It is a hot and steamy night, the humidity blankets Red Hook, and since I can't sleep because of the 'freaken' heat I'm just lying here wet from head to toe thinking of who knows what.

My body naturally tries to help me cool off with perspiration that is not doing much good. So now I'm not just hot I'm wet too. I wish that Mom would let me sleep on the fire escape like my teenage friend Roger does who lives directly above me. When I ask her she just yells at me...

"Whata you crazeee, you can falla off anda breaka you neck."

Maybe I should do it anyway. But if she finds me out on the fire escape sleeping my Mom will break my neck anyway. So, I'll just lay here and try to think about how nice and cool Roger must feel.

No matter what I do I just can't sleep from the all too present heat that engulfs my apartment, it's just too damn hot! I'm here

Red Hook Brooklyn Dock Workers.

in the middle of the dining room on a cot that miraculously converts into my part-time bed when the lights go out. I'm thinking I'll just reflect on the good things in my world such as school is out for the summer. It's July and my buddies and I have to get ready for the big 4th of July celebration. After all, I'm the first American born to my family. I just keep thinking about the

fireworks, big explosions, and the smell of gunpowder. What a wonderful feeling, maybe with any kind of luck I may fall asleep with a smile on my face.

But no such luck. My body is running out of hydration as I'm perspiring and I have to refill it or dehydrate. After all, I do not want to disappoint the mosquito vampires who love to suck my blood from my wet hot body. "Sleep, get up, fireworks, sleep, drink water, get up", I tell myself over and over again. I keep telling myself to just get out of bed and get some water from the kitchen sink and then maybe I'll fall asleep.

So, I'm setting the plan in motion. Heading towards the kitchen I keep thinking to myself. "Don't forget to make some noise, but try not to wake everybody up and get some water." Yes, noise is important to let the mice and cockroaches foraging for food know you're on the move. Although water is my goal this hot humid night I also have to remember to rinse the water glass several times so that I do not swallow any roach protein in the process.

Good work! I've made all the right moves without waking everybody up or stepping on a mouse and inadvertently eating a cockroach in my quest for water. So now I'm back in bed, oh sorry, my cot, it's about 2 AM and still not asleep. I keep thinking of all the good stuff and adventure that I planned for tomorrow morning when I hook up with my best friend Pecker. I'm so tired, even with all the heat, sweat, and bugs all over my body, it won't stop my eyes closing and I finally… drift into a sweet, deep sleep.

Chapter 2
Deposit Bottle

I can smell espresso coffee brewing this morning and it is calling me to rise. Generally, around 7 AM it's ready for consumption. My mother would call me "Pepkeenooo" to get out of bed but not this morning since there is no school today, or for the next several months for that matter. I am ready to rise and shine as quickly as possible from my cot to meet up with my friend Pecker. Pecker is my friend's nickname. We all have one and I don't really knew why. It is a neighborhood thing I guess, kids labeling each other with nicknames in order to give a picture of a weird or exaggerated visual description of a person without their birth name.

For the most part, nicknames are not complimentary.

The kids I hang out with sometimes call me "Lollypop Head" or "Keyno". My "Keyno" nickname came about because of my mother's Italian accent. When supper is ready, and everyone in

Mom Calling Pepkeeenooo Home

my family is about to sit at the dinner table, my mother calls out for me to come home. She screams as loud as possible, from our second story window

"PEPKEENOOO!"

This is her attempt to get me to come home for our family dinner as quickly as possible. So my friends who hear my mother screaming out my name will then, in turn, say to me:

"Hey, Keenooo, your mother is calling you".

My Lollypop Head nickname was descriptive because my head is way too large in proportion to my skinny body.

Pecker is a tall skinny kid about 9-years old, with blond kinky hair; he has light skin, with freckles on his face and he sort of walks like a chicken. I think that's why the Pecker nickname suits his appearance and movements. Pecker's last name is Parker and when anyone in our gang is pissed off at him for whatever reason we called him: "Pee Pee". Pecker and I are planning to meet no later than 8:30 AM this morning to seek out an illegal fireworks dealer in some smelly basement or shack on President Street. During the past several months we were collecting glass two cents deposit beer and soda bottles from the longshoremen after they finished their lunch break at Nick's sandwich shop on Columbia Street. There is a lot of competition in collecting these valuable cash refund bottles for all the kids.

If we are lucky on occasion we can snag a five-cent deposit quart beer bottle. No sooner than a grungy hard working dockworker exits the sandwich shop we are all over him begging, dancing, and fooling around to get his attention as our reward for waiting until after he is fished eating his lunch. The dockworker, also known as a longshoreman always owns a big cargo hook hanging from his belt. He must always be careful when sitting on the curb to eat his lunch because the cargo hook has a sharp point and it could stab him in the leg if it isn't turned away from him. Sometimes Pecker and I will split up to cover more territory. We do this and succeed in spite of the heavy competition from the other kids who want to snag these deposit bottles for themselves. After doing battle for several months we managed to squirrel away $18.50 to buy the fireworks we plan to burn and shoot off during the 4th of July celebration. This is going to be a big deal for us to have as much firepower as possible so that we can show up our buddies.

Meanwhile, my mother is making my breakfast that consists of a half a cup of espresso coffee heated with milk and four tablespoons of sugar. We sometimes have some leftover bread with our coffee along with jelly. There are also times during the winemaking season we will dip our bread into some homemade wine for breakfast. After consuming my jolt of caffeine, milk, sugar, and bread my 90-pound body is in overdrive. I'll tell my mother that I am going out to meet Pecker and proceed to bounce and jump down two flights of stairs to hook up with Pecker. Pecker is waiting for me with the loot we have accumulated for our trek toward President Street to seek and find a fireworks dealer. It is going to be a hot day so we are dressed in shorts, T-shirts, and Ked's sneakers.

"Hey, Pecker are you ready to go?"

He"s not giving me much of a response with the exception of a shrug and wave of his hand.

"Okay!"

We are walking north on Columbia Street towards President Street. I am thinking that Pecker most likely did not get much sleep during this heat wave. Pecker lives with his alcoholic father, no mother and he also has to take care of his younger brother. Primarily Italian immigrants settled our neighborhood and we could generally tell the birth country of a kid's parents. But Pecker was a mystery. Pecker did not resemble his brother in any way. We never knew his mother and we all speculated that his Father came from Ireland.

Who cares?

Pecker is one of the peewee gang members. We all seem to have fathers and mothers that would provide us with shelter, food, clothing or whatever. I just think that Pecker has a lot of responsibility for a 9-year-old kid.

The sun is out and the heat wave isn't letting up, as we continue walking toward President Street.

Chapter 3
Looking to Buy Fireworks

Columbia Street, paved with the cobblestones of old Red Hook warns you of the cars and trucks rumbling while approaching from several blocks away. The peddler guides his horse-powered wagon selling fruits and vegetables, calling out to potential customers with a cry for attention. "Yes, I have fresh fruits and vegetables today".

Most windows have to be open because of the hot sultry weather and no air-conditioning. The sound of the peddler's cry and the clop, clop, clop of the horse's huffs announces his arrival and alerts housewives to hurry and buy their daily produce before the sun takes its toll and wilts everything on the wagon. The horse pulling the wagon will leave a residue of urine and manure as it travels along the cobbled stone streets. Combined with the 90-degree temperature, we experience the pungent scent of livestock smack in the middle of Red Hook!

Continuing our journey we pass a large number of condemned three and four-story apartment buildings scheduled for demolition to make way for the construction of the new Brooklyn Battery Tunnel. Even in the daylight, these abandoned buildings looked haunted, the dark empty void that emanates from behind each window intrigues our young imaginations. The security guards are not very diligent and many of the kids in the neighborhood will sneak into these buildings during the day and at times during the night to strip them of copper and lead or anything else they can find to turn into cash. It beats collecting 2-cent bottles. My mother warned me that I better not follow the older boys into these dangerously dilapidated buildings where I could fall several stories and break both legs or even die.

She also says that if by chance I survived the fall I would face the death penalty when the police brought me home, so, either way, I am dead. My real fear is that she would kill me but I am still tempted to one day sneak into one of these buildings and gather whatever valuable materials I can find on the ground floor. I daydream that I will collect a mother load of copper and lead, bring my stuff to the junkyard and walk away with as much as $50.00! I can then buy a new bike to replace the old bike I don't have.

I am in a state of the never-never land, daydreaming of all my loot and what I can do with it.

"Hey, big head what the hell are you thinking of? At this rate, we're never gonna find this guy."

"Okay, okay, I was just thinking of how many ash cans, cherry bombs, whistlers, and firecrackers we could possibly buy."

So he is giving me a look and I know that I better stay focused on our important mission.

Louie Serves The Best Hot Dogs With Onions In Brooklyn.

As we cross Carroll Street we can see the corner of Columbia and President Street where Louie the hot dog guy is setting up shop. Louie boils the best hot dogs in Brooklyn with or without sauerkraut. But his homemade red sauce and spicy onions are the best he has to offer. Louie stacks his homemade onions onto his unbelievable hot dogs and my mouth starts watering just thinking about having one. People come from all over, dock workers, factory workers including their bosses and line up for lunch at his hot dog stand. Louie's customers will order at one time as many as three or four hot dogs with sauce. I will stay hungry just smelling the aroma of Louie's tasty hot dogs.

I keep thinking over and over again, hot dogs or fireworks? Okay, should we get hot dogs or fireworks? But we can't afford to give in to this temptation and waste part of our loot just to stuff our faces with Louie's hot dogs. We saved our money for months and after all, the 4th of July holiday only comes around once a year.

"Hey, Louie!" I am trying to get his attention.

"How many? How many?" asked, Louie.

"No hot dogs today Louie, we're just trying to find the guy who is selling fireworks. Can you point us in the right direction?"

"No way, you're too young to be shooting off fireworks. If I tell you where to go and you blow off one of your hands or lose an eye, your father will come looking for me and smash my head in."

"Come on Louie we're old enough. We saved our money and we've been looking forward to buying and shooting off these fireworks for months now!"

"No way kid, use your money to buy a hot dog or egg cream or just go to the movies. Hopalong Cassidy is playing around the corner at the Happy Hour Theater. I can't help you and even if I could I wouldn't tell you where to buy fireworks."

Strike one: Louie will not help us. So, Pecker and I will lay low walking around President Street looking for teenagers with brown bags. A teenager with a brown paper shopping bag could be a solid clue as to where we should look for our fireworks dealer. I needed Pecker to have a keen eye of an eagle, even though he looks more like a chicken, in order to spot the building where the teenagers are coming from. As I am going over our strategy with Pecker I spot 'Fat ass' Roger walking toward us with an overstuffed brown paper shopping bag, this may or may not be the big break we need to find the fireworks dealer.

Chapter 4
Finding the Fireworks Dealer

Roger is about 15-years old, of average height and a kind of chunky teenager, sporting a large rear end with dark almost black dirty hair, partly hanging while covering his eyes and a black, seemingly penciled in, mustache. Roger lives with his family in the top floor apartment of my building. He is walking on the sidewalk with a cigarette hanging from his mouth. I don't know if he realizes that if a hot ash from the cigarette by chance fell into his shopping bag, he is likely to start a chain reaction by igniting his stash of fireworks and blowing himself up. What a

Cooling Off On Fire Escape

show that would be to see Roger trying to put out the fire and explosions taking place as he is running down the street with his shopping bag all ablaze! On the top floor of our building where Roger lives is always very hot in the summer. Roger and his family try cooling off out on our building's fire escape. I think he's crazy when Roger tells me that he sometimes sneaks out there at night to sleep. It can be dangerous, if he makes a wrong move or turn, he can slip and fall and kill himself. Some nights when it's so hot and I can't sleep, I'm tempted to sneak out there with him. Anyway, so much for my daydreaming.

"Hey, Professor!"

I immediately catch his attention.

Everyone we know calls Roger the 'Professor'. He is smart, inventive and he can solve almost any mechanical problem presented to him. Roger also has the ability to manipulate and con you into joining him in various borderline illegal schemes. Roger will always try to separate you from your money or have you help him do the same to others. Bottom line, Roger is a lot smarter than he seems to look!

"Keyno, what's up?"

"I notice your shopping bag and it looks like you connected with the fireworks dealer. Can you help us out by telling us where we can find him?"

"I sure can big head. If you give me fifty cents I'll tell you where."

"Okay."

"You better not let on to anyone that I gave you his location. Not even the dealer since he may kick my ass around the block for telling you kids where to find him. Your mother and father will kill me if they found out that I helped you find the fireworks dealer. Anyway, go to number 36 down the basement and ask for Stevie, also known as Blackie Parisi and show him your money right away. He may let you buy some fireworks if things are slow. I can't guarantee that he will let you into his hideout to show you his stash of fireworks. Even though he's connected with the mob who would sell fireworks to anyone, Blackie doesn't like to sell this stuff to kids. But you can give it a shot but remember you better not tell him who told you where to go. So, pay up I'm getting hungry."

"Okay, Okay, I heard you the first time."

I give Roger fifty cents from our fireworks money for the location of the dealer. No sooner than Pecker and I turned around to look for number 36 I can see through the corner of my eye Roger at the hot dog stand asking Louie for a couple of dogs with onions no doubt.

We find number 36 is a two-story dirty light blue wood building that seems to be falling apart. The four steps leading to the ground floor of the building are made of brick covered in concrete that is chipped and broken. There is a wrought iron gate running along the front of the building that has parts of it missing due to rust and decay. The windows are in no better condition, a part of the glass in each window is missing and the window shades, which must have been white a hundred years ago, have various blotches of dirty brown covered with dust and spider webs. The window shades are uneven with tears and holes from every direction. The columns holding up the roof to the front door entryway are ready to crack and fall. I hope we don't have to go into the building that way. There are no signs that anyone lives in this rat hole except for some noise coming from the basement.

I think that if Roger the Professor gave us the right information and the fireworks are in this dump, what a fire-trap! This place looks like the buildings that are condemned to make way for the Brooklyn Battery Tunnel. We look down the basement filled with garbage, old tires, and rusty hubcaps and smells of urine. The basement door is open so I turn to Pecker:

"Looks like this could be the place! One of us has to go down there to see if Blackie is around. Let's flip for it."

"No friggin' way I'm going into this rat hole alone! This is your idea and you have the money we saved so you go down there and give me a holler when you find Blackie."

"Pecker, you know, you're just chicken shit. We made a deal months ago to collect the deposit bottles, cash them in, save our money so that we, partner, could buy fireworks for the 4th of July. I'm not too cool in meeting this Blackie guy. If we're still partners then let's just go in there together."

Pecker knows I am right and he doesn't know what to say. He is just flipping his hand and agreeing.

"Okay, as long as we do this thing together, count me in."

So, down we go, me first with Pecker holding up the rear position, into the Hell-hole. As we go to the basement level the smell and the garbage is giving me a nauseous feeling, but I don't want to insult Blackie by walking into his abode holding my nose while puking all over him. I'm at the doorway.

"HELLO? HELLO, anybody here?"

"Yeah, shit head, what do you want?"

There he is, all six two and about two hundred and fifty-pounds. He is as dark as can be; (now I could see how he got his nickname.) His nose looks like it was smashed several times and his green eyes glowing like they were shooting red flames as they reflect the sun beaming through the broken window. My guess is that his about forty-years-old.

Blackie is wearing a dirty white coffee stained athletic T-shirt, blue jeans and motorcycle boots that have seen better days. His body is covered with dark black hair. His body hair is so thick that you can barely see the tattoos covering his arms and chest. Blackie looks like a tough biker dude who can kill you and never give it a second thought. I don't know how Pecker is holding up, I'm afraid that he will bolt and make a run for it. Even though I am scared out of my wits, I am trying to stay and look as cool as possible.

The smell is just as bad in the apartment. I don't think that Blackie has washed in weeks. I hold out my hand.

"I have this money here and we're looking to buy some fireworks for the fourth of July, can you help us out?"

"WHO SENT YOU?"

"Nobody, really, we overheard some kids talking about getting some fireworks on President Street. So, Pecker and I started banging on as many doors as possible to try to find where we could buy these fireworks."

"BULLSHIT!"

At this point, I am shaking and start to back away.

"Sorry to bother you, Mister. We don't want to cause any trouble. We'll just try another building."

"Wait up kid, show me your money again. Just how much money do you have?"

"Uh, about eighteen bucks."

"Okay, I don't believe your bullshit story but you have money and I have nothing better to do. I don't like to sell this stuff to kids, and you better not tell your folks about me and if you do I'll hunt you down and KILL YOU. DO YOU UNDERSTAND?"

"Yes, sir, we wouldn't tell anybody where we got the stuff. We promise."

"Okay, follow me."

Chapter 5

Buying Fireworks From Blackie

One of New York's long forgotten forts on the corner of Van Brunt and Dikeman Streets in Red Hook carries the name of a café. Old Pier 39 faces Upper New York Bay, while the Louis Valentino Jr. Pier is named for the hero firefighter who sustained fatal injuries in the Canarsie blaze of 1996. The Statue of Liberty, Upper New York Bay, Governors Island and lower Manhattan adorns your vision, as the pier juts into the western end of the Buttermilk Channel, named because its rolling and turbulent waters churn milk, or so the legend goes. But to Pecker and me, the real legend or hero is- Blackie!

Following Blackie's lead, we are heading to the backyard of the building. Exiting the yard, it looks more like a garbage dump except for the eye-candy of a motorcycle. Blackie's bike looks totally out of place. It stands out like a ray of the sunshine or a crown jewel with its beaming metallic red color, sparkling chrome with leather saddlebags. Wow! I can't believe that I am looking at this beautiful machine amid all this junk!

"Hey, Blackie, is this your bike?"

"Yeah, stupid, do you see anyone else around here?"

It is the killer bike, Indian red, in perfect condition. Pecker and I can't take our eyes off this thing as we are hearing Blackie.

"Come on stupid I thought you wanted to get some fireworks?"

Still awed by the bike we are practically walking backward and almost falling over the garbage scatted all over the yard. We finally turn and notice that we are being led to a washed out gray colored shack that is the size of a small barn. As we are approaching the shack Blackie is slowly removing the padlock from the door.

"You got ten minutes to look for what you want and get the Hell out of here."

As we are cautiously entering the shack we are being presented with a marvelous display of fireworks. The colors are overpowering reds, yellows, and blues, making for such a beautiful sight!

We are dumbfounded! Not only are the fireworks display a thing of beauty, but even the gunpowder smells good! There is every firework explosive device you can imagine, displayed is a large variety of missals, mortars, Roman candles, rockets, sparklers, M-80s, cherry bombs, ladyfingers and mats of firecrackers. I keep on thinking how Blackie got a truckload of fireworks here on his motorcycle. There are boxes everywhere. I'm not about to ask Blackie how he manages to put this stuff together. It is at this point I feel someone pushing me forward towards the display and he is yelling:

"Come on kids I haven't got all day."

It is like being in a candy store with a nickel and trying to choose from the fifty-penny candies. We would just drive the candy man crazy going back and forth from one candy to another constantly changing our minds, saying "this one, no... a... that one or maybe this one"!

I have a feeling that Blackie does not have the patience of the candy man and if we do not make a quick selection he will just throw us out of his pyrotechnic wonderland. So I'll ask Pecker...

"What do think we should buy?"

Pecker is going right over to the M-80s and firecrackers. Blackie gives us a brown paper shopping bag. We fill the bag with a mat (80 packs of firecrackers, 16 firecrackers to a pack), a dozen M-80s, a dozen cherry bombs and a couple of Roman candles, bottle rockets, and motors. We pass on the sparklers that are okay for little kids. That was all our eighteen bucks can buy. We are in a euphoric state. Meanwhile, Blackie doesn't waste any time in getting us out. As we are leaving we notice eight or ten teenagers loitering near the front entrance undoubtedly waiting for Blackie to usher them in to buy their stash of fireworks. Pecker and I are so happy that we can barely contain ourselves. We are laughing and jumping for joy, we must look like a couple of goofy kids. I think that we can't believe that we're able to pull this off. This is our first successful seek and buy mission for illegal fireworks. I can't get over this feeling of accomplishment it is like we are now teenagers. What's next, girl's maybe? It was too good to be true.

Finally, it is dawning on me we better be careful heading back home. I'll remind Pecker that if any teenagers get wind of our success in buying these fireworks they will gang up on us and steal them without much of a fight. So now we are in a panic mode. After all the planning and effort to accumulate enough money to buy these fireworks we do not want to lose our bounty. We stop the laughing, jumping, and start running south on Columbia Street to get home as quickly as possible. Our goal now is to hide our stash of fireworks in a safe place. Once we are able to hide our stash we can then ration a number of fireworks that we can shoot off at any one time and minimize our exposure to being ripped off by the older kids in the neighborhood.

Making it back home without getting ripped off, the next step is for me to get into our apartment while my mother is out shopping and hide the fireworks under my parent's bed. I have no problem doing this. The next couple of days are critical to our plan. I am just hoping that my mother will not do a major cleaning that would involve dusting under the bed. If she happens to find these fireworks my parents will kill me. Now we have to move to the second phase of our plan of action that is to put together cans and bottles that we can blow up with our firecrackers and M-80s.

Chapter 6

Lunch & Simba The Killer Cat Is Ready to Attack Me

We are hungry for some lunch so Pecker and I are splitting a roast beef hero, stuffed with fried eggplant and hot salad from Nick's sandwich shop. The hero sandwich goes along very well with two ice-cold "Manhattan Special" coffee sodas. Good thing we held back a little money from Roger for paying off the Professor and what we paid Blackie for the fireworks so that we can buy some lunch. It is dirty work to accumulate the stuff we

Nick's Sandwiches AreThe Best

needed to blow up with our assortment of M-80s and cherry bombs.

We finished lunch and it is late afternoon, the heat must be up to nearly 100 degrees! We have yet to pick through garbage cans around the neighborhood to find anything useful. It isn't much fun to pick through the garbage in 100-degree weather especially right after lunch. But I must confess that our lunch was great!

There is nothing better than Nick's sandwiches with an ice-cold Manhattan Special. If we had the money we would buy lunch every day but we shot our load on the fireworks. At least we got to enjoy one lunch out of the deal. We agree to start our quest by picking through Nick's sandwich shop garbage around the corner from Columbia on Luquer Street.

There are about six metal garbage cans lined up near the back entrance of the building in addition to several boxes filled with garbage. This garbage is an accumulation from the sandwich shop and tenants who live above the sandwich shop in the same building. It looks like we didn't get there first. There are six or eight alley cats already rummaging through the garbage cans for scraps of food. These city cats are no pushover. If you got close to them while they are eating they will jump on you with all claws, scratching and biting your face off. It doesn't matter to them whether it is a man, dog or another cat, these street cats will attack anyone, as a matter of day-to-day survival. So, I point this out to Pecker, and there's no need for any explanation what-so-ever, he knows the drill already.

If we manage to chase away the alpha cat, which is the largest and toughest cat in the group, the other cats will scatter. We identify the alpha cat that must weigh about twenty pounds. It is a big male dirty orange color striped cat we named Simba. This big cat has only one good eye since the other eye was likely lost in a fierce battle. Simba looks like a monster with scars all over his face with pieces of his ears missing. His dirty tiger looks orange striped fur if you call it fur was matted and revealed gaps of skin with scars made by various bite marks. If you were to meet up with this killer alley cat one night by accident I would urge you to run like hell.

Pecker and I are setting our plan in motion. First, we will separate and approach the cats with caution. Then we will look for an opportunity to toss the alpha cat. The toss method was developed many years ago and passed down from one generation of kids to another. It does not matter who does the tossing. It involves speed, a firm grip, and strength to toss a twenty-pound cat ten to twelve feet away.

The technique is simple; we will look for Simba to be distracted and engrossed in eating a morsel of rotted food while he is deep in the garbage can. The only thing you will see is Simba's tail sticking up like a submarine periscope, above the lip of the metal garbage can. The speed of action and timing is essential. Pecker and I are on opposite sides of the garbage can waiting for the opportunity to toss Simba and scatter his gang of cats. If Simba's tale is close to Pecker he will grab it or if the tale is closer to my location then I will have to run, grab and toss. If we miss or if we do not apply the toss method properly, one of us will have to fight off Simba and his gang. It would not be a pretty sight. I am a little shaky with the thought of not applying the toss properly. Even though I am deathly afraid of Simba I am also excited about the thought of beating this big guy.

So here we are creeping up to the garbage can one step at a time. Step and freeze, step and freeze, almost there, step and freeze. I feel like we are tracking big game deep in the jungles of Africa. Finally, it looks like I am closer to Simba's tale than Pecker. I start to shake all over while I run towards the garbage can. I'm telling myself: Don't miss, don't miss or there will be pain and blood everywhere.

As I get closer to the garbage can Simba hears a sound, turns and comes up from the garbage looking right at me with that evil eye. All I can say is: "HOLY SHIT!" Good thing Pecker is there to back me up! As Simba is ready to pounce on me Pecker grabs a stick that is lying on the ground and starts swinging it at the metal cans. The noise is so loud that it startles all the cats. As Simba jumps past me he manages to swipe my hand with one of his sharp claws. Even though I was in pain I start to kick the garbage cans to shake up and discourage any other cats from attacking.

"Thanks, Pecker, you saved my ass."

Pecker is turning to me with a concerned expression.

"Do you need a band-aid for that cut on your hand?"

"I don't think so. I'll just keep the pressure on it until the bleeding stops."

With that, we start looking for discarded tomato sauce cans, soup cans or anything else we can blow up. As we go through the metal garbage cans and various boxes stacked against the wall for disposal, we notice that one box has four empty glass gallon pickle jars with lids. This is a real find!

"Wow! Pecker we can make some real money this summer!"

Chapter 7

Pickle Jar Game-Peashooter

Sometimes in the 1940's and 50's, it was a little boy's world, filled with adventure and fun with a cocktail of mischief. To tease or torment was the by-product of boredom or just a chance to change the pace, your target was usually a sister or unsuspecting girl on the block, maybe even your best friend.

In the drone of a Friday afternoon class deep into the school year, one's mind wandered to the streets and the two days off just hours away. Looking to enhance that spirit of the coming freedom was a chance to start the celebrating early.

The tools of mischief were usually simple in nature, a rolled up piece of paper juiced for immediate and long-range delivery was all one needed. A quick motion of the hand as you pitched it across the room into some-one's unsuspecting noggin usually created a sense of confusion and then suspicion, and if you didn't have your poker face on retaliation in a silent war-like atmosphere. Out of the classroom, the arsenal of mischief was expanded to more deadly weapons of torment with the peashooter, more accurate and evasive weapons that defied detection as it made it's way to the intended target almost at the sound of speed, delivering a sting and eliciting a cry of surprise and pain!

Then there were the more deadly appliances mainly the slingshot and the more popular carpet gun, as you will see later in this book created to hone mayhem and pain, all from an innocent little 9-year old learning from his elders on the streets of Brooklyn.

Penny Pickle Jar Game

The glass gallon pickle jars are in very good condition! The metal lids are a little dented but will not present a problem as long as each lid seals the glass container. I'll ask Pecker to store the cans and glass jars at his house since I know that my mother will be very upset if I try to bring this garbage into our apartment for storage. She will never allow me to do this.

"I have a good hiding place for this stuff in the cellar of my apartment building Keyno. No one ever goes down there since it's full of junk and they're afraid of the rats."

"Okay let's do that. Meanwhile, I'll take one glass jar home with me so that I can clean out the pickle juice and put a coin slot in the metal jar lid."

The next step is to convince my mother to let me borrow one of our whiskey shot glasses. I'll tell her that we plan to get together with our friends to have some fun to play drop the penny in the shot glass game."

We have no intention of playing this game for fun. The men who come to the sandwich shop for lunch are from the docks and the factories in the area. After eating a half loaf Italian hero sand-wich and completing a 32oz. bottle of beer most men are willing to try their luck and gamble a few pennies. Especially when they see a couple of bottle collecting kids running the penny shot glass game and can win five cents payback in return.

The way the game works is first you have to be lucky enough to find an empty glass gallon pickle jar. You then have to clean out the jar of any remaining pickle juice. Remove the paper liner from the metal jar lid. After the paper liner in the lid is removed you then turn the metal lid upside down, a punch a coin slot into the lid with your father's screwdriver and hammer. When you complete the cleaning and the coin slot in the metal lid you then fill the glass gallon with water and insert the whiskey shot glass right side up into the water centered at the base of the gallon jug.

The purpose of the game is to slip a penny into the coin slot and if the penny floats into the shot glass "YOU WIN!" five pennies. Of course, if the pennies do not float down into the shot glass Pecker and I get to keep them. The odds are very good that we will be able to make two or three dollars in about two hours. When the lunch crowd started to gather around our jug some men will ask:

"Hey kid, is the water salt-free?"

"Yes sir, the jar was cleaned before we put in the fresh water. Do you want to taste it?"

You guessed it; some men will say yes and stick their finger into the water to taste it. It better be salt-free otherwise some big guy may just kick you in the ass and break your jar. But if my parents or sister just happen to see me surrounded by a group of longshore-men or factory workers I'll have to run like Hell.

Once you have all your stuff ready you need at least one dollar in pennies and nickels to bankroll the game. Since we spent all our money on the fireworks and lunch we are broke. So, the game will have to wait until after the Fourth of July when we can collect and cash in enough deposit bottles to put together our bankroll.

So, now we'll have to lug the empty tomato and soup cans along with the three glass gallon pickle jars down to Pecker's cellar. I'm not too happy about going down his cellar. The rats down there are so big they can eat Simba the cat for lunch.

I first have to go up to my apartment and leave one glass container in the hallway near the entrance door. I do not want to bring it into our apartment just yet since I know it would take me some time to convince my mother to let me clean out this dirty glass jar in our laundry basin. I just hope that she doesn't see it before I get back home.

I'll drop off the jar and run down two flights of steps and rejoin Pecker. It's now late afternoon and I see Pecker!

"Come on, we better hurry up and get this stuff into your cellar, before you know it my mother will be calling out our window for me to get to the dinner table."

Pecker turns with his cheeks puffed up.

"Yeah, yeah… you Italians are always eating: food, food that is all you think about."

"Oh yeah, it's better than eating a peanut butter and jelly sand- wich every day, shit head."

I guess Pecker's father doesn't cook much with the exception of a can of soup every now and then. Anyway, after our little exchange is over we get down to business and we are walking on Luquer Street towards Peckers on Hick's Street where he lives in an old building near a vacant lot across the street from the Cardinal Tank factory.

Walking with our hands full of cans and glass pickle jars I feel this sharp pain in the back of my neck. The pain was more like a sting too light to be a mosquito but maybe it is a wasp. There it goes again, now it's my leg, again now it's my back. I asked myself what the Hell is going on?

"Look out, Ricardo Six Fingers is shooting at us with a peashooter!"

Ricardo Six Fingers is a deadly shot with a peashooter. Most kids don't walk around with a peashooter in the summer. If it was the peashooter season and I wanted to buy one, I would go to our corner candy store and buy a plastic straw and a small bag of dry peas for about 10 cents. To shoot a pea: put one into your mouth, then put your lips around the straw and maneuver a single pea with your tongue into the straw. Then blow as hard as you can and you will shoot the pea in any direction the straw is pointing. If you shoot and hit someone with the dry pea it can really hurt and it means WAR! It will cause your best friend to become your enemy. Even though Ricardo is not my best friend I just want to kill him right now.

Ricardo (Six Fingers) Lopez is about 10-years old with a dark complexion, close-set dark eyes and a wide forehead leading up to a shortcut kinky black hairline. His tiny frame made him look like 7-years old. We called him 'Six Fingers' because, yes, he has six fingers on his left hand. On his left hand, the sixth finger is located just beyond his pinky finger between his knuckle and wrist. He can't move his extra finger at all and it just looks like a hook finger growing out of his hand.

It gives me the creeps, and he knows it. He will chase me up and down the block while he is trying to rub his extra finger hand on me. It's almost like playing tag but I'm afraid of his six-finger hand. I am afraid Ricardo will touch me while I am yelling and trying to run away from him. I have a weird feeling about that one touch of Ricardo's extra finger anywhere on my body will transfer some kind of a voodoo spell and his hook finger will grow on my body or even my face. I think that Ricardo's weird hand gives him power over me, and most of the kids on the block.

We never asked but we all think his parents with Ricardo's sister Maria originally settled in Brooklyn from Puerto Rico. Maria (head lights) Lopez, is about fifteen-years old, head lights are what the older teenagers on the block call her, she is a looker. If by chance Maria would glance at me with her beautiful green eyes, long jet-black hair, shapely body, I would just stand there paralyzed and unable to move my mouth open!

Her brother 'Six Fingers' Ricardo is not a member of our gang but he keeps on trying to get noticed by shooting me in the head with his pea shooter or chasing me around the block with his weird finger. I guess that is his way of trying to make friends. I can't take it anymore.

"Hey Ricardo, cut it out! I don't have time for this bullshit."

Wham! Another hit with his peashooter. I'm hot, all sweaty from carrying this garbage; I lose it and started yelling:

"If you don't stop shooting at me I'm gonna drop this garbage and chase you down and shove that DEAD FINGER OF YOURS WHERE THE SUN DON'T SHINE! Got that Lopez?"

I think that he sees the rage in my eyes and has decided to run home because he knows that I am out for blood. Pecker just stands there laughing his ass off at my reaction and what I just said to Six Finger, Lopez.

"What the hell is so funny Pecker? Let's get this stuff into your cellar so I can get home before my mother has a fit."

31

Chapter 8

Pitching Pennies-Storings Jugs

Pitching Pennies GameWinner Takes All

As we approach the corner of Luquer and Hicks street there are four kids standing outside the grocery store. They are pitching pennies by standing in the street and throwing the pennies over the sidewalk to the building. I do not have the skill that some of the older kids have in playing this game. Some of these kids are very good at launching a penny to get as close as possible to the building so they can win the round and collect the pennies, as much as eight to ten coins are tossed by the other players that lose the game.

It is amazing to watch when a player sends a penny flying towards the building and not only come close but actually stand the penny on end leaning vertically on the building. If someone happens to stand a penny on its end against the building, during the game, the other players will do their best to knock it down when it is their turn to toss, otherwise, they will lose their pennies for that round.

The kids that are pitching pennies on the corner turn to look at us and no doubt they are trying to figure out what the Hell we are carrying. We turn the corner onto Hick's Street and cross onto the broken flagstone sidewalk as they resume playing. I can see Pecker's house, a two-story wood clapboard gray house positioned immediately after the vacant lot littered with old discarded ice-box coolers, worn out automobile tires and assorted junk. Many homes in this area do not have a modern all-electric refrigerator to store food.

Before the war people could not afford refrigerators, so they had to rely on an icebox that required a one-foot square ice cube every 2-3 days to maintain a cold temperature, thereby preventing or minimizing food, such as milk, cheese, eggs, meat, etc. from rotting during the warm months of the year.

There are ice delivery wagons all over the city, especially during the summer. The ice wagons are a welcome sight not only to the households that require a new cube of ice for the old ice box but also to many of the neighborhood kids who chase these wagons during the hot months of July and August hoping to grab a chip of ice to suck on. It doesn't matter if the chip of ice was filthy dirty when it falls off the ice wagon. If you are lucky enough to get one just wipe the dirt off with your hand and then suck on it to cool off. Every now and then one of the ice delivery guys will break off some ice for the kids following the wagon. Most of the time during the winter months as long as it is not freezing temperatures there is little or no need to buy ice for the ice-box cooler. My mother would store food on the fire escape or on our windowsill.

Now that the Great Depression and WWII are over most people have set aside enough money during the war years to buy a new refrigerator and discard the old ice box. That's why we see so many of them abandoned in almost every vacant lot around the neighborhood. Even though it is dangerous many of the little kids will sit in the old icebox imagining they are shooting from a tank when playing war. Many parents will break off the doors of the old icebox so that a kid can't accidentally lock himself in and suffocate.

Playing war is one of our favorite games; we choose sides and pretend that we were fighting the Nazis or Japanese. Of course, the Nazis and Japanese are always on the losing side.

Pecker and I are really starting to lose it. We are so tired from the heat of the day and carrying this garbage for over an hour.

As we start to go into the entrance of Pecker's dilapidated building that has no front door, you can look into the building straight through to the back-yard exit that does not have a door either.

"Pecker let's get this thing over with. I'm tired and I have to get home for dinner."

"Here we go again, you can't stop thinking about food."

"Listen, Pecker, it may seem that way but my mother likes to have us all together at the dinner table. She says that dinner is our family time and she also reminds us that she has spent most of the day planning, shopping and cooking our meal."

"Okay let's move, the cellar entrance is in the backyard."

We are walking through the hallway directly into the backyard that doesn't look much different than the vacant lot next door which is full of junk and an old "outhouse" better known as an outdoor potty. We are making our way to an old wooden broken cellar door lying flat on the concrete ground.

Pecker pulls the door open and exposes the steps leading down to the cellar.

"Okay, Pecker you lead the way."

"Shit NO! There are no lights down there and I don't want to run into any rats that will bite my ass off!"

"Yeah, chicken shit now you tell me, buck-buck, buck-buck."

"Okay, I'll go down there but you better be right behind me. First, let's throw some rocks down there to scare off any rats that may be lurking in the dark."

That's what we will do, collect about eight rocks and start throwing them down the cellar steps and yelling as loud as we can. We hear a lot of tapping and scraping sounds. The sounds must have come from a pack of rats running to get away and hide in their rat holes. We start descending into the dark, damp, smelly cellar. I'm thinking to myself that Blackie Parisi's basement on President Street smells better that Pecker's cellar. We only have some day-light to illuminate the entrance of the cellar. Not only are there rats down here but I can see a weird movement of giant water bugs about ten times the size of a cockroach. There is also an assortment of spiders and spider webs everywhere. The spiders must have very good hunting grounds down here. I can also see the reflection of an old partially filled coal bin on the far side of the cellar.

The houses do not use coal much anymore for heat. In my house, we heat the apartment with a kerosene heater, as do most homes in the area. The coals in the old coal bin make it a good hiding place for the rats.

"Pecker, I not going all the way in the cellar. Let's leave our stuff a couple of feet in from the entrance. I doubt it if anyone will be coming down here."

Pecker is quickly agreeing and we put down our gallon glass jars along with the empty cans about three feet in from the entrance. We will then get out of there as quickly as possible and start for the front entrance of the building.

"Wow! It was nasty down there. I hope that none of the critters that live in your cellar visit you at night. They give me the creeps."

"Yeah, like you live in a palace."

"I'm going home, I'll see ya tomorrow."

"See ya."

Chapter 9
Pigeon Flying Sport

Pigeon breeding became popular in Brooklyn by Italian and Irish immigrants. The practice developed among the middle and working classes. A dying art now, by the 1950's Pigeon breeding was a sport and science to those who practiced it.

Roof Top Pigeon Coops In Old Brooklyn

I'm leaving Pecker's building and hearing the flutter of about a hundred pigeons taking off from the pigeon coop located on the roof. The sound surrounds you as they simultaneously lift into the air! There are two or three pigeon coops on every block in our neighborhood. Some coops are on the roof of a building over-looking Red Hook and some are located almost secretly in a back yard. In most cases, the building may be falling apart but the pigeon coops are a work of beauty.

These pigeons are not rat pigeons. The rat pigeons are pigeons you see looking for food in the streets. These rat or street pigeons usually have gray and black feathers in a variety of designs a telltale sign being that they are rats is their "red eyes". The way I understand it, based on what I overheard from the pigeon guys, is that they call the street pigeons rats because they are the lowest of the low in the pigeon world. You don't want any rats in your coop mingling with your pure breeds.

Men mostly are into flying pigeons. There are men who are breeding racers and others who fly a flock of pigeons. The racers are specifically bred homing pigeons that find their way back to their home coop after flying long distances. It is unbelievable that a bird can fly 20, 30 or 40 miles and come back home without resting. Many pigeons have special tags attached to their leg that will clock into a timing machine to record the time a bird came home and entered a coop.

Homing pigeons are also used to deliver messages during the war from behind enemy lines. If a soldier happened to see a homing pigeon during the battle he would try to shoot the pigeon out of the sky and intercept the message it was carrying to the enemy.

The benefit of having the fastest pigeon in any competition involves bragging rights for having the fastest bird in the neighborhood. It is like having a thoroughbred horse; you can then breed your top racer and sell the offspring for top dollar. But the race mostly involves winning a substantial cash pool for the winner of the race. This sport involves cutthroat competition.

On the other hand, the men and older teenagers who are raising pigeons to fly in a flock enjoy a different kind of competitive sport. These people have up to two hundred pigeons of every variety in their coop. Some of the Pigeon breeds include Copperheads, Tiplets, Nuns, Teagasc, Capuchins, Tumblers, Persian High Flyers, Rollers, Pure Whites and Fan Tails. This flock sports objective is as follows; first, you feed your pigeon's very little food before each flight, then you release your flock and urge them to fly by creating a loud noise with metal pot covers, screams, whistles and waving both arms wildly while holding two white empty pillowcases. All or most of your pigeons will take flight usually led by the Persian High Flyers. Fan Tails, who do not fly well, stay on the ground or rooftop close to the coop while all this is going on.

All the other pigeons will do their best to keep up with the Persian High Flyers. Once your flock is high and circling widely around the home base where the coop is located, other flocks located within several blocks will also take flight. The purpose of this sport is to encourage two or three flocks of pigeon to intermingle into one large flock. Then the fun begins! Each coop involved will now try to lure their pigeons back to their home base. This is done by whistling a familiar tune and shaking a can of pigeon corn feed. It's a call for your pigeons to come home for dinner. Meanwhile, the flying pigeons hear the signal and see the Fan Tails pigeons on the ground eating some of the food put out by the handlers. Then the largest flock of pigeons starts to break up into three individual flocks. The Tumblers will start to descend quickly by tumbling and look like they are falling out of the sky. The Tumblers are now in a race to get to the food as fast as possible and feed before the other pigeons get there. The Copper Heads, Nuns, Pure Whites, and Persian High Flyers follow the Tumblers in a race with the others to get back to the coop for dinner.

The object of the sport and the challenge of the game for owners is to capture as many disoriented pigeons as possible and hold them for ransom. Generally, what happens in a rush to go back to their coop for dinner, some pigeons inadvertently land on a neighboring coop where traps are waiting to capture them so that they can be ransomed for cash or other pigeons in trade if their rightful owner feels that they are worth the cost for their return.

I would like to get my own pigeon coop someday even though my mother would kill me. My mother hates the pigeon sport. You can well imagine when she works all day hand washing clothing, underwear, socks, or whatever and then she hangs her wash out on our clothesline to dry. By the time a large flock of up to 500 pigeons completes their flight some of our garments will undoubtedly be soiled with pigeon poop. It just drives her and all the women in the neighborhood crazy when that happens. It is also common knowledge that these flocks of pigeons have on occasion pooped on many bystanders. So, you really should not look up when these birds are in flight.

Roger told me several times that we could build a coop on our roof. I really would like to partner up with Roger someday and build a small coop with a couple of dozen birds. Maybe my mother and the landlord will not notice such a small flock of birds. I realize that I am daydreaming again. I'm thinking that I better get home I'm already late for dinner. My mother must be tired by now calling out for me to come home from our second story window.

Chapter 10
Vegetable Peddler-Home Cooking

Brooklyn in the 1950's was covered by a fleet of peddlers, slowly passing through the streets on a wagon pulled by a horse with a signature clop, clop, clop, with the tell-tale sign of horse poop left behind. You could get a ragman in the early hours, or a vegetable man or even a fishmonger by shopping your sidewalk. If you were a kid and Mom needed something, she would call out for you and toss coins wrapped in a dollar or two to make her purchase from the upper stories of your building.

And so it 's about six in the afternoon and I haven't been home all day. I'm turning the corner on to Luquer Street heading towards Columbia Street, passing the horse stables that is home to several fruit and vegetable peddlers and I can hear someone calling out:

"Hey, Keyno!"

It's old Mr. Pauli the peddler. Pauli 'Hook Nose' Mengiano is about 75-years old with pure white hair, brown eyes, and always has a three-day-old facial hair since he doesn't shave much. He always has a dark tan in the summer and winter, his tan, I imagine, is due to the fact that he spends most of his time outdoors selling his fresh produce. Mr. Pauli always has a De Nobili cigar stuck and twisting in his mouth, always wearing the same old red plaid shirt every day over his dirty, torn, brown pants and unlaced black combat boots.

Mr.Pauli is a nice man even though he smells like his horse Pinto. He is always good to the kids in the neighborhood and sometimes at the end of the day, Mr. Pauli will give us his left-over produce to bring home. When he gives us leftover potatoes and carrots we will build a fire in a vacant lot and pretend that we are in the woods camping. If the tomatoes are too soft and almost rotting we can't help ourselves, we throw them at each other. It is quite a sight to see all these kids reeking and covered from head to toe in rotten tomatoes. Mr. Pauli is sitting on top of his green wagon.

"Hi, Mr. Pauli!"

I would not think of ever calling him Hook Nose.

"Do you need any help in unloading your wagon?"

I always addressed him as 'Mister' as a sign of respect and I think he likes that.

Mr. Pauli's De Nobili Cigars Smell As Bad As His Horse, Pinto.

"No Keyno, I'm done unloading for the day. But tomorrow … I will have a big load of green melons to sell and if you want to make some tip money you can come along with me to carry the melons home for the ladies. The ladies will probably give you ten cents to bring the melon up the stairs to their apartments and if you're lucky they may give you fifteen cents for helping them."

Wow! My mind is racing ahead of me. I'm thinking of the bankroll needed to finance the drop the penny in the jug game.

"Yes, sure!, I would like to work with you tomorrow. What time should I meet you in the stable?"

"The truck is scheduled to deliver the melons around 7 AM so I think we can start selling melons around 9 AM."

"Okay, I'll meet you just at 9 am."

The timing could not have been any better.

It's hard work for a little kid like me to carry a heavy melon up several flights of stairs. I just hope that it's not too hot tomorrow.

My mother is gonna be pissed off, so I better start running as fast as I can to get home. I made it! My home is at 379 Columbia Street, two flights up over Nick's grocery and sand-wich store on the ground floor. I don't think my mother likes living over a grocery store located at a busy intersection. Trol-leys will ring their bell along with cars and trucks rolling by on cobblestone streets every few seconds. There's aways too much noise and activity all day long. During lunch, you will also see as many as 30 to 40 men sitting on the sidewalks, boxes, and steps leading into the building eating lunch. Many times you will literally have to step over these men to exit the building. But for me, it is great to have a grocery store in the building. If I have to buy some groceries for my mother, I will only have to run downstairs to buy them.

I'll go into the front entrance of our building that has an outer and inner door to get into the hallway. Not like Pecker's building that has no entrance door at all. I like to jump two steps at a time up the two flights to our apartment entrance. I'll pick up the dirty glass pickle jar that I left on the landing outside our apartment and enter without a key to get in since our door is never locked. My mother, Francesca is standing there in the kitchen with her arms folded. This is not a good sign, even though she is angry at me for being late for dinner. She stands there with a mean frown on her face that is not pretty but she looks beautiful to me. She has blue eyes, light brown hair, dressed in a powder blue smock decorated with tiny white flowers. She doesn't speak much English, and that is okay in our neighborhood since mostly everybody who lives here emigrated from Italy. Since my sister and I go to public school we are the only two in our family who can communicate in English and Italian. At home, for the most part, we talk to our parents and ourselves in tour parent's native tongue, Italian.

Our parents do not like it if my sister and I are talking to each other in English and leave them out of the conversation. Even though I know that my mother is not happy about my being late I can tell by the look in her eyes that she is glad to see me. She says:

"Perche e piu tardi per cena? Lei e troppo magro e Lei ha bisogno di mangiare. (Why are you late for dinner? You are too skinny and you need to eat.)"

"Mamma, lo sono spiacente che io sono in ritardo per cena. (Mama, I am sorry that I am late for dinner.)"

"Perche ha bisogno di questo vaso di vetro sporco? (Why do you need this dirty glass jar?)"

"Io ho bisogno di questo vaso di vetro giocare un gioco coi miei amici. (I need this glass jar to play a game with my friends.)"

"Buono, pulisca il vaso e l'esca dalla casa. (Good, clean the jar and get it out of the house.)"

Meanwhile, I can hear my sister Isabella playing her big band records in the other room so I asked my mother...

"Dove e mio padre e quando generera ritornato a casa? (Where is my father and when will father come home?)"

"Suo Padre e non senta lui lavorera ogni notto e sara a casa di mattina.(Your father is not here he will work all night and be home in the morning.)"

"Buono, io sono pronto ora mangiare.
(Good, I am ready to eat now.)"

Even though I need a bath I am too hungry at this point to do so, I just wash my hands and sit at the table in our kitchen with a fork and spoon at the ready. Since it is way pass our dinner time I am the only one who did not have anything to eat. Therefore, my sister and mother do not join me at the table. My mother gives me a bowl of pasta and fagioli with some bread. Not my favorite meal but it is hot and the garlic smells good and it is better than Pecker's peanut butter and jelly sandwich, so I'll dig in complete my dinner and my mother says:

"Ora venga qui! (Come here now!)
Lei e sporco, Lei ha bisogno di orafare un bagno.
(You are dirty; you need to take a bath now.)"

I am not thrilled with the idea of taking a bath but I must admit that I smell pretty bad. We don't have a bathtub and our toilet is in a closet off the kitchen. Our baths are taken in the laundry washbasin located in the kitchen.

This washbasin is not very big and not very private so whoever needs to take a bath asks everyone else to stay out of the kitchen while they were bathing. I am the only exception since I am small enough to sit into the washbasin and my mother will insist on scrubbing me with Octagon soap.

It seems to be taking forever but now I am washed up and ready for bed. It is still too early for my mother to pull out my cot into our family room so I'll sit by the radio and listen to the Lone Ranger and his adventures.

I am turning off the radio and since it isn't getting any cooler we will all go downstairs to sit outside on the stoop with chairs my father brought down from our apartment the other night. It isn't all that much cooler than our apartment is. We are meeting with a bunch of other families doing the same thing it seems. This always gives my mother an opportunity to socialize with friends and dishwater relatives about how good it was in back in the old country. I often asked myself: Why did my father and mother leave the Garden of Eden in Italy for a ghetto in Brooklyn? I'm thinking that they miss their friends and family they left behind. I'll just sit here listening to all the stories. I'm getting bored and am now daydreaming about my going with Paulie tomorrow to sell watermelons. Of course, there is the Fourth of July celebration coming up the day after and the fireworks we plan to shoot off.

Yes, the fireworks! Thanks to Roger the professor and Blackie, Pecker and me are ready to do some real damage with our arsenal of fireworks!

Chapter 11
Selling Watermelons with Mr. Pauli

It's about 8:30 AM at Mr. Pauli's stable and I am a little early. As I'm walking I see several men unloading green watermelons from an old red truck onto the peddler's wagon. The next thing I expect to see is Pinto the horse being hooked up to the wagon to pull that heavy load of watermelons around the neighborhood.

The 90-degree heat wave is not letting up, seeping into my clothes and my neck and brow are turning into a waterfall.

Pinto is a strong horse but in this heat pulling the heavy wagon will take its toll on poor Pinto. Mr. Pauli will have to load extra water on his wagon for Pinto. I must admit that I am not looking forward to carrying heavy watermelons to apartments that are two or three stories high in this heat. But I am excited about riding with Mr. Pauli up high on the wagon. I feel like we are on a stagecoach, heading west and if we run into any outlaws I know that the Lone Ranger and Tonto will come to our rescue. But just in case the Lone Ranger is busy I carry my trusty pearl handle silver six-shooter cap pistol with me to protect our load of watermelons from outlaws.

As we are getting closer to the stable Mr. Pauli turns towards me with his ever-present De Nobili cigar in his mouth.

"Good morning, are you ready to go to work? It looks like it's going to be a very hot day and if we don't sell most of the melons before noon I may have to dump the hot and rotted melons by this afternoon!"

"Don't worry Mr. Pauli I think that they will sell fast since everybody is off work tomorrow looking forward to the big Fourth of July celebration."

"Okay, Pinto is set so we better get moving. Come up on the wagon and sit next to me."

"Yes, sir."

So, I'll climb up on the wagon with Mr. Pauli and sit next to him like he said. Mr. Pauli is whipping the leather reins gently on Pinto's hind coaxing: "Git-te-appa." Pinto isn't able to pull the loaded wagon so after a couple of seconds and more gentle coaxing from Mr. Pauli, the heavy wagon is coming alive, slowly moving forward. We are pulling away and Mr. Pauli is calling out in a loud "MELONS, FRESH MELONS, COME GET THEM WHILE THEY LAST. COME ON PRETTY LADIES BUY YOUR MELON TODAY AND WE WILL CARRY THEM HOME FOR YOU!"

He is calling out with his peddler-man pitch, while several housewives are calling from their upper windows for Mr. Pauli to wait for them to come down to select a melon. Mrs. Marguerite, a heavy-set woman is approaching the wagon wearing a soiled white apron with red stains that are most likely tomato sauce, the badge of honor of her past labors.

Selecting the largest melon on the wagon that must weigh 20 pounds she is asking me to carry it for her to her second-floor apartment. I'll cradle the large melon in my arms like it is a new-born puppy and follow Mrs. Marguerite about a hundred feet to her doorway. I don't think I can do this all day long. I am stronger than I think, and after my delivery, Mrs. Marguerite gives me 20 cents. WOW! This was a great start! Calculating to myself…10 melons, times 20 cents equals two dollars. 20 melons times 20 cents equals four dollars. This is going to be a great day if I don't die from exhaustion or a heart attack!

No such luck! My euphoria is quickly diminishing and reality is setting in. I'm receiving tips that are ranging from a nickel to ten-cents. Not everyone is as generous as Mrs. Marguerite.

Several hours have gone by and it looks like more than one-third of the melons are sold. Mr. Pauli is optimistic in thinking that we will be completely sold out by early afternoon. Pinto, Mr. Pauli and I have to keep drinking a lot of water as the hot sun is beating down on us and the temperature is lingering over ninety degrees. We are eating slices of a watermelon Mr. Pauli cut up just to keep us cool.

We are passing my grammar school and I see my friends Jimmy Pizza, Henry, Reno and a bunch of guys playing stoopball opposite the Cardinal Tank Factory. It is a great location for stoopball even though it isn't much of a stoop to play off. The

School PS #27 On Nelson Street

stoop has only three steps and if you hit the ball on the stoop at the right angle the ball will fly over the roof of the factory which is over a hundred feet high. It is exciting to hit this 'home run' but we lose a lot of balls up there. Sometimes, Mike the watchman, Henry's father, will go on the roof and throw down about 10 or 12 balls that he finds there. Most of the balls Mike the watchman finds on the roof are rotted out and discolored from the weather, and some are as hard as a rock. But we are happy to get 2 to 3 good ones.

Mike is very thoughtful and kind man. He knows that kids in the neighborhood can barely afford to buy one ball to play with. Passing the school, I hear Jimmy call out:

"Hey, Keyno, let's hang out together with Pecker for the 4th of July. I'll come to your building to call you".

"Sounds great to me, see ya".

We are traveling about ten blocks in a full circle when I admit to Mr. Pauli:

"Sorry Mr. Pauli, I don't think that I can do this much longer."

"Okay kid, I know that you're working hard and that you're killing yourself to make the delivery in this heat. But It looks like we're almost sold out and It's time for us to stop at Nick's for some lunch. It's my treat."

I am very thankful since I am just about all out of gas. Mr. Pauli and Pinto didn't look so good either. We stop in front of Nick's sandwich shop and wouldn't you know it, the longshoremen having lunch there are buying the rest of the melons from Mr. Pauli and have given me a tip even though I don't have to deliver any melons for them.

Mr. Pauli, Pinto and I are very grateful. I don't think that I am the only one who is running out of gas. We enter into the sandwich shop and I order my usual roast beef hero loaded with fried eggplant and hot salad and Mr. Pauli gives me the okay to buy not one but two ice cold Manhattan Special coffee sodas. After that, I'll have a big slice of watermelon to top off our lunch.

Mr. Pauli and I are sitting on the flatbed of the wagon, that is now empty, watching the traffic and Saturday workers are going by as we are eating our lunch. I notice that there is one melon left. This melon is the largest and seems to be the best of the lot that once was, but I am too hungry and thirsty to make a comment to Mr. Pauli about it. As I am eating and drinking my ice-cold Manhattan Special soda, I am thinking to myself that Mr. Pauli must have saved this melon to take home to his family.

It is now mid-afternoon and we are finishing our lunch. I'm wiped out, and I need a bath and after eating my big hero sandwich and drinking two ice-cold Manhattan Specials I feel like I can go to sleep. Mr. Pauli, is looking at me as I am dosing off in the corner of the wagon.

"Come on kid, wake up! This is where you live right? We sold all the melons there is nothing to unload. So, it doesn't make sense for you to come back to the stable with me."

"Yeah, this is where I live, a couple of floors above Nick's sandwich shop. Thanks, Mr. Pauli for letting me work with you today. I haven't counted all my tips yet, but thanks to the longshoremen I think I collected over five dollars total! I'm so tired but it was a very good day for me."

"Okay kid, I hope that you can carry one more melon." he continues by gesturing toward the one lone melon left on the wagon.

"Here, this melon I saved for you is to take home. Give it to your mother with my regards. Your parents are lucky to have a son that is such a hard worker."

I suddenly wake up.

"Thanks, Mr. Pauli! My mother will be very happy!"

I am now full of energy. Quickly jumping off the wagon Mr. Pauli is handing me the melon. Even though it is the largest melon on the wagon it seems as light as a feather and I am springing up the stairs to present it proudly like a bouquet of flowers to my mother.

Chapter 12

Johnny Pump-Ice Chips to Cool Off

I'm entering our apartment with the huge melon from Mr. Pauli the peddler in my arms. I'm a little disappointed that my mother is not here to greet me. The weight of this melon is starting to get to me and I think I am going drop it at any moment. I just don't know where to put it so I will lay it in our sink, this way my mother will immediately see it when she walks into our apartment. Boy, will she be surprised!

It is just too hot for me to stay home even though I need to wash and clean off the sweat and grime I accumulated in delivering the melons from Mr. Pauli's wagon, I think I'll venture out for some relief from this heat in our apartment.

I'll run downstairs and make a quick exit onto Columbia Street. After only a few steps away sits the delivery ice truck parked on Luquer Street and a bunch of kids begging for some ice chips.

One kid is standing out from the rest since he is about one foot taller than all the other kids around him. It's Nunzio (Superman) Rizzo looking to grab some ice chips to cool off from the heat. Nunzio is a big kid about a year older than the rest of the gang. Not only is he tall he is as strong as any man in the neighborhood. He has light brown hair, straight eyebrows and light green eyes with a flat nose and a pointed chin. He was dressed in blue jeans, white T-shirt, and sneakers. He standing next to Reno (the Greek) Paulettio who is the shortest kid in our gang. Reno is very dark skinned with a bushy mop of striate jet black hair, black eyes with a thin nose. He is wearing blue shorts, probably cut-off jeans, with his light blue T- shirt white socks and sneakers. His brother Henry is two years older and looks pretty much like Reno but only taller. I don't see him in the crowd of kids fighting for the ice chips. It is so funny to me to see 'Superman' and 'the Greek' standing next to each other; they looked like Mutt and Jeff. I don't want to fight this battle so I'll turn the corner onto Columbia Street.

As luck would have it I'm hearing a commotion and notice a bunch of adults, teenagers and little kids yelling and screaming as they are splashing themselves with an open Johnny Pump. The water is gushing so fast and furious out of the fire hydrant and when anyone tries to stand in front of it, water pressure tosses them onto the ground. Who cares, with the heat wave pushing 100 degrees everyone is just trying to cool off as best as they can. The fire department and the police are not too thrilled about losing all this drinking water in addition to having reduced water pressure that can hamper their efforts to put out a house or factory fire. The traffic is starting to back up on the street as it slows down. If you are in a car or truck you have to stop and roll up your windows to prevent the water from coming in. The trolley conductor is also alerting passengers to close the windows of the trolley on the side of the open Johnny Pump as they are going through the cascade of water

Cooling Off With The Ice Man

coming down upon them. Several teenagers and men are taking turns squatting down behind the hydrant and putting an open-ended metal can onto the water gushing out directly in front of them directing the water flow like a giant hose twenty to thirty feet into the air. It is quite a sight to see and hear tons of water crashing into the cars, trucks, and trolleys that have to pass through the gushing water. When this tremendous water pressure hits the side of a truck the metal cab vibrates and makes all kinds of loud deafening sounds echoing and vibrating against the buildings and windows in the neighborhood.

People are screaming and yelling from the thrill of seeing and hearing the water show. As I am approaching the active zone I get kidnapped by a bunch of teenagers who are carrying me toward the gushing water. I am squirming, fighting, and yelling as loud as I can in protest, but there was no way to escape the inevitable. I am too small to fight off my kidnappers and my yelling is lost in the roar of the gushing water. Then it is happening, Brrrrr... I am suddenly cold as the water hits my overheated body! The water pressure tosses me over and over again in the street. I feel like I am riding rapid waves and crashing into a number of giant rocks in some Colorado river. It is worth it as I stop moving forward and I land motionless, lying face up in a pool of water and I feel both cool and numb all over. Suddenly I am being dragged by the neck out of the street and onto the sidewalk only to realize that I am being hustled out of the way of on-coming traffic and imminent danger. My clothing is soaking wet but now I can join the water kidnappers and do my part to capture unsuspecting bystanders and hustle them into the ice-cold water.

I am late and so tired tonight that I hardly notice the big grin on my Mother's face. She is so happy that I brought home a watermelon for the 4th of July celebration!

Even though it is late I still have time to turn on the radio to listen to several of my favorite radio shows. So, I'll pull up a chair next to the radio and just like the RCA dog put my ear right next to the speaker. The first radio program is **The Lone Ranger** and after that, I am

Shooting Water From The Johnny Pump

looking forward to listening to my all-time favorite, scare me out of my mind: **The Inner Sanctum**. Well, I'll never make it since I will fall asleep leaning against the radio right after I hear the Long Ranger call out...

"High-O-Sliver".

My Mom pulls me gently into my cot and even though it was still a hot night I have no trouble falling asleep, my body exhausted from an exciting day and cool finish!

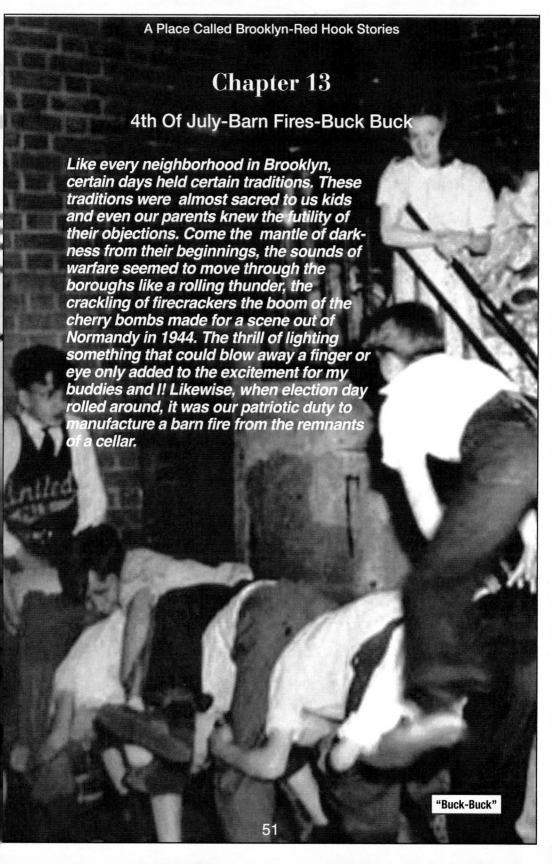

Chapter 13

4th Of July-Barn Fires-Buck Buck

Like every neighborhood in Brooklyn, certain days held certain traditions. These traditions were almost sacred to us kids and even our parents knew the futility of their objections. Come the mantle of darkness from their beginnings, the sounds of warfare seemed to move through the boroughs like a rolling thunder, the crackling of firecrackers the boom of the cherry bombs made for a scene out of Normandy in 1944. The thrill of lighting something that could blow away a finger or eye only added to the excitement for my buddies and I! Likewise, when election day rolled around, it was our patriotic duty to manufacture a barn fire from the remnants of a cellar.

"Buck-Buck"

I'm still recovering from my day with Mr. Pauli yesterday as I am waking up. I have sore muscles and pain all over my body. I figure we sold about 150 watermelons and I must have delivered about half that amount. But it is the 4th of July and the big day is finally here! It's about 9 AM and Jimmy is already waiting on my doorstep for me to come down to meet him.

Jimmy 'Pizza' is a skinny sort of kid with my build and a normal size head. He has jet-black hair with a crew cut with big dark, almost black, round eyes.

Most of the time he likes to play war with sticks that look like guns. He always wants to be the bad soldier and torture his enemy. I think he is a little weird. Jimmy's parents and aunt, who is my Godmother, are close friends of my Mom and Dad. Unlike my parents, Jimmy has a big family in the U.S. with loads of aunts, uncles, cousins and a grandmother. My Parents' families live or come from both Italy and Argentina.

I think that Jimmy's parents are rich since his father and mother own Rosie's Italian Restaurant and Bar. Once in a while, we stop at Rosie's Italian Restaurant and Bar, sometimes Jimmy will ask his father to make us a pizza for lunch, it's always a great treat for me.

We don't have a solid plan for our day, but we do know that we intend to blow up half the neighborhood come sundown.

"Hey, Jimmy what's up? Are you ready to do some damage today?"

He's looking at me with a big smile on his face.
"No shit, I bought a load of fireworks on President Street last week".

'No doubt from Blackie Parisi.' I think to myself.

"Me and Pecker got a bag of fireworks and cherry bombs too! Let's go find Pecker and figger out when we should start this war."

We are walking toward Pecker's house together. The neighborhood seems so quiet! All the factories are closed, and the longshoremen have the day off while Nick's Sandwich Shop is also closed for the holiday. We know that each street will do their best to have a bigger and louder display of fireworks than the next block just for the fun of it.

The main source of wood comes from the condemned houses that are being torn down to make room for the Brooklyn Battery Tunnel. Another great source is all the empty wooden grape boxes stacked up in front of the many houses during the wine-making season or any wooden bench, cellar board covers or wood pallets that we happen to find.

Come Election Day, people will stack up all this junk and wood on every corner and the pile will be over twenty feet high, they soak it with gasoline and light it.

Each block will do their best to try to outdo the other, like some sort of competition or contest. Every year some kids burn their hands or clothing by getting too close to the fire in order to throw more stuff on the blaze.

Wow, I don't know how the firemen keep up with all these fires going on at the same time. It is quite a sight, as sometimes these fires will set off a building fire.

But today we're looking to do our best to set off as many fire-works as possible. We turn the corner to Pecker's house and start calling out his name.

"Pecker get the Hell down here."

"It's too early to start shooting off our stash of fireworks!"

So, we'll look around if there is anyone else hanging out on the corner. We see Reno, his brother Henry, Mikie, Vinnie, Nunzio and a couple of other kids hanging out. We'll hook up the rest of the gang and choose sides to play "Buck-Buck". There are five of us on each team. Each team will have a Captain and a 'pillow kid'.

I am the Captain of my team and Henry is the Captain of his team. We are playing on the sidewalk near Hicks and Nelson Street against the wall of the Cardinal Tank factory building. My team is up first. Reno, a short kid is the 'pillow' of Henry's team; he has to put his back against the wall. Next, Henry and the rest of his team line-up bent over holding each other to form one large horse. The first kid on the line is bent over holding Reno, the 'pillow's' waist, while he is standing upright with his back against the wall. There you have it, four kids bent over holding Reno against the wall.
Now the action starts.

The first team is lined up back in the street about twenty feet away. I will direct the smallest kids to run as fast as they can and jump on the horse. I'll save Nunzio, who is the tallest and heaviest kid for last, that's why we call him "Superman". After my team is all on the horse I'll yell out:

"Buck-Buck how many horns are up?"

The first jumper on my team will hold up his hand and show Reno his fingers - anywhere from one to four fingers. If Henry calls out the right number their team goes next. If the horse gives way before the number is called because of all the weight on them, well, we go again. The horse is holding long enough for Henry to make the call. "Four Horns" It's the right call confirmed by his team member, Reno the pillow, looks at the first jumper as the call is being made. We'll play this game for a couple of hours until it will start to get dark, then it will be time for us to start our 4th of July celebration.

Chapter 14

Baseball Cards - Fireworks Celebration

It is getting darker but not dark enough to shoot off our fireworks.

"Let's play picture cards while we're waiting for it to get real dark."

The Kids Can't Wait For The 4th Of July Celebration To Start.

"Great idea Jimmy, I'll go home and get my baseball cards and meet you and Pecker back here in ten minutes."

Running upstairs I get my shoebox full of baseball cards that I put under my sister's bed. It takes us less than ten minutes to meet at the corner of Hicks and Luquer Street in front of 'Chickie's' grocery store. I don't know how much time we have to play this game before it gets dark enough to shoot off all our fireworks, but we need to pass the time and not burn our fireworks until it's really dark outside.

So here we are, Jimmy, Pecker and me flipping picture baseball cards. I like to play this game. We like to buy these picture cards hoping that we would find our favorite baseball players when we open the 2-cent bubble gum wrapper with the gum and baseball card in it. I like the bubble gum too!

The gum is the size of the baseball cards and when you put this wad of gum in your mouth you can blow bubbles all day. Pecker and I are Brooklyn Dodger fans, "Dem Bums", but Jimmy is always rooting for the Yankees. I don't think of anyone I know who is a New York Giants fan. The game starts by each of us shuffling, ten baseball cards face down with the three of us in a small circle.

I start by flipping two cards that land face up on the ground. Pecker now tries to flip his two cards to match mine. If his cards

You Can Trade Then Them Or Flip them & Get Free Bubble Gum Too.

land face up he wins that round if he doesn't match my cards, I win. The winner of a round always goes second trying to flip and match the cards lying on the ground. Pecker does not match my cards so I win this round. Now it's Jimmy turn to flip and lay two cards on the ground. When one of us wins we take a close look at the cards we won to see if any favorite baseball players are in the stack. If we see one of the players we need to complete our team, we set the baseball card aside for our collection. It's a cutthroat game; everyone wants to have all the players of the team they're rooting for. Roger showed me how to play this game and he always tries to con me out of the best baseball cards. Roger is a deadly flipper. He tries to make me lay down six cards and you know what he will flip and match all of my six cards every time! I don't play with him anymore.

We are all looking at each other and agree to stop playing the baseball card game. It's now dark enough and it's time to start blowing up our fireworks! Jimmy, Pecker and I collect our stash of fireworks from our hideout. In order to keep lighting the fireworks as fast as we can we light up slow burning punks. They smell better than some of the cigars that many of the teenagers were puffing on. We started blowing up the smaller ladyfingers and firecrackers first. We would go slow and easy so we could make the fun last as long as possible.

Ladyfingers are tiny little firecrackers that you can light up and hold on the tip of two fingers and when they go "Bang" the pain on your fingertips is not so bad. One pack holds about eighty ladyfingers. Each pack of ladyfingers and firecrackers are supposed to go off at one time. But we will unravel each pack so we can light up one ladyfinger or one firecracker at a time.

After an hour or so we are lighting up the small stuff one at a time as we are bored. We want to up the action so we start throwing packs of fireworks at each other. It's like an army of soldiers that are shooting machine guns at you. Once we start it won't take us long to burn through the small stuff.

It has a life of its' own. We always start slow and easy, one little bang at a time, like machine guns, then faster. The fast and continuous 'BANG-BANG-BANG!' goes on until a whole pack is finally spent.

Now comes the color phase of our celebration! Roman candles and rockets, and it's really starting to get dangerous! If anyone of us gets hit with these Roman candles or rockets we will end up in the hospital with serious burns and if we survive we would be scarred for life. I'm yelling at Pecker.

"Stop the shit…. Don't point that Roman candle at me or I'll put this cherry bomb up your ass!"

I think he got the message. I must say that the colors are beautiful. The whole block is aglow with bright colors that seem to be everywhere.

Here we go… first small ladyfingers, second firecrackers, then Roman candles & rockets. What's next? You guessed it! The "BIG" Bang! We are throwing cherry bombs, ash cans, and mortars. It is getting louder and LOUDER! Roger is throwing his cherry bombs off the roof. We are ducking more than once. Explosions echo off the buildings again and again. The sounds make your ears ring and your body shake. What a great feeling.

Jimmy is the igniter. Pecker and I are placing a cherry bomb under an upside down tin can with the fuse sticking out. Jimmy will light the fuse with his punk and then… "BANG". The can goes flying up two hundred feet or more. It doesn't get any better than this.

It was almost midnight and we are sitting on the sidewalk, out of ammo enjoying the light show. I am sorry to think that this 4th of July is about to end. But the good news is that the summer is just starting and going back to school is a long couple of months away!

"Wasn't this the best show ever?"

"Yeah Jimmy for me too, but you say the same thing every year. I only wish it gets a little cooler this summer so that we can hang out without this heat killing us." Pecker jumps in.

"I've had it for this year. I'm going home. Let's get together tomorrow."

Chapter 15

Lead & Copper $$$ – Egg Creams

If you grew up in Post-War Brooklyn, the favored treat for the kids on the street was an egg cream. This magical concoction, brewed behind a soda fountain counter by a soda jerk was an eggless wonder that filled generations of kids' appetites. One could try to create one in The Bronx or Queens or even Staten Island, but it would never taste as good as it did in Brooklyn.

We spent all of our deposit bottle money on fireworks, so Pecker and I have to come up with a new plan to build up our dollar pool. It is about 9 A.M. we are sitting on the stoop on Nelson Street and my cousin Johnny is walking by. Well, he's not really my aunt or uncle's son but he's what we call a dishwater cousin, which means we're not related at all. His mother and my mother are great friends, because they're like sisters. That's why Johnny and his brothers and sisters are all my cousins. He's much older, like 15 going on twenty. We all look up to him. He looks much older than his age, a good-looking guy and the girls are always all over him. He has black hair slicked back with pomade jell. Today he's wearing a white tee shirt, black pegged pants and sneakers. I'm thinking that maybe he could help us put together some cash. After all, Johnny always has a scam going and he has more street smarts than all the kids I know.

He comes up to us.

"Hi, Johnny, where you heading?"

As Johnny is sitting down on the stoop he is saying...

"Nowhere in particular. You guys look down and out, what's up?"

"We burned all our money on fireworks and we're trying to think of a way we can get some cash to fill our pockets again."

"Ha, well, maybe you can hook up with me. I plan to head over to the dilapidated buildings and rip out as much lead and copper I can find. Then I'll head over to the junkyard where they pay cash for the stuff. That's where the BIG money is!"

All those dollar signs have gotten the best of me. I can see Pecker Face who has his eyes wide open.

"It sounds good to me, but my mom told me that she would kill me if I ever went into those condemned buildings, they are just too dangerous to fool with."

"Are you crazy! We can never get that kind of cash collecting 2 cents deposit bottles. We can earn 10 to 20 times more than penny-pinching empty deposit bottles. Well you're getting older and it's time for you to take some chances!"

"OK, let's do it. Can you show us what to do?"

"It's a dirty job, but if you strike a good lead and copper mine it's worth the risk."

We jump off the stoop and start on our way toward the Brooklyn Battery Tunnel construction site.

"Pepino, we better be a little careful! We have to be on the look-out for the watchman, cops, and gangs of kids looking for the same prize as we want."

At this point, I want to cut and run.

But the dollar signs are too strong and the three of us keep moving. We find two targets. Both buildings have broken windows from kids having target practice with rocks or slingshots. The doors are ripped out and there are piles of junk everywhere. We'll be lucky if we don't get cut from all the broken glass or fall a couple of stories from the holes in the floors.

Suddenly its hitting me!

What happened to all the families who lived here once? I start remembering stories of U.S. Marshals pushing people who had little or nothing into the street in all kinds of weather. What happened to them? Where did they go? I got a sick feeling that the next time it could be my family. I snap out of it when we get inside the building.

"First we start looking for the bathrooms or kitchens that have not been picked clean" handing us a couple of rusty cast iron pipes he picks up.

"These pipes are the tools of the trade. We can use them like hammers to crack open toilets, sinks, and bathtubs."

We find a toilet, which to our surprise, is untouched. Pecker is the first one to give it a whack with his pipe. Now there was stuff flying everywhere. After an hour or two banging away at anything we can find, we are covered with plaster dust, dirt and some goop that smells like shit.

The smell of piss mixed in with the dust is so strong that I can't stop choking. My eyes are burning and snot is gushing out of my nose. Johnny wasn't kidding when he said it's a dirty job!

After we put aside as many lead pipes we can find, Johnny is now showing us how to rip out BX cables from the plaster walls and start stripping them for the copper wires inside. All in all, it is a good day's work. We put together about forty pounds of lead and twenty pounds of copper. We managed to avoid the watchman and police but we do notice a gang of young kids tearing out linoleum to make ammunition for their carpet guns. They don't even look at us.

Moving as fast as we can, we are dragging our loot to a vacant lot where Johnny is starting a fire. He is explaining that we need the fire to melt down the lead and burn the casing off the copper wires. We will spend the whole day working our butts off.

Johnny brings the lead and copper to the junkyard where he collects ninety dollars and some loose change. He comes back and shows us the money. WOW! Pecker and I are so happy until it comes to splitting up the loot. Johnny keeps fifty dollars for himself and gives us twenty bucks apiece.

It's not exactly a three-way split. We'll use the loose change to buy egg cream sodas for our ratty looking crew. We go to the candy store that has a soda fountain. Why they call this soda an egg cream I'll never know. We sit at a small counter and ask the kid behind the counter to make us three egg cream sodas.

An Ice Cold Egg Cream Is the Best Treat

Good thing the owner of the candy store isn't there because he would have thrown us out we smell so bad! I just love to watch them make this soda that has no eggs in it. The kid loads a glass of Foxes-U-Bet chocolate syrup then puts a splash of milk on the syrup. Then comes the tricky part, he will tilt the glass and shoot seltzer into the mix holding a spoon while mixing. The syrup, milk, and seltzer are starting to foam up. There it is, a chocolate soda thing of beauty called an egg cream! We'll finish the sodas in about thirty seconds.

I am still upset about the split but I realize that we won't need Johnny to help us on the next job. We have our money. Now, I have to go home and try to explain to my mother how I got all this shit on my body. I don't think she will buy any story I tell her so I better be ready to face the pain of the wooden spoon.

Chapter 16

Octagon Soap & Rubber Band Carpet Guns

It is almost dinner time as I am trying to sneak back into my apartment. My Mom is putting together a meal of vegetables and macaroni. It doesn't look like we will have any meat tonight. She is cleaning the veggies when she looks up. She has a look of horror on her face. I am a sorry sight. My skin and face are covered with dirt, plaster and a smelly goop. My clothes are also dirty and ripped when they got caught onto the sharp wood and nails that were sticking out of the floors, walls, along with broken glass. My dirty arms and legs are covered with cuts, scratches, and blood. I am a bloody mess. I look like a crazy wounded alien from outer space. She is yelling out:

"Madonna Mia! Cosa un fatto." In English "Oh Blessed Mother, what did you do?"

I stand there frozen, unable to move. I close my eyes, waiting for a whack from the wooden spoon.

I am shocked as she runs over and hugs me. I think for sure that she is going to kill me. She is shaking and crying. She keeps on saying over and over again:

"Figlio Mia, Figlio Mia (My Son, My Son.) "Cosa hai fatto mia figlio?" (What did you do my child?)

I think she thinks I am badly injured. My Mom is so upset. I feel so bad that I hurt her. I'd rather take a beating than doing this to my mother. It takes fifteen minutes for her to calm down. She checks my cuts and scratches, rips off my tee shirt, shorts, underwear, sneakers, and socks.

I am standing naked in the middle of our kitchen. She puts the boiling macaroni water and some cold water into the laundry basin and starts scrubbing me down with Octagon Soap. My Mom uses this brown soap to clean our laundry and scrubs it on her washboard. My father will wash up with Octagon Soap when he comes home from doing a dirty job on the ship he is working on that day. There are times when my father comes home late from his ship-scrapping job, his face and body are so covered with so much black soot that I do not recognize him. When someone in our family is constipated, Mom will heat up a pint of water and dip the Octagon Soap in warm water for an enema. I hate enemas! My sister will not go near Octagon Soap. The princess would only use Lifebuoy Soap to wash her skin.

I am thinking that it is a good thing I hid my loot before I came home. Otherwise, it may have gone into the garbage along with my dirty clothes! Mom manages to get me squeaky clean and turns her attention to my wounds, treating them with Iodine. The sting of the Iodine is so painful that I would be happier to take the sting of the wooden spoon instead.

It was a good thing my father isn't home yet. I don't know what he would have done to me. After I am clean and medicated, I put on a clean T-shirt and shorts. I sit at the kitchen table. It is quiet, very quiet, no sound at all except for the running water. My Mom just continues to clean the vegetables. No yelling, no beating, just like a war movie when the Japanese were trying to get information out of a prisoner of war. The prisoner was not allowed to move, talk, or drink, and had to sit for hours until he spilled the beans. I am confused and sad as I stand there watching my mother preparing dinner. She never tells my father about how bad I looked when I came home that day.

Dinner is finished and I turn on the radio to listen to some of my favorite programs. I like to listen to **The Lone Ranger** and **Inner Sanctum**. **The Lone Ranger** stories are adventures where I imagine that I am his sidekick in chasing and capturing the bad guys. My body can feel and my mind can see the action all at the same time.

Meanwhile, **Inner Sanctum** show will scare me to death. Even the commercial for Bromo Seltzer at the beginning of the show is scary. I just can't get enough of the suspense and mystery stories that will make my imagination go wild. It is getting late and my sister assembled my cot in the living room so that I can go to bed.

The Lone Ranger
Radio Show

I am lying on my cot but I can't go to sleep. I keep on thinking about the events and adventures we had today and how badly I upset my mother. I can't change what I did so I start thinking about meeting Jimmy, Pecker, and Mike tomorrow. We made plans to work on making some rubber band carpet guns so that we could play "WAR".

Roger the 'Professor' lives in my building and started teaching me how to make carpet guns about a year ago. He is known in the neighborhood as the expert gun maker. I never made these guns on my own. I do believe that if we put our heads together we can start to make a few carpet guns tomorrow.

I have a plan; first, we have to go to Mike's family barn on Luquer Street and get some empty lettuce crates. Mike is Paulie Mengiano (hook nose), the peddler's grandson. The barn houses several horses and wagons. Paulie and his son Ju Ju, Mike's uncle, sell fruit and vegetables from these wagons all around the neighborhood. So there is a good chance we can find a few leftover empty lettuce crates there. Besides the lettuce crate, we need to get rubber bands, nails, close pins, a saw and of course, linoleum ammunition for the pistols. We also have to find some three-foot sticks to make rifles.

If we plan to make a cannon, we'll need a couple of two by fours and an old bike tube. I'm not sure how to make a trigger for the cannon. I'll have to ask Roger for some help. It may take a couple of days for us to put this stuff together before we can start making these carpet guns. I think that the pistols will be easy to make if we find the lettuce crates. It's the frames that hold the crate together, is what we need first. Each crate may have two or three frames. We can make four pistols from one frame. That means we may get eight or twelve pistols from one lettuce crate. According to Roger, we can nail three or four pistols together to make a machine gun. That Roger is a genius. He just comes up with these ideas and then makes it happen.

Chapter 17

Making Carpet Guns

It is morning and I'm at Luquer & Hicks Street. Pecker is already here waiting for me. I can see Jimmy Pizza is walking towards us from Columbia Street. Henry and his brother Reno haven't shown up. Mike Tomato is down from his apartment above his granmother 'Chickie's' grocery store on the corner. I wonder why everyone calls his grandma 'Chickie'. There are three wooden buildings in back of the store along Luquer St. One building has two wagons and equipment for the horses to pull. The second building stores the fresh fruit and vegetables that have to be sold today. The last building or barn has two stalls for the horses.

On top of these buildings, Mikey and his younger brother Vincent have put up a large pigeon coop. They get to the coop by stepping out of their apartment window directly above the store and in line with the rooftop of the outbuildings. They can fly as many as 100 pigeons at a time. It is exciting to watch all these pigeons coming down and landing at the same time. I feel a little jealous that Mike and his family have their own business and all that property.

It is quite a setup except for the smell of the horses in the barn. I think they put the horses in the last building to keep the smell far away as they can from where they live.

We are short by two guys but the rest of the crew is ready to work on making the carpet guns. Mike is smiling.

"Guess what? I put aside a lettuce crate my uncle Ju Ju gave me when he came home last night."

I Smack Mike on the back.

"Great! Now we have to get a saw, rubber bands, and nails."

We have to split up so we can cover more ground. Mike thinks that he can get a saw from his grandfather's tool shed behind the wagons. I will go to Nick's sandwich shop to see if he can give me some rubber bands. I also plan to get clothespins from my mother's laundry basket. Jimmy Pizza and Pecker have to find nails and linoleum. This means that they are going to eventually search for this stuff in some of those condemned buildings at the Brooklyn Battery tunnel construction site.

After what happened yesterday, I'm not ready to go anywhere near any of those dilapidated buildings.

It's about 10:30 AM and we all get back together again.

Pecker and Jimmy find some nails and rip out a big square of linoleum from one of the old buildings. They also found two sticks that are about the right size needed to make carpet gun rifles. I ask Nick at the sandwich shop if he will give me some rubber bands. He says that he thinks he has some put-away and is starting to look around the sandwich shop. He gives me six rubber bands he finds in his junk drawer. Nick is such a nice man. He always looks after the kids on the block and will never let us go hungry. Going upstairs I look for the clothespins.

Mom isn't home, so I'll take three clothespins from her basket. I don't think she will miss only three clothespins. Mike Tomato gets the hammer and saw from the tool shed. We have collected all our stuff and go to the vacant lot across the street.

The vacant lot is a dump site for all kinds of junk. There is a collection of old broken ice boxes, assorted soda boxes, old car and truck tires, old window frames with broken glass sticking out all over. The lot is also a dumpsite for old broken pieces of lumber with nails sticking out, rusting empty paint cans and rotting fruit and vegetables. The smell is pretty bad but we need a place to work.

We settle on a spot where we can use an old icebox as a work-bench. The icebox is pretty level even though all the doors are missing. Since Mike has a saw and hammer he is in charge of taking the lettuces crate apart. Mike has to be careful not to damage the wood frames. Meanwhile, the rest of us are working on the old linoleum.

The old linoleum is very brittle so we can break it into tiny squares by bending it with our hands. We can also use these pieces for the ammunition we need for both the pistols and rifles we are making. We have finished about one hundred little squares for the ammo. Mike did a great job. We have three wood frames to work with. Mike is using a pencil to mark off the cuts he is going to make with the saw. As he starts cutting the pistols, I will hold the wood frames steady for him on our icebox workbench.

We have completed twelve rough-cut pistols. Now comes the hard part. Mike has to precisely saw the joint of each pistol on two sides at a 45-degree angle. It's a delicate cut since the wood is glued together at that joint. If you cut too far it will destroy the trigger and we will have to throw it away.

We are all coaching Mike as he is thinking he is cutting too deep. It turns out some of the cuts are too deep. We have to throw away two pistols out of twelve. OK, we've got 10 guns to work with. Pecker nails a rubber band on the bottom of the barrel. He is nailing some on the bottom of the barrel and he is nailing a few at the tip of the barrel. When complete the rubber band has to be pulled as tight as possible around the tip of the barrel until it hooks onto the back nib left by the joint cut. We complete one pistol and cock the rubber band. I then slip a piece of linoleum into the rubber band and with my thumb pushed the rubber band off the back of the pistol where it is being held ready to fire. 'SNAP!' The linoleum bullet flies about 20 feet. Not too accurate of a shot but who cares if it works.

We are all quiet while watching the carpet fly off the pistol.

"Holy Shit! It works." I yell in amazement.

Carpet Gun Pistols & Rifle
Can't Shoot Straight

Then we all start yelling, screaming and jumping around.

Now for the rifle. Jimmy meanwhile is nailing the clothespin that has a spring action about one-third the away from the back end of the stick. He is now lacing three rubber bands together tight as he can, around the stick until they reach the clothespin or trigger. He is working the rubber bands over and around the clothespin to make it a tight fit. This way when you work the last rubber band into the clothespin trigger, it will not slip out. You need to make it tight enough that it will be ready to release only when you're ready to shoot. We are now ready to go to war! As for the cannon, well, we have to wait for Roger to help us. Henry and Reno have to make their own guns.

Chapter 18
Hopscotch & Roger's Cannon

Hopscotch, an ancient children's game is nothing new and can be traced back to ancient Rome before it ever came to Red Hook for it was Ancient Rome where children played it first. The kids in my neighborhood, however, were not the first English speaking children to play, that honor goes to the 17th-Century English children, who named it: "Scotch-hop" or "Scotch-hopper" as they sometimes called it.

It's a long day but it is worth it. We've finished six carpet gun pistols and two rifles. We break up for the day and as I am starting toward home I notice that Joanie and some other girls are playing "Hopscotch". I will not admit it to my friends but I like playing Hopscotch with Joanie. Joanie is about ten years old and lives across the street from me on Luquer Street. Joanie is a pretty girl, and she's a little taller than me. She has brown eyes and brown hair, made up in pigtails. She likes to wear farmer jeans and sneakers.

I am calling out to her "Hello".

"Hey Pippino, come play Hopscotch with us."

Well, I'm looking around and I don't see any of my friends hanging around, so why not?

"OK."

I'm running over to her side of the street and she is giving me a roller skate key to play with. The Hopscotch boxes are already laid out in chalk on the sidewalk with boxes numbered from one to nine and a winner box at the top. You can play with two, three, or four people. The first player has to toss a bottle cap or roller skate key into the first box. Then hop with one or two feet over and around the box with the key in it. You are not allowed to have two feet in a box or touch any lines with your foot when hopping or you're out and the next player gets a turn. If you hop into each box, turn and hop all the way back you go again and toss your key into the next numbered box (#2). If you don't make any mistakes you can continue to the next box (#3). If you are able to hop in all theboxes before anyone else can, you are the winner of the Hopscotch game!

I'm pretty good at this game but I can't beat Joanie (a girl). If my buddies find out that I lost to a girl they will laugh and tease me to death. That's why I play this game when my buddies aren't around. Joanie and I play a couple of games and Joanie wins every game hands down. I've have enough, being whipped by a girl is no fun so I'll cross the street and go home.

As I am climbing the stairs I can hear Roger talking to his mother Emma. So I keep on climbing the stairs all the way up to the top floor apartment where Roger lives. I never knock on Roger's apartment door, as it is always open. So I walk in and

The Carpet Gun Cannon Design Will Be Like The Rifle

ask Emma where Roger is? "He's in his laboratory".

Roger's family has a double apartment or a total of eight rooms. It is big but it always looks crowded to me, after all, nine people live here. Roger's laboratory and bedroom combination is a small room about eight by ten feet. The room is located away in the back with one window. Roger notices me coming into his room.

"What's up Keyno?"

I tell him what our gang is working on all day and that we are making carpet gun pistols and rifles.

"WOW! You guys had a busy day!"

"Yeah, but we're stuck on how to make a carpet cannon."

"Well maybe I can design one for you."

He sits at his little table while I sit on his bed. He takes a pad and pencil and starts drawing. Quickly transferring one idea after another, ripping at least six or eight drawings before he's finally done.

"I GOT IT!"

It is amazing to see all the details and instructions he is putting together on his drawing.

"WOW! This looks great but I don't know if me and my pals can make this thing?"

"I make the Cannon pretty much like a rifle. The big difference will be the size and the fact that we will use an old bicycle tire instead of a rubber band. I have to work on the trigger because the clothes pin is too small to hold a tire tube. Just put all the materials together and I will be there to help you guys make this cannon once I figure out how to make the trigger. You need to find a couple of two by fours, an old bicycle inner tube, nails, some small sticks, a rubber ball, rubber bands, and some rope or twine."

"Roger, wait a minute, I'll never remember all this stuff."

"OK, OK, I will make a list for you to follow."

"Thanks, Roger, I can't wait to work with you on this new carpet gun cannon idea."

Roger looks like he wants to ask me something.

"Hey Roger, do you have something on your mind?"

"Matter of fact I do. What would you say if I asked you to help me build a small pigeon coop on our roof?"

This takes me by surprise, I am lost for words and it takes me a couple of minutes to respond.

"I had dreams about making a coop on our roof, but for one thing my parents will be against it. The Defonte's who own the building will be against it. The women in the neighborhood will be against it. I will be scared shitless trying to sneak all the wood, tarpaper, shingles and chicken wire to the roof. Then there's all the banging to put all this stuff together to make a coop. If we could do all this without getting caught, then there's the money we need to buy all this stuff not to mention the cost for the birds and the feed."

Roger doesn't say anything until I finish talking.

"You know what, you're such a shit head. How did you come up with all this stuff? Maybe you should go hide in the toilet. Look at you! You had the balls to go find Blackie Parisi in that shithole on President Street to by fireworks. You may be just a kid but you have to take some chances in order to get what you want. Just think about it and try not to pee your pants. Meanwhile, I will work on putting some money away for the material and the birds. So maybe one day when you stop being afraid of all this stuff we'll talk about this again."

Stunned, I won't say another word. I'll go downstairs to my own apartment on the second floor, I have dinner and then listen to some radio shows before I go to bed.

Chapter 19

Kids at War

Suddenly, it is morning and it feels like it's going to be another hot day. I can't help thinking about Roger's plan to put a small pigeon coop on the roof of our building. I know I'm just a kid but I still feel that we will catch Hell from our family and a whole lot of people in the neighborhood. I'm sure that Roger will keep the pressure on me until he gets me to go along with his plan. I don't want to think about this anymore. I'll just have a quick breakfast because I'm in a hurry to meet up with our gang.

"I'm running downstairs and as I turn the corner and start to walk on Luquer Street towards Hicks Street, I can see the gang waiting for me. (Pecker, Jimmy, Mikie, Reno, Henry, Nunzio, Ricardo Six-Finger and even Vinnie The Coop are there.) Ricardo and Vinnie are both the best Peashooters on the block. Everything else that we throw at each other in our war games like water balloons, carpet guns, tomatoes or even slingshots generally never hit their targets dead on. Vinnie is so good he can hit a rat that's trying to get into his pigeon coop from thirty feet away. He hits the rat so hard the rat jumps high into the air and then runs into his rat hole. It would be deadly if they both end up on the same team so we try to keep them apart so that everyone has a fighting chance."

The word is out that we plan to have a carpet gun war. There now are another four kids who I don't know. They come from a couple blocks away, closer to the Red Hook Projects. They are asking if they can join the action. We agree and start choosing sides; there are about six kids in each army, and each army has to make a flag and collect any junk they can find to make a fort. Collecting junk in our neighborhood is not hard to do. The cannon has to wait for the next war since the invasion is about to start.

Even though we don't have time to make the cannon for this war, we do have lots of firepower. We have put together carpet pistols, machine gun, rifles that were made the other day and linoleum for ammunition. We also collect an old icebox, a bunch of old tires, wood pallets and boxes, doors and assorted lumber. We make two forts, one on each side of the street. Along with the carpet guns we have, we also have slingshots, small rocks for ammo, waterballoons, pea shooters (good thing Ricardo six fingers is in our Army), tomatoes, potatoes, carrots and any rotted vegetables that Mr. Pauli is throwing away.

We even found some old pots and pans that we can use as helmets. We decorate our faces and bodies with charcoal like war paint. It is quite a sight. On one side of the street is the Red Flag Army and across the street, they are facing the Black Flag Army. It is hot mid-afternoon summer day and both armies are ready for some action.

Without warning the war starts when each army throws water balloons at each other to helping to cool off on this hot day. Each army has about two hundred rounds of carpet ammo, and every carpet pistol, machine gun, and rifle has a two-guy team. One member of the team loads and the other fires as fast as he can. There are bits of carpet flying everywhere, yet the shooters have no idea if the bits of carpet they are firing will hit anyone as they just keep blindly aiming at the fort across the street. The carpet shot is not accurate like a bullet; it just flies in all kinds of crazy directions.

If you are unlucky and one of the bits of linoleum bullets hits you, it could and will cut you. So you better keep your head down as much as possible. The old pots and pan helmets can help protect you from all the stuff that's flying around but if one hits your eye it will get you a trip to the hospital ER. That goes for the slingshots and peashooters as well.

We are hot and heavy into the action with: carpet guns, water balloons, peashooters, slingshots, and my favorite, rotted tomatoes, potatoes, and vegetables, and there's nowhere to hide. I get hit with a couple of tomatoes and it looks like there's blood all over me. I can hear the pinging echo of peas and rocks hitting my helmet. There are bits of carpets lying all around me. I can see Pecker picking them up and reusing them to fire back at the enemy. Our black flag is all messed up with rotted vegetables. Some kids were crying and in pain from getting hit with bits of carpet and rocks from the slingshots.

They may be hurt but no one is stopping, we just keep shooting and throwing everything around us at the enemy. WAR is great! Now, for the final charge! We will use sticks with a sharp point as swords and run at the enemy's fort as quickly as we can. To win the war we have to get to the enemies red flag before they get to ours. I yell:

"CHARGE!"

All our soldiers are picking up their swords and running at the fort across the street. The desperate hand-to-hand battle is now beginning! Good thing we have Nunzio and Pecker who are the biggest and tallest soldiers in our army. I can see that our army has a chance to win this battle! With our swordsticks hitting each other and more rotten tomatoes along with carrots being thrown at us I yell out to Nunzio:

"GRAB THE FLAG!"

Nunzio turns and is knocking over Mikey and Henry and grabs the red flag claiming:

"VICTORY!!!".

Everyone has stopped while we do our victory dance. It takes about ten minutes for us to settle down. We are sitting on the curb looking at the mess all around us. I turn to Pecker:

Red & Black Army
Flags Ready

"WOW! It was a Hell of a battle. Look at all this shit. Is anyone hurt?"

Pecker, looking at Nunzio utters:

"Yeah, I think Nunzio is hurting bad!"

I am walking over to where Nuzzio is sitting:

"Hey, Nunzio, are you okay?"

"I don't think so. My hand hurts like hell."

He is showing me his hand. There's a big bump on the back of his hand between his thumb and first finger. Turning his hand over I see that there is a hole in the palm of his hand with a piece of wood sticking out of it and blood all around it. It's making me sick to even look at it.

"We better get you home right away, Nunzio!"

We get up from the curb and walk to his house. I knock on the door and his mother opening it looks at us.

"WHAT HAPPENED TO YOU KIDS?"

We are all wet and covered with rotten vegetables.

"Aw, we were playing war. I think Nunzio is hurt. Can you please check his hand?"

Well, she is letting out a scream looking at it. Crying and yelling.

"NUNZIO GET IN HERE! I have to get dressed and take you to see the doctor right away!"

She doesn't say a word to me and just closes the door. I stand there transfixed at the closed door for a couple of minutes, then, leaving, I'll go over to where the rest of the gang is sitting. I am very upset because Nunzio is hurt.

"I took Nunzio home and his mom is upset and rushing him to the doctor's office!"

I think Pecker is going to start crying, too.

"Don't worry Pecker, I think he'll be OK. He must have been stabbed with a wooden sword when he went to grab the red flag and it broke off in his hand."

Pecker has his head down. I put my hand on his shoulder.

"I'm heading home, OK?"

Pecker is shaking his head.

I get home and it is a good thing my mother is still out shopping. I run over to the laundry sink and wash up a fast as I can. I throw my dirty clothes under my sister's bed and I put on a fresh pair of socks, clean shorts, and T-shirt. I hope my mother doesn't notice the cuts on my arms. It could have been the greatest day ever if Nunzio didn't get hurt.

Chapter 20

Superman-Lash La Rue-Charlotte Russe

It is a long night. I just cannot stop thinking about Nunzio and how his Mom screamed when she looked at the hole in his hand and saw all that blood. I always look up to Nunzio after all he is Superman. I keep thinking about how he got hurt so bad. He didn't even cry out in pain, he just held his hand and said:

"It really hurts so bad."

It's morning and the summer heat is still with us. I think I have to visit Nunzio to see if he's okay.

I checked my box of comic books that I hide under my parent's bed. I find a couple of Superman comic books that I bought from Roger last month. Roger is always trying to sell me stuff. I like to read comic books but mostly I like to look at the colorful drawings. One book is about Superman fighting a bunch of aliens from outer space.

Nunzio is just like Superman, he's always trying to save the day and keep us from getting hurt. The other Superman comic book is a story that tells how Superman fought off man-eating giant worms by throwing them into the sun. I hope that Nunzio will like to read these comic books as much as I do.

I'll go down to Defonte's Sandwich Shop and buy a Devil Dog. Nunzio loves Devil Dogs. A Devil Dog is a long chocolate cake shaped like a hot dog and filled in the middle with a white cream. I'll try my best not to eat this dog before it gets to Nunzio. As I walk to the middle of the block on Luquer Street where Nunzio lives, I have the comic books tucked under my left arm and I'm holding the Devil Dog in my left hand. Knocking on Nunzio's ground floor apartment door I hear feet walking towards the door and Nunzio's Mom calling out

"Who is it?"

"It's me Pepino, Mrs. Rizzo."

"Okay, I'll be right there."

Mrs. Rizzo unlocks the door with a big smile on her face. Phew! I was so scared that she is blaming me for that deep cut on Nunzio's hand.

"Pepino! Come in, come in. Nuzzio is in the kitchen eating his breakfast right now."

I find Nunzio sitting at the kitchen table eating a couple of eggs with his right hand and a sling holding his left arm. He has a big white bandage wrapped around his left hand.

"Hey, Nunzio how are you doing?"

He is looking at me with some egg on his chin.

"Wow! I never thought that I could get hurt this bad. My Mom rushed me to the Doctor's office and he put me in his car and took me to the Hospital ER. They had to cut the back of my hand to pull out the pointed broken stick that was stuck there! It was a piece of a broken wooden sword that looked about two inches long. I was screaming when they pulled it out, it hurt like hell. Then they cleaned the wound and put fifty stitches to close the hole in the top and bottom of my hand.

The pain was more than I could stand. They gave me a shot, wrapped my hand and put my arm in a sling."

Laughing he is asking me:

"What's new with you?"

I'm just standing there looking at the runny egg on his chin.

"Ugh, I brought you some Superman comics and a Devil Dog. I hope you get better soon."

"Thanks, I sure feel better today than yesterday. I wish you could have seen your face last night when you checked the cut on my hand. I thought that you were going to pass out."

Putting my hand on my forehead I tell him,

"Nunzio, you're Superman; I could not believe that you could get hurt so bad. I don't think that we will ever have another war game again. All our friends were scared for you."

"I'll be okay. You have to admit that it was the best war game we ever had."

"Our gang wants to get together tonight to play Ring-A-Leave-E-O I don't think that you will be in any shape to defend against anyone trying to release prisoners of the captured team."

He stops eating his egg and says:

"My Mom doesn't want me to play any games until they take out my stitches."

Mrs. Rizzo walks into the kitchen.

"Yesterday, seeing Nunzio hurt so bad was the worst day of my life!"

She takes two dollars out of her apron pocket and puts the money in my hand.

"What is this for?"

She looks at Nunzio.

"Well, now that Nunzio is feeling better, I would like you boys to go to a movie this afternoon."

I cannot believe what she is saying! I just sit at the kitchen table staring at the money.

"Thank you, Mrs. Rizzo, I'll be happy to go to the movies with Nunzio today!"

Happy? I can dance on the kitchen table! I tell Nunzio that my favorite Cowboy "Lash La Rue" is playing at the Happy Hour Theater on Columbia Street. I'll go home to kill some time before I come back to meet Nunzio, then we'll go to the movies.

My sister is home listing to Big Band music.

"What are doing home on a hot summer day?"

I tell her about Nunzio's hand, the war games, and his trip to the hospital and that we are planning to go to the movies this after-noon. I don't think that she is much interested in what I'm saying since she continues to shadow dance around the room. I go into the kitchen and look into our junk drawer. I think that I might as well bundle the Ronzoni coupons. We have pasta dinner every day of the week.

Sometimes with vegetables or tomato sauce, if my father has a good job that week we will have pasta first and then some chicken, fish or beef after the pasta. My Mom will cut out the Ronzoni coupons from each box of pasta and put them into the junk drawer. My job is to bundle these coupons so that my mother can turn them in for credits or kitchen stuff.

There must be three hundred coupons in the junk draw ready for me to bundle. It will take me an hour to bundle all the coupons.

It is now lunchtime and I am hungry. I am looking around the kitchen to see if there is anything for me to eat. I take some Italian bread soak it with olive oil, cut a tomato, put it on the bread and have lunch. I now am ready to meet Nunzio for our trek to the movies. I find Nunzio waiting for me outside his apartment. We walk up to Columbia Street past Carroll and President Streets. When we get to the Happy Hour Theater I see that the candy store right next to the theater has a glass display case right out front with Charlotte Russe cakes in it.

They looked so good! The Charlotte Russe is a vanilla cake about one inch high. The cake is wrapped in a tall paper cylinder and loaded with about three to four inches of whipped cream and a big red cherry to top it off! There is nothing like it. I look at Nunzio:

"I don't know if we have enough money to pay for our movie tickets, some popcorn, a soda and the Charlotte Russe cakes. Let's go see Lash La Rue, buy some treats and when we come out of the movies we'll see if we have enough money left to buy us two cakes. What do you think Nunzio?"

Charlotte Russe Cakes Are A Great Treat

"That's Okay with me."

Well, we are in the movie, have all the treats and yes, we stuffed our faces with two Charlotte Russe cakes. I hate to say it but Nunzio's getting hurt turned out to be a good thing!

Chapter 21

Roller Skates - The Milkman

I don't know why I am up so early this morning. It's 7 AM, and my Dad left for work, Mom is working in the kitchen and my Sister is still asleep. I think that the summer heat just got to me last night. It's too early to go out to meet up with my friends. So, I'm lying here in my cot thinking how great it was hanging out with Nunzio yesterday. I'm so happy that his hand is getting better. I hope that seeing all that blood when Nunzio got hurt doesn't stop our gang from playing war games.

Anyway, it sure worked out for the best. Nunzio's Mom is so happy that he is okay she cannot do more to make us happy, like money for the movies and treats. I know it is a bad thing that happened to Nunzio in our war games. I just don't understand why I keep feeling so happy!

I'll get up and have some toast and jelly with a shot of espresso with milk and lots of sugar, then I'll get dressed and go see Jimmy Pizza this morning. I still remember what he told me a couple of days ago that his sister gave him an old pair of street skates. If the wheels of the skates are not worn out maybe we can use them to make a couple of scooters!

Old Roller Street Skates If You Want To Make A Scooter

I should get Roger to help us but he will ask us to pay him for his ideas. We're all just tapped out of cash, so we have to do it on our own.

I'll get up from my cot, have breakfast and then walk to Jimmy Pizza's apartment building on Columbia Street. It is still early as I am at number 369 Columbia Street. I don't want to call up to Jimmy because it is so early, so I'll sit on his stoop to wait for him.

It is kind of quiet, not many people walking around, no peddlers calling out for attention. The sun is rising just above the building across the street, getting into my eyes as I sit here. Any of the kids I know are either asleep or just getting up. So, I'm sitting here feeling how hot it is and wouldn't it be great if my sister takes me to Coney Island and lets me jump into the ocean to cool off. I have to work on her to take me.

There is a good chance I'll get to go with her since my Mom will never let her take off to Coney Island unless she goes with a grown-up or someone like me who will "Rat" on her if she tries to hook up with some boys. If I go with her my Mom knows I will give her up in a minute. I think that my sister will say it's okay for me to tag along because she thinks that she can keep me from ratting her out. She thinks she's so smart. Ha! I have more power than she does since I can blackmail her anytime I want to. Anyway, I'll fight this battle another day.

Today I will hang out with Jimmy and Mike Tomato, maybe we can cool off with some ice chips if we spot the ice wagon coming down our block. Sitting here for about 10 minutes I notice Joanie and her friend Janie walking down the block. Even in this heat, Joanie is still wearing her farmer jeans.

"Hey Pepino, what the heck are you doing sitting there so early in the morning?"

I tell her about Jimmy and his sister's roller skates. I asked her where she is heading.

"Somebody took off with our milk this morning and my Mom asked me to go over to Aunt Rosie to borrow some. My Mom wants to bake a cake for my Dad's birthday today."

"How can somebody steal your milk from your icebox?"

She looks at Janie as if I was asking a stupid question.

"Well, we have a milkman you know, who delivers two or three bottles of milk on our doorstep every other day. How do you get your milk?"

"Wow! Your parents must be rich. I have to get up early every morning while it's still dark and carry my bucket over to Mr. Pauli's barn on Luqure Street. Mr. Pauli has a couple of goats there. I sneak into the barn and take the milk from the goats while they're sleeping. I hope Mr. Pauli doesn't find out."

Joanie looks at me as if I am crazy and then she and Janie start to laugh. They are laughing so hard that they start to cry. Joanie rubs her eyes on the shoulder of her tee shirt and walks away. She is looking back at me while walking away.

81

"Baaaaaaaaaa".

I can't wait to ask my Mom why we don't have a milkman. She will smack me on the head and say,

"Whatta u crazzzzie?"

No sooner am I finished thinking about my Mom giving me a smack on the head I'm hearing Jimmy's steps behind me.

Chapter 22

Street Skate Scooters

"I heard you talking to Joanie from my open window. What was all that milkman stuff about?"

"It will take me too long to tell you the whole story, Jimmy, forget about it. Tell me about your sister's street skates. Do you have them? Are they in good shape?"

"Yeah, yeah, I got them, take a look."

"Wow! They're in great shape! Why is she giving them up?"

"Well, she's 16 now and let's say that she is more interested in how she looks and acts. She doesn't want to skate around all pretty and fall down in front of any good-looking boys. You get it?"

"Yeah, I get it. She sounds a lot like my sister. Let's go find Mike and work on a plan to make us a couple of skate scooters."

We are at Mike's house and he is flying pigeons with his brother Vincent off the roof of the barn. As it's a clear hot day once again, the sun is starting to squeeze little beads of sweat from my brow. Mike and Vincent have a huge flock of birds that just take off without warning! What a beautiful sight seeing and hearing these pigeons flap their wings!

"Hey, Mike! Are you ready to work with us on making a couple of street scooters?"

"Yeah, I'll be right down."

His brother Vincent keeps on flying the pigeons while Mike is crawling into his apartment window facing the roof of the barn. It doesn't take long as the door opens and Mike comes out and meets us.

"What ya got?"

"Look at these skates they're in great shape! I think we can make two really great looking scooters."

Mike takes the skates from Jimmy's hand.

"You're right. They look almost new!"
The three of us are now sitting on the curb of the street in front of Mike's house.

"We have to find some strong wooden boxes, some lumber for the base and nails. Then we will need a hammer to put all the parts together."

"I can get a couple of Pepsi Cola soda crates from my grand-mother 'Chickie's' grocery store. Those boxes are heavy duty and they can take a lot of punishment."

"That's great! Now, all we need is some two by fours which we can probably find near or in one of those condemned houses at the tunnel job site, Mike!"

"Okay, I'll go there to look for the lumber Jimmy!"

"Kool, I'll get the hammer and nails from Mr. Pauli's tool shed in the barn."

"Okay then, Jimmy, Mike, let's meet here in about an hour and put these scooters together."

Everything is falling into place. We all are meeting again near Mr. Pauli's barn with the parts we need for the scooters. Jimmy brought a couple of two by fours from one of the dilapidated houses. They are nice, straight, and strong but they are too long for the base of the scooter. We didn't think about it at first but now we know that we need a saw to cut the lumber to the right size. It's as if Mike is reading our minds-

"Yeah, I know, I'll go look for a saw."

He found one in the shed and gives it to me. I'll cut the lumber to the right size of about five feet long. Jimmy is taking the skates apart. Each skate disassembled gives us two parts with two wheels each. Mike turns the front part of the skate upside-down and nails it about three inches in from the end of the two by four. This will now be the front of the scooter. He is also nail-ing the back of the skate to the other end of the wood.

Handmade Street Roller Skate Scooter

Turning the board with the skates nailed in place we give it a test to see if it rolls on the street. Perfect! We are testing the wheels and Mike nails the box to the board to the front end about three inches in from the end with the open end of the box facing the rear.

We are finished! We're all standing here looking at our first street scooter. Mike is asking:

"Okay, who is going to ride this baby first?"

"I'll give it a try."

I'm putting my right foot on the board, hold the top of the box with one hand on each side and pushed off with my left foot. Wow, I think. "This baby can really move!"

Jimmy and Mike are yelling and jumping up and down. They both take a turn.

After we all have a test-ride we will get to work on the second scooter and finish it in about forty minutes. We will each take turns riding the second scooter, all the tests have worked out just as we planned.

I'm screaming. "ROGER! EAT YOUR HEART OUT, YOU BIG FAT SHIT HEAD!"

We are putting the finishing touches on our creations, as we are making handles for each scooter. The handles are made of two pieces of wood twelve inches long, two inches wide and about one inch thick.

I am nailing one handle on each side of the box sticking out about eight inches towards the rear. These handles will give us better control when making the scooter turn left or right. We are also collecting about one hundred bottle caps from Nick's sandwich shop to use later.

We find some small nails in the tool shed and nail the bottle caps to the front of the scooter to form a number one on the first scooter and number two on the second scooter. We are each taking turns nailing more bottle caps all along the sides of the two by fours for decoration.

Parking the scooters side-by-side on the street along the curb, we step back about ten feet looking at our work. They look beautiful. We must be standing looking at this scooters for more than ten minutes by now!

Chapter 23

Stoop Ball - Puppy Love

35

Playing Stoop Ball With My Friends in Brooklyn

We had a great time yesterday making our street scooters. Pecker and Reno came by early this morning to see what we made; the scooters are a thing of beauty. Jimmy is riding scooter number one and I will take number two for a spin. Pecker is now complaining:

"Hey, you guys, what about us?"

"Well OK, I'll let you have a ride in a couple of minutes."

Jimmy let Reno try number one and I gave Pecker number two. They had so much fun! Reno pulled up next to me.

"I think that my uncle has an old pair of street skates. If he gives them to me will you help Pecker and me make our own scooters?"

I cannot help thinking that I might be turning into an inventor like Roger the Professor.

"Sure I'll help you but you better ask Mike Tomato if you can borrow the tools you'll need in Mr. Pauli's shed. We will continue taking turns riding the scooters most of the morning.

Reno gets an idea.

Reno's "Spaldeen"

"Let's park these scooters and play some stoop-ball. I fished a Spaldeen ball out of a sewer the other day and can't wait to try it out."

I am getting tired of the entire scooter riding and by playing stoopball I don't have to run a lot.

"Yeah! It sounds good to me. Nunzio's apartment building has a great stoop and we don't get much traffic on Luquer Street."

Reno is going home to get his Spaldeen ball while the rest of us are sitting on Nunzio's stoop to wait for him.

If Reno's ball is a high bouncer we can hit a home run without trying too hard. Stoopball is a great game; all you need is a ball and a stoop with sharp steps. We will choose sides.

Let's say it's Jimmy and me against Pecker and Reno. The rules are almost like baseball. The team that's up first will have one player on their team throw the ball as hard as he can against the stoop aiming for the sharp edge of a step. If he hits it right the ball will fly over 200 feet for a home run. If he doesn't hit a home run the other team for an out may catch the ball. If the other team drops the ball that means there's a man on base. No ground balls are ever allowed; you get two turns throwing the ball against the stoop. If you hit two ground balls you're out. If you hit a home run with a man on base your team gets two points. If your team makes three outs the other team gets a turn. The team that makes fifteen points first wins the game.

I can clearly see Reno running back down the street with a ball in his hand.

"Hey guys here's the ball, let's get started."

After choosing sides by throwing our hand out with one finger or two fingers showing ("one-strike-three, shoot!") we settle on our teams, Pecker and me against Reno and Jimmy. I'm up first and hit a dinghy, the ball is flying across the street about 300 hundred feet right into Mrs. Folly's open window! We are suddenly hearing a loud scream and screech:

"WHAT THE HELL IS THIS SHIT!?"

We are all looking at each other as we take off running towards Columbia Street, stopping in front of Nick's Sandwich Shop laughing like crazy. Pecker is out of breath and gasping:

"Wow! That was some shot, it's the longest stoopball home run I ever seen! Mrs. Folly must have been shocked to see our ball flying through her open window and bounce all around her apartment hitting God knows what."

"You're right, Reno, that Spaldeen ball you fished out of the sewer must have been a new ball to fly like that! Are you going to ring Mrs. Folly's doorbell and ask her to give you your ball back, OK?"

Reno is turning to me with his eyes wide open.

"HELL NO!!! I'll just have to keep fishing for a new ball. It's too bad you hit that ball so hard. I don't think I'll ever find another Spaldeen ball like that one again."

We are all laughing when I spot Joanie coming toward us with her farmer jeans and all. But this time it looks like she has a new friend.

"What's so funny? I've never seen you boys laughing so hard!"

"Can you do us a favor, and ring Mrs. Folly's doorbell and ask her to return our ball?"

She is wrinkling her nose at us.

"It sounds like a trick question. She lives way up there on the third floor, why would she have your ball? It sounds like you want to send me into some sort of trap."

She's too smart for us and I don't think she will do it anyway.

"Forget it I'm just playing with you. About the ball: well I hit the ball so hard on the stoop that it just flew like a rocket right into Mrs. Folly's open window!"

"Wow, I would have liked to see that."

"I don't think any of us will see a ball fly like that ever again. Who is your new friend?"

"Doesn't he look great? His name is Joy he's my new dog and he is a full-breed Boxer. He is only three months old but if you look at the size of his paws you can see that he has a lot of growing to do. My Mom and Dad gave me Joy for my birthday. What do you think of him, huh?"

It is Love at first sight. Joy doesn't just look great; he's beautiful.

I bend down and start petting him with both my hands. He is all over me licking and jumping. I think he likes me.

"When Joy is about six months old my Dad will take him to the Vet to have his ears and tail cut."

She sees the look of horror on my face.

"Cut, what do you mean? Like, cut off? Why would anybody do that to such a beautiful animal?"

She tries to calm me down.

"He's a Boxer' All Boxers have that done to them. That's the breed."

I think I am going to throw up. I can't hear this stuff anymore. I'm turning and walking away thinking: How can anyone do such a terrible thing to this beautiful animal, why anyone would allow people to cut up a little dog just for a certain look on a breed!?

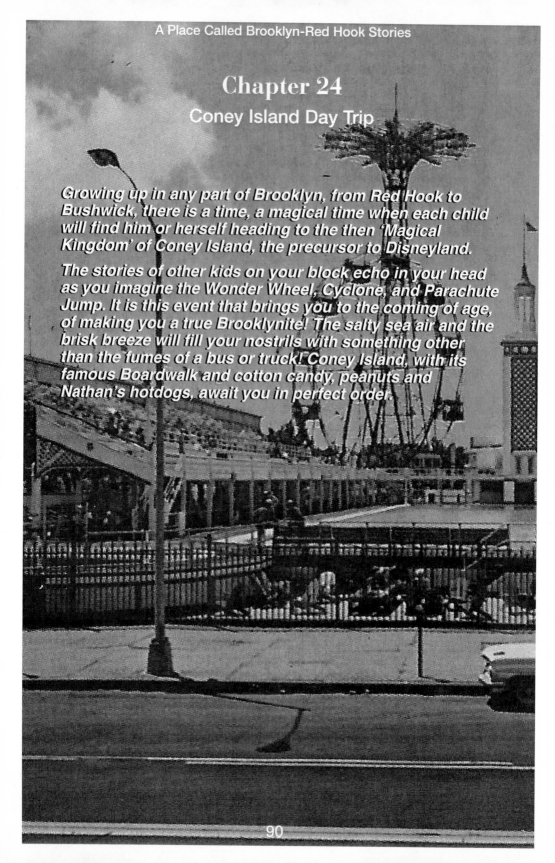

Chapter 24
Coney Island Day Trip

Growing up in any part of Brooklyn, from Red Hook to Bushwick, there is a time, a magical time when each child will find him or herself heading to the then 'Magical Kingdom' of Coney Island, the precursor to Disneyland.

The stories of other kids on your block echo in your head as you imagine the Wonder Wheel, Cyclone, and Parachute Jump. It is this event that brings you to the coming of age, of making you a true Brooklynite! The salty sea air and the brisk breeze will fill your nostrils with something other than the fumes of a bus or truck! Coney Island, with its famous Boardwalk and cotton candy, peanuts and Nathan's hotdogs, await you in perfect order.

My First Coney Island Day Trip On The Subway

I couldn't sleep last night thinking about Joanie's Boxer, Joy. I still can't understand why anyone would allow people to cut up a little dog just for a certain look on a breed! Joy is such a pretty puppy and when you look into his sad eyes you just want to hug him and whisper: "Everything is going to be all right!" I don't think I can do or say anything to convince Joanie's parents to not let anyone cut that poor puppy.

I am rubbing my eyes of sleep as I walk into the kitchen hearing my sister begging my mother to let her go to Coney Island with her girlfriends.

"Ma, Ma, Ma, please, please, the summer is almost over and I promise I'll be a good girl. I won't get into any trouble. I promise I will not look or talk to any boys."

My Mom says:

"No, no, I ya no trust-a you. You justa boy craaazy."

At this point, my big sister is running into her room crying.

I follow her into her room and whisper:

"Why don't you ask Mom to let me go along with you?"

She looks up from her bed interested and wipes away her tears with a smile on her face.

"Okay, okay, I'll ask her."

Getting up she is heading back into the kitchen.

"Ma, if I take Pepino with me to Coney Island, will you please let me go?"

My Mom turns with her right hand waving in the air.

"My God youa NEVER stop! Yes, you canna go but you and you friends gotta watch you brother!"

My sister is happy! I know that she thinks she can control me. She thinks that she can go off with her friends, and hang out with boys and leave me on the beach blanket to wait for her to come back for me.

She is calling out to me:

"Hurry up Pepino, and get your bathing suit and towel. We have to meet Frances, Millie, and Maria on our way to the subway at Smith and Ninth Street to catch the D train!"

I'm telling her to hold on. Just so she knows that I plan to go for a swim and then hang out at the penny arcade:

"I don't plan to sit on the beach blanket all day long waiting for you to come back from playing with the boys."

Smith & 9th Street Station

She gives me a piercing look. Pointing her finger at me:

"Listen, squirt; remember I'm taking you only because Mom gave me the okay."

I give her a quick 'yes' only because I can always rat her out and hold it over her whenever I want."

We are packing our beach stuff and taking some bread and fresh fruit for lunch with us. We can always get some water from a drinking fountain at the beach. We don't have much money, but I saved four dollars by collecting deposit bottles, looking at it as four hundred pennies for the arcade. I'm thinking my sister has ten dollars and maybe I can get her to buy me an ice cream or maybe a hot dog at Nathans.

We meet her girlfriends on Luqure and Hicks Street on the way to the subway. They are all so happy giggling and laughing like teenage girls do thinking about all the great looking boys they plan to meet at the beach. We are arriving at the station on Ninth Street, and it looks far from a 'subway' that I always think of as underground. This station is about four stories high. As we get to the top, we can see Manhattan on one side and the Statue of Liberty on the other. It's a beautiful day and a lot cooler than last week. There are maybe a hundred people waiting for the D train to pull into the station platform.

I'm hearing a rumble as I see the train coming. It looks full of people with all their beach stuff already on board. The train pulls in, the doors open and the girls and I push our way in. Whew! We made it! We're packed in like a can of sardines, with a hot bunch of sweaty people squished around us. The overhead fans on the train don't help much. The fans just seem to blow around these weird odors that are making me feel sick. We can't move and my four-foot body with all these taller people surrounding me makes me feel like I am drowning in a sea of sweat. I'm thinking to myself: "Hold on, only an hour to go!"

We are arriving at the Coney Island station and its' about 10 AM. We are getting off the train and I feel the cool ocean breeze and it smells so good hitting me all at once!

"Hurry up, Pepino! We have to get a good spot on Bay 14 for our beach blanket!"

The law of the beach is that every neighborhood in Brooklyn has a claim to a beach location. Our neighborhood camps out on Bay 14 near the pier and the Parachute Jump Ride on the boardwalk. I don't know how these rules started. All I know is that if you're from Red Hook you better not put your blanket on Bay 13 or Bay 15's beach. If you do you better be ready to fight your way back to the boardwalk.

We are hopefully looking for a spot on the beach close to some shade near the pier. The beach is packed with people and it isn't easy to find an empty spot of sand. We got lucky finding a small spot of sand and lay out our blankets; I undress and run into the water. My sister is yelling out:

"PEPINO, STOP! Get back HERE. You CAN'T go into the water without ME!!!"

WOW! I didn't think my sister really cares that much about my safety. I stop and we all jump into the cool ocean together. It feels so good splashing around and jumping into the waves. The weather is so nice and warm and not too hot and my sister is having a great time with her girlfriends. We have some bread and fruit for lunch but I am still hungry. I'll ask my sister if I can buy some cotton candy.

"No, that's junk I'll buy you a hot dog at Nathans."

Wow, that sounds good to me.

A guy by the name of Nino asks my sister to go with him for a ride on the Steeple Chase. She is looking at me probably thinking that if she says 'Yes', I will rat her out to my mother. She gives me two dollars to get a hot dog and she gives me the okay to meet her on our beach blanket when she gets done with her horsey ride with Nino. My sister knows I'm weak; money will always buy my silence.

Off she goes with Nino and the girls to the Steeple Chase Park. I'll have my hot dog and play all the penny games at the arcade.

It is still early as I get back to the blanket. I fall asleep on the blanket. Next thing I know, my sister is shaking me to wake up!

We are packing our stuff and will make our way back to the subway. The ride home isn't so bad; we even manage to find a couple of seats next to a fisherman who is heading home from a day of fishing at Sheepshead Bay. He had a good day too, I could tell because of the stack of fish on the seat next to him. I think we got some seats on the train because of the strong fish smell. After a while, the smell isn't too bad. I least I'm not being crushed to death by a herd of sweating, smelly people. I start looking at the "Good Luck" horseshoe-shaped piece of metal with a shiny penny stuck into its center that I bought at the penny arcade. Looking at my good luck charm I had a great day!

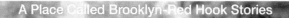

Chapter 25
Stickball - Jacks, A Girl's Game

You Can Also Play Brooklyn Stickball & Run Bases When You Have 8 Guys On Each Team.

If there was one thing that kept us happy as kids, it was the magic of our inventive minds and ability to put our imagination to good use. As city kids went, we were poor and from humble families that made the best of what we could afford. A ball was not complete without our inventiveness to create games of competition or small toys that kept us busy for hours. Stoopball, stickball, hand-made wooden scooters and pick-up jacks, and jump rope kept our attention from early morning to after supper. No rain or snow could convince us that there was nothing to do or somewhere to do it, from the streets to the sidewalks to the hallways of our apartment buildings, and it was all magic to us!

where three sewers is deep center fi

I woke up this morning hoping that I'd feel much better today. It's not that I'm sick with the flu or infection it's just this damned sunburn I got two days ago when I went to Coney Island with my sister. I had such a great time splashing in the ocean and jumping into the waves. The sunburn is so bad I just can't move without feeling sharp pains in my back and legs.

My Mom is so pissed-off at my sister for going off with some boy she met and leaving me alone and asleep to fry on the beach blanket!

My sister really caught hell from my Mom and Dad. Don't get me wrong, except for the pain; I love all the attention my parents are giving me. For me, the icing on the cake is that my sister is now in the "Shit House."

These last two days in our apartment are starting to make me crazy. I don't want to show my parents that I am feeling a lot better. I think the Noxzema my Mom put on my back and legs made the burn just about go away. The problem is that once I tell them that I feel better and I want to go outside, the sooner my sister will be out of the "Shit House."

I don't know why I can be so mean sometimes. She did take me to Coney Island, she bought me a hot dog and she gave me money for the Penny Arcade so now I feel guilty. Okay, okay, I better let her off the hook. I am thinking about all this stuff and I can hear Pecker
who is calling out to me from my open window,

"Hey, Keyno, where the Hell are you? I haven't seen you for days; get your ass down here."

"Hey Pecker, I'll be down in about fifteen minutes."

I tell my Mom that I feel much better and she looks up and says:

"Getta outta here."

It's the way she says it that makes me think she has had enough too. So I'll get dress and run down the steps as fast as I can.

I find Pecker around the corner with Jimmy Pizza and Henry.

"What's up Pecker?"

"We haven't seen you for so long we thought you were dead."

"Dead? Well, you see I went to Coney Island with my sister three days ago and had a great time. We went on the parachute jump, the cyclone roller costar ride, the giant Ferris wheel, and the merry go round."

They are both looking at me with their mouths open wide and then in the middle of my Coney Island story Henry says:

"Stop! You're so full of it, Pepino!"

"Yeah, but I did get to go to the Penny Arcade and I did jump in the ocean to cool off. But I got such bad sunburn, I couldn't move for days. You guys have any plans for today?"

Pecker, is tilting his head to one side:

"Yeah, we're meeting up with our gang to play stickball some-time this afternoon."

"Wow, stickball!" Henry adds:

"Reno fished another Spaldeen ball out of the sewer yesterday and I found an old broom that I cut so we have a bat to play with. All we need is a flat brick wall and some chalk."

We are walking to Nelson Street and meet up with the guys.

Luckily we find a wall we can use at the Cardinal Tank factory across the street from P.S. 27. Jimmy Pizza brought some chalk to draw the box on the wall for the strike zone. Stickball is a little like baseball and stoopball combined. Just like baseball, the batter stands in front of the strike zone box we chalked on the wall. There could be three or four player on each team and one umpire. Like stoopball, we have a home run zone, triple zone, and a double zone. Then we set up one base to run to just in case the batter hits a ground ball. If the batter hits a fly ball and it's caught, you're out. If it's not caught the batter tries to get to the base before being thrown out. If you reach the base without being tagged you're safe and there's a man on base. No one stays on base.

A team can only have a maximum of three men on base at a time. If the batter hits the ball into one of the high fly zones he will get either a home run, double or triple automatically. If your team has any base runners at that time, depending on the zone the ball is hit into; can bring home one, two, or three runners scoring. Don't forget, we also have a strike zone and an umpire calling strikes

I Wouldn't Play Because Jacks Is Aa Girls Game.

and balls. We always give the umpiring job to one of the old guys hanging around the neighborhood. Just like Baseball there are three strikes and you're out or four balls will put a man on base and if your team gets three outs the next team gets their chance at bat. The team that reaches 21 points first wins the game. We choose sides and have four men on each team with Papa Joe as the umpire. The game is going on for almost three hours and we don't break any windows on the school building. Vinnie, of course, managed to hit two balls over the roof. Our team, Reno and Jimmy Pizza, Vinnie the Coop and me rule the day. Vinnie is so talented, he's an expert when it comes to flying Pigeons, he can fish a ball out of the sewer, shoot a Rat with his Pea Shooter and whack a ball with a Stickball bat so hard over the roof of the school building that you will never find it again. Good thing he is on our team today. Henry, Pecker and six fingers Ricardo are the losers. By the end of the day I will be wiped out. The sunburn is not completely gone and running around playing stickball for almost three hours is too much for me. So we do our victory dance and I tell the guys that I am heading home.

I'm on the way home and now I see Joanie, Janie and a couple of girls playing jacks with Joy the Boxer lying down next to them.

"Hey Pepino come play with us."

"No way; I can't be seen playing a girls game, the guys will laugh me out of the neighborhood."

She keeps on taunting me.

"Come on you can do it."

To tell the truth I wouldn't play with them even if I could because they will whip my ass. The girls will bounce that little red ball and grab one jack and catch the ball before it hits the ground, then do the same and grab two, then three, then four jacks until one player misses. The player that bounces that little red ball and can grab all the jacks before the ball hits the ground is the winner. I don't think I can stand losing to those girls and that's why I don't play with them. Just call me "CHICKEN!" I wave back to Joanie and continue on my way home.

Chapter 26

Radio Stories & Spin The Top Games

Before television there was radio. If there was one invention that helps build the imagination of a young boy in the 1940's, it was the box that sat somewhere in the darkened living room or kitchen, a glow emanating from its' dial talking to you and holding your attention and loyalty, night after night.
The adventures of the Lone Ranger or the forbidden 'Shadow who knows', produced in every young mind in every state of the Union the same scenes and visualizations and words with different young stage directors and in their collective minds, separate presentations. THAT was radio's heyday!

Radio Stories Are Best Listened To In The Dark

It is still early and I am home. I want to play the Jacks game with Joanie and her friends, but it's a girl's game and if the guys I hang out with see me playing this stupid game, they will make fun of me for weeks. Mom's dinner is ready so I'm ready to sit down and eat. Mom and my sister are joining me at the kitchen table and I have a bowl of broccoli rabe mixed with spaghetti, olive oil, and Parmesan cheese, sitting in front of me. Dad is not at the dinner table so I'm guessing he's working late again. This spaghetti and vegetable dish is not my favorite meal so I sprinkle some hot pepper on the pasta and vegetables.

My Mom knows I load hot pepper on a meal if I don't like the taste of what she's serving. For me, the hot pepper cuts the bitter taste of the broccoli rabe. My Mom does not like my loading hot pepper on her food, so she looks at me while squinting her eyes and is predicting:

"You knowa, when-na you grow up-a you willa liker this food... BETTER than you likea meat."

I'm thinking to myself:

"Yeah, fat chance, if it wasn't for the olive oil and all the spices on this shit I wouldn't be able to eat it at all."

I just smile and kept on eating.

Dinner is over so I'm going into the living room, which is my part time bedroom, and sit next to the radio and listen to stories of Superman and Suspense. The Superman stories are exciting and fun to listen to, but the Suspense and *Inner Sanctum* programs are my favorites, they always scare the hell out of me. I think I'll shut all the lights except for the little light glowing from the radio so I can listen to these programs in the dark! Then when all my radio stories are over, I'll go to bed.

I Get A New Spin Top
For My Birthday

I'm lying in bed thinking that the summer vacation from school is moving too fast. I only have about three weeks left before I have to go back to school. Wow! Why does time go by so fast when you're having fun? I know I will soon fall asleep.

It's morning, I'm up having breakfast, and will go out to look for Nunzio. My godmother Concetta gave me a new spin top for my birthday and I want to hook up with my friends to play our Spin the Top war game. Nunzio is sitting on his stoop. He looks okay and he doesn't have any bandages on his hand. I'm hoping that his hand healed 100% from that stab wound he got from the wooden sword when we had our carpet gun war. Thanks to Nunzio and his charge to get the red flag, we had a great victory.

"Hi Nunzio, how's your hand?"

"I feel great and my hand is just like it was before I got stabbed!"

"I got a new spin top for my birthday and I thought it would be great if we could put together a spin top war game this morning. Do you have a spin top?"

"Yeah, I have an old one that's still in great shape. I'll go get it."

Nunzio running into his house and comes back out within five minutes with his red top in his hand.

Walking up the block to find Pecker, Reno, and Mike Tomato, we find all them sitting on the corner of Hicks and Luquer Street. It doesn't take long when all the guys find their spin tops and we start playing our war game. I'll take a piece of chalk and make a ten-inch circle on the smooth blacktop surface in the street. We can't play this game on a cobblestone street. You need the smooth surface for the top to spin without any interference. We will start by competing to see who goes first, second, third, whatever. We do this by aiming our tops to hit the chalk circle. Whoever lands his top directly in the circle goes first. If you miss the circle you have to wait for the second or even the third round before you try to hit the circle again. If everyone hits the circle before you and it turns out that you're dead last, you have to lay your top into the chalk circle.

Reno's bad luck makes him dead last. So now he's putting his green top in the chalk circle for everybody to shoot at. All the tops are made of wood and they spin on a sharp metal tip at the base. We sometimes sharpen the metal tip by scraping it along the concrete sidewalk. Each player is throwing his top as hard as possible at Reno's top in the circle. If they hit his top they wait to go again at the end of the line. If the player misses hitting the top in the circle and his top is still spinning, he has to slip the spinning top into the palm of his hand. While the top is spinning in the palm of his hand, he rushes over to the target top in the circle and throws his spinning top at the top of the circle. He has to hit it before his top stops spinning.

If the player who threw the top makes it in time he has to wait for the next round to go again. If the player misses the target he has to put his top in the circle. Now Reno goes free and it's his turn to throw the top at the target.

It's now my turn, I'm twirlling the string all around my spin top. I'm easing my middle finger into the loop at the end of the string. Some tops have a button at the end of the string that you can place between your fingers.

I want to hold the top upside down with my fingers as tight as possible. Bringing my arm way over my head I whip my arm in a downward motion with all my might at the target. If I hit the target directly, with my top's sharp metal point, it can and will split the target wood top into two pieces.

That is why we call it a War game because we are all doing our best to "Destroy" the other player's spin top. After a couple of hours, two tops are destroyed in our war game. Nunzio and Mike Tomato will have to buy new tops for the next time we play this game. Many times, we see the teenagers play this game with money on the line. If you lose, not only is your top destroyed, you then have to pay a dollar or two to the winners. That's when it gets real ugly and fights break out. Our guys don't have much money to bet on the tops game so at the end of our game we will head to the Candy Store to buy some treats.

Chapter 27

Candy Store-Smoking-Ring-O-Leave-E-O

The 'Spin Top' game is a lot of fun for me. My top came out of the war without too many scars, but I don't think that my top can take another direct hit. Too bad Nunzio and Mike Tomato aren't as lucky. I don't know why it feels so good when my top makes a direct hit and Nunzio's top explodes into four pieces. It's like WOW! That's the way the game goes. It's just about lunchtime, and we don't have enough money for a sandwich or a Devil Dog so we're heading to the candy store to buy some penny treats like Sugar Daddy pops, Mary Jane's, Sugar Dots on paper, Toot-

sie Rolls and anything else we can afford. The old candy store has seen better days.

The old couple Larry and Mindy who run the place sell cigarettes, cigars, newspapers, penny candies, and kid toys like yoyo's, pea shooters, kazoos, clay, checkers, balsa wood airplanes, marbles, Chinese finger games, chalk and a bunch of magic games.

We are turning the corner on Columbia Street and see Roger and a couple of teenagers standing in front of the place smoking some cigarettes.

"Hey, big head, Pepino, where you going?"

"We're just going to buy some candy."

"Why don't you grow up kid and have a smoke with us? I'll sell you guys these cigarettes for two cents each or three for a nickel. Are you ready to make a move up, little man?"

"Listen, Roger, we only have fifty cents between us and we're hungry, I don't think that blowing smoke is better than candy. Even if we had enough money we would not buy your ciga-rettes, we would rather go to Nick's and spend our money on a hero sandwich and soda. This way our bellies are full and we don't smell like shit."

"Yeah, big head! Grow up; look around you, if it's so bad why is everybody smoking?"

I won't even answer him. We are pushing our way past him and his friends walking into the candy store. They think they're so "cool" all dressed in a shirt, jacket and cap in the middle of the summer. These guys are just want-to-be men, all grown up, smoking their brains out to impress the girls. Roger is the smartest one in the bunch. He is always looking to make money. He buys a pack of cigarettes for twenty-cents and sells them loose to the 'want-to-be men' kids and makes himself forty cents and doubles his money.

Mrs. Mindy is behind the counter and is greeting me.

"Hey, Pepino! What are you up to?"

"We want to buy some candy Mrs. M."

There are about fifty different candies in her display case. This is not going to be easy for the four of us to pick out what we want. But Mrs. Mindy knows the drill and she will give us all the time we need to make a selection. After about a half hour of giving me that one, no-no this one, no-no, again that one, we finish our back and forth selections and walk out and sit on the stoop next door to eat our treats. I like the sugar high better than Roger's smoke high.

My father likes to smoke his Lucky Strike cigarettes. I hate it when his friends come to visit, they spend their time talking and smoking for hours. Even after they all go home the apartment smells like a sewer in the room.

We are sitting on the stoop and having our candy. I bought Bazooka Bubble Gum, Sugar Dots on paper and Sugar Juice in little wax bottles. It isn't much to eat but sugar treats always make us happy. The best treat of all is Bazooka Bubble Gum. As we are sitting on the Stoop chewing our Bazooka gum and seeing who can blow the biggest bubble we are reading stories about Bazooka Joe on the inside of the wrapper. Suddenly I see a bunch of guys are walking up Columbia Street. It looks like Jimmy Pizza and four of his cousins are coming our way.

Jimmy Pizza is stopping in front of us.

"Hey Keyno, do you guys want to play Ring-O-Leave-E-O?"

"Okay, looks like we have eight guys with your cousins."

It's Jimmy and his cousins against me and Nunzio, Mike Tomato and Reno. The teams are a little light but four kids on each team are about the bare-minimum number of players. Columbia Street is too busy with all kinds of traffic so we will walk to Nelson Street near PS 27, and find a spot-on Nelson and Hicks Street for the home base. You need two teams to play Ring-O-Leave-E-O. You choose sides and one team has to chase and find the members of the second team. When you grab one of the team members you're chasing you have to hold him and yell out "Ring-O-Leave-E-O, 1, 2, 3" at that point he becomes your prisoner. You then take your prisoner to the established home base that is our 'jail'. Let's say your team has two prisoners to guard. One of your team members has to stay with the prisoners at all times to prevent the second team from trying to set them "Free". They can set their team members free by trying to run around the guard, stepping into the jail box and yelling "FREE!" If their team member can step into the jail box to free his team members, the guard can capture him by yelling "Ring-O-Leave-E-O. 1, 2, 3." It's not that easy to capture the guy who's trying to free the prisoners because two of them generally rush the guard at the same time and you can't stop them unless you have help from one of your team members. If the prisoners are set free you start all over again. There is a lot of running and fighting in trying to capture the second team members. This game can and does get pretty ugly at times but we love it.

Sugar Juice Wax Bottle, Just Bite & Drink

Jimmy's cousins are so fast that they seem to free the prisoners at will. Our team is starting to run out of steam and we are conceding victory to Jimmy and his cousins. We all sit down on the curb to rest. We are all covered with sweat, most of our T-shirts are torn to shreds and some of us are bleeding from scratches we got from struggling to get free. We all look and smell pretty bad. It is getting late so I'm telling the guys that I am heading for home.

As I'm going over to Luquer Street towards Columbia. I can see Joanie and her dog Joy sitting on the stoop of her building.

"Pepino, what the Hell happened to you?"

I'm telling her I was playing Ring-O-Leave-E-O with Jimmy Pizza and a bunch of guys over by P.S. 27.

"Wow! You guys must have been running and fighting for hours. Who won?"

"Well, Jimmy and his cousins beat the Hell out of us. So, I guess you could say that the victory was theirs today but I'm looking forward to a rematch before this summer is over."

"I'm sorry you didn't win the game. But good thing you came by because I wanted to ask you something. The thing is that I'm going to visit my aunt Lora on Long Island for a week so I won't be home to walk my dog, Joy. You think that you can walk him for me in the morning and again in the late afternoon? My Dad said that Joy is my dog and he will not walk the dog while I'm away. It's just one week. Can you please do that for me?"

I can't control the smile that is coming across my face. I'll try to stay calm and easy.

"I think I can do it."

I hope Joanie didn't see all the dancing and my jumping going on in my mind. Wow! I love this dog.

Chapter 28
Walk The Dog-Skully Street Game

I can barely sleep during a long hot night. Just thinking about walking Joanie's Boxer, Joy, has me all excited. Joy is still a puppy and he looks so beautiful. Every time I see him with Joanie I just want to hug him. Now that Joanie is visiting her aunt on Long Island I will have Joy all to myself for a whole week! She told me to pick up Joy at 9 AM and walk him for an hour and then come back again late afternoon to walk him again.

It's 8:45 AM. I'm ringing the doorbell at her house on Luquer Street and her father Bruno is answering the door and greeting me with:

"You must be Pepino, Joanie said you're walking the dog while she's away this week. Just make sure that the dog poops and pees before you bring him home. Okay?"

"Yes, Mr. Bruno. I will make sure he does his stuff before I bring him back home."

"Just remember, kid, I don't want this dog to shit all over the house. If he does his stuff in the house I'll kick your ass all around the block. Understand!"

"Yes-sir, yes-sir."

He has finished his little talk and is giving me the leash with Joy on the other end. I'm taking the dog and going to Columbia Street and walking towards Coffey Park. It's a nice day and I think that Joy will like to run around in the park with me. It's taking us ten minutes to get to the park because Joy is stopping a few times to do poop along the curb. Lucky for me the dog takes no time to do his stuff. We are at the park now and Joy is pulling on the leash, I can tell he wants to run without the leash. If I let him go who knows if I'll ever find him again. If I lose the dog Joanie will be upset, and more importantly, her father will kill me. So I will hold onto the leash for dear life.

No way am I going to let go of this dog. Joanie's father is a tough guy; he's over six-feet tall, with black hair slicked down with Vaseline, he has big black eyes and a very dark complexion. He wears an athletic T-shirt to show off his muscles and his skull tattoo with bloody sharp scissors stuck in its head, and there is a tattoo on his right arm. I've seen him beat the shit out of a few guys in the neighborhood because they owed him money. Joanie's father is the neighborhood bookie, he takes bets on horses and he also collects money from his runners for the numbers game. No one ever talks about it but some of my friends tell me that he runs the neighborhood gambling, loan sharking and other stuff that I don't want to know about, for the Mob. So, after I run all over the place with Joy I'll bring the dog back home.

I'm walking up to Hicks street and see Pecker and Henry on their knees drawing a big box on the street black top with a piece of chalk in hand.

"Hey, Pecker, what are you guys doing? Are you praying or something like that?"

"NOOO stupid! We're drawing a Skully box."

"What the Hell is a SKULLY box?"

"I know this kid who lives in the Red Hook Projects and he told me about this game he played in The Bronx before he moved here. The rules are kind of complicated, so he asked his mother to write them down for us. So Henry and me are making this box and start line to see if we can get the hang of it."

I take a look at the rules.

"Wow! It's a lot of stuff to learn, I don't want to work this hard to learn this stupid game. I feel like we're back in school again!"

Pecker and Henry are laughing.

"Come on don't be such an asshole. If we don't get it we'll make up our own rules as we play the game."

"Okay-okay, what do we do first?"

"We make the Skully game, six-foot by a six-foot box with this chalk on a smooth surface so that we can drive the bottle caps when we snap our fingers like this."

I take another look at the rules and I am more confused than ever. What the Hell? I'll just have to read this stuff over and over again! The instructions go on to say you need a bottle cap

108

that you can weigh down with an orange peel, crayon wax or some clay so the cap doesn't flip over when you hit it with your fingers.

With the chalk, we'll continue to make 12 smaller boxes in the perimeter of a large six-foot by the six-foot box. Then make number 13 box in the middle of the square surrounded by a dead zone or skull.

We start the game by aiming for the number 1 box. If you get in and you're not touching any lines you can continue to shoot your cap to the next box. If you miss or you are on the line, the next player goes. You can shoot your cap at any player in the box you're aiming for and knock his cap out of the box as far as possible. After you move your cap from 1 to 13 without getting knocked out (in which case you have to start again) you have to go back from 13 to 1. Then you shoot for 13 again or the "Skull" in the dead zone, only then your cap has the power to hunt and kill the other players. You can also hunt other killer caps by hitting their cap three times. The last player left in the game is the "Winner".

Looking over these rules I can see why every neighborhood makes adjustments for what they think the rules should be. Anyway, we play this game for hours and I think that we stuck to the rules listed as close as possible. Henry came out on top this time. With some practice, I think that the next time we play this game I can kick Henry's ass.

I picked up my cap with the orange peel in it. I put it in my pocket and start walking to Joanie's house to pick up Joy for his afternoon walk.

Chapter 29

Kick The Can - Spiderman Swing Jump

Many a neighborhood had its own culture. The way we played and said things, almost a foreign language to a kid in another section of Brooklyn. What was red in Red Hook was orange in the Bushwick section. Black and whites were variables and not constants.

Game rules were decided on by what was available to poor kids of the streets in Brooklyn; there was no want, only inventiveness and the simple joys of living. So, let's see what games like 'Kick the Can' and Spiderman Jump was like in my neighborhood.

COFFEY PARK

My week of walking Joanie's dog, Joy, is over. Joanie is back from visiting her aunt on Long Island. She asks me if I had any problems in taking care of Joy while she was away. I tell her that the poop patrol went well and that walking and playing with Joy is fun for me. I also tell her that if she needs any help in taking care of the dog for any reason, that I stand ready and available to do the job

Joanie says that her dad likes me because I am always on time. He also told her that he doesn't have to kill me since the dog did not have any poop accidents in the house. Phew! I am glad to hear that. I love that dog. I still get upset when I think of his going to the Vet to have his ears and tail cut so that he can look more like a Boxer. But that is out of my control.

Walking up the block I notice a bunch of guys are playing 'Kick the Can'. We play this game when we don't have a ball and with nothing else to do. Jimmy Pizza found an old empty tin can of Spaghetti-O's near Nick's sandwich shop. He calls a bunch of our friends together to choose sides to play the game. 'Kick the Can' in our neighborhood is played like any baseball game only difference being you have a tin can instead of a ball and you don't use a bat.

The kids from the Red Hook Projects that moved here from The Bronx tell me that the 'Kick the Can' game they play is a combination of Ring-O-Leave-O and Hide and Go Seek, which is a completely different game from what we know as 'Kick the Can' to be. In our neighborhood, we use a can when we don't have any money to buy a Spaldeen ball or when we can't find a ball to fish out of the sewer.

Our game in Brooklyn has anywhere from four to six guys on a team. The team that's up first will kick the can as hard as they can and run the bases. If the can goes up in the air and is caught by the other team playing the field you're "out". When you kick the can and it rolls on the ground, the team playing the field has to grab it and either run to a base before you get there to tag you out or the player who picks up the can will have to toss it to a teammate at the base for the out. If you beat the throw or the tag you stay on base waiting for your next team-mate to kick the can. At this point, all the baseball rules apply. If your team makes three outs the other team gets their turn to kick the can. Playing this game with a can instead of a ball can be dangerous. When a big kid kicks the can with all his might and it's flying at you, you don't have much time to grab the can to make an out. If you miss it, the can will smack you in the face, arm or leg. I've seen kids play this game get hurt because of the metal the can is made from. Many kids are cut and bruised and run home bleeding and in pain. But it looks like Jimmy Pizza, Mike Tomato, Henry, Reno and the others are having fun. I don't know if they will get to play much longer since the Spaghetti-O's can they're using is all dented.

I am sitting here watching them play for about ten minutes as they are giving up the ghost. The can is too crushed for them to continue the game. But the good news is that Jimmy's team wins the game 16 to 4.

"Hey, Jimmy, doesn't look like your team had much competition?"

"Yeah; we were playing against a bunch of pussies. These guys were so afraid to charge the can when we kicked it to them."

"Do you have any plans for this afternoon?"

"We were thinking about going to The Clinton Movie House to see the Tarzan movie. But most of the guys don't have the cash for the movie and treats. So it looks like we'll head over to Coffey Park and play on the swings. I don't know if any of these pussies will come with us."

I think I know why Jimmy is saying this because when we go to play Spiderman on the swings in Coffey Park, we stand on the swing like a trapeze artist and fly as high as possible just before we jump off the swing. We do this when we're way up in the air and push our bodies towards the twelve-foot chain link fence that surrounds the playground. At this point, you better grab onto this twelve-foot fence as soon as you hit it or you will fall about ten feet and crash into the concrete pavement below, and if you miss and fall you will be lucky if you walk away with a couple of bruises. The kids that aren't so lucky will wind up at Long Island College Hospital with broken bones. Then your father will have to leave work early and go to the hospital to get you, that's when it really gets ugly! About six of us have agreed to go to Coffey Park to play the Spiderman swing game. The game also reminds me of Tarzan flying through the jungle grabbing onto trees and vines with his best friend Chita the Chimp. It takes about fifteen minutes to walk to the park, and most of the swings are free. Most kids must have gone to the Red Hook Pool to cool off instead of playing on these swings this hot summer day. There are only a couple of teenagers doing some crazy stuff to impress girls that are sitting there. I don't get why they do all this crazy stuff just to make girls smile at them. Anyway, we take turns on the four swings that are free. The best jumper turns out to be Pecker. He may look like a chicken but is no chicken when his long skinny body jumps and flies like Spiderman as he hits and grabs onto the twelve-foot fence. I am really impressed; he has this weird angry look on his face like he is daring the fence to hurt him. After an hour of jumping like crazy people, we leave the park and head back to our neighborhood.

Chapter 30

Working At Defonte's-Game Of Marbles

Home from Coffey Park my mom tells me that Mr. Nick from the sandwich shop downstairs is looking for me. He's asking my mom if it would be okay for me to work in his store on Saturday and Sunday. Wow, I work for Mr. Nick? That's a first! Mr. Nick is always very nice to the kids in the neighborhood. I ask my mom what kind of work he wants me to do. She has no idea, but she says that she told him it would be a good experience for me to have a little job.

Danny Defonte, Mr. Nick's Son Is Sick

I am so excited because I never had a real job, except when I work with Mr. Pauli delivering fruits and vegetables for tips. I run downstairs as fast as I can. I walk into the store and Mr. Nick calls me over to talk.

"Hello Pepino, did your mom talk to you about working in the store starting tomorrow afternoon?"

"Yes Sir Mr. Nick, what do you want me to do? I never had a real job before and I hope I can do a good job for you".

"Ha-ha, Pepino don't worry I'll teach all you have to know. Your mom does not want you to work with knives or the slicing machines. I assured her that you would not work with anything that can hurt you. I have sandwich orders for two big weddings this weekend and my son Danny is sick so I need you to help me assemble about 500 sandwiches for these weddings. You think You can do that."

"Yes, Sir Mr. Nick. What time do you want me to startwork?"

"Come here about twelve o'clock, I'll make you a sandwich before you start work."

Nick's Sandwich Shop Has Great Food

I have this big smile on my face and thank Mr. Nick, running out of the store hoping I will see some of my friends so I can tell them about my job and the sandwich too. I just can't believe it myself! My Friends will just freak out. None of my friends are around so I'll go home, have dinner, listen to my radio programs and go to bed.

I had another sleepless night thinking about my new job and wondering what kind of sandwich Mr. Nick plans to make for me.

So, I'm up early and have five hours to kill before I report for work. I can't wait for my friends to show up, so I go to Jimmy Pizza's house and start yelling in his hallway for him to come down. Jimmy calls down to me:

"What are you crazy it's seven o'clock in the morning and my parents are going to kill you?"

"Please tell your parents that I'm sorry to wake them up so early, but I have some important news to tell you."

After about fifteen minutes go by I can hear Jimmy running down the stairs. I can see that he put on his clothes in a hurry and he didn't comb his hair.

"Okay, now that my family is going to kill me what's so important?"

"You're not going to believe it! I got a real job!"

I give him the whole story about Mr. Nick talking to my mother and my meeting with him and I am also telling him about the sandwich. Jimmy's mouth is wide open the whole time.

"Holy Shit! That's unbelievable! When do you start your new job?"

"I've got about four more hours to wait before I go to the store for lunch AND my new job."

I can't help myself by rubbing it in a little.

"Well, I planned to call you this morning anyway because my sister gave me a sack of new marbles for my birthday yesterday and I was going to ask you if you wanted to set up a game this morning?"

My head is still spinning about my job as I come down to earth.

"Yeah that sounds like a good idea, it will keep me busy while I wait for Twelve o'clock to report for work. Let's get a hold of Nunzio and Pecker to see if they want to play marbles with us?"

Before we go to call Nunzio and Pecker I'll stop by my apartment and get my box of marbles. We get Pecker and Nunzio to come out and they are very happy to set up a game of marbles with us. I also give them the complete story about my new job at Defonte's Sandwich Shop. But time is running out for me, I have only three hours left to play marbles with them.

We have to decide which game of marbles to play because there are so many to choose from. We can play Poison, Potsie, Google, Dropsies, Fox Hole, Puggy or about five other games I can think of. Today we are settling for our favorite game "Potsie". We are going over to a vacant lot across the street from the sandwich shop so we can play on a patch of dirt. First, we have to chase away four kids about five-years-old who are hunting for bugs in the lot. This was not a big problem for us. We just tell them to move their ass out of there and find another place to go bug hunting.

They are leaving and we are clearing an eight-foot by eight-foot area that will be free of grass, weeds and any garbage that happens to be lying there. I find a stick and make a two-foot circle in the middle of the square, and scratch a starting line about six feet from the circle. Okay, the field is now ready for play.

We are each putting five of our marbles in the circle and spreading them apart. When everything is in place we will choose which player goes first, second, third and forth. Jimmy won and will go first. Standing behind the line in the dirt he throws or tosses his shooter marble at the circle. He has to be very careful not to put his shooter marble into the circle. If it goes into the

Marble Potsey Knockout Game

circle he has to go to the back of the line. This round we all toss our shooters at the circle and no one lands in the circle. The next round is to shoot your marble at the marbles in the circle in order to knock out of the circle as many marbles as possible.

The fact that Jimmy won the first toss does not mean that he is shooting first at the marbles in the pot. The new rotation is set up by the players' toss. The player who is the closest to the circle goes first. I am the closest one and I shoot as hard as I can and I manage to knock out three marbles that are now mine. I will keep shooting until I miss or get stuck in the circle. If I miss, the next player will go. If I get stuck in the circle I have to put two marbles back into the pot and start over from the line. This game can go on and on for hours until all the marbles are knocked out of the circle, that's when the game is over. But my time is running out I will not play until all the marbles are knocked out of the circle. So I'm calling it quits, picking up my marbles and walking across the street to report for work.

Chapter 31
Football Wedding-Boxball Game

It is a long weekend that started with our marble game this morning and then going to my new job at Nick's sandwich shop. I'm at my new job and Mr. Nick is calling to me by waving me around the counter where he is serving customers. I was never behind the counter before and it feels strange. I am now part of Mr. Nick's crew. Mr. Nick notices that I am very nervous being here. He starts to laugh and is putting his arm around my shoulder to calm me down a bit.

"Okay Pepino, what would you like for lunch? You have to eat before I show you how to make and assemble the football wedding sandwiches."

I am still shaking a little.

"Okay, Mr. Nick. Whenever I have some money I come here and order a quarter of a loaf with fried eggplant, roast pork and your famous hot salad put right in the sandwich."

He cuts the Italian bread, slices it open and puts in the stuff I asked for. He looks at me smiling.

"There, here's your sandwich and what would you like to drink?"

"Can I have a Manhattan Special soda?"

"You sure can."

I had my sandwich and soda and now I follow Mr. Nick to the back of a large counter where he is inviting me to sit on a stool.

Ice Cold Manhattan Special, It's Like Espresso Coffee In A Bottle'.

"Pepino this is your work area. Have your lunch and when you finish eating I will show you what I would like you to do."

"Okay Mr. Nick, thank you for the sandwich and soda."

I am finished eating and cleaning my spot standing up waiting for Mr. Nick. He now notices me standing and is coming over to the large counter. He is showing me six large boxes at the end of the counter that is filled with freshly baked sandwich rolls.

There must be 100 rolls in each box.

"Do you know what an Italian football wedding is, Pepino?"

"Yes Sir, Mr. Nick, my parents took me to one about a year ago. Everybody was invited, family, relatives, friends, kids, and anybody who lived on the block. There must have been over 300 people in the church hall. It was so much fun being there. We had loads of sandwiches to eat that were dumped in the middle of the table we were sitting at.

Everyone would throw a sandwich at each other across the table if they wanted a certain cold cut sandwich that was at the other end of the table. My Sister told me that a long time ago someone made a joke that this looked like an American football game. And like everything else in Brooklyn the name stuck. She said that anytime there's a wedding with sandwiches they call it a 'Football Wedding.' My parents had homemade wine and beer to drink and the kids had a soda from large bottles. Everybody was dancing to Italian music. The band never stopped playing. I hooked up with a bunch of kids and we ran all around the church hall. We sometimes ducked under a table to eat our sandwiches, sugar-coated almonds called Confetti, assorted cookies and wedding cake it was like we had our very own clubhouse."

At this point, Mr. Nick put up his hand to stop me because I would have spent the whole afternoon talking about the football wedding.

Mr. Nick is smiling and says:

"I could not have described it any better. Sounds like you and your family had a lot of fun there. Now you have to wash your hands, then open the first box of rolls and lay out the bottom part of the roll on this large counter. I will bring you a large tray with different cold cuts for you to put on each roll. After you put the meat and cheese on each roll you have to put the top of the roll on top of each sandwich. Over here you will find Defonte business cards and paper already cut into sandwich size squares. You assemble the sandwiches, place a business card upside down on the paper, then place a sandwich upside down on the business card and wrap the whole thing like so. It will take time and practice for you to do this, don't feel bad if you're moving slowly at first. Just keep doing it, Okay?"

Wedding Sandwiches Are Tossed Around The Table Like A Football.

All this time Mr. Nick is talking I just stand there with my mouth open. Holy Shit! What did I get myself into? It is taking me a while but I snap out of it and am assembling. Much to my surprise, Mr. Nick is right; I'm really moving faster and faster. I look up at the clock and noticed it is 5 o'clock already! I packed five boxes loaded with 400 assembled sandwiches! I finish the first wedding and I go back to work the next day and assemble another 500 sandwiches. Mr. Nick is very happy with my work and gives me $20.00 for working the weekend. I am so happy, I run upstairs to show my mother my first paycheck. She is so happy to see me so excited about working for Mr. Nick. This weekend just flew by, and I know I will sleep like a rock tonight.

It's Monday, and I have big money in my pocket. My mom urges me to put half of my pay away for another day. So I will, I'll keep $10.00 for myself and stashed the other $10.00 in my secret hiding place. It just feels so good to have walking around money in my pocket! I eat a quick breakfast and run down the steps to greet the world.

I walk around the corner to Luquer Street and I see Joanie is playing a box ball game with her friend Jenny on the other side of the street. Walking over to watch the game I notice that Joanie has a great eye for this game. She just looks up for a second and hits the ball with the ice cream stick for another point. When it's Jenny's turn, she misses the target. The game is going on now for a few more minutes and it looks like Joanie's friend can't hit the side of a barn. It doesn't take long for Joanie to reach fifteen points and win the game. Box-ball is a great game for girls to play. You don't have to pitch a ball at 90 miles an hour or hit a ball with a bat for a home run. All you need is a ball, a penny or a flat ice-cream stick and a smooth sidewalk to play this game. Most of the time there are only two players but you can play this game with up to four players.

You put a penny or ice-cream stick on the line in the center of the two boxes. Each player stands in front of their box, the player with a ball in hand is ready to throw it at the target first. If the penny or stick is hit, one point is scored. Each player gets a turn to throw the ball and so on. The player who reaches 15 points first wins the game.

The game is over and Joanie comes over to me.

"Hey Pepino, why do you have this big smile on your face?"

"Huh, big smile, I didn't notice! Maybe it's because I have ten bucks in my pocket."

She is laughing.

"Yeah, I know the whole story. My aunt Marylyn went to Defonte's to buy some cold cuts Saturday afternoon and saw you working there assembling sandwiches for a football wedding. She then stopped over my house and told my mother what she saw. So now you're a big shot?"

"No, I guess I'm just happy about getting my first real job. It feels good and my face shows it."

Joanie looks right into my eyes.

"I think that's great Mr. Big Shot! So maybe now you can buy me an ice cream?"

My face turned beet red and I'm mumbling nervously:

"Ah, okay let's go to the candy store."

Meanwhile, Jenny is laughing so hard she is crying.

Chapter 32
Ice Cream & Joanie-Chinese Handball

I am going with Joanie to the candy store for ice cream. We are both getting vanilla ice cream in Dixie cups that we can eat with wooden flat spoons. I have never gone to a candy store with a girl before. We are sitting on the stoop finishing up without talking and I think it is a good thing Jenny went home. But now I'm thinking maybe it would have been better if Jenny stayed with us. I wouldn't feel so silly just sitting here like I do now. One of us has to break the ice, so…

"Hey Joanie, how is your dog, Joy? Did you have his tail and ears cut by the Vet so he can look like a Boxer, yet?"

She doesn't look at me, she looks down at the ground and says:

"Well, it was pretty bad.

I went with my Dad when we took Joy to the Vet. The dog was so upset like he knew what was about to happen. I didn't want to go into the room with my Dad; I just started crying. My Dad told me to wait in the lobby. He told me that the dog will be put asleep and he will not feel any pain. I couldn't help it, I cried the whole time. About a half hour later my Dad came out with Joy in his arms. Joy's ears and tail were all taped with a white bandage. When we got home that after-noon Joy was still asleep and I fell asleep too."

I am getting sick just listening to her story and wish I hadn't asked her about the dog. I'm telling her that I am sorry and I hope that Joy is okay now, I get up from the stoop and say that I have to meet Pecker at his house and just walk away. I don't think she believes me when I said that.

Walking to Hicks Street I find Mikey Tomato, Reno the Greek and Nunzio Superman sitting in front of Mikey's grandmother 'Chickie's' grocery store.

"Pepino, Who died? You look so sad."

I'll sit down next to him.

"I saw Joanie and asked her about her Boxer Joy.

CALL FOR *Elsie* ICE CREAM FROSTICK!
WORLD CHAMPION OF THE TASTE LEAGUE

Sold at: Ebbets Field!

Frostick

Elsie

I Bought Joanie An Ice Cream At The Candy Store.

She was so upset that her dog had his ears and tail cut off so that he would look like a full breed Boxer!"

"Booooo Hoooooo, she was sooooo upset. Face it stupid, you really like her. That's why you're always talking to her and taking care of her dog."

"If you don't SHUT UP; I will kick your ass around the block. Ass Hole!"

He looks really shakened!

"OK, Ok, don't get crazy!"

I'm thinking to myself that maybe he's right about my feelings for her. I can't let on that I really like to be around her because my friends will tease me to death. Joanie is always nice to me and she's so smart. I am still thinking about her and Nunzio jumps up.

"I've got a ball, how about we play Chinese handball?"

Everyone agrees that it is a great idea. We haven't played this game in a long while. I will tell the guys that we need to play Chinese handball against a building that has a flat wall and smooth concrete sidewalk in front of it with sharp lines so we can get a box for each one of us.

Mentioning that the factory building on Columbia Street on the same block as Defonte's was rebuilt about six months ago. A machine manufacturing company called the Triangle Tool and Die has just moved in. I think that this building and the smooth sidewalk they made would be perfect for Chinese handball. We all get up and start walking to Columbia Street.

Chinese handball is a Brooklyn game. Up to six guys can play. If you play Chinese handball with only two players it's not as much fun. We draw lots and each kid has his own box in front of the wall of the building.

Since Superman has a Spalding ball he gets the first box or ace box. The Greek is in the second box or King box and then the Queen, Jack, etc. We are not playing American handball. If we are playing American handball we will slap the ball and hit the wall on a fly. When we play Chinese handball the Ace serves first and slaps the ball on a bounce against the wall to another player. The ball can land in the King, Queen or Jack box.

Whoever receives the ball has to slap it in one bounce back to the other players. The game continues this way until one of the players makes an error. The player who has the ball in their box does not have to immediately slap the ball to another player. He can keep the ball in his box but he has to keep slapping the ball in one bounce against the wall until he is ready to hit the ball to another player.

When you slap the ball to another player up or down the line and if your ball hits a rock or bottle cap that happens to be on the court and goes cuckoo, you can call a "do-over." The point of the game is not to make an error. If and when you miss a shot you lose your box and have to move to the end of the line and you receive a penalty numbered '1'. The Ace is the only player that can make an error lose his box and not be charged a penalty number. If anyone makes seven errors they're out of the game. The players continue to play until the one player is left and declared the winner. The number seven is not a good number when you're playing Chinese handball. This game has players who develop different strategies when hitting the ball. You can "blast" the ball hard to another player or slap the ball with a "spin" down or up the line. Each player develops his or her own technique on how to slap the ball. Yes, even "girls" can play this game.

We play two games and Reno the Greek is the big winner as he took both games. At the end of the second game, the non-winners all sit along the brick wall and watch Reno doing his victory dance.

"Hey, Pepino, I heard that you were working at Defonte's this weekend. One of my cousins saw you working with your head down assembling about a hundred sandwiches. He told me that you never looked up to say hello."

"Yeah, it was my first job. Mr. Nick paid me 20 dollars; I never had that much money at one time."

Mikey laughs.

"Why don't you buy a used bike? I know that you don't have one, and I can teach you to ride on my bike while you're looking for your own bike."

"Gee, thanks, Mike, I would like that. I'll check with my parents and get back to you."

I start daydreaming about riding my dream bike...

Chapter 33

My First Bike Ride-Tarzan Movies

I am so happy that Mike Tomato promised to help me learn how to ride a two-wheeler bicycle. I never had a chance to get on a bike before. When I get home for dinner I'll ask my mom if she is okay with the idea.

Mom is sitting down on a kitchen chair facing me and wiping her hands on her apron saying that I am too short to ride a 26-inch bicycle because my feet will never touch the ground when I stop the bike. I'm telling her that 'yes', my feet can't touch the ground, my friends who are about my height ride and stop their 26-inch bike close to a bench, curb or stoop and put their foot out so they won't fall over. Sometimes when they're not close to a curb, bench or stoop and they have to stop, they still put a foot out towards the falling side of the bike and do their best to hold the bike to land on an angle. I know it will take time and practice but I can do this with Mike's help. She is agreeing to let me practice on Mike's bike as long as we're riding in the schoolyard. If anyone tells her they see me riding on the street she will shut me down for the next year.

I'm telling her that I will not ride in the street. Now I can plan to hook up with Mike tomorrow morning for my first bike-riding lesson. I go to bed and have a dream that my whole family is riding bikes and before I know, it is morning.

After breakfast, I run down the steps and crash into Roger the Professor who is just coming into the building. I fall on my ass but Fat Roger is still standing looking down at me.

"What's wrong with you Shit Head? Why don't you look where you're going?"

I am still in a daze looking up at him, telling him that I'm sorry that I crashed into him.

Giving him the whole story of my new job, the money, Mike and the bike lessons and my hope to buy a bike, while looking into his eyes, I can tell he is thinking about the money and how he can get some of it. I don't trust him for a second. He grabs my hand pulling me up from the floor.

"I can see why you were in such a hurry to meet Mikey. Let me know when you're ready to buy a used bike. I will help you; I

Brooklyn Kids Line Up For A Matinee At The Clinton Theater.

know where I can get one for you real cheap."

Telling him that I will see him around, I take off to find Mike Tomato.

Going down to Luquer and Hicks Street I can see Mike and his brother flying their pigeons on the roof of his grandfather's barn. I am calling up to him and he waves to me and comes down to the street.

"Hey Pepino, are you ready for your bike lessons?"

"Yeah, Mike, I'm ready, but my mom told me that I'm only allowed to ride in the schoolyard. If she finds out that I rode the bike on the street she will kill me."

Mike didn't care where we went so he got his green and white two-wheel bike and we walk to the P.S. 27 schoolyard on Nelson Street.

"Pepino, listen, it's not hard it's all in the balance. Just remember how you balance yourself on the street-scooter, well you do the same thing when you ride a bike.

You don't look down, you look forward and get a feel for when to move your body side to side for balance. Just keep pedaling the bike, if you're going too slow the bike will tip and fall."

I understand his instructions. Mike holds me as I get on the bike, I start to pedal and I go forward. Mike runs with me as he's holding the bike that helps me keep my balance. After two or three tries I'm moving solo without my having any support from Mike! WOW! What a great feeling, it's like you're set free from gravity! I fell a few times but I get back on the bike and keep trying. Before I know it, I am ready to get my own bike!

After an hour of riding around the school playground, we are walking back to Mike's house. I put my arm around Mike's shoulders and thank him for teaching me how to ride his 26-inch bike. He is right about the street-scooter and knowing how to keep your balance, that is a big help.

I am so happy that I'm asking Mike to come with me to see a Tarzan movie at the new Clinton Theater. I'm telling him that I will pay for the movie and treats. He smiles and thanks me.

"That's great! I hear that both the Happy Hour and the Lido Movie House can fit into the Clinton Theater with room to spare. Not only is the new theater huge, it has a balcony too!"

We plan to meet after lunch about 1:00 P.M. so we can walk and be there way before the 2:00 P.M. matinee starts.

I am home for lunch now and telling my sister what Mike and I plan on this afternoon. She is telling me that the Clinton Theater is a new and very modern design theater with air conditioning.

"What's air conditioning?"

"It keeps you cool, Stupid!"

She goes on saying that the Clinton is the largest neighbor-hood theater in Brooklyn. It can hold 1,000 people on the ground floor or orchestra and almost 700 people in the balcony. The people who own the place built the theater because of the Red Hook New York City Projects being built nearby. When the

I Paid For some Good & Plenty Movie Treats.

Projects are completed 2,500 poor families will live there. So that's why the Clinton Theater is so big. The owners expect a lot of customers will come there from the Projects to see the movies and buy treats.

Lunch is done and I will go meet Mike Tomato and walk to the Clinton Theater. As we are turning the corner of Huntington Street we can see a crowd of about 300 kids standing in line waiting to get into the theater. We wait in line and finally get in. I treat Mike to a bag of popcorn, soda and a box of Good & Plenty. We sit in the kid's section and watch coming attractions, a newsreel, and some cartoons before the Tarzan movie starts.

The Tarzan movie is fun watching, and almost two hours long. The movie shows us that when Tarzan was a baby he got lost in the African rainforest.

A wolf pack finds him wandering around and a mama wolf adopts him, feeds him, raises and protects him. So when Tarzan is a teenager he thinks he's a wolf. He hunts and howls like a wolf. There is lots of action with his animal friends, Cheetah the Chimp, Mogador the Lion, Juba the Elephant and others.

Tarzan does not know he is human and when the natives try to hunt and kill his animal friends he will come to the rescue screaming and yelling while swinging from tree to tree. This is his way of warning his animal friends that they are in danger so they can run or hide from the natives.

We are standing in the lobby thinking about all this stuff and Mike looks at me.

"You know that we have to go home sooner or later. I think that the theater manager is about to throw us out!"

"Yeah, you're right Mike. But it's still hot outside and I can stay in this air conditioning forever. It would be nice but I don't think that they will let us sleep here tonight. Okay, let's go home and tell the guys all about the Tarzan movie."

Chapter 34

Jungle War Dance-Hunting Party

Mike Tomato and I are still flying high from the Tarzan movie as we get to his grandmother's grocery store on Hicks Street. Sitting out front of the store is Pecker, Nunzio Superman, Reno the Greek and Jimmy Pizza. We are sitting next to them and telling them all about the new Clinton Theater, the cool air conditioning, and the Tarzan movie. We are also talking about how Tarzan lives in the jungle and how he is lost, and how wolves find and raise him as part of their family. Tarzan makes friends with a lot of different animals in the jungle, Mogador the Lion, Juba the Elephant, Wolves and his close friend Cheetah the Chimp.

When the natives try to hunt the animals Tarzan does his best to save them by yelling and swinging from one tree to another. Mike Tomato stands up and suggests:

"Hey, why don't we put together our own native hunting party tonight? We can make some spears, and use garbage can lids as shields and paint our faces like the natives do in Africa. We can then build a fire in the lot across the street so we can do a war dance around the fire before our war party takes off to hunt the animals."

Everybody is yelling and jumping up and down like they think the African natives do it.

"Mikey, what are we hunting? I don't see any jungle animals hanging around Luqure Street."

"I see lots of jungle animals. Look at the Tigers, Lions, Leopards, and Wolves that live here." Jimmy is yelling.

It finally dawns on me that he was pointing to all the alley cats and stray dogs that are always knocking down the garbage cans looking for food.

"Mikey! You mean like Simba the tiger cat who can kick your ass."

"Yeah; I think that the Red Hook Jungle animals will start running when we chase them yelling like African Natives banging our spears against our garbage can shields."

So that's what we will do. We will collect a bunch of small trees that are growing in the vacant lot like weeds to make spears. Getting six garbage can lids that are in front of the apartment buildings, we also borrow old lipstick and make-up from our sisters and mothers' junk drawer for war paint. We build a fire and start to do a war dance around the fire. We look like a crazy bunch of kids. After the war dance, we form a line and walk side-by-side towards Columbia Street, yelling banging our shields and screaming our heads off. And you know what; Sumba the cat and his gang and all the other stray cats and dogs are running for their lives. It is so funny to see them scatter like real Jungle animals. We are now on Luqure and Columbia Streets and there isn't a jungle animal to be seen! Our war party is sitting on the curb of the street laughing our heads off. Every time we try to say something we can't stop laughing to get the words out.

Joanie coming out of her house to walk her dog Joy stands there staring at us.

"What are you guys nuts, screaming and yelling with all that paint on your face?"

She doesn't stop walking to wait for an answer because we are still laughing like crazy people. I know that this giddy feeling will not go away. Now, every time the guys look at each other we will not be able to talk because we will start to laugh for no reason. It will take some time for this giddy feeling to go away.

Roger coming over wants to know what the commotion is all about. I tell him the whole story about the Clinton Theater, the Tarzan movie, our war party and how we chase the neighborhood jungle animals up and down the block. Roger can't control himself either. He is laughing too!

"You guys are something else. How do you come up with these crazy games?"

None of us can give him an answer from we are still laughing so hard.

Roger tells me that he is looking to find me a used bike. He thinks that his friend Joey Hook Nose has an old bike down his cellar that hasn't been used in years. I tell Roger that I am still interested in finding one and to let me know how much Joey Hook Nose wants for it and when can I see his old bike? Roger doesn't say it, but I know he will do what he can to separate me from my money.

I tell the guys that I am going home to wash my face and take off all this war paint. We all are leaving the corner and agree to meet again tomorrow to play a game of 'One and Over', or if we can buy a pimple ball we can play Fist Ball. The summer is almost over and we will have to go back to school in a couple of weeks. The good news is that when the summer is about to end our neighborhood church celebrates the feast of the Madonna, a tradition that

Mola De Bari Italian Festival Street Procession

came to Brooklyn, New York when my parents and their friends moved to the United States from a small town in Italy called Mola DeBari.

It's really a fun time of year. It's a big deal to go to church and parade with the saint on your shoulders all-around the neighborhood. We all get dressed up for the parade and march with all the Italian-American Molesi people. We will walk what seems like a hundred blocks with a band playing Italian music and then the parade stops in front of homes where families have made large money donations to the church to shoot off fireworks. When the Madonna stops people will come up and pin money donations directly on the Madonna's clothing. It's quite a sight: the marching with thousands of people, the music, the fireworks and the street festival will go on for three days and nights! As I walk up the steps to my apartment I'm also thinking that I have to stop by Defonte's to ask Mr. Nick if he needs me to work for him again. I can really use the money for some stuff for myself.

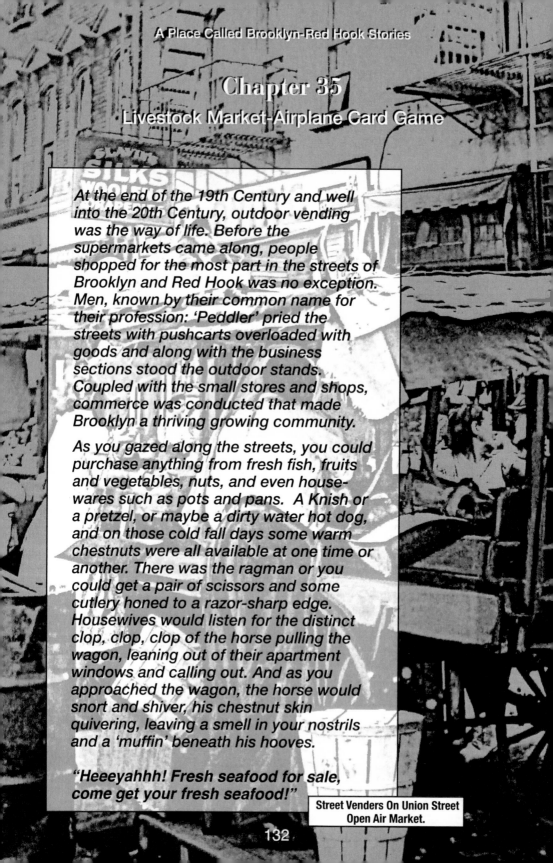

Chapter 35
Livestock Market-Airplane Card Game

At the end of the 19th Century and well into the 20th Century, outdoor vending was the way of life. Before the supermarkets came along, people shopped for the most part in the streets of Brooklyn and Red Hook was no exception. Men, known by their common name for their profession: 'Peddler' pried the streets with pushcarts overloaded with goods and along with the business sections stood the outdoor stands. Coupled with the small stores and shops, commerce was conducted that made Brooklyn a thriving growing community.

As you gazed along the streets, you could purchase anything from fresh fish, fruits and vegetables, nuts, and even house-wares such as pots and pans. A Knish or a pretzel, or maybe a dirty water hot dog, and on those cold fall days some warm chestnuts were all available at one time or another. There was the ragman or you could get a pair of scissors and some cutlery honed to a razor-sharp edge. Housewives would listen for the distinct clop, clop, clop of the horse pulling the wagon, leaning out of their apartment windows and calling out. And as you approached the wagon, the horse would snort and shiver, his chestnut skin quivering, leaving a smell in your nostrils and a 'muffin' beneath his hooves.

"Heeeyahhh! Fresh seafood for sale, come get your fresh seafood!"

Street Venders On Union Street Open Air Market.

132

As I am walking into our apartment, Mom is greeting me by telling me not to make any plans for tomorrow morning. She's telling me that my sister is going out to buy school clothes tomorrow, so she can't go with my mom to shop for food that day. Mom needs me to go with her to shop for food at the open-air market on Union Street. I really don't want to go with her but I won't argue because I know she needs my help to carry home the shopping bags loaded with food. I say okay but ask her if I can visit Mr. Nick before we go.

She knows I want to find out if Mr. Nick still needs my help in assembling the football wedding sandwiches next weekend. She says okay but not to make it too late because the heat will start to rot the fruits and vegetables at the open-air market before we get there. We are all sitting down for dinner except for my father who is still working.

I hardly ever see my Dad; he's always working. When he gets home late at night he washes up, eats and goes to bed for a couple hours of sleep, he then gets up early and goes back to work. I'm thinking to myself and hoping I don't have to work that hard when I grow up. It's after dinner, I'm washing up in the laundry sink, taking off the rest of my war paint, putting on clean clothes and sitting by the radio listening to the adventures of Batman and Robin. I love to listen to the action radio programs. Closing my eyes, I can hear and see Batman jumping and flying over the rooftops chasing after the bad guys bringing them to justice.

The Batman stories are over and I'm nodding off and I can't seem to stay awake long enough to listen to Roy Rogers and Dale Evans riding after more bad guys and singing western songs. I'm just too tired from running and jumping around like African natives chasing the Luqure Street jungle animals up and down the block, so I think I'll go to bed.

It is morning and my Dad took off for work. I have breakfast and go downstairs to talk to Mr. Nick about assembling sandwiches. Mr. Nick is having coffee as I am walking into his store. I sit next to him and ask him if he needs me next weekend. He tells me that he has a sandwich order for only one wedding so he will need me to work on Saturday. I thank him and tell him that I will report to work at 11 AM Saturday. While I'm leaving the store, I notice a new kid about my age throwing a soccer ball against the wall of the building and hitting it with his head. I stand there looking at him and he stops, and walking over to me says: "Buongiorno" which means "Good day" in Italian. Answering in Italian he looks a little surprised that I know the language. We are introducing ourselves and he tells me his name is Michael Della Pesca. I tell him that in Brooklyn he will be known as 'Mike the Fish'.

We both laugh and I tell him that I have errands to run but I can hang out with him later this afternoon or tomorrow. I take off to meet my mother and go shopping with her on Union Street. It is

Hicks Street Live Market with Chickens, Rabbits, etc

a little after 9 AM and already crowded with people! You would think the vendors are giving the stuff away. My Mother is stopping at a food vendor's cart to buy vegetables. She is now talking to the vendor about the freshness of his produce and fighting over the price. While I'm standing next to her I notice my cousins Frankie and Albert, Johnny's brothers, working the crowd selling paper shopping bags. They buy a hundred bags for 5 cents each and then sell them to the shoppers for 10 cents each. When they're not selling bags, they shine shoes for 25 cents to make extra money. I wanted to join them a couple of times but my Dad told me that he will kick my ass if he found me selling bags or shining shoes. He doesn't want our neighbors and friends to think that he could not take care of us.

Meanwhile, if my mom ever settles on a price with the vendor we will need a couple of shopping bags to carry the fruit and vegetable she plans to buy. So, I touch her shoulder and ask her to give me 50 cents to buy shopping bags. She looks up to see Cousin Frankie and Albert walking towards us. She reaches into her pocketbook and gives me 50 cents to buy the bags. It takes several hours for my mom to get the fruit and vegetables at the right price. We now have 4 shopping bags to carry home. We're not done shopping yet!

We walk over to Hicks and Union Street to buy two chickens. We go into the Acqua Caldo (Warm Water) live market. This place is like a zoo! They not only have live chickens for you to buy, they have rabbits, turkeys, pigeons, ducks, piglets, and other strange looking animals. The sounds and smells of all this livestock are making me sick. My mother talks to the owner Joe the 'Geep' and selects two fat chickens. Joe drags the chickens out of their cage by their legs and gives them, as they're squawking, to the executioner behind the counter. This guy is dressed in a rubber suit with tall rubber boots. He is so fast; he grabs the chickens and cuts their throat with a sharp knife. He then throws them into a barrel to die. It seems like it takes forever for the chickens to stop jumping around in the barrel while they're bleeding to death.

After a minute or two the executioner takes the chickens out of the barrel and dips them into boiling hot water, then hangs them upside down to take the feathers off, cuts them open to remove their guts and then asks my mother if she wants the chicken head, feet, liver and heart to make soup. My mother is saying yes and the man then cleans everything in the boiling water, and packs the chickens and innards in paper and gives it to my mother. While all this was going on I watch the executioner kill and skin rabbits. He kills the rabbits with a knock on the head with a large wooden hammer, then guts and skins them while they are still alive. I hate to go to the live market with my mother. It's like watching a horror show. I'm glad it's over and we now take all the food we brought home with us. I help my mother carry everything to our apartment and then I take off to meet Pecker and Jimmy Pizza.

I find them in front of Jimmy's building on Columbia Street tossing picture cards against the wall, sort of like pitching pennies. As I am walking up to them they are asking me why I have a sick look on my face. I'm telling them about my trip to the live market and as I'm done with my story Pecker and Jimmy look sick too.

The game they're playing is with airplane picture cards, instead of baseball cards. They toss three cards each time in turn towards the brick wall and the closest to the wall wins all the cards on the ground. I don't like this game all that much because the picture cards really get beat up and are not worth keeping. I rather flip the cards instead of tossing them against a brick wall.

After 20 minutes, they stop playing the game, now that summer is almost over, we sit on the curb talking about the street festivals and going back to school.

Chapter 36

Buying An Old Bike-One And Over Game

I come downstairs this morning only to find Mike the Fish aka the new Italian kid still banging the soccer ball against the wall with his head. So, I'll call out to him.

"Ciao, Mike, you like to play soccer?"

He looks at me with a crooked smile and it dawns on me that he doesn't understand any English. So, I'll tell him in Italian that my family came to the USA from Mola di Bari and I am born in the USA a couple of years after they came here. He is happy to hear that since his whole family is also from Mola di Bari. I'm telling him in Italian that I can and will help him learn the English language. He thanks me in his native language and goes off to meet his father and brother to do some shopping.

Just as Mike the Fish is leaving Roger is coming over to me.

"Hey Keyno, do you want to take a look at the old bike in Joey Hook Nose's cellar? Joey told me that if you're interested he will give you the bike for fifteen dollars."

Wow, fifteen dollars! I have enough money to buy this bike.

"Yeah sounds good to me."

We'll walk over to Huntington Street to find Joey. On Huntington Street, we are walking past PS 27 School while we head towards Clinton Street. As we get to Joey's dilapidated house Roger knocks on Joey's door. The door is opening I see two beautiful blond teenage girls standing there, and one of them says:

"Hi, Roger, where have you been? I haven't seen you around that much lately."

Roger irritated, responds: "Cut the crap Ginger. I have to talk to Joey. Where is he?"

She looks disappointed.

"He's in the backyard screwing around with some old bike he found in our cellar."

I think to myself that Roger is crazy not to cozy up to Joey's beautiful sisters. Both girls have their blond hair pushed back

136

into a ponytail. They both have green eyes highlighted with eye-liner and their lips stand out with bright red lipstick. Ginger is wearing an extra-large white T-shirt, which stops just above her knees and her sister is wearing a red shirt and very tight jeans. Wow, I just can't take my eyes off them, as Roger yells:

"Hey, Pepino, do you want to look over this bike or not? Get your ass over here."

We walk to the backyard where Joey Hook Nose is doing his best to clean up the old bike. This is the first time I have met Joey. His hooknose isn't just big it's gigantic! His nose hook is so bad it almost covers part of his mouth. I never notice the bike he is cleaning. I just stand there looking at Joey with my mouth open when I hear Roger say:

"Isn't it a beauty?"

I turn to look at Roger and wonder "Huh?" I think he is talking about Joey's nose. But no, he's pointing to a piece of shit he calls a bike. The bike they are showing me is falling apart.

"Roger this is a joke, right?"

You can't expect me to pay you guy's fifteen dollars for this piece of crap."

Roger is putting his arm on my shoulder and saying in a low voice:

"It just needs a little work. I'll help you spruce it up. When we get done even Joey's sisters will want to ride with you!"

He is pointing to the girls who are standing there, giggling and smiling at us. I'm seeing myself riding around the neighborhood with two beautiful girls following me on their bikes. All my friends will be SO jealous! Roger can really be convincing.

"Okay, I'll give you ten bucks."

Joey and Roger agree immediately and take my money before I can change my mind. Here I am, walking home with this rusty, squeaky, old bike with flat tires.

I am at Grandma 'Chickie's' grocery store and find Pecker, Jimmy Pizza, and Reno the Greek with Mike Tomato sitting in front of the store. As soon as I get up close to them they start to laugh and Jimmy is giggling.

"Where did you find this piece of junk. Did you find it in some vacant lot or something?"

"No, I bought it from Roger and Joey Hook Nose."

They all continue laughing all the harder. I'm MAD now.

"Yeah, you'll see how great this bike will look when I get finished sprucing it up. It will be the best-looking bike on the block."

I really don't believe it, I just feel so stupid that Roger conned me again. So, I'll put my head down and just keep on walking home.

I"m at Nick Defonte's sandwich shop on Columbia Street, leaning the bike against the brick wall and sitting on the curb looking at it. I can't believe that I can be so stupid to let Roger pull this over on me. He's such a shit. Well, now I'm stuck with this old bike and I'll be damned if I'm going to give up on it. I will work on fixing this thing even if it kills me. I can't look at it any longer so I'll wheel it into my hallway and store it behind the ground floor staircase.

I think I'll go back to find the guys who are teasing me about this old crappy bike.

I'm on Hicks Street and they are still sitting there. They won't give up on it so I have to stand here a take some more teasing until they settle down. It is still early so I'll ask them if they want to play One and Over. They are all jumping up at once, so, we pick the first 'horse', Pecker.

One and Over is a simple game, it's almost like follow the leader. The 'horse' Pecker steps into the street and bends his body and head, way down looking at the ground. They agree to make me 'the stupid one' and the leader, in the first round.

Now I'm backing up to the wall of the building facing the side-walk and Pecker the 'horse' who is bent over in the street is right up against the curb. Yelling out: "None" I will run and jump over Pecker with my hands on Pecker's back as far as I can. When I land on the street I mark that spot with a chalk, rock, stick, or anything that's handy. Jimmy Pizza, Reno the Greek, and Mike Tomato, will follow and jump over Pecker the same way I do. We all finish jumping over Pecker and he is moving to the spot on my first jump. Now, as the leader, I have to make a new call, if I feel I can make it I will call "None" again. Now that Pecker is further away from the curb the leader may call "One". Okay, I'll stay with "None"; I run and jump off the curb, take one step in the street and jump over Pecker again.

If I make it without knocking him over we set a new mark. Everyone has to obey the command and follow. If I called "TWO" everyone is allowed two steps before jumping over the horse. If the leader calls "THREE" you're allowed three steps before you jump and so on. If any of the players including the leader, can't make it and they crash into the horse, Pecker is released and the player who made the foul is now the new horse. Now we start all over again and I call "None". I like this game; we managed to play into the night.

Going home I am running into Roger. He says that he means everything he said about helping me fix the old bike. We shake hands and he gives me a bunch of his comic books as a peace offering. He tells me that we have to fix the tires first and take the bike for a road test. After the road test, we can then start sprucing it up. It may take a couple of weeks before we can make this bike look like something.

Chapter 37

Playing Checkers-Visitation Church

It's morning and I'm getting ready to report to Defonte's Sandwich Shop to assemble a couple of hundred sandwiches for a football wedding Mr. Nick hired me for. It is still early so I don't have to report to work until 11 AM. I hear a knock on our door. I open the door and Roger is standing there.

"What do you want? Did you come down to screw me out of more money? If you did I'm sorry to say I'm all tapped out of cash."

He is looking down whispering:

"No, no, I thought that you might want to play a game of checkers with me this morning. My uncle Sammie gave me his old checkerboard and an old set of wood chess pieces. I know how to play checkers but I never played Chess before. What do you say?"

"I know what checkers is. What the Hell is Chess? And what makes you think that I would spend time with you playing any game?"

Roger can feel that I am still pissed off at him, because of the screwing he, and his friend Joey Hook Nose, gave me yesterday. He's trying to calm me down by reminding me that he will work with me to spruce up that old Bike. Anyway, I have to kill some time before I report to work, so I'll say okay.

We are walking up to his apartment, which is upstairs from mine and enter into his bedroom at the far end of the building. I like Roger's room, it's so private, and it's not like my bedroom in the middle of our living room. We are sitting at a little table in his room, which doubles as his laboratory. Roger is so smart, he is always working on some invention he thought up. He puts out the white and red Checker set on the table and starts to explain to me the rules of the game. He tells me that you can only move one checker at a time, forward in the black boxes on the board. If your red checker lands next to the other player's white checker he can jump over your red checker and take it off the board. If there is the room he can also double jump your checkers and take two off the board. If one of your red checkers manages to go all the way to the end of the board in front of you, you can call out "King Me". The guy that's playing against you now has to place a red checker on top of your checker.

The King checker can now move in any direction around the board when a single checker can only move forward. The winner of the game is the player who jumps and clears the board of all his opponent's checkers. We play this game for a couple of hours and Roger wins every game, but with a little practice, I think I can beat his ass. It is getting late so I'm getting up from the table and telling Roger that I have to go to work at Defonte's. He nods okay and promises to teach me how to play Chess the next time we get together again.

I went to Defonte's and work for almost six hours. I am getting very good at assembling the wedding party sandwiches. It is an order for 350 sandwiches, not the 200 I had thought the order called for. But it doesn't matter; I am assembling sandwiches so fast that Mr. Nick gives me an extra two dollars. Wow! Now I have twelve dollars, plus five left over from my last job for a total of seventeen dollars. I go up to our apartment and my father is still at work, so I'll have dinner with my mom and my sister, listen to the radio and then I'll go to bed around 10 PM.

I get up this morning to the smell of tomato sauce cooking on the stove, realizing it must be Sunday morning. Every Sunday my mom gets up at dawn to crush the tomatoes, mixed them with olive oil, basil, spices, and meatballs. My Mom tells me that making tomato sauce is an art. Every Italian family has their own tradition on how to make the tomato sauce, no two families make it the same way. Even if you're related, the mother's sauce will be different from her daughter's tomato sauce. You would think that the daughter's sauce would taste the same as her mothers since her mother taught her how to make it. But no, there's always a difference, it could be lighter, thicker, hotter, sweeter or spicier. My mom and grandmother and many other Italian generations of our family before us say that the perfect tomato sauce has to cook slowly for a minimum of six hours. That's why my Mom gets up so early. Every Sunday we have our dinner in the afternoon so we can get out of our apartment and chat with our neighbors. I get to the kitchen and find my mom making fresh wide noodles.

Wow! We're going to have lasagna today! My Dad has been working crazy hours for weeks, which means that we have a little extra money for food. I can't wait to sit down at our dinner table to eat this meal. But, not so fast, my mom is getting ready for church and it looks like she will drag me along with her. So, she is getting after me to put on a clean pair of shorts and a white shirt with sleeves and collar. I really don't want to go with her but if I say no she will whack me with her wooden spoon and I'm not in the mood to lose another fight with her.

Visitation Roman Catholic Church in Red Hook Brooklyn.

I'll get dressed and go downstairs to wait for her. She comes downstairs and takes my hand and we walk to Visitation Church near Coffey Park. It's a beautiful day, and I think that I'm the only kid going to Church with my Mom. I love God, but I'm not crazy about Church.

As we arrive my Mom is meeting a number of her friends from our old town in Italy. After they talk about how great it is back in Italy, I often wonder why in the Hell did they leave such a beautiful place to come here?

We're in Church and it's so boring. I don't understand a word the Priest is saying. I sit when they sit. I stand when they stand. I kneel when they kneel. I even make believe I'm praying in Latin, I don't think that anyone around me understands it anyway. They all seem to go through the motions of doing what they think they should be doing when praying to God. But all I can think about is getting home to eat the lasagna my Mom is making for our afternoon dinner. After dozing off a few times my Mom shakes me to tell me that mass has ended and we're finally going home.

As we cross the street next to Coffey Park I'll tell Mom that I will run in the park ahead of her and meet her at the other end, a block away. It's such a beautiful day she lets me go into the park. I like to run in the grass but I have my good shorts and clean white shirt on so I can't roll in the grass the way I would like to.

So, I'm running around with a bunch of kids that I don't know and I climb the metal statue of a World War I soldier that was put there in the memory of those who died fighting for our country. What I can't understand is that if all those men died to keep us free why did our soldiers have to fight again in World War II? Maybe my teacher can tell me the answer when I go back to school next month.

World War I Statue In Coffey Park This World War I memorial was originally dedicated in 1921 in Coffey Park. It was moved to the VFW Post 5195, in or about 1972 after having been vandalized in the park on multiple occasions.

Augustus Lukeman, later hired to carve the country's largest Confederate monument on the side of Stone Mountain, Georgia, sculpted the 'Doughboy'.

143

Chapter 38

St. Stephens Church-Flattened Pennies

Home from church my sister and dad are setting up the kitchen table for our afternoon dinner. It's such a beautiful day my sister is opening all our windows to let the fresh air into our apartment. The radio is playing music from an Italian radio station and the sauce with meatballs is cooking on the stove. The lasagna is in the oven and it will be ready to eat around 1 PM. The wonderful smell of all the cooking is making me hungry. I just can't wait, so I'll rip off the heel of the fresh Italian bread on the kitchen table. I'll walk over to the stove and dip the bread into the saucepot. I've decided to crawl out our window and sit on the fire escape eating my bread coated with warm sauce. It's such a great feeling to enjoy the bright warm sun on my face, with the smell of all the cooking along with the Italian music. I'm closing my eyes and imagining that this is how it is in Italy when all my relatives get together for a Sunday afternoon dinner.

I doze off for a while and hear my mom call out "Pepino!" Which means dinner is on the table. So, I better rush in and sit at the kitchen table with my family. The dinner is perfect; my Mom is such a great cook! Finishing dinner, my dad and I are going out to visit with his friends from the old country. Every Sunday my Dad gets all dressed up in a suit, polished shoes, white shirt, tie, and dress hat to hang out with a bunch of men who smoke Lucky Strike cigarettes. They all talk to each other in Italian. This is all going on while my sister and mother are cleaning up the kitchen and putting away the leftover food. They will meet their friends after the kitchen and the apartment are all clean. Dad turns to me and says that all the men are making plans to meet at St Stephens on Summit and Hicks Street later this week for the procession of Mola di Bari Santa Maria Addolorata and the three-day street festival. Wow! I can't wait to tell my friends about the plans for the parade and feast. This day comes to an end after dad and his cousin's family meet at our apartment for espresso, biscotti, and cookies. They sit in the living room and talk over me late into the night, while I sleep on my cot.

It's Monday Morning, I'm meeting Roger to start sprucing up my old bike. Roger tells me that he happened to find a leftover can of black paint that we can use for the bike frame and fenders.

So, I'll take the bike from behind the stairs of the first-floor hallway and roll it out next to the side of our building on Columbia Street. Roger just stands there with his hands on his hips looking at the bike.

It is a sad sight to see this broken down old bike leaning against the building. Roger explains:

"Okay, we have a lot of work to do to whip this bike into shape. First, we have to take it completely apart."

Roger has his toolbox and we are turning the bike upside down and taking off the wheels, fenders, handlebars, peddles, drive-chain, and seat. Roger has a patch kit to fix the

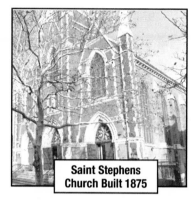

Saint Stephens
Church Built 1875

flat tires and shows me how to use a screwdriver to separate the tire from the rim so I can pull out the inner tube. After taking out the inner tubes we walk over to the gas station across the street. The guys at the Gulf gas station are very nice to us, they let us use the air pump to fill the tire tubes and test them for leaks in a bucket of water. We find two slow leaks in each tire tub and we use Roger's patch kit to fix the leaks.

We'll go back to the unassembled old bike and start working on putting the bike wheels together again. Roger deflates the inner tubes of all the air we pumped into them. He then pushes the inner tube back into the tire and tells me to take the assembled bike wheels back to the gas station and fill them with air.

Roger opens the old paint can and starts to paint the bike frame and fenders black. He gives the parts one coat and he then tells me that we have to wait a day for the first coat to dry before we give it a second coat. I stand back and look at the painted frame, fenders, and inflated bike wheels and much to my surprise they start to look pretty good. While Roger and I are working on the old bike, a tall skinny teenage guy is walking up to us. He has long, dirty, black curly hair down to his shoulders and some of his hair falls over his face. He has dark skin and green eyes. He looks like he came straight out of a horror movie. I can't take my eyes off his face when Roger suddenly says.

145

"Hi, Moon Face! This is my friend Keyno. Where are you heading?"

"Hey Professor, what ya doing? Fixing this piece of shit bike? You guys are going to be here for days!"

"Yeah, I know there is a lot of work to do but when we get this thing put together it will look pretty good."

"Well, I'm going to the railroad freight yards down at the docks to flatten a bunch of pennies for my girlfriend. She likes to make girl stuff, like jewelry with them."

Roger is asking:

"Is it okay if we go with you? I have a bunch of pennies and I would like to flatten them too."

"Yeah, yeah, it's no big deal; I'm not going to rob the freight train."

I have no idea who this guy is and how they plan to flatten a bunch of pennies and why.

All I know is that this is one ugly guy! Roger is directing me to put the painted bike frame into the backyard and all the other bike parts and tools down our cellar. We are down the cellar, away from Moon Face, and Roger tells me to be careful because this guy is crazy.

All the Pennies Were Flattened By Train

"His whole name is Charlie Moon Face. He's a member of a street gang called the Dukes. Charlie and his gang are always fighting the Black Panthers from the Red Hook Projects. The project teenagers are new to the neighborhood and they want to keep Moon Face and his gang out of their territory. One night during a gang war Charlie tried to throw a firebomb at the Panthers but the flaming rag that was stuck in the gasoline bottle came loose. As Moon Face went to throw it, the gasoline spilled on his face and back and the fire was all over him. The Dukes jumped on him and put the flames out but his face and back have all kinds of ugly pockmarks on them, now you know why Moon Face looks the way he does. So, don't mess with him."

Wow, I heard about these gang wars but I never met a guy who was in one.

It is a long walk to the freight yard at the docks. Ships were being unloaded, trucks and rail cars are moving in scrambling patterns all over the place. We won't go into the restricted area, we'll stay back outside the gates right along the railroad tracks. Roger and Moon Face kneel by the railroad tracks and lay a bunch of pennies with scotch tape on each rail.

We all sit on the ground and wait for the freight train to come out of the dock area and crush our pennies under the wheels of the train. The trains are coming out every half hour. Now it is time to collect the pennies and see if the train wheels crushed the pennies flat. Charlie finds about twenty flatten pennies and Roger finds about a dozen.

They are happy with the results and Moon Face is taking off to find his girlfriend while Roger and I are walking back Home.

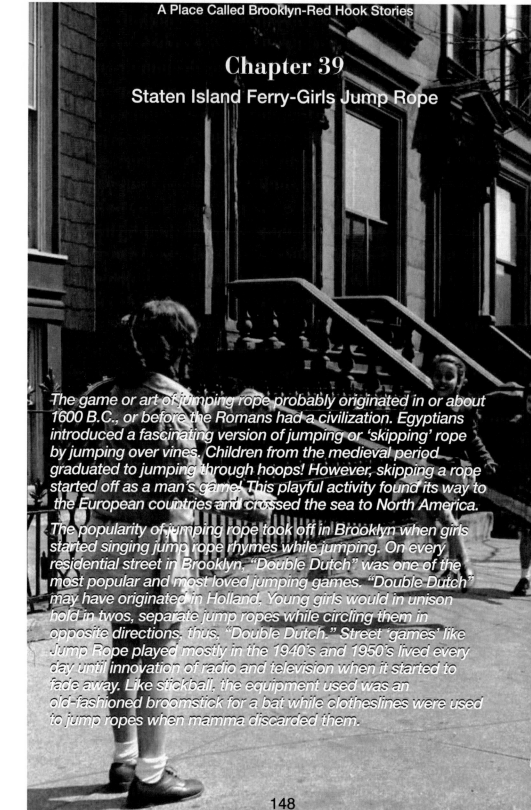

Chapter 39
Staten Island Ferry-Girls Jump Rope

The game or art of jumping rope probably originated in or about 1600 B.C., or before the Romans had a civilization. Egyptians introduced a fascinating version of jumping or 'skipping' rope by jumping over vines. Children from the medieval period graduated to jumping through hoops! However, skipping a rope started off as a man's game! This playful activity found its way to the European countries and crossed the sea to North America.

The popularity of jumping rope took off in Brooklyn when girls started singing jump rope rhymes while jumping. On every residential street in Brooklyn, "Double Dutch" was one of the most popular and most loved jumping games. "Double Dutch" may have originated in Holland. Young girls would in unison hold in twos, separate jump ropes while circling them in opposite directions, thus, "Double Dutch." Street 'games' like Jump Rope played mostly in the 1940's and 1950's lived every day until innovation of radio and television when it started to fade away. Like stickball, the equipment used was an old-fashioned broomstick for a bat while clotheslines were used to jump ropes when mamma discarded them.

148

Roger and I are home from flattening pennies on the railroad tracks with Moon Face Charlie and it is getting close to dinnertime. We agree to call it a day so we are getting the painted bike frame from the backyard and putting it in the cellar for storage with the other bike parts. Roger says if it doesn't rain we can try to put the bike together tomorrow. I'm okay with that and I'm going upstairs to my apartment. It is a weird day; I can't get Crazy Moon Face Charlie's ugly face out of my mind. To top it off he has a girlfriend and I wonder what the hell she looks like? What kind of a girl would go out with this crazy guy who throws "Fire Bombs" in a gang fight?

Walking into our apartment I'm surprised to see my father all cleaned up and sitting at the kitchen table. He is sitting there reading *El Progresso* an Italian newspaper. My Mom tells me to wash up for dinner. This can't be a good thing. I haven't seen my father home when it's a workday in months. Our family is sitting at the kitchen table ready to eat as Mom tells my sister and me that my father's job ended at noon today and that if he doesn't get another job soon he may have to collect unemployment insurance. We are all sitting there without saying much, and, Mom tells me that Pop wants to take me for a ride on the Staten Island Ferry tomorrow. Wow! That sounds great; I never went on a ferry before. Even though I liked the idea of going with my Dad on this ferry ride I am not happy about him being out of work. I can see why my Mom looks so upset, even with unemployment money she will have a hard time paying the rent and putting food on the table. She wants to buy my sister and I some new clothes when school starts next month. Then there's the festival of our Madonna coming up just before school starts.

My parents also planned to make a monetary contribution to St. Stephens Church and to the Mola Di Bari Parade Association that they belong to. If my father is out of work, that is going to be very hard for them to do. After dinner, my father goes back to reading his Italian newspaper. My sister is going out to meet her girlfriends at the ice cream parlor and I will sit by the radio listening to the adventures of the Green Hornet.

It is morning and my Dad is up early. He had his breakfast and is waiting for me to wake up and eat my breakfast. We will leave our apartment about 9 AM and start walking toward Van Brunt Street to catch a bus to Bay Ridge where the Staten Island Ferry comes in to dock at the 69th Street Pier.

It seems like a long bus ride, Dad isn't saying much to me except for a "yes" or "no" to my questions. We get off the bus and walk to the ferry landing, and as we do, the sunny day is hot but the wind is cooling, and the seawater smells so good. Dad buys two tickets and we get on the ferry. I'm getting excited at the prospect of being on the water on a ferry for the first time! I eagerly ask Dad if I can sit on the top deck so I can see all the sights. He agrees as long as I sit next to him. The ferry makes a large moaning roar and water is starting to bubble all around the bow and stern of the boat as we are departing from the dock. I watch as the boat is parting the water as if plowing its way through thousands of bubbles creating a mesmerizing foam. As the boat moves forward a strong wind is blowing in our faces.

The smell of the seawater getting even stronger as the Captain is steering the ferry towards Staten Island. I ask one of the ferry crew-hands how long the trip will take and he informs me:

"A little over a half hour, young man!".

Wow! I want the trip to take longer, because I love the vibrations, the sound of the engines, the wind, seagulls, the smell of the saltwater and the sun beating down on us, on this cool day as the ship roars forward.

I am so happy that my father has taken me on this trip. As we get to the next landing and after we dock, we have to wait for cars to be unloaded before we can walk off the boat. As we get off the boat I see another ferry docked close-by. This other ferry is much bigger than the one we sailed on, so, I ask Dad about it and he says that that's the ferry to Manhattan and we will take a ride on that one too!

Wow, this is unbelievable! I can't wait to ride that big ferry to Manhattan! We get on the Manhattan ferry and are riding almost forty-five minutes, passing the Statue of Liberty, heading toward Manhattan. I want to do this all day long. We dock in Manhattan and we stay on the ferry and return to Staten Island. We pass the Statue of Liberty once again; it is such a beautiful sight, her torch held high as a beacon in the harbor, but I don't know why I almost start to cry? When we return to Staten Island we got back on the ferry to Brooklyn.

As Dad and I board the bus, my father starts talking about the days he served as a sailor in the Italian Navy fighting with the Allies against Germany during World War One. He was assigned to a Battle Ship and saw lots of action in the Mediterranean. I never knew that my Dad was in the First World War fighting with the Americans. I guess being on the water on such a beautiful day with his son brought back some memories he wanted to share.

It is late afternoon and we are home. I run out of our apartment to find my friends to tell them all about my trip on the ferries to Staten Island and Manhattan and back again. I get to Jimmy Pizza, Mike Tomato and Nunzio Superman's apartments, their mothers tell me that the gang is cooling off at the Red Hook Swimming Pool near the new Projects. They should be home in a couple of hours. So, there I am all pumped up about my trip with no one to tell it to. That's when I notice Joanie and her sisters jumping rope in front of their home on Luquer Street. I'll walk across the street and sit there watching the girls jumping "Double Dutch".

Okay, my friends are away at the pool, so I think I'll do the next best thing and tell Joanie and her sisters all about my Staten Island Ferry adventure. The girls are very good jumping Double Dutch.

They are so fast and they have a good rhythm keeping time while the jumper sings "My name is Joan-a, I come home-a for some Bologn-a, but nobody is home-a to give me the Bologn-a…." And soon, it's such fun to watch them do their thing. I remember that I once asked my sister about who started jumping rope and she said that she once looked it up at the library. She told me that the encyclopedia said that this game started way back when with the Egyptian and Chinese rope makers. She doesn't think that anyone knows for sure when jumping rope turned into a kid's game. Rumor has it that the Dutch brought the game with them when they settled the town of New Amsterdam. I guess that's why they call it "Double Dutch" because there are two ropes spinning at the same time while you're jumping. I could never tell the guys that I jumped a single rope with the girl's months ago. It was a lot of fun, but there's no way I could do this Double Dutch thing. The girls stop jumping rope and I sit on the stoop with Joanie and tell her all about my adventure to Staten Island.

Chapter 40

Fixing The Old Bike-Making A Go-Cart

I had so much fun yesterday going on a ferry ride with Dad to Staten Island, Manhattan, and back again to Brooklyn. I am still excited after seeing the Statue of Liberty from the upper deck of the ferry ride to Manhattan. I get a chill when I think about it. I just want to tell everyone or anyone who will listen to my story. So, I'll get up this morning and run upstairs to call Roger to tell him all about it. I knock on his apartment door and his mother Emma answers:

"Good morning Pepino, if you are looking for Roger he's in his room in the back, but, you better wake him up otherwise he will sleep the whole day away!"

Mrs. Emma is such a nice lady; she treats me like one of the family. I'm walking quickly towards the back bedroom passing through Roger's three sleeping sister's bedrooms. I opened the door to his room and I whisper:

"Roger, Roger, are you awake? It's me, Pepino!"

"I am now, shit head. What the Hell are you doing here so early in the morning?"

"Well, it's not that early. I wanted to get an early start so we can finish sprucing up that piece of shit bike you sold me."

"Okay, Okay, you're never gonna let me forget it, are you? So, I better get my ass moving. I just want to finish painting your stupid bike so that you'll stop bugging me about it."

Roger is moving very slowly but this gives me a chance to tell him all about my adventures on the ferry rides to Staten Island, Manhattan, and the Statue of Liberty. He's not even looking at me, just keeps nodding his head. I don't think he hears one word of what I am saying! It doesn't matter whether or not he hears me, I am just happy to tell him my story.

We are going downstairs to pull the bike frame and all the unassembled parts from the cellar. He gives the bike frame and fenders another coat of black paint. After it dries we will start to reassemble the bike. You know what, that piece of crap I bought, really looks pretty good! I walk the bike over to the schoolyard for a test run. I don't know what it is; maybe the fresh coat of paint, but it rides like a new bike! I can hear Roger say:

"What do you think about your spruced-up bike now, SHIT HEAD?"

He is right, but I don't want him to see how happy I am, so I just keep on riding all around him.

"When you're finished riding around Big Head, get off the damn bike so you can help me build a Go Cart and wagon from a couple of old baby carriages I found."

Old Carriage Wheels For Go-Cart & Wagon

So, I'll ride the bike on the sidewalk back to our building on Columbia Street. I'm thinking that I'll buy a new bike seat, and handlebar grips with streamers, and maybe a bell, too! Roger helps me put the bike in the cellar for safe storage.

Out to the backyard again we are opening the old shed that is filled with junk. Roger is starting to clear out a bunch of lumber and wheels from an old baby carriage, rope, nails, long bolts with nuts, washers, along with old paint cans.

"Roger, how long have you been collecting all this crap?"

"Yeah, it's a lot more than I thought it was too! It has to be almost two months that I got the idea about making a wagon for my little sister Diane and maybe a go-cart for my cousin Jeffry. Last year I made Jeffrey a big cardboard red airplane that he could slide over his body and run like he was flying."

"Wow, do you have a plan on how to make this stuff or are you just playing it by ear?"

"What do you think Big Head? I've been making drawings for weeks on different designs and I think now that I have all the material we need, we can start putting the wagon and go-cart together. Just so you know, we have a deadline to meet! We have to build the go-cart first so that Cousin Jeffry can race in Sloan's Ice Cream Parlor race against all kinds of wheels the neighborhood kids race this afternoon."

"This afternoon; what are you crazy, there is no way we can complete a go-cart in time for this race!"

Roger starts to laugh and says: "Do you doubt me?"

I think to myself, well 'no', not Roger the professor. He can do anything he puts his mind to.

He is pulling out his tools and starting to work!

First, he is making a plywood platform on a 2'x4' frame. Now he extends one 2'x4' right down the middle of the frame about one foot. Everything is nailed in place. He is taking two separate 2'x4s about two and a half feet long where he anchors the wheels and axles from the baby carriage. He is now nailing one set of wheels on the back end of the frame. He is drilling a hole through the extended 2'x4' in front of the frame and drilling a second hole in the center of the beam with wheels so that he could assemble it with the bolts and washers to the front of the beam extended from the frame. This will allow the front wheels to move side to side in order to direct the go-cart to go left or right. Roger said that "Jeffry is a small kid but a little on the chunky side, that's why we call him, "Fatso".

It may be tight, but he will have to lie flat on his belly on the frame facing the front wheels and put one hand on the right end of the wheel beam and the other hand on the left side of the wheel beam. Now Jeffry can make the go-cart go left or right just by pushing the wheel beam with one hand or the other. For power to move the go-cart, you can push Jeffry or find a street or road on a hill that can make Fatso move as fast as gravity can pull him downhill."

Roger steps back looking at his creation, a slight smile of accomplishment on his face.

"Hum, not bad. All we need to do is grease the wheels and Jeffry is good to go. It's getting late and my sister's wagon will have to wait for another day."

I ask Roger if it is OK for my gang and I to compete in the Ice Cream Parlor race.

"The race is open to any kid who shows up with a three-wheeler bike, street scooter, go-cart, wagon or anything small kids can ride or push down hill."

"Me and my guys made a couple of street scooters. I'll call Mike

Tomato and ask him to go with me so we can ride our scooters in the kid's race, Where, is it?"

"Its way up on Court Street and a great place on top of a hill for a downhill race."

No sooner Roger tells me about the location of the Kids race, Jeffry shows up with his dad Larry BB. Jeffry is all dressed like a fighter pilot, with goofy looking goggles, airman hat, and leather gloves. Jeffry's dad is talking to Roger for a while and is picking up the go-cart and is walking with Jeffry towards Court Street. Meanwhile, I'll run like hell to find Mike Tomato. I can see Mike on Hicks Street; we will get our street scooters and start walking toward Court Street.

It takes about fifteen minutes to get there and it is crazy to see about sixty kids with parents and friends getting ready to plow down Court Street to the finish line on Fourth Place and Court. We are late in getting in line so our location in line sucks. We are four rows behind the start position. The horn blows and suddenly all the kids take off downhill towards the finish line. Even though we never come close to winning it doesn't matter. It is such a thrill to ride our street scooters with all these crazy kids who have no idea what the Hell they are doing.

We do manage to get a free ice cream cone from the sponsors of the race, while walking home holding our street scooters in one hand and licking our ice cream treat with the other hand, it is a good day!

Chapter 41
Bicycle Motor Sounds-Haunted House Tag

I had a lot of fun yesterday watching Roger make a go-cart for Jeffry with old carriage wheels he found. To top it off, Mike Tomato and me had a chance to test our street scooters at The Court Street All Wheels Downhill Race. The free ice cream cone was good too! I dragged my spruced-up black bike from the cellar this morning and walked it over to the schoolyard. Even though I'm upset that Roger sold me a piece of a shit bike, he

Attach Playing Card Or Balloon For Motorbike Sound

did make it up to me by sprucing it up like new. I hate to admit it, but I always respect Roger and yes, I do like him like a big brother. I get to the schoolyard and start to ride my bike around and I hear sounds that a motorbike might make.

I thinking, why would anyone have the balls to ride a motorbike in the schoolyard with all these little kids playing here? I see Joanie riding what looks like a new bike towards me. I notice that the motorcycle sounds are coming from her direction!

Sure enough, the sounds are coming from her bike.

"Hey, Joanie, What's with your bike? It's making all these motor-bike sounds and that it isn't a motorbike!"

"Pull over and I'll show you!"

So we pull over by a chain link fence. She gets off her new bike.

"Take a look at my back wheel. You'll see that my Dad attached a playing card and balloon with clothespins to make motorbike sounds when I ride my bike forward. The sound comes from the bike's wheel spokes when they hit against the playing card and balloon. Isn't that a cool idea?"

Wow! It's so simple and it sounds great! You would think that Roger would come up with an idea like this. I have to tell him about it. Joanie and I get back up on our bikes and I follow her and her motorcycle-sounding bike around the schoolyard. All the kids are looking at us going around and around. Finally, the balloon on Joanie's bike pops and the playing card comes loose and falls to the ground. Waving at me she is motioning that she is heading home. So I'll wave back to her and head back toward home too. I'll put my bike back in the cellar and then I'll go to Hicks Street to look for my friends.

I'm on Luquer and Hicks Street and I have found the whole gang standing in a circle talking. I'll push my way into the circle to find out what they are up to. Sure enough, they are talking about playing "Haunted House Hide and Go-Seek." They are trying to decide which condemned house in the construction site for the Brooklyn Battery Tunnel, would make a good target for this game. It looks like we have eight players. One of the players will be it! After we draw lots Reno the Greek comes up short. The game starts and Reno turns against the wall and counts to fifty, while the other players run into the selected dilapidated building to hide. Meanwhile, you would think that the security guards could keep the kids out of these dangerous broken down buildings before a kid falls through a hole in the floor, killing himself.

But no, most of the time the guards are sitting around drinking beer. If they happen to see you sneaking into a condemned building, they will yell at you but they will never chase you into the building. They won't take the risk of hurting themselves by chasing a stupid kid into one of these buildings. For the little money they are paid to do this work, in their minds, it just isn't worth the trouble.

All the kids know that there is little or no risk of getting caught by these guards. Too bad, over the past year I know of ten kids who went to the hospital with cuts and broken bones, but none of this is going to stop us from playing "Haunted House Hide and Go-Seek." Hide and Seek, is not as dangerous as "Haunted House Tag" in this game there are eight or ten kids being chased through the haunted house by the tag leader. If you're caught he will hit you with an old sock full of cornstarch. At least in Hide and Seek you find a good hiding place and wait. When you play tag you run up and down the building that is covered with broken glass, old pipes, plaster, old sinks, and toilets, mixed in with the smell of poop and pee. I hate to play "Haunted House Tag".

We walk down Hamilton Avenue to find the haunted house we are looking for. The outside of the house isn't so bad except for the broken windows and fire damage, but the inside of the house is creepy. The smell of the place can make a kid throw up. Over the months when this house was condemned a lot of kids, including my cousin Johnny and me, ripped out all the Lead and Copper we could find.

Just for the Hell of it, some kids think it pretty funny to pee all over the place. I stop thinking of all this stuff when Reno is starting the game by counting, "One, two, three, four", and so on. We are all running like Hell to find a hiding place that isn't loaded with the smell of pee. I get lucky and find a broken closet that the pee brigade did not put their mark on. Out of seven kids that are hiding Reno only finds five before his time is up. So we all will come out from hiding and Reno will have to start counting all over again. This is going on for two hours now, so, we'll finally give up the ghost and call it quits. I am fairly clean, but some kids aren't as lucky. They smell so bad we aren't about to let them come near us. Three of the guys have to go home to face the music and get beat up with the wooden spoon for being so stupid.

Reno the Greek, Jimmy Pizza, Pecker and me have enough money in our pockets to pay for some treats and a movie. Jimmy says that a new Ali Baba movie is playing at the Ledo Theater on Columbia Street. It is taking us fifteen minutes to get there for the 3 o'clock show. I love the Ali Baba movies, I like it when Ali Baba and the Forty Thieves get to their hideout and he yells out: "Open Sesame!" The ground shakes and then the big rock doors of the mountainside open to a large cave and Ali Baba and the Forty Thieves rush into the cave on their horses, and the rock doors then close behind them. They go deep into the cave, then light torches on the wall and you can see all the treasure laying on the ground: gold coins, diamond jewelry, rubies, pearls, gold robes, piled up and overflowing in open gold and silver chests. What a beautiful sight it is to look at all the Ali Baba treasures.

The Forty Thieves then unload the loot that they took during the latest battle with the King's tax collector, putting their bounty on to the pile of loot already there and ride off again to fight against the evil kings who tax their people into poverty. I like to watch Ali Baba battle against the King's army. The Forty Thieves mainly fight with bows, arrows, and swords. The poor people rise up to fight with them using rocks, knives, and pitchforks.

After they win the battle, Ali Baba turns to help the poor people giving them the gold and jewels that he and the Forty Thieves took from the evil king. This way they can start a new life with their families. It feels so good to see Ale Baba kick ass. After we leave the movies we start playing that we are in the battles with Ali Baba and the Forty Thieves against the evil King.

Going home we make wooden swords and are running through the streets, yelling and screaming. People are watching us like we're crazy. I get home and yell "Open Sesame!" to the front door of our apartment building. The doors open to my command and I step into the hallway, there is no treasure to be found. Oh, well, we live to fight another day.

Chapter 42
Diane's Carriage Wagon-Chess Game

As you stroll through the parks of Brooklyn and many other cities on a sunny day, there you will find people of all ages engaging in the ancient and still respected game called Chess. A game of strategy and careful planning, you will find both the old and the young engaged in this pastime. Skill is acquired by experience, and that mirrors real life.

In the 1950's, it came to Brooklyn and became like baseball a pastime for the young as well as the old. Both young and old could play the game on an equal footing, as well as the big, small, weak or strong.

No one can prove how the game of chess originated or where it came from, some think it India. No matter its origin, it found its way to the Middle East in Persia, and "Shah mat," which is Persian for "the king is finished" was the essence of the game. In Europe where the English took the game of chess and restricted many moves while establishing other of its rules. However, in the fifteenth century, it was the Italian influence that made the game interesting when the Italians changed the rules somewhat by enabling the pawn the option to advance two spaces on the first move of each pawn and allowing the queen piece to become the most powerful on the chessboard.

This morning I'm up and discover I don't have anything to do! The weather is not as good as yesterday, clouds cover the streets like a mantle and with it is a cool light rain. I'm thinking I can get a bunch of my friends together and play handball today. But if it keeps raining I don't think the guys will want play handball. Anyway, I'll go downstairs to see if anyone is around. Leaving the building I'm hearing a banging noise coming from the backyard. While I walk to the back of the building I see Roger nailing together a bunch of wood and it looks to me that he is

You Need Old Carriage Wheels to Make Wagons

finally making the wagon he promised his little sister Diane. He doesn't notice me.

"Hey Roger, are you putting together the wagon for your sister Diane?"

"Yeah, I want to finish this project once and for all."

I'm impressed:

"Wow! It looks like you have the platform ready to assemble the old carriage wheels you found!"

He is laughing at me.

"Well, it turned out to be a Hell of lot more work than I bargained for. No matter, I won't disappoint my little sister."

He is looking down and is banging away. Even though he is busy putting this wagon together I'll keep talking to him. As I'm chatting away about riding my bike in the schoolyard with Joanie yesterday, I'm telling him all about the motorcycle sound coming from her new bike and how her father attached a playing card and balloon to her back wheel to make the motor sounds. I'm also telling him about the "Haunted House, Hide and Go-Seek" game we played in a disgusting, smelly, condemned house at the Brooklyn Battery Tunnel construction site. I mention that we went to see the new Ali Baba movie.

I'm going on and he looks up again, his hair wet from the rain, water dripping down his face and points the hammer at me, and yells:

"WILL YOU SHUT UP ALREADY? I can't concentrate on making this wagon and listen to you babbling all your crap. I just don't give a shit. You HEAR ME!"

"OK, ok, ok, don't get your balls all twisted. I'll be quiet while you finish your stupid wagon."

I'm just sitting near him with my arms folded and won't say another word. Roger is finishing putting the carriage wheels on the platform, and now he is putting on a little seat on the back of the platform that will hold his sister's butt in place.

He is tying a rope on each side of the front wheels so his sister can steer the wagon left or right. With all his bitching and moaning the damn wagon looks pretty good! For a summer day, with the clouds and rain, it is actually getting cold. Roger's sister Diane and two of her friends come running from around the corner straight at us. They are dressed in coats. Wow, I don't think it is that cold!

"Roger, Roger did you finish my new wagon?"

Roger smiles and with a happy voice he says:

"Come on Diane it's time to give your wagon a test run. Sit Here, your little friends have to push you, okay? Grab the rope and pull it from side to side when you want to turn your wagon."

Diane is getting on the wagon in a flash, as the two little girls with her are getting behind the wagon and start pushing it.

Wow, that wagon can really move, racing up and down the sidewalk. With one quick pull on the rope, Diane turns the wagon into the street and Roger just goes nuts. He is running like a bat out of hell, while he is screaming and yelling at her to "STOP!" He chases after her as fast as he can, finally catching up to her and makes her get back onto the sidewalk. He walks back to where I am standing and says:

"Come on, let's get out of here. Follow me upstairs I have to get out of these wet clothes. I want to show you what I learned about playing the Chess game my uncle gave me. It's a lot more complicated than playing checkers."

So, I follow Roger into our building and stop at my apartment to get out of my wet clothes too. I put on some dry clothes and run up to Roger's apartment.

He is still getting dressed so I go back to his room and will push him along.

"What's your hurry? You must be really interested in learning how to play Chess."

"I'm not that interested in the game but I would like to know more about the pieces that your uncle Sammie gave you. I've never seen anything like them before."

We are sitting at Roger's little table in his room and he puts the Chessboard and Chess pieces on it. He looks at me and states:

"It's not like playing checkers. The board may look the same but the pieces can move in all kinds of different directions based on what they are."

Roger is holding up each piece and instructing me.

"The Pawn is this little guy who is basically a foot soldier. The soldier may only move one or two squares at a time forward on his first move. After that, the soldier can capture any enemy piece on a diagonal square.

This guy is called the Bishop. He has a pointy hat and he can move any number of squares diagonally anywhere on the board to block or capture the enemy.

This is the Knight. You can tell it's a Knight because it looks like a horse. This piece moves into 'L' shapes, one square and two over or two squares and one over like this. The Knight can also jump over the other pieces on the board to capture the enemy or to a blank square.

The Rook, which looks like a Castle can move any number of squares, up or down or side to side on the board but it can't move on a diagonal like the Bishop.

The Queen can move like the Bishop and Rook piece anywhere on the board.

The King can only move one square at a time anywhere on the board. Now that you know how these pieces can move and fight each other what do you, think?"

"Wow, I'm so confused."

"It's really a simple game once you know how to make the

pieces move around the board. You see the object of the game is to get to the King. If any of your pieces can trap the King and he cannot move out of your trap it's called a Checkmate and you win the game. Each player has to do two things. Number one is to attack trying to trap the enemies King. Number two is to work up a defensive plan to keep the enemy from trapping your King. Do you see how simple it is?"

"Roger you're out of your 'friggin' mind if you think I can play this game like I can play checkers. It will take me forever and a day just to learn the moves. I will never be able to protect my king against an enemy attack."

"My uncle Sammie gave me this game and told me that if I really learn how to play it and think ahead of every move I make, playing Chess or in life, I will do well no matter what I decide to do. Because if you study and think ahead of time on how every move you make will affect the outcome you will make fewer mistakes. Then you have a better chance to protect your King and that's how you can win the game of life."

I wish I knew what the hell he is talking about. I'll leave Roger more confused than ever. I don't know if I'll ever learn how to play this stupid Chess game.

Chapter 43

The Feast Of The Blessed Mother-Handball

It's Friday Morning and I get up finding my Dad at the breakfast table. I still can't get used to the idea of having breakfast with Dad. He can't find any work; most of the time he tries not to show it, but I know this is making him very unhappy. I notice that this morning he seems to feel a little bit better. As I'm about to leave our apartment to find my friends, Dad stops me and reminds me, that we have to get dressed this afternoon. We will then go to Saint Stephen's Church to assemble together with other Italian Americans from my father's village of Mola De Bari.

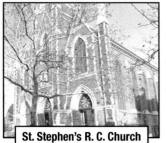
St. Stephen's R. C. Church

There are many different villages in Italy where people left for a new life in America. My Dad's village is only one among many who celebrate their village traditions with a street festival and a patron saint in their Brooklyn neighborhood. My Dad, his cousins, and friends are members of the Molesi Social Club; they will all assemble to form a parade outside the Church. The Priest and many other religious people from his congregation, who are originally from the Italian Village of Mola De Bari, will gather, pick up the statue of the Blessed Mother, and carry her through the streets of our neighborhood.

This is a big day for my family and friends. The parade also includes prayers, music, and fireworks, as we will march through the streets with a police escort. When the parade gets back to the Church, this will signal the beginning of a three-day festival, with more Italian music, food, games and carnival rides. I tell my Dad that I will be back in time to meet him this afternoon to walk with him to Saint Stephen's Church.

I am running down the steps of our building and I find Pecker and Jimmy Pizza waiting for me on my doorstep.

"Hey, Pecker, what are you guys doing here so early this morning?"

"Well, we haven't seen you for a couple of days and we thought the only way we could hook up with you was to sit and wait for you on your doorstep."

Wow! I didn't realize they missed me so much!

"Sorry guys, I've been doing all kinds of stuff the last couple of days.

165

A Fast Game of Street Handball Game.

I rode my new bike, I helped Roger make a wagon for his little sister, I am learning how to play a stupid game called chess and I helped my mother with stuff around the house. The time really flew by so fast, but I'm happy that you came over to find me this morning Jimmy."

"Wa, wa, wa, MISTER big shot. You're SOOO busy that you forget all about your friends!"

"No, no, I didn't forget about you guys. I was thinking about you guys the past couple of days. I wanted to play handball with you. But you're right, I was running around all over the place and I didn't think that we could play handball in the rain. So here I am, ready for some action."

They are all getting up from sitting on the steps of my building and we are walking over to find Nunzio and Mike Tomato. They are happy to join us for a game of handball. We get to the schoolyard and find Reno the Greek and his brother Henry slapping a ball against a brick wall. It is like they are reading our minds. We now have more than enough guys to play this game. Handball is a great game; all you need is a good pair of sneakers, some chalk, and a ball. Looks like we will have to play doubles and some of us will have to sit out of the game and challenge the winners when the first game is over.

We're lucky that the wall at the schoolyard is a nice flat wall to play against. But sometimes we have to settle to play against a wall that has cracks and is all uneven; when you hit the ball against the uneven wall it makes the ball bounce like a Mexican jumping bean moving all over the place.

Taking a piece of chalk we are drawing a short line about four feet from the wall and a long line about twenty feet from the wall. Once you set the boundaries, short, long and side-to-side, you choose sides and the server starts the game by slapping the ball within the boundaries to the other players who have to hit the ball back at the wall on a fly. After the ball is in play there is no restriction on the short line. If any player hits the ball out of bounds, over the long line or the side-to-side boundaries they lose a point and the right to hit the ball first as the server.

Handball is a fast game, points are made when anyone makes an

166

error by not hitting the wall on a fly, or missing a shot completely, or hitting a ball out of bounds and so on. The winner is the team that reaches fifteen points first. If both teams manage to reach a fourteen-point tie, the winning team has to reach sixteen points first. If the teams tied again at fifteen the winning score changes to seventeen and so on. We play handball for three hours, and Nunzio and I win most of the games. Good thing Superman is on my side.

It is getting late so I better rush home to meet my father. As I get to our apartment and my father is already dressed and waiting for me. I dress in no time and we start our walk to Saint Stephen's Church. We get there and it seems like there are a couple of hundred men and boys, all dressed up and ready to march. I realize this festival tradition is mostly a man thing. My father has a ribbon with the image of the Madonna pinned on his suit and he calls me over to pin the same ribbon on me. A group of eight men are going into the Church and picking up the statue of the Madonna for the march through the neighborhood. The Band is playing music to march to and we are all walking in the street behind the statue of the Madonna. There are lots of people on the sidewalks watching the procession and praying to the Madonna. After a short walk, the parade is stopping in front of a building that has a special cross in front of it. The men turn the statue to face the building. The music stops and then you hear loud sounds of fireworks going off right in front of the building.

My Dad tells me that the people who live in that building make a large donation to the Church for this special honor and blessing from the Madonna. The fireworks are ending, now the band starts playing and we are continuing our march with a police escort to the next house with a special cross displayed in front of it. We are stopping again and more fireworks are going off. This honor and blessing must be given twenty times during our march through the neighborhood. Each time the parade stops to turn the statue of the Blessed Mother, many people standing on the sidewalks come up with the statue and pin dollar donations onto the clothing of the Blessed Mother statue. Before you know it the statue looks like it has clothes made of money. The parade continues for miles, we march for six hours or more. We are now full circle back to Saint Stephen's Church for a special blessing and more fireworks. Wow, I feel like such a big deal marching with my father and our Italian friends!

**Mola di Bari Italy St. Maria Addolorata
Procession In Red Hook Brooklyn**

Chapter 44

Italian Street Festival-Playing Poker

You can fly to Boston on Monday, San Francisco on Tuesday, and back to Brooklyn on Thursday and attend a feast day in the Italian neighborhoods of those cities, and you will swear you are in the same place each day. The color and passionate devotion to a patron saint and the joy of being Italian or with Italians will always feel special yet seem the same!

The peppers and sausage sandwiches, the zeppole and the various traditions of the Old World foods and music, replanted from city to city from Italy to America will instill a sense of joy and enchantment, a singing voice of the local neighborhoods of Italian Americans, their devotion to the church and one-another always will be present.

After six hours walking in the parade with the Blessed Mother, St. Stephen's Church is a welcomed site. I am tired and hot from marching all dressed up in a suit and tie. I can't wait to get home and get out of these clothes.

The Molesi men carry the statue of the Blessed Mother, who is covered in a ton of paper money, back into the Church. I am standing on the steps of the Church where I can see a platform built for the bandstand. Once it gets dark the band will climb on the platform and the festivities will begin. The street is covered with multicolor lights, and many of the vendors are putting the finishing touches on the food carts and food trucks that will be serving all kinds of Italian delights to eat. Other vendors will be selling gifts and trinkets with the image of the Blessed Mother. There are games to play that test your skills or good fortune. If you're lucky, you can win a stuffed animal or live goldfish to take home.

A bunch of kiddy rides like a mini carnival for the little guys and girls is set up. Everything is so colorful and the smell of the different foods cooking is making me hungry. I am walking home with Dad, and we are shedding our suits to more comfortable summer clothes. Mom and my sister are walking back to St. Stephen's Church with us where the street festival is starting up, but it is getting dark. Colorful lights are beaming brightly and you can appreciate the colors, the music, the food cooking and the festive mood of the crowd. Everyone seems so happy to be here, and even though Dad is out of work and doesn't have much money he still manages to scrape together four dollars to give me to spend at the feast. I feel a little guilty taking the money, but I know that it makes my Mom and Dad happy to have my sister and I enjoy this great celebration. This feast is part of their heritage that they brought with them from the old country. My sister tells me that when people move to America from countries all over the World they continue to celebrate their customs and traditions. For example, the Irish celebrate Saint Patrick's Day, the Chinese celebrate their New Year, the Jewish people celebrate Hanukkah, the Germans celebrate Octoberfest, the Italians celebrate Columbus Day and so on. Just like all the people who immigrated to America before them, my parents do not want to forget the family traditions that they enjoyed as children in their little hometown of Mola De Bari. When we get to the steps of the Church we are separating, Mom and Dad will go to meet their cousins and friends and listen to Italian music while eating traditional Italian foods.

My sister is going with her friends to seek the company of good-looking Italian boys to talk to. As for me, I'll find a bunch of my friends, Pecker, Mikey, Nunzio, Reno, and others. We are playing every game of chance we can find, and stuff our faces with sausage and pepper sandwiches, funnel cakes, nuts, pop-corn, zeppoles and all the pastry delights we can find. I think I'm going to be sick from eating all this crap. I keep telling myself that this festival will go on for three days and I don't want to waste my energy and money on the first night of the festival. We call it quits around 11 P.M., and my family and I are walking home. We can still hear the Italian music playing and the crowd cheering the band on from blocks away.

We all got up late this morning. Yesterday was too much for me. The handball games, the parade and the night at the festival, I don't know how I can do it all over again tonight? I meet up with my friends and it's about one p.m. and we are sitting around in front of 'Chickies' grocery store on Hicks Street talking about all the fun we had last night, but none of us have much energy left. Jimmy Pizza thinks it would be a good idea to play a game where we don't have to jump or run like crazy. Pecker suggests:

"My Dad has a deck of cards we can play with. We can play

poker for pennies, baseball picture cards or bottle caps. I'll run home to get them."

Go back thousands of years and you will find one thing in common with today: the game of Poker.

Poker is a game that has crossed several continents and cultures where it finally settled in Brooklyn. The Chinese had an emperor that in the 19th Century played a game like it, maybe its roots. Some claim it is a Persian game: 'As Nas' that dates to the 16th Century.

Once it arrived in Europe in the 17th Century France, it got the name of 'Poque' or the German equivalent, 'Pochen'. The Spanish had their own name for the game: 'Primero'. But it was thanks to the Louisiana Purchase and the French settlers who populated Louisiana that Poque became 'Poker' when Americans began to get interested in it.

Everyone agrees that this is a good idea so we all are going home to get whatever we can to put into the pot for the card

Visitation Church

game. It takes us about fifteen minutes to get back to Hicks Street with our booty. We have decided to play our card game in front of one of the houses that has a high stoop. Most of the time a high stoop has a wide landing at the top and it's great to sit on for playing a card game. The girls on the block also look for a high stoop when they play Jacks. The best house is the one next to the stable on Luquer Street. We all pick our spots and sit there waiting for Pecker to bring the playing cards. Pecker gets here with the playing cards and we are all agreeing to play "Five-card Draw Poker".

Five of us are sitting on the stoop while Pecker is shuffling the cards. Jimmy Pizza now cuts the deck. We are all dropping one penny into the pot. Pecker is dealing out five cards to each player. Draw Poker is an interesting game when you get your five cards, you check your hand to see if you have a pair of Jacks or better to open or be part of the game. If you don't know anything about the game of Poker, you need to know the basics of the game.

First, you have to know that anyone playing in the first-hand needs a pair of Jacks or better to continue the game. If you have a pair of Aces, you can open the game by saying: "I open or I'm in". At this point, you have to put an additional penny in the pot. Everyone playing has to follow your lead or drop out of the hand. If everyone does the same then you can hold on to your pair of aces and give the other three cards in your hand back to the dealer. Then the dealer will give you three new cards. Everyone playing can decide what they want to keep or which cards they want to give back to the dealer. You're allowed to give up on four cards to the dealer for replacement cards. Then you check your new cards and decide if your hand is worth gambling for a win. If you get another ace as a replacement card, you then have three aces, which is a strong possibility of a winning hand! All the other players will do the same. Some players will drop out because they don't think they can win the pot with their hand. If you think you can win you put more pennies in the pot and say: "See you". Then everyone who is still playing must show their cards to the other players to stay in the poker game.

If no one has a hand that beats three aces, you win the pot, but it looks like Jimmy Pizza has four two's and that hand beats three aces. Jimmy Pizza collects all the pennies in the pot. Even though two's alone have the lowest value in the deck of cards, but since Jimmy has four two's in his hand his cards are of greater value than three Aces. When you play "Draw Poker" it's important to know the value of the cards in your hand. There are many combinations that can be a possible winner. Such as pairs, two pairs, three of a kind, four of a kind, low straight, high straight, straight flush, royal straight flush, flush, full house, etc. It will take time for you to learn all the combinations of possible winning hands and the best way to learn is to play "Draw Poker". Today Jimmy Pizza turns out to be the big winner in our card game.

Chapter 45

Nunzio-Superman's Killer Darts

Playing "Draw Poker" with the guys the other day was fun. Too bad I lost all my pennies and eight baseball picture cards to Jimmy Pizza. I don't have any money left and I dip into my bicycle reserve fund that I am saving to dress up my new bike. I feel that going to the last day of the Italian festival is a once in a lifetime thing. I'll take out six dollars from my stash and stop myself from taking the eight dollar balance, that, I put back under my mattress hiding place in my mother's bedroom.

I'm thinking that I will be going back to school soon and I want to hang out with my friends as much as possible before I'm stuck with having to do all kinds of school work. I found myself some fresh tomatoes that I am slicing and putting on Italian bread with olive oil, salt, and pepper for lunch. Even though I am trying to save some money for the last night of the feast, I can't help myself. I'll run downstairs to Defonte's sandwich shop and buy an ice-cold bottle of Pepsi to wash it down. Man is it good!

I'll go over to Nunzio-Superman's house to see if he has any plans for the afternoon.

As I'm knocking loudly on his door, Nunzio opens it with a big grin on his face.

"Hey, Nunzio, why do you have a big smile on your face? You look like you swallowed a canary or something."

Putting his finger up to his lips he pleads:

"Shush, my mother is not home right now. If my Mom finds out what I plan to do she will kill me."

With his hand, he waves at me to come into his apartment, so I'm following him in. Nunzio walking into his mother's bedroom kneeling down on the floor and sticks his hand way-under his mother's bed. He takes his hand back out and he is holding an old T-shirt that is wrapped around something. He is still sitting on the floor near the bed and unwraps the T-shirt showing me what he is hiding. I see what he has in the T-shirt, and jump back:

"Holy Shit! You have darts. HOW THE HELL DID YOU GET THEM!!!?"

I know that our parents would never allow us to play with darts. Every parent in the neighborhood keeps warning us about kids who were badly hurt when they were playing with the stupid darts.

Nunzio's grin is still on his face as he is whispering to me.

"My cousin Vincent and his family came to visit all the way from Long Island yesterday because of the Italian Festival. Vinnie, who is almost thirteen years old, always wanted my collection of Superman comic books. So, when he was here he pulled out these six darts from his little bag and asked me if I wanted to make a trade for the darts? I never gave it a second thought. I got my Superman comic book collection, gave it to Vinnie, and I said: Hell YEAH! I said to Vinnie:

'You better take these comics before I change my mind.'

So we made a trade, my comics for his darts."

Meanwhile, as Nunzio is telling me his story, I can't help thinking about a movie my sister took me to see last Christmas. The movie was about Laurel and Hardy being toymakers for Santa. The movie is called: "Babes in Toyland", but some people call it 'The March of the Wooden Soldiers'. It was a really fun movie to watch. I enjoyed the part when they were fighting the villain, Barnaby, and the Bogeymen as they attacked Toyland.

Stannie Dum and Ollie Dee use a gross of darts to fight them off. There are darts flying everywhere. Ollie sets up the darts and Stannie Dum is using a stick to hit the darts at the evil villain Barnaby and his gang of Bogeymen. After Stannie and Ollie realize that they can't win the war with darts alone, they decide to push the button on the backs of each wooden soldier so they can wake up and fight the Bogeymen. The Soldiers do their job, saving Bo-Peep and drive Barnaby and the Bogeymen out of Toyland. Stannie Dum tells Ollie to shoot the cannon loaded with darts at the Bogeymen as they were running away from Toyland. But something goes wrong and the cannon flips over and shoots all the darts at Ollie's rear end. The movie ends with Stannie pulling each dart, one at a time, from Ollie's butt. I know that this movie is all 'make believe' and that no one gets hurt, but it makes me think that a kid seeing this movie could feel that it may be okay to throw darts at another kid. Now I know why our parents don't want kids to play with darts. Oh, what the Hell, my parents will never find out that I'm playing with darts. I can't wait to throw these darts at something.

Nunzio finishes his story and is giving me one to hold, and it is beautiful! The dart looks so big and the wood is so smooth to the touch. There is a very sharp piece of metal that looks like a thin nail, sticking out of the nose. Touching it with my finger I feel it pinch me. I see now why the pointy nail could cause some real damage if it hit somebody. I like to run my fingers through the feathers at the tail of the dart because they're so soft! But Nunzio is starting to yell at me:

"Hey, it's not a kitten! STOP PETTING THE DAMNED THING and let's go find a place where we can throw these suckers!" He takes the dart I am holding from me and wraps it with the other darts in his old T-shirt.

Leaving his apartment and walking around the corner towards the Brooklyn Battery Tunnel construction site, our best bet is to find one of those dilapidated houses that will be torn down soon. We are lucky that the watchmen are having a two-hour lunch break, instead of the one-hour lunch they are allowed. Entering the condemned house, it smells bad as we notice a couple of rats running for cover. So, we'll make a lot of noise to scare off any more rats that are hanging around. Walking into what was an old kitchen is a broken wooden door lying on the floor. I kick off the trash and broken glass and lift up the door from the floor to put it against a wall near a sink.

"This wooden door can be our target, Nunzio!"

Nunzio takes three of his darts and gives them to me to hold. We stand back about ten feet, Nunzio taking aim, throws a dart at the door. WOW! What a beautiful sound it makes when it hits and sticks deep into the door! We take turns throwing the darts into the door.

I go get my darts out of the door, and they were buried so deep that it takes me a few seconds to wiggle the darts free. Man, these things are so sharp I bet you can kill a rat with them. After hitting the wooden door target with the darts for a half hour, we look around the shit house for new targets to throw at. We start throwing the darts at anything and everything we think the dart will stick into. We have a great time playing this stupid game for more than two hours.

We have enough, Nunzio now gathers the darts and wraps them into his old T-shirt. He'll run home to hide them under his mother's bed before she gets home from shopping. Good thing there are only the two of us throwing darts in the dilapidated smelly rat house. I think that if there were three or four of our gang throwing these darts in every direction there would be a good chance one of us would get hit with one of these 'friggen' darts. Then if we got hit with a dart we would run home crying and bleeding. Our parents would rush us to the hospital to get stitched up. When we get back home they would kick the shit out of us and for added punishment, make us wash the stairs and hallways in our building for God knows how long.

I'm not following Nunzio home. I'll go looking for some of my friends so that we can hook up to go to the last night of the Italian Festival. I find the guys but can't tell any of them about the darts, because if I do tell them, Nunzio-Superman, will break my neck. After all, we agreed that the dart throwing we did has to be kept a secret.

Chapter 46

Pick Up Stix-Italian Festival's Last Night

I keep thinking about the dart game and that we can't tell anyone about our secret. I'm not good at keeping secrets but I don't want Nunzio to get pissed off if I spill the beans.

As I am walking to find my friends so we can go to the last night of the feast together I see Joanie sitting on her stoop with her dog, Joy.

"Hey, Pepino, where are you going? Do you plan to go to the feast tonight?"

"Yeah, I'm looking for Jimmy Pizza, Reno the Greek and Pecker to go with me."

"It's still kind of early, I like to get there when it's dark and all the lights are on. If you're not in a hurry how about playing a game of 'pick up stixs' with me?"

She's right about the time. It's only four o'clock and the feast doesn't get rolling until eight o'clock.

"Okay, I heard of the game but I never played it before."

"Pepino, it's not that hard to play. I play this game with my four-year-old cousin and she doesn't have a problem getting the gist of it."

"If your four-year-old cousin can beat you I think I can beat you, too."

"Wait a minute; I didn't say that she beat me. But I'll have no problems kicking your ass in this game."

"Wow, that sounds like a challenge to me."

As Joanie and I are going back and forth about who can beat who, Joy the dog keeps moving his head from looking at Joanie and then back to looking at me and then Joanie again, as we argue about who can beat who. It's as if the dog is watching us play a ping-pong game. I'll sit down next to her on the stoop, ready to play her stupid game and show her who is boss.

We are sitting kind of close as she takes out a cylinder about ten inches long with a label saying 'Pick Up Stixs.' We are so close to each other that I can't help but notice that she smells so good. She takes out a bunch of colored sticks that look like eight-inch long thick toothpicks in different colors. She separates ten sticks each of two different colors.

"The blue sticks are yours and the yellow ones are mine."

She's giving me a red stick and telling me that I have to use the red stick to pick out my blue sticks without touching the yellow sticks. I'm thinking that this game is more complicated than I thought but if a four-year-old can do it so can I.

Joanie takes the blue and yellow sticks and mixes them together in one bunch. She holds the bunch in her hand upright and drops them on the stoop. They fall into a crazy pattern all blue and yellow mixed together laying on the stoop.

"Okay, now you have to take your red stick and try to separate your blue sticks from my yellow sticks without touching or moving my yellow sticks. If you touch my yellow stick with your red stick you lose your turn and then I get a chance to try to separate my yellow sticks from your blue sticks without moving them. The player who can get all their sticks out of the pile first wins the game".

After three hours, Joanie is ahead five games to my one game. I guess I showed her who's the boss. I'm thinking that her four-year-old cousin could probably kick my ass too. After being embarrassed by a girl, I say goodbye to Joanie and go look for my friends.

I catch up with the guys and we all are walking towards Saint Stephen's Church and the Italian street festival. Crossing over the highway we can hear the Italian music and the crowd of people singing along with the band. We now hear that the feast is in full swing so we all are running as fast as we can. We don't want to miss any of the action. As we are getting closer I smell the sausage and peppers cooking mixed in with the smell of funnel cakes, making me hungry. We are about a half a block away and I see that there are so many people crushed together it looks like a wall. It is so exciting: the music, and the food, the colorful lights, the crowd singing and cheering the band for more! The vendors are doing their best to keep up with people who want to play the games and buy balloons for their little children who are screaming their heads off.

The carnival rides are going strong too, with the Merry Go Round, the Ferris Wheel, the Whip and more. There are so many teenagers and kids my age pushing and shoving for a place on the line to get on the rides. We push our way through the crowd trying to get to the guy cooking the sausage and peppers. Pecker gets there first and I'm yelling for him to order me a sandwich and I shove two dollars between two guys who were standing behind him, he takes the money and is yelling back:

"Okay I got it."

Pecker squeezes back with two sandwiches in his hand and pushed one into my face.

"Here, are you happy NOW?"

I grab the sandwich.

"Shit yeah, I'm so hungry that I thought I was going to pass out."

We are standing here crushed by the crowd eating our sandwiches as fast as we can. I'll yell back at him again:

"Let's find a food stand where we can buy a drink and keep a look-out for Jimmy Pizza and Mike Tomato. I think I saw them back there waiting to get on the Ferris Wheel."

We are pushing our way through the crowd again and I can feel a soft sweater almost like a pillow in my face. It is a little hard to breathe when I looked up and realize that my face is buried right in the middle of Maria (aka, Headlights) Lopez's chest. I think I am going to die right here and now, with this huge crowd around me. She smells so good! All of a sudden I am feeling a strange sensation in my body as I rub up against her. It is a weird feeling but I liked it. My face is still nuzzled in her chest as I looked up and she looks down at me and says:

"Hello, Pepino, are you having fun?"

If the crowd wasn't pushing me I could pass out and fall on the ground! Pecker, who is a witness to my good luck, is laughing so hard, he is crying. I'm doing my best to back away from her, but the pressure of the crowd is

Mini Merry Go Round At The Italian Festival

180

keeping me there with my face stuck between her boobs. I just can't move while mumbling:

"Hi... hi, Maria, sorry, I just can't move. Is your brother Ricardo here tonight too?"

She looks at me with her beautiful green eyes as she brushes her jet-black hair away from her face and giggles:

"Ah-huh, I think that he's right in back of me. If you want I can try to turn around so you can see him."

Oh God, if she turns, her boobs will rub up against my face! But what the HELL!

"Yes PLEASE!!!"

She does as I ask and it is WONDERFUL! Now I can see six-finger Lopez and I say:

"What's up Lopez?"

"What do you think, shit head? I'm pushing my way through the feast just like you are."

At this point the crowd releases me and I can see Maria walking away in her pink high-heel shoes, looking like a movie star. She has a body that girls would die for. She is wearing a tight light pink short sleeved sweater, with tight white shorts, and every guy and man at the feast turns to look at her.

Pecker stops laughing and turns to me saying:

"You're the luckiest 'friggin' guy I know. Not only are you having a great time at the feast, you then find a way to bury your face in Maria Lopez chest and rub your cheek against her boobs! What was that all about?"

I'm thinking to myself, I don't know but I enjoyed every minute of it. I won't answer Pecker. I'm still pumped up because of my face-to-chest meeting with Maria Headlights Lopez! We walk over to the vendor cooking Zeppoles and I buy nine deep-fried dough balls and I eat all of them in ten seconds. I wash them down with an ice-cold Pepsi. We find Jimmy Pizza and Mike Tomato by the carnival rides and I'm telling them all about my lucky face to chest accidental meeting with Headlights Lopez when all Hell breaks loose. Explosions and lights flashing like lighting are all over the place! The fireworks show is starting;

they are being launched from behind the Church. This show marks the end of the Italian Street Festival. It is beautiful to watch the lights from the fireworks flashing around the Church's steeple. Every time there are a few seconds in between the loud booms, I'm doing my best to tell my story about Headlights Lopez, to Mike and Jimmy but they can't hear me because of the loud booms. So, I give up and just watch the show. I realize at that moment, not only is the feast over, but the summer season is over too!

Fireworks Mark the End of The Italian Street Festival

Chapter 47

Back To School PS 27-Chinese Finger Trap

Even though I have to go to my first day of school tomorrow we all get home pretty late. My family and friends don't want to give up the great time we all had at the Italian Street Festival tonight. We squeezed out every last moment we could. I'm in bed at midnight but can't sleep! I keep thinking about all the fun we had this summer and next summer is still a hundred years away! It seems as if the 4th of July was only a few days ago. All the summer adventures we had, all fun games we played, are now just memories and will be replaced with schoolwork. It's hard to believe that the summer slipped away so fast. I feel so bad about stuff, like my father not having a job, or

Sister Taking Pepino To P.S. 27, 4th Grade Opening Day Of School.

how my mother will pay the bills, and what will become of us? My parents try to keep a happy face but I can see them worrying about our family. I keep on going in and out of sleep all night long.

Thank God, it's morning. I'll get up and walk into the kitchen. My mother can only put together some bread with butter and coffee for breakfast.

My sister is dressed and ready to go to work. She

PS 27 Grammar School Red Hook, Brooklyn Founded 1890

is very good at sewing things but she doesn't get paid much for the work she does. My mother tells me to put on the dress shorts, white shirt, tie, knee-high black socks with black shoes that she laid out for me so I can go to school dressed like a gentleman. I'm upset and yelling at my mother that we don't live in Italy. I can't go to school looking like I'm attending an Italian Prep School! Even though I'm now in the 4th grade, I will run into the older 6th graders who will laugh at me and then they will kick my ass. I tell her that there is no friggin way I will go to school dressed like a little Mama's boy! Well, she gives in because she recalls all the bumps and bruises I came home with last year. She finally says okay and agrees to let me dress in long pants. I also warn my sister not to walk with me to the PS 27 schoolyard entrance. The school is only one block away, so she agrees to walk me to the corner of Columbia Street and Nelson Street so that she can see me walk into the schoolyard. My mother kisses and hugs me goodbye before we leave. Everything is going pretty much the way I planned.

I leave my sister on the corner and am running as fast as I can towards the PS-27 schoolyard entrance. I'm there just in time to meet Jimmy Pizza and Mike Tomato and don't run into any of the 6th-grade bullies. We will all walk into the schoolyard together to line up for our classes. As the bell rings the lines of kids standing are starting to move into the building with the teachers leading the way and directing us into our assigned classrooms.

I get to my classroom number 207 and all the kids are scrambling for seats. The smart-aleck kids, who think they're so smart, want a seat in the front rows, as close as possible to the teacher. This way the teacher will notice them first when they raise their hand to answer a question. The rest of us want to sit as far away as possible from the teacher in the back rows of the classroom. We sit down but there are still kids standing without a seat. By my count, there are 35 seats and 38 kids assigned to this 4th-grade class. The teacher is walking out of the room and returns quickly with three little chairs for the kids who are standing. I'm thinking to myself it's better than last year when there were five kids left standing.

The teacher goes to the front of the class and turns to face the blackboard. She writes her name with chalk on the blackboard,

"Welcome, my name is Miss Kent."

She is turning to face the class again to take attendance. I get a good look at her. Wow! She's beautiful! She's kind of short but she has a great looking body and shows it off with her tight sweater and skirt. She has great looking legs too that look great with her high heel shoes. Miss Kent has a beautiful smile that makes her glow. She has light brown hair down to her shoulders. I think that I'm in love with her! Now that I see her, I should have fought the smart-aleck kids for a front seat so I can look at her up close all day long. The teachers never give us work to do on the first day of school. Each of us gets up one at a time to introduce ourselves to the rest of the class. Then Miss Kent tells us the subjects she plans to teach us this year. The day goes by so fast and I get home a little after three in the afternoon. As I get home, my father is sitting by an open window smoking his Lucky Strike cigarette. He doesn't look happy, he is just sitting there looking out the window and puffing his cigarette. He doesn't say hello or anything, he just keeps looking out the window.

I'll change into my street clothes and go out to find my friends.

Turning the corner on Luquer Street I see Joanie sitting on her stoop with her dog Joy. She is waving at me to come over. So, I'll cross the street and sit next to her and ask her about her first day at school.

"I like my 3rd-grade teacher, she knows a lot of stuff and I feel good about learning all the things she talked about today.

How about you, did you like your 4th-grade teacher?"

I didn't want to tell Joanie that I'm in love with Miss Kent when I first looked at her, so I tell her that my new teacher is okay. Joanie smiles and offers me some of the animal crackers she is eating out of a little red box. I take some of her animal crackers and we sit there with her eating them. I must be hungry; I wolf down about ten crackers in no time. We sit there for quite a while. Even though I am dying to tell someone, anyone, about things that happened the last couple of days, I can't muster enough courage to tell her about the darts that Nunzio gave me, and for sure, I can't tell her about my lucky face-to-chest meeting at the Feast with Headlights Lopez. So,

"Hey, Joanie, wasn't the feast at Saint Stephen's Church a lot of fun? I never ate so much food! I played a lot of different games, too! The one game I like to play is the one where you try to throw a wooden ring onto a brown beer bottleneck. I got six rings to start and if I was able to collar four beer bottles with the rings I could have won a stuffed animal! If I collared three beer bottles I could have selected a smaller prize. But I had bad luck because I was only able to collar one beer bottle. So, I lost fifty-cents because I kept trying to win the big prize."

I am finishing telling Joanie my story and she is jumping up. "Oh, oh… I played that game and I won one of the smaller prizes. Wait here, I'll be right back."

She runs into her house while I'm sitting here with Joy, waiting for her to come back. She's now back within ten-seconds with two colorful soft-tube-looking things in her hand.

"Look! Look, I played the same ring on the bottle game and I won these bamboo Chinese Finger Traps! Aren't they great!?"

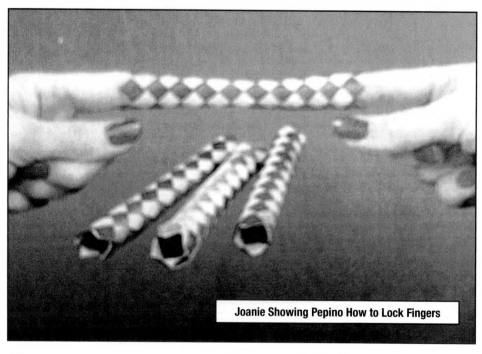

Joanie Showing Pepino How to Lock Fingers

They don't look like much of a prize.

"So, what do you do with these soft tube things?"

She says she learned how you can tie one finger from one hand to a second finger on the other hand and this bamboo tube locks your fingers together. Once you lock the fingers together the trick is how you go about trying to unlock them. Joanie puts the bamboo tube on her fingers to show me how they lock. I look at her hands with this Chinese finger trap.

"Hey, you know what? They should call them finger cuffs! Let me try them."

She struggles at first to unlock them from her fingers. Unlocking the damn things she gives them to me and I put them on one finger on each hand.

"Wow, these things are cool! We could lock prisoners' fingers together when we play Ring-A-Leave E-O." It isn't easy to get this finger trap off my fingers. I'll get up from the stoop and give the finger-ma-jig back to her.

"Thanks, Joanie, I've got to run, the guys are waiting for me in front of 'Chickies' grocery store. See you around."

I'm off down the street towards 'Chickies'.

Chapter 48
Daisy BB Gun-Dodgers & Ebbets Field

Brooklyn, New York has a uniqueness that defies explanation, a place with personality, Old-World charm, and a language all its own. The 'Borough of Churches', trees, home of educators, writers, actors, and various enter-tainers, a place everyone in the world has heard of. But if you think it ends there, then you need to have lived in the 1940's and 50's, and experienced two sacred places, maybe more sacred than the Vatican or the Wailing Wall. They are icons, one that sadly exists no more and one that exists to this very day. Both will live on forever.

As a child growing up in Brooklyn, Ebbets Field was a real field of dreams. It was home to the beloved Brooklyn Dodgers, 'dem bums' and both field and team resided in our collective hearts. We lived and died each year, facing great triumphs and eventual failure at the hands of the hated New York Yankees. But we always had a hope on our lips of:
"WAIT 'TIL NEXT YEAR!"

When our hearts became aware of other things, it turned to Coney Island, to a place on the Brooklyn shore and with the boardwalk and Nathan's hot dogs, a teenager's field of new dreams, the field of romance.

As young teenagers we invited our best girl or guy for that special day on the beach, lying with the crowds on the white sands listening to both the ocean and Rock 'n Roll from our transitor radio, then, a stroll along the Boardwalk and a stop at Nathan's, always a must.

Walking towards Hicks Street to find my friends, I'm thinking about Joanie's bamboo Chinese finger trap game. I wonder how the Chinese came up with this game. Maybe a Chinese dad made it for his kid for his or her Birthday. I have to ask my sister about it, she seems to know a lot about this stuff. Like when I went to Coney Island with my sister and her girlfriends this summer: I asked her if she knew why everyone calls that part of Brooklyn, Coney Island. Well, she said,

"I asked myself the same question so I went to the Brooklyn Public Library and looked it up in the Encyclopedia Britannica. The book explained that a long time ago when the Dutch settled in Brooklyn to farm the land they couldn't plant much on this is-land because it was too sandy. But they were able to hunt small animals for food. They found that mainly Rabbits lived on the sandy Island. So when a Dutchman was going there to hunt he'd tell his wife that was going to Rabbit Island or 'Coney' Island, which is Dutch for Rabbit.

The name stuck, and then everyone started to call this place Coney Island, even though over the years all the rabbits are now gone. Years later, it became a fun place for city people to get away to play at the beach, swim or go on carnival rides.

The very first roller coaster was built at Coney Island in 1884 and it kept on growing with all kinds of new rides like the 'Parachute Jump'."

I have to ask my sister about the Chinese finger trap game. Maybe she can look it up for me the next time she goes to the Brooklyn Public Library. Then I'll know how and why this game came about in the first place.

I'm on the corner of Luquer Street and Hicks but my friends are not here! So I'm going home. It's about four o'clock and I want to see what Roger is up to. I'll go up to the top floor of my building were Roger lives with his family. I'll just walk right in without knocking. There are so many people living in his apartment they never close or lock the front door. I walk all the way to the back bedroom looking for Roger. I know that there is a good chance he will be here if he isn't out trying to con some kids out of their money.

Roger is sixteen-years-old, dropped out of school and doesn't have a steady job. But Roger is smart and he manages to get money one way or another. When I walk into his room I am shocked to see him cleaning a Daisy Red Rider BB Rifle.

"Roger, how in the Hell did you get your hands on a Daisy Rifle?!"

He is looking up without our eyes meeting-

"Well, it's a long story. I made a bunch of trades and then I conned Crazy Joey Hook Nose into giving me this BB gun. Do you want to shoot it?"

"Hell yeah, I always dreamed of having a Daisy BB Rifle, ever since I saw the Christmas ads for it in my comic books. I never thought I would be able to shoot one. Come on and let me hold it."

Roger pulls the gun next to his chest.

"Not so FAST Pepino! If you want to shoot my beautiful Red

Any Boy Who Reads Comic Books Dreams Of Having His Own BB Gun

Rider BB gun it will cost you ten cents a shot."

"Haha, What, ten cents a shot? One BB costs less than a penny. That's not fair."

"Ha! You can't shoot a BB without a BB gun and I have the gun, stupid."

Wow, I told you Roger is smart. He's going to make a fortune off of this scheme he thought up!

It looks like he suckered me into being his first customer. So, I'll give him the three dimes I have in my pocket for three shots. He takes my money, opens the bedroom window, and gives me the rifle to fire.

"Go ahead, now you can shoot the rifle. But, you better not hit any cars or people walking down there with your three shots."

I take my time and aim the gun at a broken window in the vacant lot across the street and press the trigger. Puff, Puff, Puff, the shots ring out and I can hear glass breaking. It takes me less than ten seconds to blow thirty cents!

But the thrill of shooting a Daisy BB Rifle is worth it. It is a better thrill than throwing darts with Nunzio. I give Roger his rifle back.

"Listen Pepino, since you are my first customer, I have some good news for you. You may remember the go-cart we made last week for Fatso Jeffery. His Dad Larry BB was so happy with the go-cart he asked me to go with him and Fatso Jeffrey to see the Dodgers play at Ebbets Field this weekend. He said that I could bring a friend with me. Guess what friend? Would you like to go with me?"

"WOW! YES! Yes, I'd LOVE to go!"

I'm not sure whether my Mom and Dad would let me go to a major league baseball game with Roger. I am so excited that I will keep on begging Roger to take me with him. If I know Roger he will milk me out of every last dollar I own for God knows how long, but it's worth it. I hear so much about the Dodgers and I never thought I could ever get to see them play at Ebbets Field! Even if my Dad had the money he would never take me to see a major league baseball game. My Dad's sport is soccer or as he calls it: "Football". It's the only game he and his friends talk about.

My First Baseball Game At Ebbets Field

It's the following day and I come home from school and tell my mother and father that I am invited to go to the Dodger baseball game at Ebbets Field on Saturday. My mother doesn't jump for joy when I say that Roger is taking me to the game. My mother doesn't like Roger, the fact that Roger is a teenager and not an adult scares her even more because we were going to a place she has never been to. I know that she will feel this way so I tell her that Roger's adult cousin Larry BB is also going with us with his son Fatso Jeffrey, but she still doesn't agree to let me go to the game.

She tells me that she wants to talk to Roger's Mom, Emma about this trip to the ballpark. Another day has gone by and Mom sits me down and tells me that it is okay for me to go to the game. Roger's Mom says that she would talk to Larry BB to make sure that he will keep an eye on me so I don't get lost in the crowd at the big stadium. Wow, I'm in! Now I'm getting pumped up.

Finally, Saturday is here; the day of the baseball game has arrived! It's ten-o'clock in the morning and Roger is knocking on my door telling me that we will hook up with Larry BB and Jeffrey in an hour and we will all go together to catch the bus to Ebbets Field. The Dodgers are playing the Giants and the game starts at two o'clock.

"Wait a minute Roger; I never asked you before about Larry's name, what the Hell does BB stand for."

"Haha! Just take a good look at Larry with his big belly and you can see what the 'BB' stands for!"

Yeah, now it all makes sense to me. I am ready to go, Roger goes back upstairs and I go to my mattress-hiding place to get five dollars to spend at the game.

Jackie Robinson
Baseball Trading Card

I took out money for the Feast last week and now I'm taking another five dollars for the baseball game that only leaves me with three dollars to spruce up my bike. Oh well, I'll just ask Mr. Nick if he has some work for me to do at the sandwich shop so I can make some extra money.

I go downstairs and meet Roger in front of our building and we are walking together to Hamilton Avenue to meet Larry BB and Fatso Jeffrey to catch the bus to Ebbets Field. I love the bus ride; we are passing so many places that are new to me, like Prospect Park, I heard about the park but I never knew how big it is. Now I know that the park is huge! Prospect Park has a zoo, a big lake, boats, horseback riding, a museum, and paths that go on for miles.

I have to ask my sister to take me to Prospect Park. I would love to see the animals at the zoo and roam the park with her.

We are arriving at the stadium and it is about one o'clock. Larry BB gives each of us a ticket and we enter Ebbets Field to find our seats. As we enter, we walk through the rotunda that dominates the main entry with everything baseball! We look for the seating assignments on the tickets and follow the instructions posted for each section. We climb the ramps and come to our section entering the walkway, the greenness of the field and it's manicured grass with perfectly white baselines take away my breath! We have found our seats on the upper level above the stadium's entrance. The Dodgers take the field and I see Jackie Robinson, Pee Wee Reese, Roy Campanella, Gil Hodges, Carl Furillo, and the Duke of Flatbush; Duke Snider and other team members getting ready to play ball. I get goosebumps when we stand up to hear the National Anthem, I am so proud to be an American.

Seeing Jackie Robinson live for the first time is really something! I have his rookie baseball card at home but it's no substitute for seeing him in person running onto the ballfield.

I hear so many good things about Jackie when he came to join the Dodgers last year. The game has started and the Dodgers are playing great. I hear a Giant fan yelling out bad things against these Brooklyn 'Bums'. I'm getting upset at that!

"Don't get crazy, the name calling is all part of the game!" says Rodger.

As the teams are fighting it out we are eating hot dogs, Cracker Jacks, popcorn, ice cream and we wash everything down with an ice cold Coke. The best part of the baseball game for me is seeing Jackie Robinson run so fast in the outfield and around the bases. It amazes me that a player can have such lightning speed. Jackie Robinson tops it off for me by hitting a home run into the leftfield stand's upper deck! The Dodgers have won the game six to four. We get home and my mother is so happy to see me come back alive and well, she runs up to me and hugs me so hard that I can't breathe. It is such an exciting and long day, that I have some pasta for dinner and then I'll crash, falling asleep on my cot.

Chapter 49

Mexican Jumping Bean Game-Eating Chicken Feet

Even though it was three days ago, I am still glowing from my trip to Ebbets Field with Roger. I can't believe that I got to see the Dodgers and Jackie Robinson live and in person. Roger is a pain in the ass most of the time when he is out to screw me out of the few dollars I saved, but I will always be grateful to him for inviting me to go with him to see my first major league baseball game.

At school today, Miss Kent is so easy to listen to, giving us a social studies lesson and it's like hearing a great story, as I'm learning a lot about American History. I like looking at her, as my teacher is so beautiful. Before I know it, the bell is ringing and it's three o'clock, time to go home. I'll drop off my books at home and go out looking to find my friends. No one seems to be outside, so, they're probably doing homework. I am just about to give up and go home but now I see Joanie sitting on her stoop.

"Hey Joanie, what are you doing?"

"Not much, just waiting for Jenny to come over, she's got a new board game she wants to play with me. Did you finish your homework?"

"No, I plan to do it tonight. I'll just sit with you to wait for Jenny. I would like to see the new board game she's bringing over."

So, we are sitting together for about fifteen minutes and watching Jenny as she comes up the block with another girl.

"Hi Pepino, this is my girlfriend Frances. Ya wanna play this Mexican jumping bean board game with us?"

I'm thinking to myself, 'Damn straight I want to play with you'. Her girlfriend, Frances is a beauty. Frances is a little on the short side, she looks great in her tight blue jeans. She has a cute face that glows when she smiles at me. I love the way her dark brown hair is pulled back into a ponytail. I think that she r eminds me of a young Miss Kent.

Jenny laying out the board game on the stoop gives each of us a bean.

"Okay, we all have to put our Mexican bean in the center of the circle at the same time. We have to hold our bean upright with our finger. When I say 'Go', we take our fingers off the bean and watch the bean wiggle all over the place. The first bean to wiggle out of the circle gets the points closest to the bean.

We are doing the same thing and when a bean reaches a total of twenty points, you win. It's a crazy game because none of us has any control over our Mexican bean. Sometimes they move fast, sometimes they move slowly and sometimes they don't move at all! Jenny is right: it's a crazy game. When we release our beans, each one of us starts yelling and screaming for our bean to move, as if the bean could actually hear us.

Frances is laughing out of control. I love it! The only bean that seems to hear and jump towards the line is Joanie's bean. It looks like it moved and stopped at Joanie's command. It is like an invisible hand or ghost is moving the bean for her. Joanie wins all three games with her magic bean.

As we all go home for dinner I'm hoping that I get to see Frances again. I am upstairs and my Mom doesn't look happy at all! She tells me to wash up and sit at the table. I get it. My dad is still out of work and my Mom has to put something on the

Chicken Feet Tastes Great When You're Hungry

dinner table for us to eat. She doesn't say much as she puts a bunch of fried chicken feet and a pot of chicken bean soup on the table. The soup is made from chicken guts that my Mom's friend at the live market gave her.

We have no bread, no butter, or wine, just water to wash everything down with. But I must say that even though my Mom got this so-called food from the garbage can at the chicken market it is tasty and not that bad to eat. My Mom must have been cleaning the chicken feet and chicken guts all day longing for it to taste good! I like the fried chicken feet, except when my Mom misses cutting the nail off the foot. When I eat the soup, I try to pick out the chicken livers, I don't like to eat the heart either because it's like having a piece of gum in your mouth, it's much too chewy.

It is after dinner and my Dad is telling us that he thinks a large ship is about to arrive in the next several days and his contractor told him that he may have a job for him. says the only problem that may prevent him from landing this job is the fact that there are many more Italian Immigrants looking for work than there were a month ago. Things in Italy are so bad that young Italian men are doing everything they can to leave Italy for better-paying jobs in America, Canada, Argentina or wherever. If they're lucky and they manage to get to America legally or illegally they are desperate to find work. Many contractors are taking advantage of the new immigrants and paying them well below the current wage scale. So, my father can only hope that his contractor will keep him on his work crew.

After eating my fried chicken feet, I'm parked by the radio to listen to the adventures of Sherlock Holmes. My sister told me about this radio program and now I try not to miss any of the many mystery broadcasts.

All the characters are fun to listen to. Sherlock has a super brain and he is able to solve crimes based on deduction, whatever in the Hell that means. The other programs I like to listen to are;

Dr. Watson & Sherlock Discussing A Murder

Superman, Batman, Spiderman and most other superheroes who need to beat the bad guys with their strength and not so much their brains. That's why I like Sherlock Holmes, he reminds me a little of Roger, He's always thinking about stuff, and Roger couldn't fight his way out of a paper bag. I like Sherlock's sidekick, Dr. Watson, too! He has a gun and he's not afraid to use it when it comes down to protecting Sherlock from the bad guys. When I listen to the story on the radio, and Sherlock goes into his deduction crap and he finds the answer to the crime, I don't know why I really get excited. Then the Scotland Yard Inspector Lestrade gets all the credit for solving the crime. I still can't figure out the bad guy called Moriarty, who is as smart if not smarter than Sherlock Holmes at times. Sherlock Holmes stories when on the radio keep me glued to my seat.

The radio programs are over, so I'll sit down to do my homework. Opening my Social Studies textbook I know that in ten minutes I will fall asleep with the book in my hand.

197

Chapter 50
Fist Ball Game-Rubber Band Pistol

This morning my beautiful teacher, Miss Kent, is not happy with me because I haven't handed in my homework. No, the dog didn't eat it because I don't have a dog and that is a lame excuse anyway. So, I'll tell her the truth that I put off doing it until late last night and I just fell asleep before I could get to it. Miss Kent gives me a beautiful, knowing smile.

"Pepino, I suggest that you hit the books first thing when you get home. Don't, I repeat, DON'T wait until late evening to start doing it. Do you understand what I'm saying?"

She is very sweet as she scolds me in front of the class. I tell her that I will follow her instructions and she seems to be satisfied with my response. I don't like the sick feeling of knowing that she is pissed off at me. Oh well, I will do anything to stay on her good side. I go back to my desk and finish the homework I should have done last night. I am looking at Miss Kent, daydreaming when the three o'clock bell rings. I can't believe this day went by so fast!

I'm home and finished my homework in twenty minutes, so, I'm going out looking for my friends. I find the guys on Hick Street in front of 'Chickies' Grocery store.

Soft Pimple Ball Is Great For A Fist Ball Game While Spalding High Bounce Ball, Is Too Hard On The Hands

"Hey, Mike, what's going on?"

"We're all going to Nelson Street where the guys from our neighborhood team, the Rio's, plan to play a money game of Fistball against the Dragons from the Red Hook Projects. They will all put up five dollars each in the pot and the winners take all!"

The 'fistball' game is sort of like baseball, some neighborhoods call the same game 'punchball'. You have a home plate, first, second, and third, base. There is no pitcher like in a stickball game. Most of the time there are six to seven players on the field. The teams toss a coin and the winner goes first to hit the ball. The teams are not the only ones placing bets on the game. Everyone is placing side bets on the game, like adults, other teenagers who are watching the game and yeah, kids like me. They play only seven innings in a fistball game. The game of 'fistball' is played with a soft white ball with bumps on it. They call it a 'pimpleball'. We don't play this game with a Spalding ball because it's too hard to hit with your bare hand. The pimpleball is soft and easy to hit with your fist or open hand. At Nelson and Hicks Streets are a good location to play fistball because of the sewers and manhole covers located there, making a perfect infield diamond.

One manhole cover is home plate and another manhole cover is second base. One sewer on the right of home plate is first base and the sewer on the left of home plate is third base. I hope you get the picture of what the ball field looks like from home plate. Hicks Street crosses Nelson Street just beyond second base like a "T". The players in the field set themselves up. One at first base, one at third base, one at second base, and one behind the second baseman in short center field. The outfield is set up with one player in long center field because Nelson Street is a narrow street, the right field and left field players are positioned like the top of the "T" on Hicks Street. There are no shortstops because of the narrow infield. The third baseman also acts like a shortstop because the first baseman holds his position and he does not chase the ball. There are no balls and strikes in fistball, that's why there is only one umpire who will call a hitter safe or out. When a team makes three outs they will take the field and the opposite team gets to punch the ball. A right-handed 'batter' will toss the ball up with his left hand while punching the ball with his right hand as hard as he can. The left-handed player does the opposite from the left side. Many players will just punch the pimpleball with a closed fist. If they hit it right the pimpleball can really fly a long distance. That's why there are short and long center field positions.

Some players can hit the pimpleball with a cupped hand and the ball will curve right or left depending which hand you use to hit the ball with. If someone is on base, players will simply slap the ball on the ground with an open hand to drive his teammate home. These fistball games are serious business in Brooklyn. Each team has professional T-shirts made up of the team colors and team name printed on them.

The Rio's T-shirts are green and white while the Dragon's T-shirts are red and white. Fights break out between the teams when a player running the bases is knocked-down by a defending player and everybody goes crazy. The players gang up on each other and the people watching the game jump in too. It may take twenty minutes for everyone to calm down and continue the game. It's a beautiful day and the game goes on for about three hours with only two fights. The Rio's win 15-11 and take home the money pot. We are all yelling and cheering the winning team. I collect my two-dollar side bet and excitedly walk back to 'Chickie's' grocery store with my friends. When I'm a teenager, I hope they will let me join the Rio's fistball team.

We are all sitting here for a while and Jimmy Pizza pulls out a bag full of rubber bands!

"Let's play War!"

Finger Shooting Rubber Band Pistol

We have eight guys choosing sides and Jimmy is giving each of us six rubber bands. I love to play this game. There are two teams, one team is the 'Defenders' and the other team is the 'Invaders'. It's sort of like 'Hide and Go Seek'. I am on the 'Invaders' team. The 'Defenders' have ten minutes to hide in the Brooklyn Battery Tunnel construction site area that is filled with all types of building material. Metal I-beams are stacked up high, huge bins, some filled with gravel and others filled with sand, metal core rods to reinforce the concrete, stacks of bricks, cinder blocks and lumber and other stuff that I don't have a name for, litter the area. The ten minutes are up and the 'Invaders' go looking for the 'Defenders' with their rubber band pistols. When you shoot another kid with the rubber band it doesn't hurt that much, it only gives you a little sting. Since all the players have imaginary bulletproof vests, that's why you can only kill a soldier with a direct shot to the face.

I load two pistols: one pistol in my left hand and the other pistol in my right hand. To load the pistol, you take a rubber band and hold it with your lower three fingers in the palm of your hand. Then you stretch the rubber band around the back of your thumb and hook the rubber band onto the tip of your extended index finger. Now your hand looks like a pistol. You can shoot the rubber band at your target by releasing it with your lower three fingers and directing the shot at the target with your index finger. Remember you can only 'kill' someone with a shot to the face. If you miss each other you are allowed to pick up rubber band ammunition that may be laying around in the heat of battle. The 'defenders' team has the advantage because they know you're coming for them and if they find a good hiding place: surprise, surprise, 'You're Dead'!

Suddenly, Jimmy Pizza is jumping out from his hiding place behind a stack of bricks! I shoot first with both pistols and hit him in the neck. But Jimmy gets the kill shot by hitting me right in the middle of my forehead. We do our best but the 'Defenders' kick our ass. This is such a fun game of trying to outsmart each other, but it is getting dark so we'll all go home to eat dinner and plan to fight another day.

The Brooklyn Battery Tunnel Construction Site

Chapter 51

Prospect Park-Balsawood Airplane

Prospect Park Day Trip

Even though Jimmy Pizza shot me dead yester-day in our rubber band hand-pistol war game, I had a ball trying to outsmart him. I like to play this war game because playing hide and seek without a rubber band pistol is so boring. I plan to challenge Jimmy to a rematch and I will get a second chance to kick his ass. It's Friday and I have all weekend to plan my revenge.

I'm home from school and cracking the books open pushing myself to finish my homework. This way, my weekend will be free of worry by getting my homework done in time before I go back to school on Monday. I'm putting my books away and my sister is arriving home from work.

"Hey Pepino, you know that I always help Mom clean the house on Saturday. I asked Mom if I could skip working with her this Saturday because I want to take you to Prospect Park tomorrow. She told me that she was OK with the idea. So, don't sleep late tomorrow!"

"I think we should leave for the Park around 8 AM. This way it will still be cool enough for us to walk around the park. There are a lot of things I would like you to see."

As she is catching me by surprise, I'm just standing here without saying anything for a minute or two. I'm now dancing with some real excitement!

"Wow! That's great! Is anyone else coming with us?"

"Yes, I asked my girlfriend Frances if she wants to take her little sister with us. She loves the idea, so it will only be the four of us going on this day trip to the park."

Oh well, Frances' little sister Mary Jane is only seven-years-old and she is always talking and asking questions. I hope she doesn't drive me crazy! I won't say another word to my sister about Mary Jane coming with us because I am just so happy that I am going to Prospect Park for the first time!

This morning is Saturday and mom is sitting at the kitchen table having a cup of coffee. She is smiling and giving us the good news that dad started his new job yesterday and that he will be working all weekend. I can see a calm feeling come over her face. We are so happy that she gives us the good news before we leave for our day trip to Prospect Park.

We are outside of our building and find Frances and Mary Jane waiting for us. Mary Jane is a skinny little girl with a big mouth. She is kind of pretty with her bright red hair in a braid running down her back and her sky-blue eyes looking at you. You would never think that Mary Jane has Italian parents. We are walking together to catch a bus on Hamilton Avenue.

We are on the bus and Mary Jane is asking how long it will take for us to get to Prospect Park. My sister is telling her that it will take about forty-five minutes to get there. Mary Jane is continuing to talk on and on about anything and everything that pops into her head. I have stopped listening to her altogether. I just look out the bus window and am day-dreaming. It doesn't seem to take that long and my sister is pulling at my shirt and says:

"Okay guys, we're HERE!"

We are getting off the bus and found an empty bench close to the entrance of the park. It's a beautiful day, not too hot and it's just cool enough for us to walk around the park. Prospect Park is a big place so we are all sitting there while my sister starts making a list of what we should see.

As my sister is talking to Frances about what we should see first, I am looking at the park entrance. I can't believe how BIG this place looks! Everything is so green, the trees, the grass and all the colors of flowers that are blooming everywhere I look! I can't help thinking how lucky we are living near such a beautiful place.

Frances is suggesting: "Isabella; why don't we go to the zoo first. After we see the zoo we can walk around and find a place where we can sit and have lunch?"

My sister agrees.

"Great idea, the kids will love to see the animals!"

So, we are walking to the zoo and the park is so big that it is taking us a half-hour to get there. As we are walking I'm looking at all the people in the park, it's a Saturday and there are so many people here! We get to the entrance of the zoo, and it is starting. Mary Jane is asking how big the park is. My sister is telling all of us:

"I looked it up in the Encyclopedia. Prospect Park is about six hundred acres and the man-made lake is about sixty acres". Mary Jane then asks:

"What's an acre?"

"Well I'm not sure, but I think it's about the size of one city block."

Wow, that's huge. If it's that big we will need to spend days here seeing everything!

As we are walking through the zoo entryway I see the monkeys first. The monkey cage is indoors and as we are walking into that area the smell of the urine and monkey shit starts getting to me. The smell takes me back to that smell in Blackie Parisi's fire-trap basement on President Street. Only the monkey cage is ten times worse. All the monkeys in the big cage are screaming, swinging and jumping all over the place. As we get close to the cage a black and white monkey spits at me. All of a sudden, Mary Jane is crying and sobbing out of control. Frances grabs her and pulls her out of the monkey cage area and we follow her. The rest of the zoo is mainly outdoors so the smell of animal crap and piss is not so bad.

The animals themselves are beautiful to look at. There are lions, chitas, water buffalo, elephants, zebras, gazelles and my favorite: sea lions. It's much better to see the animals live instead of looking at picture-books or magazines. The sea lions are a lot of fun to watch as they jump in and out of the water, play with each other and juggle a big ball on the tips of their noses. I am so happy my sister took me to see the animals at the zoo.

We now walk out of the zoo and are passing people on horseback riding slowly on trails, more people at the boathouse and people in

Flying A Balsa Wood Airplane In Prospect Park

paddle boats on the lake. Everyone is out enjoying the day in the park. We find a bench to sit on, close to the food-stand and my sister buys me a ham sandwich, potato chips and a Coke for lunch. Like the people around us, we sit on the bench enjoying our lunch and the magnificent view!

I finish eating, and my sister takes a paper bag she is carrying and gives it to me and surprises me with:

"Here is a little something you can play with, in the meadow!"

I opened the bag and find a balsawood airplane kit with a rubber band propeller.

"Wow! THANKS! This plane is perfect to fly here!"

I am assembling the plane with the propeller rubber band engine that's included in the cellophane wrapper. I am turning the propeller with the rubber band attached to it as tight as I can.

"OKAY! Let's go fly this thing."

Mary Jane smiles and jumps off the bench to follow me into the meadow.

"Are you ready?"

She is looking up towards the sky as I am releasing the airplane. That sucker flies faster than I thought it can! Mary Jane comes running after it as it is landing about thirty feet away.

It is great to watch Mary Jane be so happy, laughing and having fun with me. We launch the plane time and time again and watch it come down for a soft landing in the rich green grass of the meadow. We can never fly this Balsawood plane on the streets where we live because as it comes down it could hit the hard concrete pavement and be damaged or destroyed. The only place we can fly this plane is in the soft grass of Coffey Park.

My sister is calling us over and says that we will walk over to the Botanical Garden to see all the beautiful flowers in bloom. I'm not too thrilled to go see a bunch of flowers but how can I give my sister a hard time about it, after all, she went out of her way to take me on this day trip to Prospect Park.

Chapter 52
Homemade Wine-Bocce Ball Game

Emigrating to America, or South America or even Australia for Italians meant coming with their customs and past-times. That little bit of home that was ingrained in them as they set out for the new world brought comfort to them. The Dutch brought bowling to America and the Italians brought their Bocce, their form of bowling.

Once the 'boccino' (little bocce ball and object of the game) was tossed, all bets were on, and so began the serious business of playing Bocce, accompanied by skill, proper technique and the ingrained use of Italian verbal and body coaxing to accompany the bocce down the corridor of this ancient sport.

It is appropriate that the Romans would bring the sport from the Middle East, that was perhaps borrowed from the ancient  *Greeks and have it settle in Italy, then France and Europe, then finally in America.*

Sentenced To Life In A Cage
in Prospect Park

Last week's trip to Prospect Park was so much fun. It just blows me away to see this beautiful park right in the middle of Brooklyn! The zoo is the best part of the trip for me. Seeing all the animals is better than looking at them in pictures. At the zoo, I get to see them moving around, eating and sometimes I get to see them playing with each other. The only cage I'm not too thrilled about is the Monkey Cage. Once I get over the smell of all the pee and poop I look at them and you know what, they look back at me! That's when I get the feeling that the Monkey's know that we are the enemy that put them in a cage. When I look deep into their eyes I can feel the hate they have for mankind, who could blame them. The other animals at the Zoo just seem like they gave up! They just eat and sleep their lives away in a cage. I do enjoy seeing all the animals but I can't shake the sad feeling I have about them being in a cage for the rest of their lives.

The park is so big that we can't get to see it all in one day. I hope that my sister will take me back there one day soon.

Wine has been around since almost the beginning of time. Cultures from the Far East to the Middle East across and all sides of the Alps have imbibed in the ancient art of drinking wine and winemaking. Europe has wine regions just about everywhere one will travel. It is the signature of cultural pride and the daily substance for both adults and children from a tender age.

The Bible makes many references to wine and in both the New and Old Testaments it is reverently referred to. The process of making wine evolved slowly with the same basic concepts, for the most part, a pit or barrel or basin to hold the grapes and filter the juice from the waste where the juice fermented and turned eventually into wine by crushing the grapes by foot or some other method favored by the local populace.

My father is telling me this morning not to make any plans with my friends this weekend. He says that he will not be going back to work until Monday because he and his friends are getting together to make homemade wine. They pooled their money to buy a truckload of red and white wine grapes and they are expecting the delivery of the grapes this morning, Everyone has to get together to unload the truck and put the wine grapes into the cellar of our building. Wow! The summer flew by so fast and I don't realize that the grape season is here already!

I love the grape season and I am ready to help my dad with it any way I can. We go downstairs to meet my dad's friends, their sons and our cousins to wait for the truck. I am happy to see Jimmy Pizza waiting there with his dad.

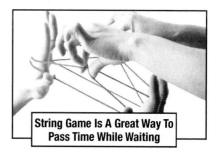

String Game Is A Great Way To Pass Time While Waiting

While we sit there waiting, Jimmy Pizza takes a string about eighteen inches long out of his pocket and folds it in half. He then takes the two ends and ties them together forming a circle. Now he takes the string in a circle and starts to work it with his fingers into a rope design. Wow! My sister Isabella told me about the string game but I never actually saw one. Jimmy turns to me with his hands out.

"You go first, put your pinkie fingers here and there and swoop both hands down and then around under the strings and pull back."

I'm doing what he says and I see the two parallel strings in Jimmy's hands turn into a web design in my hands.

"Holy Crap, I did it!"

Going back and forth playing this game for twenty minutes and nowsuddenly I hear the rumbling of a truck approaching. The truck is arriving with a shit-load of grape crates on it. The men are taking charge and unloading the grape crates onto the side-walk near the entrance to the cellar. All the kids are picking up a forty-pound grape crate and sliding them all one by one down the chute into the cellar. We are separating the red grape crates from the white grape crates, stacking them next to the ancient hand-crank grape crushing machine.

The grape crushing machine is on the top of an empty barrel. The machine is centered in the middle of the of the barrel's opening ready to crush the grapes that will fall into the Barrel. I'm not counting them but there must be a couple hundred grape crates down here. Each person in our group both adult and kid is assigned a different job. Some open the wooden wine crates; others dump the grapes into the grape crusher, while the strongest of the men in our group turn the wheel of the grape crusher. Kids like me have to gather the empty wooden grape boxes and stack them in the backyard. This is going on for most of the day. We crush all the grapes into six wood barrels of red and three barrels of white. In the coming weeks ahead, the grapes will ferment and turn into wine. When the head wine-maker gives us the word that the wine is ready, we all return once again to separate the wine from the crushed pulp and stems mixed in. Once that's done the wine goes back into a wooden barrel for aging. Pressing the wine is my favorite job. I will scoop up the crushed grapes from the barrel into a bucket, then I take the bucket and dump the crushed grapes into the grape press. The press will squeeze the remaining juice out of the crushed grapes.

As I lean over the wine barrel six or seven times to put the grapes into the bucket I breathe in the air from the barrel. I love the smell of the barrel filled with wine mixed in the crushed grapes, I can feel a high sensation. It's about the same sensation that comes from drinking a couple of glasses of wine. I keep working but I'm high as a kite. Every kid I know drinks a little homemade wine at dinner. My mother and Dad will only give me a half glass at each meal. Sometimes I have a little wine for breakfast with peaches. The homemade wine is very strong and when I sip it, it makes me feel warm all over. But when I suck in the air from the wine barrel, I'm drunk. So, when I start feeling dizzy I call over for another kid to come over to finish the job. The grape press is full of the crushed grapes and the men are taking over. They are turning the wine press and squeezing the wine out into a large metal bucket and pouring the pressed wine into another wine barrel for aging. I'm taking a count of all the men and boys in the cellar, and there's ten of us working together to make wine this season. It's a lot more people working down here than last year. The women help by bringing sandwiches, soda, water, pastries, and coffee. Even though we're all working, it's turned into a party.

My Father's Old Wine Press

By now, everyone is laughing, singing, telling stories and just having a great time! We're all feeling high from the smell of the new wine in the air. As all this wine-making is going on, a few men are taking a break for a smoke and playing a Bocce ball game in the backyard. I'm a little high and I feel good working with everyone when it's the wine season. We are all working hard and playing while having fun at the same time to make wine for our family and friends, there is nothing like it, except maybe, for Christmas. I take a break too and go into the backyard to watch the Bocce ball game.

My dad tells me that everyone in Italy likes to play Bocce ball. There is a total of nine balls in a Bocce set. There are eight large balls made of hardwood. Four are red and four are green the ninth yellow ball is much smaller than the other eight. You play this game with two or four people at a time. If there are four people playing, each team of two players gets two balls of the same color. They toss the small yellow ball about thirty feet, then each team gets a turn to throw their balls one at a time as close as possible to the yellow ball. The first team player throws his red ball at the small yellow ball. His ball stops about one foot away from the yellow ball target. Then the green team player goes next and throws his ball at the yellow ball target. After every player is finished throwing their balls everyone walks to the yellow ball to see which team's ball is closest to the yellow ball. If the red ball is the only ball closer to the yellow target than any of the green balls, the red team gets a point. If there are two red balls closer to the yellow than any green ball the red team gets two points. If one of the red balls is touching the yellow ball then that is worth three points. So, if one red is touching and there is another red ball close but not touching the yellow ball, then the red team gets four points for that round. It's not a complicated game to figure out the points. But if you watch them play you will see more fights about scoring points than any other game I know. As you're playing you can try to throw your ball as hard as possible to break up the other team's balls and push them away from the yellow ball. This way your ball gets closer to the yellow ball.

Italian Bocce Ball Game

They are all looking at their team balls around the yellow ball and fighting about which ball is closer or which ball is touching or which ball is not touching the yellow ball. Now the men playing are drinking wine at the same time as it's getting pretty ugly. The men are finally settling on the score for that round and picking up their balls and throwing the yellow ball in the opposite direction to start the new round. When a team gets 15 points total they win the game. I ask my dad who invented Bocce Ball and he tells me that no one knows for sure who did.

Many years ago, explorers found a painting of people playing a game that looked like Bocce in an Egyptian tomb that dates back to 6000 BC. There are stories that the game found its way to Greece around 1000 BC and later it was brought to what we now know as Italy by the Romans. He also said these are only stories about Bocce Ball that were passed down from one generation to another. The Italians love to play this game and that's why they brought the game with them to America.

Sometimes the kids get a chance to play Bocce ball after the men stop fighting over the score taking a couple of shots at it. We start playing after sucking in all the air in the wine barrels. I roll four Bocce Balls at the little yellow ball and my balls roll in all kinds of crazy directions. It is impossible for us to remember our score. So, Jimmy Pizza says:

"The Hell with this, I'm going back to the wine cellar!"

It's Sunday, and we finish pressing all the wine out of the crushed grapes. I count four barrels of red wine and one barrel of white wine set aside for aging. Come Christmas the wine will be ready to drink. That's when our fathers will pour the wine from the barrels into glass gallon jugs for everyone to take home for their family and friends. Every year I look forward to the next winemaking season.

Chapter 53

Italian White Lightning-Dance Lessons

I'm sitting with Jimmy Pizza in the backyard looking at the big pile of empty grape crates. We are very tired from working this past weekend. The winemaking season is fun but it's a lot of hard work and exhausting. We look pretty bad sitting there with our grape-stained T-shirts, shorts, and sneakers, and our faces, arms, and legs are covered with dirt and grape stains. The high we got from all the wine is starting to wear off. I'm not talking much but Jimmy is.

"Wow! Look at this shit load of wood here! All this wood will make a really great bonfire when we pile it up on the street corner for Election Day!"

"You're right. All these empty grape crates are a good start for us this year. We have to get together with Reno the Greek, Pecker and the rest of our gang to collect more wood from the condemned houses at the Brooklyn Battery Tunnel construction site. With all the winemaking in the neighborhood and all the construction going on in the tunnel, there will be gigantic fires on every block."

Grappa... Italian White Lightning

Jimmy just keeps on shaking his head up and down as I'm talking to him.

"Hey, Pepino, do you know what our parents are gonna do with all those old flat-looking grapes left over from the winepress? Do you think they'll let us burn that stuff in the bonfire?"

"Well, my father and his cousin John plan to make Grappa from the leftover crushed and pressed grape skin, seeds and stems."

"What in the Hell is Grappa?"

I'm laughing because of the funny look on Jimmy's face.

"Grappa is what is called homemade Italian white lightning! People tell me that it's like American Moonshine. My Dad let me taste it once. All I can remember is that it tastes like medicine and it makes my face turn beet red. It's powerful shit. You should ask your Dad to give you just a little taste."

Jimmy is sticking his tongue out.

"No friggin way! I hate the taste of medicine."

I'm getting up and waving my hand goodbye walking into my apartment building. I don't have any energy left even to say good-bye to Jimmy.

I better wash all the grape stains off my face arms and legs. I'm changing my clothes and see that my sister is shadow-dancing to some big band music. She owns a collection of records she calls "Seventy-eights". She never lets me go near her record collection because she thinks I might drop one. If I make a mistake and I happen to drop one of her precious records it will shatter into a million pieces. I

My Sister's Record Player

My Sister's Big Band Record Collection

can't blame her, these records scratch and break so easily. Some of the records she likes to play are 'Begin the Beguine', 'I'll be Seeing You', and the dance music of Tommy Dorsey and Benny Goodman. She likes to listen to songs from the Ink Spots and she is really in love with a new young singer from New Jersey, named Frank Sinatra.

"Come on, come on; dance with me. I'll teach you how to Foxtrot and how to Lindy."

She is pulling my arm and before I realize it, holding my hands while I face her.

"This is how you Foxtrot. One-two, feet together, one-two, feet together."

As we are listening to the music, she's showing me how to lead my partner. I'm too tired to fight with her so I'll do my best to learn this thing. But it's hard to lead your girl partner when she's much taller than you are. Now we're dancing all around the room and I'm really into this! I like this dance thing. My sister is telling me that I have a good ear for the music and rhythm too.

Anyway, we're doing this dance thing for about twenty minutes now! I'm begging her to let go of me so that I can take a rest from all the winemaking.

"Okay, you spoilsport. You will thank me when you're older and a pretty girl asks you to dance with her."

Letting go of my hands I walk into the kitchen for a glass of water. I guess my sister is getting tired because the dance music stopped playing. She follows me into the kitchen and looks at me with a serious expression on her face.

"Pepino I know that you're just a kid but I have to talk to you about our family. The other day we were all happy when Dad told us that a ship was coming to Red Hook and he was looking forward to working on this ship for the next six weeks. I overheard Mom and Dad talking last night and Dad told Mom that his contractor will not give him a job to work on this ship because all the positions were filled, and Mom started crying.

We're out of money, Mom has borrowed as much as she can from our family and friends. Dad told Mom not to worry because he plans to work as a day laborer off the books, digging ditches, painting. cleaning out sewers or whatever. It's not steady work and he doesn't know how much money he can make from doing these odd jobs. My sewing job pays very little, but we have to help out where ever we can. I'm sorry to tell you all this stuff but we're a family and I may need your help, I'll let you know if you can do anything to help out. Meanwhile, don't tell anyone about what I told you, and I mean NO one. If Mom and Dad find out I talked to you they will kill me."

As she turns around walking out of the kitchen and into her bedroom crying, I just sit here not knowing what I can say because she scared me to death. I'm thinking that I could use some of my father's Grappa about now. I'll get up and walk into the next room listen to the radio, maybe some of my radio programs will make me forget about things for a while!

I always like to listen to stories from the old west like the Lone Ranger, Hop-along Cassidy, and Roy Rogers. I remember that my friend Mike Tomato told me about a new program called Gunsmoke that just started playing on the radio. He told me that the stories are about a U.S. Marshal called Matt Dillon who has to tame the outlaws around Dodge City, Kansas, right after the Civil War. Mike tells me that it's the best radio western ever. So, I dial the radio station and tune in on my first episode of Gunsmoke. I just want to forget everything my sister told me.

Mike is right as I am glued to the radio listening how Marshal Matt Dillon and his sidekick Chester fight the outlaws in Dodge City. Matt Dillon's best friend, Doc Adams is a big help in patching him up when he's wounded in a gunfight and Doc always seems to give Matt Dillon good advice on how to get the outlaws out of town. The best part of the radio story is when there's a fight in the Long Branch Saloon and pretty Kitty Russell runs to find the Marshal for help. Kitty is the owner of the Long Branch Saloon and I think Matt Dillon is sweet on her. When I listen to these stories I feel that I'm part of the action. I can't wait to tune in for the next episode. But it would really be great if they make a movie about Marshal Matt   Dillon fighting the outlaws in Dodge City who are trying to take over the town. I would like to see all the action on a big screen. I think that all my friends would love to see it too. Good thing Gunsmoke is over, I'm still scared to death and tired, I can't keep my eyes open, so, I'll go to bed and drift away to sleep before my head will even touch the pillow!

Chapter 54

Duncan Yo-Yo Man-King Of The Mountain

I'm not too happy about going to school today. My mother pushed me out of my cot.

"You gotta go to school. Wake up!"

I'm dragging myself to the kitchen for a jolt of espresso coffee. The coffee is strong, so I'll put two tablespoons of sugar in it for energy. Now I'm feeling better but my body is not ready to move. I'll get dressed and walk to PS 27, probably in a daze, yet even though I live only a block away from my school, I'm walking slowly and will be about five minutes late! Walking into my classroom, Miss Kent, my teacher, takes one look at me and exclaims:

"Pepino, you look TERRIBLE, what happened to you over the weekend!?"

"I helped my father and his friends make homemade wine for our families. It was fun in the beginning, but by Sunday afternoon I ran out of energy. Don't get me wrong I loved every minute because it was like a huge block party with music, storytelling, dancing and we ate all kinds of treats all day long. We laughed while we pressed the wine grapes and put them into wine barrels for aging. I'm sorry that I'm so tired today, I will do my best stay awake and keep up with the class work." I don't say anything about my family's money problems and the sick feeling I have in my stomach. I have all these crazy thoughts about our having nothing to eat, not having a place to live or my family moving back to Italy, I think that scares me the most. I'm doing my best not to think about this stuff but I can't help it because it's always on my mind.

Miss Kent is giving me a big smile and is turning to write our lesson plan for the day on the blackboard. I'm dozing off a few times but I'll make it to the end of the day. The school bell is fially ringing, thank God, and is waking me up so, I know it is time to go home.

Leaving the school building I see Reno the Greek and his Brother Henry playing with Yo-Yos.

"Hey, Henry when did you get your Yo-Yo?"

"Aren't they neat? I'm just getting the hang of how to make them do tricks. I bought mine last Friday when the Duncan Yo-Yo man came to the Candy Store to show us what the Yo-Yo can do. He did a crazy routine with one Yo-Yo in each hand at the same time. It looked so easy when he was doing it so I gave him thirty-five cents for this bright blue Yo-Yo. It took me all weekend to learn how to make this Yo-Yo go up and down."

My energy is starting to come back to me. I am so excited to see Henry playing with his beautiful Yo-Yo.

"Where can I get one?"

"The Candy Store has a box of Duncan Yo-Yos on display on top of the candy counter. But if I were you I would wait for the Yo-Yo man come there before you buy one. He told us he planned to come back to the Candy Store after school on Wednesday."

Reno is talking to me and doing his best to control his bright red Yo-Yo. He is having a hard time and I know it's not going to easy to learn how to Yo-Yo, but I want one! I don't think that I can wait until the Yo-Yo man comes back to the Candy Store on

Candy Bar Reward For The King Of The Mountain Winner

Wednesday. I'll rush home to get fifty-cents from my moneybox that I hide under my parent's bed. Rushing back to the Candy Store on Nelson and Hicks Street, I'm walking into the store and find a Yo-Yo display on the candy counter, and only three Yo-Yo's are left in the display! Wow, they're almost sold out! Now I have to pick one from the pink, yellow or orange Yo-Yos on the counter. I'm afraid to take too long because another kid could come and take one before I do. I'm not going to buy the pink Yo-Yo because pink is a girl's color. Let's see, should I get the yellow one? It's kind of a bright color. The orange one looks good, so I pick it up from the display box on the counter and I pay Mr. G. the candy store owner thirty-five cents for the orange Yo-Yo. Then I get myself a Hershey Milk

Chocolate candy bar for a nickel

I'm walking over to the corner of Luquer and Hicks Streets eating my candy bar and getting to the corner I find a bunch of my friends watching Reno the Greek and his Brother Henry playing with their Yo-Yos. Hum, it looks like they learned a lot since I saw them earlier today! Now they're able to move the Yo-Yo up and down in a fast motion. Henry starts to show off by making the Yo-Yo swing out like it's going to hit me, then he swings it back real fast. If they can do that, then I can do it too! I put my finger on the Yo-Yo string and try to make it go up and down but I just can't get it going. I have to rewind it again and again. It's going to take a lot of practice for me to get to the same level as Reno and Henry. After ten tries, I finally get the knack of making the Yo-Yo go up and down. Now Pecker yells out:

"Let's play King of the Mountain!"

There are six of us on the corner and we are ready for action. The question now is where the mountain is and how does the king or queen get their rewards. Even though girls can play this game too, boys don't like it when they hone in on the action. Mike Tomato is collecting a nickel from each of us and goes to the Candy Store and he buys six treats, Hershey Chocolate bars, with and without almonds, Almond Joy, Mounds, and Snickers to hand out to the winner of each round.

Next, we have to find a mountain to climb. With all the construction that is going on in the neighborhood for the Brooklyn Battery Tunnel, we have a lot to choose from. Pecker is telling us that he found a condemned bank building that would be perfect for us to climb. The old bank building has a concrete entrance with two columns on each side; it's about fifteen feet high and sticks out two feet from the wall of the building all around, of what used to be the entrance. All the doors are gone except for the plywood boards that are nailed to the entrance to block kids and looters from getting into the building. The old bank building is only two blocks away.

We all agree that the second mountain for us to climb is the eight-een-foot-high stack of metal I-beams at the construction site. The third mountain is a twenty-foot high pile of loose gravel. The starting line will be fifteen feet from each mountain. Mike Tomato the leader is taking charge, yelling, "One, two, three, GO!" as we are all rushing to climb the mountain at once. The one kid who is able to get to the top of the mountain first will yell out: "I'M KING OF THE MOUNTAIN!" winning that round and getting to pick one of the candy treats. The old bank   entrance will be mountain number one.

We are all standing ready to go at the start line. Mike yells out "GO!" and we are all running like crazy to climb the old bank mountain. We're pushing and shoving each other to get there first, and if a kid in front starts to climb ahead of me, I will grab his leg and pull him down. Everybody's fighting, while we call each other names trying to get ahead of one another. Pecker beats us all to the top of the old bank door and he wins the first and second rounds. I have a feeling that he put one over on us. He was probably practicing his climb on this building for weeks.

Brooklyn Kids Playing King of The Mountain

I won the first climb on the metal-I beam mountain and Jimmy Pizza won the second climb. Reno the Greek, that little monkey, wins both rounds up the gravel mountain. Reno is so fast using his arms and legs rushing up the loose gravel, we can't seem to come close to beating him. Henry, Mike Tomato, and Six Finger Ricardo can't seem to win any of the climbs. We are having a great time playing "King of the Mountain." Now we're all standing on the corner again sweaty and dirty looking like we went to Hell and back.

I'm glad that I won a candy bar and that my new Yo-Yo didn't fall out of my pocket. I'm also glad that none of us got hurt clawing our way up the mountains. Nunzio Superman was the only kid who did not play the mountain game. He's too fat and heavy to squirrel his way up each mountain so he watches us compete and he gives out the prizes to each winner. After the game, I'm going home to get cleaned up, have dinner and do my homework for Miss Kent. Tomorrow is Wednesday and I hope that the Yo-Yo man shows up at the Candy Store after school. I'm so looking forward to seeing him do those tricks that everybody is talking about, with a Yo-Yo in each hand all moving at the same time.

Chapter 55
Joanie's Pink YoYo-The Hot Potato Game

It's Wednesday and I'm sitting here in class looking at my teacher Miss Kent. She is so beautiful to look at! I know that she is going over our history lesson but I'm not paying attention to what she is saying. Suddenly, she has caught me by surprise.

"Pepino, can you tell the class when George Washington crossed the Delaware?"

"Huh, The Delaware!? I... I..."

I think she is shooting a question at me because she can see that I am daydreaming. My mind is blank and the whole class is laughing at me because of the stupid look on my face. Miss Kent isn't waiting for an answer, she's just moving on and asking another student the same question. So, I'll go back to my day-dreaming and hope that school will let out soon because I am looking forward to seeing the Yo-Yo man this afternoon. It seems like it is taking forever for the three o'clock bell to ring, Ah, finally it is ringing so I'll gather my books together and run downstairs and exit the school building. I practically run over Mike Tomato who is in front of me!

"Wahoo, take it, easy shithead, you almost ran me over!"

I'll push him aside and rush over to the candy store across the street. I can see about twenty kids at the candy store trying to push their way in. The store owner is coming out, he's raising his hand and shouting to us kids waiting, that the Yo-Yo man will come outside. He will stand in front of the store and do his Yo-Yo tricks on the sidewalk so that everyone can see him. I'm watching the Yo-Yo man as he is coming out of the store, looking a lot younger than I thought he would be. He's a tall good looking guy with long dirty blond hair. There are a bunch of teenage girls here too and I don't think that they're much interested in just seeing the Yo-Yo man do his tricks.

Wow! He's starting to twirl a couple of Yo-Yo's, one in each hand, all at the same time! It's amazing because of the Yo-Yo's looking like they are an extension of his arms. All the kids watching are cheering him on and clapping after each trick. I think that Duncan will sell a hundred Yo-Yo's today! The show is now over and after fifteen minutes the kids are lining up to buy their own Yo-Yo. I have my orange Yo-Yo so I don't have to buy one today.

I see Joanie coming out of the Candy Store holding a bright pink Yo-Yo and walking up to me.

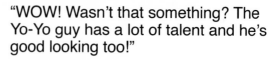

"WOW! Wasn't that something? The Yo-Yo guy has a lot of talent and he's good looking too!"

She pauses for a minute to look at the Yo-Yo guy again.

"Hey, Pepino, Jenny, and Frances are meeting me after dinner to play the Hot Potato game. We need two or three more players; can you come over with Jimmy Pizza to play the game with us?"

"Okay, but what in the Hell is a Hot Potato game?"

To tell the truth, I don't care what the game is all about as long as I get a chance to hang out with Jenny's friend Frances, any game is okay with me. Frances is so pretty to look at and when she laughs, I don't know why it just makes me feel good!

I am home now and having dinner with my family. We are all sitting around the dinner table with my father, who I barely see at the   dinner table when he's working full time. Eating pasta with beans and a little bread for dinner, I can't help but ask myself, "Is this it?" I don't think we will ever see a second dish of food until my father gets a steady job. My Dad is doing his best shaping up as a Day Laborer which is hit and miss for selection to work that day. Even though I'm still hungry I'll get up and go into our living room to finish my homework. When I finish my homework, I'll run downstairs like a bat out of Hell to meet up with Joanie. First, I'll go over to call Jimmy Pizza and

Nunzio-Superman to ask them to join us for the "Hot Potato" game. Joanie and her friends, Jenny, Frances, and Jeanette are on Joanie's stoop waiting for us.

"Hey, Joanie, I got some of my friends here with me to play that game you told me about.

Can you tell us how to play your stupid game?"

I only called the game stupid so that Frances will notice me. Joanie wrinkles her nose and says:

"It's NOT a stupid game! Jenny told me about this game the other day and I think it will be fun to play something new."

I'm not listening to Joanie because my eyes are on Frances, she has such a glow around her. Turning to Joanie I apologize.

"Okay, Okay, please tell us the rules of the game."

"Listen the rules are not that complicated. Hot Potato is a little like musical chairs. I bought this potato for me to start the game. We throw the potato from one player to another until the leader or caller says 'STOP!' The player who is left holding the hot potato at that time is 'OUT'. Then the leader will say 'START', we start throwing the potato at each other again until we hear 'STOP!' You guessed it, the one holding the "Hot Potato" is 'OUT'. We keep moving the game along until the only player left in the circle is declared the winner. Then we start a new game with all the winners and losers. It's possible for the winner of the first round to win several rounds. Now we first have to pick the leader or caller who will call out the 'START' and 'STOP' commands.

Okay, all the players are in a circle now. The leader is standing over there with his or her back to the group so that they can't see who is holding the "Hot Potato" as it goes around the circle. I will be the first leader or caller. After we finish playing this game six times we then gather the winner of each game for a playoff to find who will be the champion of the Hot Potato game.

Do you have any questions?"

Frances is raising her hand.

"Jenny, if you call out the commands for each game, when will you get a chance to play in the circle?"

Jenny is opening her eyes wide and smacking her forehead with her open hand.

"You're RIGHT! I forgot to say that when the first round is over and the first player out will replace me as the caller. Then I will have my chance to join you in the circle. Every time we start a new game the caller will be replaced by the first player or loser that has to step out of the circle. We'll keep playing until we get three different winners from the games played.

When that happens, we can then start the playoff game to see who is the "Champion".

I feel confused.

"I thought you said that this game was not complicated? I don't know how I can remember all these 'friggin' rules!"

Everybody is laughing, Jenny is raising her hand way up high yelling at me.

"STOP! You will see how easy it is once we get started."

We are calming down and forming a circle with Joanie holding the potato in her hand. Jenny is right; since we got into playing the "Hot Potato" game we are having a lot of fun. As we are throwing the potato from one player to another we are laughing louder and louder each time.

If a player drops the potato and it hits the concrete sidewalk hard, it will break into a million pieces, that's when we start to laugh like crazy people and we roll on the floor because we can't stand up any longer.

At this point, we'll have to stop playing so that Joanie can ask her Mom for some new potatoes for us to play with. Even though we smash three potatoes on the sidewalk, we managed to finish three games. I won the first game, Jenny won the second game and Frances won the third game. We three winners will go into a mini-circle to start the playoff game. Joanie is calling out the commands for the playoff to begin.

Jenny is out first and it is between Frances and me for the

224

championship round. I can't keep a straight face and neither can Frances. We are looking at each other and laughing again. This last championship round seems to be going on forever. I think that Joanie does it on purpose. As five or six minutes have now passed, Joanie finally yells: "Stop!" and I am holding the "Hot Potato" I stand there with a big grin on my face as I am watching Frances do her victory dance. Wow! This is great! We are all sitting down on the sidewalk, laughing and talking about all the screw-ups. We are all wiped out, and I never thought that the "Hot Potato" game would have so much action. I'm leaving the gang sitting here and I will go home to crash on my cot for the night.

Chapter 56
Pez Dispenser-Columbus Day Parade

Getting up late this morning I'm feeling great that we are off from school on Monday because of the Columbus Day celebration. I don't have any plans for this long weekend so I'll just sit around a while and wait for some of my friends to call me for some street games. I'm day-dreaming about playing the Hot Potato game with Frances yesterday. I had such a great time. I hope that I get to hang out with Frances again. I don't know why, but it's a magical feeling when I see her. She is so pretty, she has a beautiful smile. I love to hear her laughing and she smells great too! As I sit here in the kitchen looking out into the backyards through the window seeing all the clotheslines, I hear two loud bangs on the water pipe.

I'm jumping off the windowsill waking up from my day-dream wondering what in the Hell is all this banging about? I realize now that it must be Roger the Professor calling me to come up to his apartment. No one in our apartment building has a telephone. So, if you're not close enough to ring our doorbell or knock on our door you have to call the public telephone in Defonte's sandwich shop on the ground floor of our building. Then Danny Defonte, or one of his brother's will answer the telephone, walk into our hallway, ring our doorbell and yell for us to come downstairs because we have a phone call. It is a great system for my Mom and Dad to keep in touch with our family and friends except that they can only call us when the store is open for business. If Danny and his family are busy making sandwiches they don't have the time to pick up the phone so it will ring and ring with no answer.

So, Roger came up with this great idea of calling me or me calling him by banging on the water pipes in the kitchen. Two bangs on the water pipe mean that he wants to see me. Three quick bangs on the water pipe mean that it is an emergency alert and to rush up to his apartment immediately. The emergency alert signal means that there is a "Fire" in the building or that someone is sick and

Phone Booths In Defonte's Store

needs help.

It's a great system for the most part except when Roger gets it into his head to break my balls! Roger sometimes bangs on the water pipe with a butter knife three times; I rush up to his place like a maniac, only to find him laughing his ass off. It is just another false alarm. When I realize what he is doing to me, I curse him out and call him an asshole. This time, I hear the two taps on the water pipe and I walk up to his apartment. The door is open once again, so I walk in and find him sitting on the couch with his black cat on his lap. He notices me standing there:

"Hey, Roger, what's up? I hope that this isn't another one of your bullshit signals."

He's holding up his hand smiling.

"No, no, I just want to show you my new candy Pez Dispenser. I got it from crazy Joey Hook-Nose yesterday. This sucker is really neat!"

He holds this contraption in his hand; pressing down on what looks like a trigger with his thumb.

"Here, have a mint!"

I've never seen anything like it; it is like magic when I see this little mint pop out. So, I take the mint and put it in my mouth.

"Wow; what a neat contraption. I've never seen anything like it before. Why would Joey Hook-Nose give you this new candy dispenser?"

Roger is laughing out loud.

"Well, do you remember the Red Ryder BB gun I conned him out of? Joey really missed shooting it. He came over the other day and asked me if he could borrow the gun so that he could shoot some targets in his backyard. I told him no, that if he wanted to shoot the BB gun it would cost him ten cents a shot.

Joey is broke so he is pulling out this Pez dispenser.

"Here, I'll give you a mint for every shot."

"When I see this Pez dispenser I almost lose my cool! I say to myself: Shit, I want this contraption! So, I tell Joey, no, you can't shoot my BB gun for mints. He looked so disappointed and stupid holding the Pez dispenser offering me a mint. After Joey

Good & Plenty Movie Treats Taste Better

puts his head down I make him a counteroffer. I tell him that he can shoot as many BB's he wants to for a half hour if he gives me the dispenser. Joey put his head down again and gives me the Pez dispenser. So now I can offer you a little mint by pushing down on this lever, here; Take one."

I can't believe that Roger conned Joey Hook-Nose again. I'll take a mint and put it in my mouth. The taste is OK, but not as good as the Good n' Plenty mints. I leave Roger sitting on his couch petting his Cat.

When I get to my apartment I find my sister, Isabella, sitting at the kitchen table cleaning vegetables for my mother.

"Hey Sis, did you ever see a Pez dispenser? Roger showed me his 'Captain America' Pez Dispenser and gave me a mint. I can't get over how this contraption spits out a mint every time you push down on the lever."

"Yeah, but the dispensers I've seen are not jazzed up with the head of a superhero. They are kind of plain looking. They sell them in the candy store next to the cigars and cigarettes. A lot of women and men buy them to freshen their breath after they finish a smoke. I hear that someone in Europe, I think in Austria, invented the contraption because he was sick and tired of his wife bitching about his bad breath after he finished smoking a cigar."

I just stand there as she finishes her story about the Pez Dispenser and I think to myself; Wow, my sister knows a lot of shit.

She is looking at me again-

"You know it's Columbus Day on Monday, right?"

I'm just shaking my head up and down.

"My girlfriend Frances and I plan to go to the big Italian-American Parade in Manhattan on Monday. Frances is taking her little sister Mary Jane with her. Do you want to come along?"

"Huh? Yeah, I hear so much about the parade. My teacher told us all about Christopher Columbus discovering America and all. It will be great to see the celebration. I want to see and hear the marching bands, see all the big Italian mucky mucks marching with the Governor, and the Mayor waving American and Italian flags, instead of seeing pictures about the parade in the newspaper. I can't wait to go to the parade with you."

My sister is smiling.

"Okay, we have to get up early on Monday morning and take the D train to Manhattan so that we can get a good spot along Fifth Avenue."

I'm thinking to myself: Columbus must have been a little crazy to go to Spain after the Italians told him that he was nuts. At that time, everyone thought the world was flat and that Columbus and his ships would fall off the Earth when he got to the edge of the world. The Italians just laughed at him, no one would give the crazy guy the money to find a new route to Asia.

So, he packed all his maps and went to Spain. Just like Roger, Columbus conned Queen Isabella of Spain with a promise to bring back lots of gold, silk, and spices from Asia. So, she gave him the money and ships to find a new way to Asia. Maybe she wanted a new silk wardrobe, after all, she was the Queen of Spain. Well, my teacher says that Columbus never got to Asia. Columbus and his three ships didn't fall off the earth, and they did find North America in 1492. Queen Isabella took a long shot at this nut from Italy and she won big time. She didn't get her new silk wardrobe, but over the years she got lots of gold that made Spain the richest country in Europe.

What a story, you can't make this stuff up. I'm thinking how Columbus discovering America is such a big deal for the Italian-Americans, after all, but the Italians blew him off when he asked them for the money to buy the ships and supplies he needed for the trip. That's why he went to Spain in the first place. I'm thinking, why they don't call this parade the Queen Isabella Spanish American Day Parade. Well, there must be a lot of Italian-Americans like Roger out there who say Columbus is an Italian and it's only right to make a

Columbus Looks At Asia But Finds America

parade to honor him and all Italian-Americans. Who's complaining?

Not me, I'm going to the parade on Monday.

Chapter 57
Columbus Day-Ring Around The Rosie

Monday morning has arrived and last night I could hardly sleep laying here in bed with excitement thinking that my sister, Isabella, is going to take me to the Columbus Day Parade today!

I'll get dressed and go sit in the kitchen to wait for my sister. It's 6:00 AM and my father has already left for work around 5:00 AM this morning. My mother and sister are still sleeping, so, I'll just sit here at the kitchen table with my hands folded just like I would in my classroom at PS 27. I'm dozing off and after a while jump out of my chair when my sister finally walks into the kitchen.

"Hey, Pepino, are you ready? It looks like it's going to be a perfect day for a parade!"

I'm still dazed, so I can't say anything. I'm just rubbing my eyes trying to wake up. My sister puts together some apples, bread, jelly, and cookies for lunch. This way we will have something to eat while watching the parade.

She places our food in a shopping bag and we leave our apartment to meet my sister's girlfriend Frances. We are meeting Frances and her little sister Mary Jane on the corner of Luquer and Hicks Street. All of us are walking now to the subway station, and while walking I am watching Mary Jane and thinking

Smith & 9th Street Station

to myself, 'Wow!' with her bright red hair and blue eyes she looks more Irish than Italian. Maybe her grandmother has some Irish blood in her. It doesn't matter because she is Italian now.

The Smith and 9th Street subway station is about five blocks away. It's a cool day so the long walk to the subway station isn't so bad. We are at the station in fifteen minutes and taking the escalator up, about eight stories, to the outside subway platform to catch the D train to Manhattan. It is the highest station in the NYC subway system, at eight stories high!

The train pulls into the station and the doors open and it is packed with people. They all look Italian and you can see that they are excited and looking forward to celebrating their Italian heritage in the name of Christopher Columbus. We are pushing our way into the subway car and can't find a seat because the car is so crowded. Standing as we hold on to a pole all the way to Manhattan, I don't think that it is that bad standing on this train; at least we have a pole to hold on to. The train leaves the station heading into Manhattan and I'm thinking about our subway ride to Coney Island last summer. On that hot 90-degree summer day, we squeezed our way into the subway car with a bunch of towels, two blankets, food and whatever, heading for the beach.

The D Train Subway Trip To Coney Island

When we struggled and pushed our way into the subway car, we didn't need a pole to hold onto because there was no way we were going to fall down.

We are like sardines in a can. We even smell like rotten Sardines, I keep thinking about the heat, sweat, weird smells with my face smashed against somebody's butt for almost an hour back in July. It gave me a sick feeling and I almost threw up just before we got to Coney Island. All of a sudden the D train pulls into the forty-second street subway station, Wow, that was a quick ride! The doors are open and we push our way out of the subway car along with a bunch of Italian families with screaming kids. We all run up the steps to the street, where everybody is rushing to find a good spot on the sidewalk to see the parade.

We have managed to find our spot on Fifth Avenue near Forty-Seventh Street. It is like being in the crowded subway car all over again. It is great though, I love seeing the people marching with flags, dancing, loud music playing, seeing the floats with pretty Italian girls dressed up in costumes and to top it off I get a glimpse of our governor, Thomas E, Dewey, walking with the New York City Mayor, William O'Dwyer. Even though they are both Irish they seem to fit in with all the Italians marching with them. It isn't easy for me to see them, I'm short and skinny and there are two or three people standing in front of me on the sidewalk. To get a view of all the marchers and festivities on the street I'll keep pushing myself in between the people in front of me and jump up and down. It isn't a perfect view but I am getting to see most of what is going on. I don't know how we are doing it but we do manage to eat lunch while being squished in the middle of the crowded sidewalk.

The parade is finally over and we are on the D train going back to Brooklyn. It is not as crowded on the train this time and we even find a couple of empty seats! I am very happy to be part of the Columbus Day Parade. It doesn't take long after I sit down in the subway car that I fall asleep. It seems like it takes just two minutes for us to get back to the Smith and Ninth Street train station.

"Pepinooo..., Pepino, wake up we're home!"

It is about 3:00 PM and we are at Columbia Street and say our goodbyes to Frances and Mary Jane. I'll thank my sister for taking me to the parade. She looks so tired as she is walking up to our apartment to take a nap. I sit down on the stoop of our building and close my eyes. I doze off for a couple of minutes when I hear a bunch of girls singing:

"Ring around the Rosie, A pocket full of posies. Ashes! Ashes! We all fall down!"

I'm opening my eyes seeing Joanie and six of her girlfriends singing this song over and over again. They are holding hands making a circle with one girl in the middle of that circle with her two hands covering her eyes. The girls making the circle dance around the girl in the middle of the circle and keep singing.

"Ring around the Rosie, A pocket full of posies. Ashes! Ashes! We all fall down!"

I think I'll get up from the stoop and walk across the street to watch this 'Rosie' game the girls are playing. I'm standing here with my arms folded watching them as they sometimes change which girl will stand in the middle of the circle with both hands covering her eyes. This is going on for almost a half hour now and they are alllaughing like crazy as they all sit down on the sidewalk looking at the girl in the middle who is still standing in the circle with her hands on her face. Joanie is turnings to me...

"Hey Pepino, do you want to play this game with us?"

"Well the way I see it, I'm the only guy standing here and there's no way I'm going to play this stupid game with a bunch of girls!"

233

The Black Plague Killed Millions Of People

As I'm telling Joanie that I don't want to play this game with them they are all standing up and surrounding me, laughing and pulling my arms.

"Let go of me! Let go of me! What's the matter with you, Joanie? Have you all gone crazy? What is it with this Rosie game you're playing?"

Now they are calming down and sitting on the sidewalk together.

"Yeah, Pepino, this IS a crazy game!

One of the girls heard about this game last week. She went to the Red Hook Public Library on Clinton Street near the community center to look it up in the Encyclopedia Britannica. Well, what she found was that this game is hundreds of years old. Kids made it up and started playing this game in England a long, long, time ago. There was a plague killing thousands of people in London, England, and no one knew how to stop this disease from spreading all over the place. Men, women, and children were dying left and right. There were dead bodies everywhere, people were dying every day. Every time someone died they put the bodies in the street! You can imagine the smell of all those rotting dead bodies lying all over the place. So they picked up as many bodies as they could, they put them on wagons and piled the dead bodies up in an open field to burn them. But burning the bodies did not stop the disease from spreading and killing more people. Many of the people who lived there started carrying flowers like posies to mask the smell of the rotting bodies in the streets.

Death was everywhere, no one really knows how or when the kids made up this game called "Ring Around the Rosie". You watch us play this game and you can see what it means. The song we sing, the circle we make and the dead person standing in the middle of the circle with eyes covered, the point of the game is that anyone could die. So if you're the last one in the circle falling down, then you take the place of the dead person standing in the middle of the circle. We think that the kids made up this game because they were afraid of dying themselves and they did their best to make fun of all the death around them. The

234

Children who came to America in Colonial times brought the game with them."

Joanie is telling me about how the kids in England made up this game, and I'm sitting here listening, with my mouth open.

"Holy Shit! Why didn't they all die?"

Joanie laughs because she knows I am scared out of my mind and is reassuring me.

"Remember, this took place hundreds of years ago. No one knows the real story but people say they found out that the rats were spreading the disease. So they killed as many rats they could find but people started dying in France, Spain, and Germany, and just about everywhere else in Europe. Then they found out why this disease, called the 'Black Plague', was spreading everywhere. A sailor noticed that the rats moved from place to place by climbing up the rope into the ship tied to the dock. When they got to a new seaport, the rats would climb down the rope when the ship docked again and brought the disease with them. That's how the rats moved from place to place. The sailors made special discs that were put on every rope to stop the rats from climbing on and off the ships. It took years for the people in England and Europe to stop this plague, which they did by killing all the rats they could find and keeping the rats from moving from place to place. No one knows the real number but the stories say that 25 million or more people died during this period of the Black Plague."

Joanie really freaks me out by telling me how these kids made up this freaking Rosie game hundreds of years ago. I know that thinking about this Rosie game is going to give me nightmares tonight. I can't shake this creepy feeling I have while walking home. I keep on hearing the girls sing that stupid song in my head over and over again. "Ring around the Rosie, a pocket full of posies, Ashes! Ashes! We all fall down!"

Chapter 58

Immigration-Religious Instructions-Cardinal Sin

Coming to America took a certain kind of courage. If an immigrant had a sponsor who could afford him the luxury of a place to temporary lay his head, and that of his family, and could feed and help find a job, he was a lucky one. Those who had nothing arriving here did so in a hostile environment. Not being able to speak the native language, unable to read the street and building signs took a great deal of planning and courage for a foreigner, especially one like an Italian, Pole, or Asian not understanding English. Where did they go, how did they navigate, looking for a shelter, food and hope?

The immigrants, who settled here earlier or the people born in America hated the new wave of immigrants. The hatred stemmed from the fact that because they had nothing when they set foot on shore, the newly arrived would work for very little money. This meant that there were fewer jobs to go around and the jobs competing for, paid the least. The new immigrants dragged everyone down with them. So, when they got off the boat at Elis Island no one put out a welcome mat for them.

It is taking a couple of days to get the "Ring Around the Rosie" song out of my head. I am spooked by the game and the history behind it. Sitting in my fourth-grade class at PS 27 this afternoon my teacher, Miss Kent is telling us about the settlers who came to America to make a better life for their families. The immigrants who came here at the end of the eighteen hundred's had to deal with all kinds of discrimination. First, the good news: you made it to America. Second the bad news: the streets are not paved with gold.

New Immigrants Come To America For Work

Suddenly, the school bell is ringing! Miss Kent is stopping the history lesson and asking the Catholic students to line up. At this moment, I don't know what is going on. NOW it comes to me, it's Wednesday and the Catholic students have one o'clock early release from school on Wednesday for religious instructions.

We are lining up to leave the building and will walk from PS 27 to Visitation Church for religious instructions to prepare to receive Confirmation. I hate the fact that we have to go to Visitation Church for this bullshit. The only lucky ones are the Catholic School students at Visitation Parochial School because they get to go home early to make room for public school students who have to learn about their religion. Don't get me wrong, I Love God, but I don't love the Nuns or the Brothers who teach us at the Catholic School. As I line up I feel a spitball hit me in the back of the head. I'm thinking to myself: "What the heck is this all about?" I turn and see my school chum, Frankie 'Coochie' Coo holding a straw in his hand! I like Frankie but he can be a big pain in the ass. So, I'll turn and give him the finger. There are too many teachers around for me to give him a smack in the head. But it's a different ballgame when we'll get outside the building; there are no teachers to see me kick his ass. Once we're out of the school building we're on our own, without any supervision. I wonder who thought up that great idea?

We start walking to the Catholic School and we cut through Coffey Park, which makes our trip a little shorter. Now is my chance to pounce on Frankie for the spitball attack! He is running way ahead of me because he knows what I have in mind. Meanwhile, it's like a mob scene in the park. Mostly the boys are attacking each other, fighting and rolling around in the grass. The girls are standing there with their arms folded laughing at the boys. We arrive at the Catholic School for religious instructions and we are all messed up! We're doing our best to find the books we lost when we were fighting. They are thrown all over the park. I haven't caught up to Frankie since he ran away from me like a bat out of Hell. But I will get him one day to even the score.

Walking into the Catholic School building, our clothes are disheveled. We have dirt on our faces, grass stains on our arms and clothes, and we look like we went through World War III. Walking into the classroom, our nun, Sister Mary Catherine, doesn't waste any time. She hits us with her ruler as she marches up and down the aisles between the desks to restore order. She always has a mean look on her face: dressed in her black habit and head cap she looks seven feet tall. Her habit covers her head and only has a white opening framing her face.

She wears big heavy black shoes that make the ground shake as she's rushing up and down the aisles. The large Rosary around her waist sounds and looks more like a chain. She keeps hitting us and shouting:

"You are all **DOOMED!** You are all going to Hell!"

Sister Mary Catharine Will Teach Us A Lesson

After three whacks with her ruler, I am feeling some serious pain. We all do our best to keep quiet, looking straight ahead, folding our hands and placing them on the desk in front of us. Every student in the classroom calms down and we do not dare to make a sound.

I turn a little to my right and see Frankie 'Coochie' Coo sitting at the desk next to me, looking like an angel. Oh Crap! How did he wind up next to me?" We don't have as-signed seats in Catholic School so this shit-head is sitting next to me just to make trouble. He knows that I can't look at him without laughing out of control. If I crack up laughing, Sister Mary Catherine will surely kill me with ten whacks of her ruler. Because of this laughing problem, at PS 27, Miss Kent assigned us to seats at the opposite end of our class-room because we can't stop laughing if we're next to each other.

Frankie knows that I'm dead! But I'm not going down alone since once he looks at me he can't stop laughing either. Sister Mary Catherine is doing her best to teach us our prayers, while I'm trying not to look at shithead. It takes every bit of self-control I have, not to look at him. I'm keeping my head low but I turn a little to the right, I can't help it; it's like a death wish. Out the corner of my eye, I see him doing the same thing, turning his head a little to the left. That's it! We laugh and laugh so hard we start shedding tears. Sister Mary Catherine runs at us swinging her ruler like a baseball bat. She hits me hard, two or three times, on my back and arms, I'm in such pain. My laughing tears change into crying tears. At the same time, she reaches over, and grabs Frankie's ear and drags him out of his seat, pulling him as he's screaming in pain, to a desk at the other end of the room. Frankie still has his arms raised to protect himself, but it doesn't do him much good. I can see that his ear is beet red with a little blood on his earlobe. Ouch! Better him than me. All the kids in the classroom are scared shit-less. Our classroom goes so quiet that you can hear a pin drop!

Sister has a mean look on her face again! She is walking to the front of the class, turning to look at us and keeps slapping the ruler in her hand, daring us to make a move. She then continues her lesson about the Catechism. Why should we learn all this stuff? It's a waste of time. When my mother drags me to Church every Sunday, I sit with her and I don't have a clue of what's going on. It's all Latin to me.

The only time I do understand anything is when the priest starts to explain the sermon in English. But most of the time our priest talks about the money the Church needs to pay the bills so they can do their good work. I'd rather be outdoors playing games with my friends. It is the end of the class and a priest has come into the classroom to give us a quick quiz on today's lesson. He is telling us not to sin, like cursing, disobeying your mother and father, not going to Church on Sunday, and eating meat on Friday and so on. He is warning us to watch out for the biggest sin of all when lightning will strike you dead on the spot and you will go right to Hell. This sin that you must avoid at all costs happens when you go into a Protestant Church or Mosque, Synagogue, Buddhist Temple, or whatever.

Then he gives us this weird look, points his finger at us and says in a deep voice, ***"You better listen to me or else."*** He scares the whole class to death. I hear this warning every time I go to religious instructions but I don't believe him. First, I don't feel that God would zap a bunch of kids to death and put them in the fires of "Hell" because God loves us.

Second, I was fixing my bike one day, when a little old man started waving me to come over. I looked around and I didn't see anyone else so I went over to him. He told me that he pulled the light cord too hard and it broke. He asked me to follow him into the building, and climb on to a platform to reach for the broken light cord and turn on the light for him. He said that he is just too old to climb up on to the platform himself. I walk into the dark building with him, and it is so dark that I can barely see anything; the old man feels for the platform with his hand and says:

"Here it is. Please step up on this platform and feel for the broken light string."

I'm now on the platform, find the light string and pull on it. The light goes on and there I am standing on the platform, holding the broken light string, adjusting my eyesight to the bright light. Well, when I finally see this big room clearly, I realized that I am standing on an altar in a Synagogue! I almost shit my pants while waiting for the bolt of lightning to hit me, and the Devil to pull me down into the fires of "Hell." You know what? It doesn't happen. I get off the platform and the old man, who is a Rabbi, is thanking me for helping him. He offers me a quarter as a tip for helping him. I say: "No thank you." My mother told me never to take money from older people who need your help. That's why I don't believe the priest's warning about the Cardinal Sin.

The religious instruction class is over. I hook up with my friend, Frankie 'Coochie' Coo, putting our arms around each other's shoulders and walked home together, laughing!

Chapter 59

View Master-Horn & Hardart

In the 1940's and 50,'s the World was on the cusp of major changes in technology. With that change as America recovered from the world war, television contributes to the development of a better life at home and a glimpse of the world to come.

Computers were slowly creeping into our lives without our realizing it, and suddenly, our old values and traditions would begin disappearing. We started to look back and see no more what we once took for granted.

Two icons of the period after the war that stand out are the View-Master and strangely enough, the Horn and Hardart automat that in New York City opened in 1912. The Horn and Hardart was a place to go for a cheap lunch, quicker than a diner for food and more efficient. It could be a place for a nickel pie after a movie, a quick cheap sandwich and cup of coffee. It filled out a date or two during the war years, disappearing from the landscape by the 1970's.

As a child and for many adults, the View-Master was a new toy borrowed from an old idea, the stereoscopic 3-D cards, transformed into discs of transparent color film that continued the 3-D experiences, taking us where TV and the movies didn't.

Both bring us back to that period in our lives that help us remember best our youth.

View-Master Comic
Books Are the Best

I'm sitting on the curb on Luqure Street after school, not doing much. It's Friday and I don't have any plans this weekend. Maybe I'll call my friend Jimmy Pizza and see if he's interested in going with me to see a movie tomorrow afternoon at the new Clinton movie house. It's quiet and I'm bored, none of my friends are on the street today. They're probably home doing their homework so they will be freed up to do whatever they want on the weekend.

No, not me, I'm too smart to waste a beautiful afternoon indoors. I'll just hit the books the last minute on Sunday night just before I go to bed. I'm so stupid, I always promise myself that I will and can do my homework late Sunday night and you know what? My plan never works out that way. Come Sunday, I try to do my history book assigned reading, my

View-Master Is A Great Way To Travel

math, memorize my spelling words and I never complete what I'm supposed to do. I always end up listening to Roy Rogers and Dale Evans on the radio and before you know it, I'm too sleepy to do any homework so I'll go to bed.

It's suddenly Monday morning, and my teacher Miss Kent is giving me all kinds of grief. That's because she doesn't believe any of the bullshit stories I'm telling her! She is yelling at me and calling me a lazy, stupid kid. I don't know what the hell is wrong with me. It turns out that my friends all seem to be a lot smarter than I am. Most of them hit the books as soon as they get home from school. Not me, if I don't make up a lame excuse, I am sitting around day-dreaming about all the important stuff I'll do when I grow up. I'm smart enough to know that I'm just kidding myself, but I'm too weak. I do the same stupid things over and over again.

Anyway, school is over and nobody's around except for that new Italian kid, Michael Fish, standing about twenty feet away from me facing the wall of my building, head-banging a soccer ball against the wall over and over again. He must really have a hard head. He never misses hitting the soccer ball with his head. I wonder if he gets a headache. Just as I am about to nod off I hear somebody calling me.

"Hey, Pepino, come over here, I've got something to show you!"

As I snap out of my daydream I am noticing that Joanie Pigtails and Joy across the street are sitting on Joanie's stoop. She is waving me to come to her with one hand and she is holding something black in her other hand. I'll wave back and walk over to meet her.

"Hi Joanie, what's that weird thing you're holding?"

She keeps looking into this thing like it's a pair of binoculars. She's holding it in one hand while she's moving something with her other hand. I keep hearing a: click, click, click sound as the index finger of her right-hand moves up and down.

"Hey, Joanie is that thing you're holding a new-fangled camera? I've never seen anything like it."

She starts laughing at me as she puts the thing in her lap.

"No stupid! It's a View-Master and I'm looking at 3-D pictures through these two eyeholes here. The pictures I'm looking at look so real, it's even better than looking at a movie!"

Now I'm excited and try to pull this thing away from her so that I can look into the eyeholes and see the beautiful pictures she's talking about. She pulls the View-Master close to her body, turning to block me from getting it.

"Uh, uh, not yet: I'm not finished flipping the pictures."

I'm standing there in front of her with my empty hands open like I'm ready to receive something.

"Okay for you Joanie, what are you some Prima Donna or something? When are you going to give me a chance to look at your pictures?"

She is continuing to look through the thing.

"Okay, you're such a big baby. Here, TAKE it; I don't want to see the Italian Prince, cry."

I take the View-Master from her and hold it up to my face. Joanie puts her hand over mine and is showing me how to flip from one picture to another. Wow! It's like magic; the 3-D pictures look so real! I feel like I'm in the photo and I can touch everything that I'm looking at. Joanie is right they're so beautiful.

"OK Pepino, give it back to me and I'll change the disc from the Scenic New York City to Batman."

I'm giving it back to her and she pulls out the disc I am looking at and slides the Batman disc in its place and gives the View-Master back to me. I'm looking into the friggin eyehole again and I can't believe what I'm looking at! The colors are so bright they jump out at me! Batman and the Joker look so real my heart starts pounding so hard and I think it's going to jump right out of my chest!

I've never seen anything like this before! We are enjoying her View-Master for about twenty minutes as Joanie's father walks out of the house. His name is Bruno, over six feet tall with a muscle build, dark complexion, black beady eyes that look right through you and has an ugly skull tattoo on his right arm with a pair of bloody scissors stuck in the skull's head, pushing out of one of its' eyes. It gives me the creeps looking at it.

He is one tough-looking Dude and he scares the shit out of me. He is calling out to Joanie:

"Hey, little girl, are you ready to go to Horn and Hardart with me?"

She is turning and looking up at him.

"Daddy, can Pepino come with us?"

My heart is really beating harder now and I'm thinking what in Hell is this Horn and Hardart thing they're talking about? If I go with them will I ever see my family again? I start shaking and hoping that Joanie's father says "No". But he islooking into Joanie's big brown eyes.

"Okay, I'll take the shithead with us since he did walk the dog for me when you were away."

At this point, Joanie's dad takes the dog and puts him in the house, as Joanie follows him putting the View-Master in the house for safekeeping. Mr. Bruno then locks the front door.

"Follow me; my car is parked around the corner."

We are turning the corner onto Columbia Street and there it is, a shiny green Packard hot rod, with painted bright flames shooting out on the front hood and each side of the car. I think I'm falling in love! We get in the car, Joanie sitting in front with her dad and me jumping into the back seat. He starts the car with a big roar and peels off like a bat out of Hell. Wow! Can this car move! It's like the cops are chasing us and we're racing to get away as fast as we can. It takes only ten minutes with Bruno's hot rod roaring all the way to where we're going. The roar of the engine and shaking over the cobblestones stop.

"We're here!" Joanie is yelling out:

We get out of the car and walk into Horn and Hardart. It's a very bright place that has tables and chairs to sit and eat with a big wall that has little squares that open when you put money into a slot next to the little doors. Each square has food in it that you can see through a window in each square. Bruno is walking up to a change booth giving a guy a ten-dollar bill and the guy gives Bruno ten dollars-worth of nickels.

Wow! I've never seen so many nickels. Bruno gives Joanie a handful of nickels; she turns to me and announces:

"Come on Pepino, follow me, I'll show you how we get some food out of these little boxes."

We are heading right for the dessert section, putting our nickels into the money slots, opening two little doors and take out two big slices of chocolate cake, one for each of us.

No sooner do we take our cakes out of the little squares and close the little doors, like magic, another cake appears in the same spots. I notice people eating everything from hot soup,

Pick Your Food & Open The Little Door

sandwiches, pork & beans, meat-loaf, mac & cheese, and chicken pies with all kinds of side dishes. Almost anything you can get at a diner you can get here. Mr. Bruno has a Ham and Cheese Sandwich with Coffee. This place looks like a diner but it's not really a diner, you don't give anyone your food order, you just walk up to the wall of little square doors and pick out what you want to eat.

When you take your tray to where the drinks are, get your knife, fork, spoon or whatever and go sit down at any table and eat. When you're finished, you put your empty dishes or coffee cups back on your tray and take it to a cleanup station.

We eat our desserts and Mr. Bruno finishes his meal. We leave Horn and Hardart, go back into Mr. Bruno's hot rod and rumble back home. We arrive back home and I thank Mr. Bruno and Joanie for taking me to Horn and Hardart and tell them I will be happy to walk the dog anytime Mr. Bruno needs me to.

Chapter 60

I Hate Wakes-Nunzio's New Television

I'm up this morning finding my sister, Isabella, at the kitchen table having a cup of espresso coffee with milk. I get my coffee and sit down next to her. I want to tell her all about Joanie's new View-Master and my trip with Joanie in her Dad's Hot Rod to the Horn and Hardart Automat on Fulton Street. But she looks kind of sad when I say "Good morning" to her.

"Why are you so sad this morning?"

"I'm upset because Mom got word that her best friend, Tessie, died suddenly last night."

My eyes are going wide and my jaw is dropping in shock.

"Oh, My God! What happened? Was she sick or something? I can't believe that Tessie passed away just like that!"

My sister is looking at me, searching my eyes.

"No, it wasn't just like that and YES, she was sick for months and Mom kept it from us."

I hear about people dying but this is the first time I know some-one that died who is close to our family. My sister puts her hand on my shoulder to calm me down. She tells me that there will be a wake at Tessie's house on Monday and the funeral Mass will be on Tuesday at Visitation Church. She leaves me in the kitchen staring down into my coffee cup. I hate wakes. I hate flowers. I hate to hear people crying. I don't want to go to the wake. Holy Shit! I feel sick to my stomach. I don't know what I will do to help my mother? Since I was a little kid my mother would take me with her to a wake for people I don't know. Most of the time, these wakes, are in a small room in a person's apartment. The open coffin is always in the middle of the room surrounded by tons of flowers. Everyone there is very sad.

There is lots of crying and here I am with my mother and other women dressed in black with their little children praying for the person who died. I can never look at a dead person. I close my eyes as I stand by my mother until it is time to leave. I am scared out of my mind the whole time we are at the wake. All I can think of is the strong smell of flowers and the ladies crying around me that makes it hard to breathe. I can't wait to get the

247

Hell out of here! The more I think about it the more upset I get.

My sister walks back into the kitchen, on her way out of the apartment, and she can see the confused look on my face.

"Don't worry there is nothing you can do right now. We will all go to the wake together on Monday. Just give mom a big hug when you see her tonight. Do me a favor, go to the bakery and buy a loaf of Italian bread before you come home for dinner tonight."

She gives me a quarter, for the bread and leaves the apartment to meet my mother. My sister and my mother will be at Tessie's house to help her family any way they can. My Dad isn't around, he is working all this weekend. I'll finish my coffee and I am moping around the apartment it seems. I'll pull myself together and go out to find my friends.

I'm turning the corner and going to Nunzio's house on Luqure Street. I'll knock on his door and no more than two seconds Nunzio is opening it, greeting me with a big smile on his face.

"Come in, come in, I have something to show you. You're not going to believe it."

I am now wondering what he's talking about! As I am walking into his apartment, Nunzio is walking backward and at the same time, he is waving his hands for me to follow him. It looks like he's
directing me to follow him into his parent's combination living room/dining room and he keeps saying:

Nunzio Has the Only Television
In The Neighborhood

"YOU'RE NOT GOING TO BELIEVE IT! YOU'RE NOT GOING TO BELIEVE IT!"

We get to where he wants me to go stand with his back in front of something, blocking my view. Nunzio is a big kid, that's why we call him: "Superman." it's almost impossible to see anything behind him. From what I can see, it may be one of those new radio record player units. He is
holding his two hands out like a crossing guard telling me to stop in my tracks!

"Nunzio, cut the bullshit! Just show me the friggin' thing!"

He finally steps aside so that I can see what he's hiding with his big body. He's right, I can't believe it. Wow! It's one of those new television boxes I've been hearing about on the radio. Everybody is talking about this movie box!

"Cut the crap! When did you get it? How much does it cost? How does it work? What did you watch on this thing?"

I keep asking one question after another like a detective on a radio crime show.

Meanwhile, Nunzio is laughing out loud as he's dancing around the room with his arms razed over his head. When he finally ends his celebratory dance he is telling me,

"I can't touch it. My Mom and Dad told me that they're the only ones allowed to turn it on and off at night. But it's great to watch people dancing, singing, cowboy movies like Roy Rogers and cartoons anytime you want."

He's rolling his eyes and confessing-

"I don't know what it costs, but I know that it must have cost my parents an arm and a leg to buy this thing! This television is new to us so it will take a while before I can invite you over to watch cartoons with me."

I think I'll stop asking Nunzio questions, I'll just stand there looking at his new television and imagining something is playing on the blank television tube.

Nunzio's excitement over his new television has snapped me out of my gloom about Tessie. For these moments anyway, I forget all about Tessie' wake. What a shocker it is to see my first television box! I never thought that anyone in our neighborhood could ever own one. We both stop looking at the blank television tube and go out to find our friends.

We walk towards Hicks Street and find Mikey Tomato sitting on the curb talking to Prospector Frank from Huntington Street.

"Yo, what are you guys talking about?"

"Nothing much, Halloween is coming up and Prospector Frank here is trying to talk me into making a lean-to so that we can camp overnight on Halloween in the vacant lot near his house on Huntington Street."

"Oh, yeah, no shit! Guess what I saw at Nunzio's house?"
"OK, Big Head, spit it out!"

I'm laughing and looking at Mike and Frank and motion my extended arms wider and wider and announce:

"Superman here just got a huge television box in his apartment about this big."

Prospector Frank, squints his eyes, wrinkles his nose looking confused.

"What in Hell are you talking about? What's a Tell-a-vision?"

"I guess you haven't heard that you can buy a box with a window that looks like a movie screen and they can send a movie to your house for you and your family to watch, with sound."

Frank has this weird look on his face and he looks like he is about to pass out!

"Come on, cut the bullshit. The next thing you're gonna tell me is that aliens are sending these movies from outer space, huh? Huh?"

I'm about to crack up.

"This is not bullshit Frank! I just saw my first television box in Superman's house two minutes ago."

Frank now is yelling:

"Holy Shit! What will they think of next? Maybe they'll put a guy in a rocket and shoot him to the Moon? How about that, Pepino?"

I don't think that Frank's brain can handle this stuff. We all start laughing and making up all kinds of stuff like:

"Yeah, like swimming across the Atlantic Ocean to England."

"Yeah, or how about camping in a vacant lot on Halloween night. Boooooo!"

"Yeah Frank, maybe you will be the guy they shoot up to the Moon."

That's it! Now we can't stop laughing after almost twenty minutes. Settling down we stop laughing making plans to meet the following weekend on Halloween for fun and games. I'll leave the guys on

Hicks Street and walk about six blocks to Cammareri Brothers Bakery on the corner of Henry and Sacket Streets.

My mother loves Cammareri Brothers Bakery. There must be ten bakeries within a five-block area. Some of the bakeries are on Union Street and some on Columbia Street, Henry Street, Court Street and a few more towards Atlantic Avenue. Every Italian family is loyal to a baker who came to America from their village in Italy. I like any kind of bread that I can dip in wine for breakfast, put Olive Oil on it for lunch or dip it in the pasta sauce for dinner. I'm getting hungry just thinking about it.

I have bought a loaf of bread and am heading home. It is still early so I'll leave the bread on the kitchen table and go up to the top floor to see what Roger is up to. As I walk into Roger's apartment I find he is working on a drawing for the carpet cannon we talked about months ago.

"Hey, Roger... I thought you maybe forgot about the cannon we wanted to make!"

"No, I didn't forget. It's been bugging me on how we can make a trigger that can shoot a square piece of linoleum that measures eight by eight inches. I think I'm close to solving the problem but I don't feel like making another drawing today."

So, I'll chim in and talk about all of my adventures.

I'm going on and on telling him about the View-Master, my visit to the Horn & Hardart in Bruno's Hot Rod, Nunzio's new television box, and our plans to camp out on Halloween. I can barely catch my breath. Roger looks amazed.

"Wow, you HAVE been busy the last couple of days!"

After talking with Roger for a half-hour about the new inventions he plans to work on, I'll say goodbye and go downstairs to see if my mother is home yet.

I find Mom sitting at the kitchen table shucking peas for dinner. I don't say anything; I walk up behind her and put my arms around her and hug her tight. She looks at me over her right shoulder and starts crying out of control as I hold her in my arms, tears welling in my eyes.

Brooklyn Bread Is Better Than Dessert

Chapter 61

Shoes On The Wire-Treasure Island

If you could condense the world into a smaller area, where every culture comes together, then you would be in New York City, where it exists. At the turn of the 20th Century the influx of immigrants from Europe and Asia began in large numbers, and by the middle of the century, New York with its five boroughs had just about every ethnicity there is. A new wave of immigration also became apparent, like a tidal wave that washed one group ashore from Europe, rolled out and brought in another from the Caribbean Islands and South America.

Old neighborhoods became enclaves for new immigrants, cultures, and havens for those who did not speak the language, just as they did once for the Italians, Greeks, Poles, and Germans who came before the Hispanic populations. They all eventually mingle and become a new fabric of the America Dream. Today, it truly is: "We the People."

I don't feel like doing much this weekend. My homework is due on Monday but no way will I spend an hour or two indoors on such a beautiful day. I'll just put it off until Sunday just before I go to bed. I finish eating my olive oil and tomato sandwich for lunch and go out to scout for some of my friends. I walk over to our usual hangout in front of 'Chickies' grocery store on Hicks Street. All is quiet and none of the guys are here, so I'll sit on the curb and wonder when Roger the Professor will finish his drawing for the linoleum firing cannon he promised to build for our war games. I'm daydreaming about the War Games and how we can kick ass with the new cannon, and spot Henry Black-face, Reno the Greeks brother, walking towards me. We call Henry "Blackface" because he has shiny greased black hair and his face, well, is darker than the black-top pavement covering some of the streets in our neighborhood.

Old Sneakers Hang On A Wire Near The Red Hook Projects

"Hey, Henry, what's up? Where is your brother Reno, and the rest of the gang?"

Henry shrugs his shoulders, putting out both hands.

"I don't know for sure. They may have gone to see that new pirate movie at the Lido Theater on Columbia Street, or they may have gone to check out those old sneakers and shoes hanging on the electric wires all around the Red Hook Projects?"

"What, shoes hanging on a wire? What the Hell is that all about?"

Henry sits next to me on the curb and gives me his take:

"Yeah, there are shoes hanging all over the place. They tell me that a lot of kids and teenagers who move into the new Red Hook Projects from their dilapidated tenements in the Bronx threw them up there. It turns out that they are mostly Puerto Rican families who can barely speak any English. The Puerto Rican Teenagers joined gangs in the Bronx and when they moved to Brooklyn they were still gang members."

"Okay, what do all these Puerto Rican gangs have to do with all these shoes?"

"Ha! That's the thing, there are all these new gang members now living in the new Red Hook Projects so now they want us to know that the Projects belong to them. That's why they mark their territory by hanging the old shoes and sneakers on the electric street wires around the Projects. Now we have to be careful not to wander into their territory because the shoes on the electric wires mark the borders of their territory. If you happen to cross their territory the PR gang members will ask you to pay a toll and if you don't cough up the money they will kick your ass and take your shoes."

"My shoes! What the friggin Hell is that all about?"

"Well, if you have a nice pair of sneakers, they will keep them for themselves. If your shoes are all worn out, they will throw them on the electric wires as a territory marker."

I am really getting mad now, I can feel my face turning beet red. I put my fist up to Henry's face and utter:

"Holy shit, who the Hell do they think they are? I want to kill those Bastards."

"Calm down. They may stake out a territory in the Red Hook

Projects but the stupid jerks don't realize that they're surrounded by Italians, Irish, Poles, Greeks and our Puerto Rican friends, like Six Fingers Ricardo Lopez and his family. That's why my brother Reno, Pecker and Jimmy Pizza went over there to check out the hanging shoes around the Projects that they now call little Puerto Rico."

"HAHAHA! I get it, so when these jerks come out of the Projects to shop for food, take a subway, go to a movie, or whatever, we will pounce on them. If they don't pay us to walk through our territory we will kick the shit out of them."

Henry agrees.

"You're right, The Italian teenagers are just as pissed off as you are. They put together a new gang with all our friends to fight these assholes. They call themselves, 'The Dukes', and our gang is called 'The Midgets'. The older teenagers will do the fighting and we will help them get chains, bats, rocks, knives, zip guns or whatever they need to fight these guys."

I'm thinking to myself when the Hell did all this happen?

Here I am sitting and thinking about kids playing war games but these things that Henry Blackface is talking about will be a real war
between the Puerto Ricans living in the Red Hook Projects and the Italians living in the neighborhoods around them! I have to go see these freaking hanging shoes for myself. I'm all pumped up and ready for battle, but to tell you the truth, I'm scared too! This could be a real bloodbath. I think that Henry can see right through me. He can see that I am pissed off and scared at the same time as he says:

"Forgetaboutit, don't get your balls all twisted. When these guys get back from scouting the Projects, we'll have to have a pow-wow about all this shit. There's nothing going on here right now so why don't you come with me to the library on Clinton Street. I want to get a book about Treasure Island."

I agree and get up from the curb, walking with Henry to the library about four blocks away.

As we are getting closer to Clinton Street we can see a group of young girls walking towards us with books in their arms. They are laughing and talking to each other and they look so happy toting all these books home to read. I can't believe that they can read all the books they are carrying. I have no interest in reading a book. I have to read history books when I'm in school because my teacher Miss Kent tells me to. Some people, like Blackface Henry, read for fun, that's why he's so smart. He always gets high grades in all his subjects. I wish that I could be that smart too. That's why I tag along with Henry to the Library because I hope that some of the reading he does will rub off on me. The girls with the books pass us and I turn and walk backward next to Henry as I'm looking at them.

"What's the secret about reading a book? You seem to like it so much when for me, reading is hard work. That's why I never finish reading a book, ever."

I'm still walking backward next to Henry when he suddenly gives me a quick smile.

"You know, for me, reading is like breathing. I always think everyone can do it like I do. But my brother Reno has a hard time reading too! I tell him to go to the Library and look for a book with lots of pictures and pick a subject of fun stuff he likes. The book could be about cars, trains, boats, animals, or anything that he would like to learn about. It'll be like reading a comic book because the subject doesn't matter. That's why I'm going to the library today to get a storybook about Treasure Island. I like adventures, any adventure sparks my interest. I like Treasure Island so much I read it again and again, I love it!"

A Bunch of Girls Walking Home From The Library

Turning around I am walking side by side next to Henry facing forward once again.

"Come on, how can, you love a book so much?"

Henry's eyes are opening wide as he is looking at me.

"To me reading the book Treasure Island is like going to a movie. No, it's better than seeing a movie because I feel like I'm there sailing the high seas with pirate Captain Long John Silver and the young boy-cook he saved from being killed, Jim Hawkins. They go off together like partners with a treasure map to find a hidden treasure on some island. They face all kinds of danger because the pirates want to kill them both and keep the treasure for themselves. It's a great story." As Henry is telling me the Treasure Island story I feel like I'm in the story with the characters. We walk into the library and he is telling me that he reads every adventure story before he sees the movie because most of the time the book is better than the movie. Henry finds his book and leaves me to the library by myself. I'll keep looking at all the books to see if I can find one that reads like a comic book. As I am going through these different books I notice a funny thing: you know what? I don't know why but I like the smell of all these books around me. I don't want the Treasure Island storybook Henry talks about because it only has a few pictures in it. I'll wait until I get better at reading books without too many pictures. So, I'll get this book about the ocean and river steamboats that has lots of colorful pictures in it. I hope that someday I can read a book like Henry does so I can see and feel the action in the adventure stories the way he can.

Chapter 62
Making A Zip Gun-Drive In Movie

I go home with a steamboat picture-book that I borrowed from the public library on Clinton Street. As I am walking into my apartment building on Columbia Street I am upset about the things Henry Blackface was telling me about the Puerto Rican gangs that moved into the Red Hook Projects from the Bronx. It's like an invasion into our Italian neighborhood. It wouldn't be so bad if the new kids that moved in from the Bronx wanted to get to know us. But when they start to hang shoes on the electric wires all around the Red Hook Projects to mark their territory, it really pisses me off. So instead of going into my apartment on the second floor, I walk up another flight to find Roger the Professor to see if he knows anything about this shit.

I noticed walking into Roger's apartment his little sister Diane sitting on the couch playing with their cat Misty.

"Hi Diane, is your brother Roger around?"

She is looking up at me as she continues petting the cat on her lap.

"Yeah, my shithead brother is in the back room working on one of his new inventions."

As I'm walking into the back to Roger's room I'm thinking about why Diane is mad at her brother. Sometimes she gets mad at Roger when he doesn't stop working on his project to build her a toy, doll house or anything she wants when she wants it. Diane is so spoiled; I guess that happens when you're the baby in the family. Sometimes my older sister feels left out when my Mom treats me like a little Italian prince. Diane will not stay mad at Roger too long because he does what she wants most of the time and she knows it. As I walk into Roger's room I can see all kinds of stuff on his workbench. He's sitting back in his chair, with his eyes closed, with his hand holding his chin, thinking.

"Hey, Roger, do you have a minute, I want to tell you about all the shit that's going on in the Red Hook Projects."

Roger jumps back a little, as he open his eyes like he is waking up from a dream.

"Huh! Pepino, what the Hell are you talking about?"

Rattling off all the shit Henry Blackface told me about the shoes hanging all over the place, about the Puerto Rican gangs from the Bronx, and the money they want us to pay them, I'm talking so fast that I can, barely catch my breath

At this point, Roger is holding up his hand and exclaiming:

Roger's Work Bench Has Everything Ready To Make A Zip Gun

"Stop, I know all about it, that's why I'm sitting here trying to figure out how to make a zip gun. Our gang, the Dukes, need all the help they can get if and when we have to rumble with the Puerto Rican Killer Sharks gang from the projects."

I think to myself: holy shit, a zip gun? That thing can kill somebody. I asked Roger:

"How far did you get? How does it work? How many guns will you be making?"

Roger holds up both hands palms out and says:

"Whoa, Whoa, hold on, one thing at a time! You can make a complicated zip gun from a cap pistol which can take about two weeks or you can make a simple wood zip gun that will take about two hours to assemble once you have all the material. Take a look at the stuff on my workbench and you can see that I plan to make the wooden zip gun from these parts. I'll show you how I plan to do it. First, I make a piece of wood in the shape of a gun, some guys even decorate the handle but I don't have time for that. Then I get an old car radio antenna, a toy cap pistol, lots of tape & rubber bands. When I have all the material I go to work, I cut and tape one of the metal tubes from the antenna that has a 22mm diameter; about eight inches long and tape it to the top of the wooden pistol. Then I break apart an old metal cap pistol to get at the hammer. Then I grind the back end of the cap pistol hammer to a very sharp point. When that's complete I assemble the hammer to the back end of the wooden pistol with rubber bands and make sure that the sharp point of the hammer goes directly into the opening of the antenna cylinder. Now the zip gun is ready to shoot.

To shoot a 22mm bullet you pull back the hammer, place the bullet into the cylinder, release the hammer slowly to see if it can strike the back of a 22mm bullet. If everything looks okay you hold the gun with one or both hands, pull back the hammer as far back as possible with your thumb, point the gun at your target and release the hammer. When you release the hammer the sharp point on the hammer will strike the back of the bullet with enough force to fire the 22mm bullet with a BANG at the target or person you're aiming at. If you're shooting at a person who is charging at you with a baseball bat, you better hit him or he will crack your skull open. Because if you don't hit the guy with the bat, it takes about a minute to reload your zip gun and you will not have enough time to run away to save yourself. Sometimes the guys who shoot the zip gun set up a two-man team with two guns so that one gang member shoots while the other guy loads a bullet into the second gun. Two guys can cut the reload action down to thirty seconds.

Any questions?"

As Roger is going through this whole thing about how to make and shoot a zip gun I'm looking at him with my eyes and mouth wide open in wonder.

I just can't believe that he is telling me how his zip gun can kill somebody. I want to close my mouth but I can't!

"Roger, what the fuck, are you crazy? How can you make this thing when you know it can kill another kid? Roger is standing up with a weird look on his face and starts screaming at me.

"YOU BET IT CAN KILL SOMEBODY. IF THESE PIECES OF SHIT FROM THE BRONX THINK THAT THEY CAN WALTZ INTO OUR NEIGHBORHOOD AND TAKE OVER, THEY BETTER BE READY TO FIGHT TO THE DEATH."

I won't say anything because I can see that he has thrown all reason out the window and that there is no way I can change his mind. So, I'll turn around and leave Roger in his room with a weird look on his face and spit running out of his mouth down to his chin. I've never seen Roger so mad.

Walking down to my apartment I can smell a strong odor of cigar smoke in the hallway. It must be a White Owl cigar. That's the only brand my Mom's cousin smokes, I always know Uncle

Frank is visiting from New Jersey as soon as I step into the hallway and take a whiff of his strong cigar. He is the only one in our family who made it big. Uncle Frank is a hard-working, smart, honest, man. He set up a little construction company in New Jersey and makes lots of money.

He met and married a Dutch girl who is just as nice as my Uncle. They settled in a small town in New Jersey in a big white house with a piano and have lots of kids. Even though he has money he never looks down on the many Italians who have less than nothing. He comes to Brooklyn every now and then to check up on my mother who is his favorite cousin. The story he tells us every time he comes to visit is that he and my mother grew up like brother and a sister in Mola di Bari, Italy and to this day they are still very close. My mother doesn't say much but I know when my father could not find work for weeks on end, all of a sudden, Uncle Frank shows up and we have food on the table. He is such a bubbly friendly man and to top it off he drives a big ass, Buick! No wonder he made it big in the construction business. I just can't wait to see him.

Drive-In Movie Car Speaker

As I walk into our apartment, Uncle Frank grabs me and gives me a hug and kiss with his smelly cigar mouth. I love him so much. He always knows what I want; he pulls out his car keys, smiles and gives them to me.

"Don't go tracking any dirt into my new Buick when you pretend to drive it."

Wow a new Buick, the old Buick was only six years old. I run downstairs and have no trouble finding his new car because it's the only one on the block.

After pretending to drive for fifteen minutes I see Uncle Frank, my Mother, and sister walking out of our apartment building. Uncle Frank comes to the driver's side opens the door and orders:

"Scoot over; we're going to the movies."

Hmmm… this is not normal that we're all going to the

Clinton Theater to see a movie. We drive past the ferry landing to Staten Island, past Coney Island, where are we going?

"Uncle Frank, how far is the movie house you're taking us to?"

"It's not that far now, we can drive right into the theater when we get there because it's outside and we can park and watch the movie sitting in the car."

Drive-In Movie Theater.

Holy shit, this is my first trip to a drive-in theater. We get there in five minutes, Uncle Frank pays the admission, and we park the car and put the speaker contraption in the car window. Then Uncle Frank walks over to a building and comes back with candy, popcorn, and drinks for everyone.

We watch the Ten Commandments. What a treat it is to see a movie from Uncle Frank's car! I can't wait to tell Pecker, Jimmy Pizza, and Mike Tomato all about my trip to the drive-in movie, it is going to blow them away, that their big shot friend drove into the theater in a new Buick to see a movie. I love it...

Chapter 63

Portable Radio-Red Woolworth Diner

I had a great time and lots of fun going to the drive-in movie theater with my Uncle Frank yesterday. He dropped us off at home and told my mother that he will come to visit again in two to three weeks. He would like our family to spend a weekend at his home in New Jersey. He says that he will call us ahead of time so that we can pack with a change of clothing and pajamas for our weekend sleepover. He explains that he will pick us up in his new Buick, drive our family to his home in New Jersey and drive us back to Brooklyn Sunday night. I am so excited about going to Uncle Frank's home and spending time with his family. The last time we went to New Jersey was over six months ago. It was like a big party with lots of food, wine and all kinds of desserts, we played baseball, picked wild strawberries, went hunting for frogs in a brook that ran through his property, I even played the piano. All the adults sat around smoking cigars or cigarettes and eating, drinking homemade wine, and telling family stories.

Typha Plant Also Called Cattail Or Punk Burns Slowly Like A Cigar

The air is nice and clean there, not like the smog we breathe in Brooklyn from the trucks and factories all around our neighborhood. The only smoke I suck in New Jersey is the smoke from the campfire we make late at night to roast marshmallows and light up the Cattails we find growing in the woods. When we light up the Cattail or 'punk', it will burn with a slow glow to it and the kids pretend they are smoking a cigar. I asked my sister, who seems to know everything, about the Cattail plant and why do kids call it a 'punk' when it was lit up and glowing like a cigar. She tells me:

"Well, the Cattail plant you're talking about is called a 'Typha' plant that grows like a weed all over the world. People use this plant for decoration, some people cook and eat it, others use it for building material for constructing a hut or some people weave the leaf into baskets or burn it like incense to keep

263

insects away. The kids who burn it and call it a punk are just using a slang term they made up, pretty much like a nickname. I think the punk word started when they lit a slow-burning Cattail so they could light fireworks one after another instead of using a bunch of matches."

Wow, that was more complicated than I thought it would be! Big deal, so now I know what a Cattail plant is. We are finally in bed and all the kids sleep together and tell stories before falling asleep. It is like a vacation because I can never do all this stuff in our dirty cobblestone streets or the vacant lots in Brooklyn. Uncle Frank left late last night for his trip back to New Jersey. It's going to seem like forever now that I have to wait about three weeks before he comes back to take our family to his home. I think the wait is going to make me crazy. But I could not help but wonder if Uncle Frank helped my mother pay some bills and gave her some money for food before he left because I can see a calm look come over my mother's face. My mom could never tell my father that she accepted some help from Uncle Frank. My Dad is too proud to accept any help from anyone. In his way of old world thinking, doing so, meant, that he failed to support his family. Which is totally unacceptable.

I'm out this morning looking for someone or anyone I can tell about my trip to the drive-in movie in my Uncle Frank's new Buick. I can't find any of the guys hanging out on the corner to talk to so I walk back to Columbia Street and noticed Pick-tail Joanie sitting on her stoop holding something to her ear. Oh, well, it's better than no one, so I go over to see what she is doing. I get closer to her and I can hear her singing! She doesn't notice me, so I ask:

"Hey, Joanie, what the Hell do you have stuck to your ear?"

She keeps singing like she doesn't notice me standing right in front of her. So, I'll yell out:

"HEY JOANIE! Wake up girl."

I can see that she is surprised to see me standing there. She jumps and drops whatever it is she is holding on her lap. I'll bend down and take a closer look at this small box she dropped because I can hear music coming out of it!

"What the Hell is this thing?"

"Listen Pepino, next time, don't YELL at me. You scared the shit out of me. I couldn't hear you, to begin with, because I am listing to music from my new portable radio!"

"This little thing is a radio? How the Hell can they do that? How can they get those big radio tubes into this little box? Where is the electric wire to light it up? How did you plug it into the electricoutlet? How do you turn it on? How do you change stations?"

I am amazed; I can't believe that this little box is a radio! Even before I can finish my questions Joanie is laughing so hard that tears were coming out of her big brown eyes. All she can say is:

"It's not from outer space shithead. My dad gave me this portable radio for my birthday, stupid. You don't have to plug it into an outlet for electric power because it works on battery power. It's almost like a car radio but much smaller! I don't know how they squeeze all those radio tubes into it but as you can hear it works just fine. It has an 'off' and 'on' tuner and you can also adjust the volume with the same dial. The bigger dial here you can turn to find a radio station you like. So that's the story, shithead, do you have any more stupid questions?"

Now, I'm standing in front of Joanie with my mouth wide open. I see it with my eyes but I still can't believe I hear music coming out of this little box called a portable radio. I think that my drive-in movie story is great but this portable radio is way better. I want a radio like that one too!

I am sitting next to Joanie on her stoop and she is turning off the radio. She looks at me and listens when I start talking to her about the shit that's going on in the Red Hook Projects, the possible gang war with the Puerto Ricans from the Bronx, the shoes hanging all over the place, the zip gun Roger is making, my Uncle Frank's visit and the drive-in movie. She is so interested in everything I tell her.

"Wow, I don't know what to say, the thing about the projects scares me because we have to go to school with those guys. But at least you had some fun at the drive-in movie with your Uncle Frank. You have to put the gang war thing out of your mind for now, so why don't you have breakfast with me and my father at the Woolworth

Cafeteria?"

The last thing I expected was Joanie's breakfast invitation. I don't know that Woolworth the famous five and dime store has a cafeteria! I'm at a loss for words but I have a reflex action.

"Sure, I would love to go to Woolworth with you but I'm flat broke and even if I had the money I wouldn't know how to get there." Joanie starts to laughing again and says:

"Don't worry about that, my dad will take us to Woolworth in his new hot rod and has enough money to buy us breakfast."

Holy shit! I suddenly get this chill running up and down my spine. If I make a wrong move Bruno could break me in two with one hand. I'm more afraid of Bruno than facing three Puerto Rican gang members charging at me with baseball bats. With my voice trembling:

"Oh, oh, okay. I'mm ver veery ha haappy to goo ooh with you."

I think she can hear that I'm not exactly thrilled about having breakfast with her father. She holds my hand and says: "Don't be scared, my father is a pussycat."

As soon as Joanie finishes talking, Bruno steps out of the house with all his muscles, killer bike tattoos and stands directly over us. He spots me sitting next to his daughter, and says,

"Hey baby, are you ready to go? Please don't tell me that this shithead is honing in on our breakfast just like he honed in when we went to the automat couple of weeks ago?"

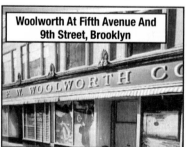

Woolworth At Fifth Avenue And 9th Street, Brooklyn

"Come on Daddy, why can't I take a friend with me? Remember the dog sitting he did for you? He was there when we needed him to take care of Joy, right?"

He is grabbing the huge key ring from his belt.

"Okay, okay, it looks like I'll be paying for him walking our dog for the rest of my freaking life. Let's go, I'm hungry."

We are all walking together around the corner to Columbia Street. Bruno walks up to a wooden gate on the sidewalk and unlocks a padlock, takes the chain off the doors and swings the gates open. I look at the lot and I see Bruno's new hot rod sitting there with a paint job that gleams like a mirror. Holy shit, I thought Uncle Frank's new Buick was something special. But Bruno's Hot Rod is like I died and went to Heaven. His new car is beautiful! We all get in the car, Joanie is sitting in the front with her father and I am sitting in the back smelling the new leather seats.

Bruno starts the engine and we rumble over the cobblestone streets up Hamilton Avenue to Fifth Avenue and Ninth Street. He parks the car and we walk about a block to a new Woolworth. We all sit at the counter, Bruno, Joanie and me. I want to order everything on the menu, but I wait and followed Joanie's lead. Bruno orders steak and eggs, potatoes, toast and black coffee. Joanie selects scrambled eggs with bacon and a glass of milk, I order the same as Joanie. All my food is delicious. Joanie and I finish first and while Bruno is still eating, we get off our stools and walk around the store looking at all the stuff they have on display. I don't know how they can keep track of all this shit. Woolworth is so clean that I feel that I can wander around the place for hours. We hear Bruno calling out in a very loud voice:

"HEY, GIRL! WHERE THE HELL, ARE YOU? LET'S GET OUT OF THIS PLACE. I HAVE TO MEET A GUY ON SOME BUSINESS!"

We rush over to meet him. We all walk over to the car and drive home. When we get home, it is still early. I thank Bruno and Joanie for treating me to breakfast at Woolworth and tell them that I'm always ready to help out with the dog, whenever they need me.

Saying goodbye and I walked to our hangout on Hick Street to find a few of my friends.

Chapter 64
Garrison Belt-Long John Silver

I'm at our gang's hangout on Hicks Street, I see Reno the Greek sitting on the curb. He is moving his arms back and forth scraping a belt buckle on the curb's stone. What in the Hell could he be doing? I'm getting closer to him but he's not stopping! Reno is scraping this big belt buckle like he is possessed by the Devil. I am watching this for a few minutes now.

"Hey, Reno, WHAT in the HELL are YOU doing?" He's stopping his scraping and is looking up at me.

"I'm getting ready for the gang war. When my brother, Henry told me all about those new kids who moved into the Red Hook Projects and all the shit they want to pull, I got blind with hate. All I can see is "RED" and I want to walk into the projects and beat the shit out of them. Who in the hell do they think they are?"

"Okay, I get it, but why are you grinding your belt buckle against the curb for?"

Reno is looking down at the belt buckle in his hand then is l ooking up again.

Huh, yeah... well I need protection when I face these guys. Manny Cross-Eyes, from the Dukes, tells me that your Garrison Belt can save your ass in a fight. Manny took off his Garrison Belt and told me to touch the edges of his belt buckle. Holy shit; when I touched the buckle with my finger, it hurt because the points on the buckle are so sharp that it almost cut me. I pulled back my finger and said, 'Wow, how did you do that?' Manny laughed at me and then he sat down on the curb to show me how to grind down my Garrison Belt buckle with sharp points like his. That's why I'm sitting here doing this shit. Oh, there's more, he showed me how to get my belt off in a hurry, wrap the leather part around your hand and swing the buckle of the belt like a whip. Keep the belt on your hand ready for combat short for one person and long for group combat. Then he told me if you're going into enemy territory and you know that there's a chance that they may bushwhack you, you have to be ready to take your belt off in a split-second. That's when I unbuckle my belt, slide it out of my pants loops and then I wrap the belt around my waist again and only buckle it in the second hole so the belt falls loosely on my hips. It almost looks the way a gun slinger's six shooter's belt falls on his hips. This way you can get your garrison belt off in one second and ready for battle if you're under an attack."

"Wow that's great, I'm going to get my garrison belt and sharpen the belt buckle too. This way I'll be able to protect myself if and when I need it. But I have a question, who the Hell is this guy Manny? I never heard about him from the other guys on the Dukes, and why did you call him 'crossed-eyed'?"

"Manny just moved into the neighbor-hood with his parents and three sisters about two weeks ago. He moved into Prospector Frank's building on Huntington Street. According to my brother Henry, he is one tough dude. He's over six feet tall, built like a shit house and he can kick your ass around the block in no time. He's Blackie Parisi's Italian cousin from Argentina, need I say more? I don't know much about the thing with his eye. From what

Whip Your Garrison Belt at Your Enemy, Short For One & Long For Group Combat

I heard his left eye doesn't line up with his right eye. Henry said that if you're looking at him he can only look at you with his right eye and his left eye goes towards or crosses over to his nose. That's why the gang nick-named him Manny Cross-eye."

I'm think the whole neighborhood is going crazy. Reno with his garrison belt, Roger with his zip gun and I hear that Reno's brother Blackface Henry is collecting bottles and rags to make gasoline bombs. I don't like the feeling I'm getting that we will kill each other in a gang war. I sit with Reno on the curb and Pecker and Prospector Frank arrive. Asking about the garrison belt, Reno tells them about Manny all over again.

Prospector Frank puts his hand on his forehead.

"Holy Crap, you can't walk around your own neighborhood with-out getting mugged or into a gang war. I hate this shit and I don't want to think about it. I say let's go over to the Lido Movie House and see the new Treasure Island movie this afternoon."

"That's a great idea! I hear a lot of good things about the movie."

We all agree. Reno puts on his garrison belt and we are all taking off for the Lido Movie House on Columbia Street just above Union Street. We are also a little hungry and Pecker thinks we should stop for one of Louie's hot dogs along the way. Wow, thinking about going to the movie and eating one of Louie's famous hot dogs with onions makes me feel a lot better than thinking about all this gang bullshit I'm hearing about.

As we walk to Louie's hot dog stand I'm telling the guys all about my events the past few days. I tell them about my uncle Frank's new

Louie The Hot Dog Man With
Killer Onions

Buick, the Drive-in Movie, seeing the Ten Commandments, Joanie's portable radio, and our trip to Woolworth's, but I leave out the part about Roger's zip gun because I have enough of all this gang shit.

We are at Louie's hot dog stand on Columbia and President Streets sitting on a nearby stoop to eat our hot dogs, and I am telling the guys about my trip to the library with Henry to get a book, Treasure Island and even though Henry is keen on reading the Treasure Island storybook, I am so looking forward to seeing the movie. We finished our hotdogs, get to the Lido and pay our twenty-five cents for admission for the matinee. The movie is everything Henry told me it is. It is the best movie that I've ever seen! I love the story about Jimmy the cook on the pirate ship. I liked seeing Long John Silver with his one leg and his sword fighting off the other pirates to save Jimmy's life. The best part of the movie is the treasure map of Skull Island and Long John Silver with Jimmy trying to find the pirates buried treasure before they do.

The movie has everything; the pirate ship, the sword fighting, the treasure map, Jimmy and Long John racing to find the treasure, and much more. We leave the movie house and I am pumped and Prospector Frank has an idea!

"Hey, I have an idea! I think we can have an adventure of our own. We can collect some of those rocks that look like silver in the vacant lot near my house on Huntington Street and make a treasure chest. I'll play Long John Silver and Reno can be Jimmy. You, Pepino are the bad Pirate Red Hook and steal the treasure chest from the ship and bury it in Brooklyn. We can make some swords from some old wood and stage some fights."

Let's Put Rocks Together That looks Like Silver & Make A Treasure Chest

"Waaait, wait a minute! Suppose I get Roger to bury the treasure chest in Coffey Park or in one of the baseball fields down by the docks. People have been telling stories about where Pirate Red Hook's Treasure is buried for years. No one knows if it ever happened, so we can make up our own story about Pirate Red Hook. I'll ask Roger to make a real looking treasure map, tear the map in four or five pieces and hide the pieces of the map around the neighborhood for us to find with clues as to where we should be looking, just like a scavenger hunt! It will take us a lot of work to pull this together but if we can make this game it can take our minds off all this gang crap, it will be well worth it."

The ideas are starting to flow like water and we are agreeing to meet tomorrow to make the treasure chest, wooden swords and anything else we need for this pirate game. You may have guessed it by now! Yes, I am elected to convince Roger to work on this project for us.

Chapter 65

Sheepshead Bay-Telephone-Camp Site

I'm on my way home and still pumped up about the idea of playing pirates and looking for the treasure chest full of silver rocks. I think this new game will work but I don't know if Roger the Professor can tear himself away from making zip guns and work with us to draw and make a Skull Island treasure map. The guys in the neighborhood know that I like to spend a lot of time with Roger. He always comes up with a solution to solve a problem and I think that he is a great inventor too. Right now, he is still angry at gangs moving into the Red Hook Projects. He wants to think of how we can stop them from taking over our neighborhood. For me, this pirate game is going to be a real challenge getting Roger interested. Making the pirate map we need and setting up the rules for this new game will need Roger's help also.

I'm home and it's time for dinner, and surprisingly see Roger sitting at our kitchen table talking to my mother. This is really a

Our Families First New Telephone Ever

shocker, Roger hardly ever comes down to visit me or talk to my mother.

"Hey, Roger, what's up? Is there something wrong?"

He knows what I mean.

"I'm sorry that I yelled at you about all this gang stuff. So I came down here to ask your mother if it would be okay for you to go fishing with me tomorrow morning."

Wow, it was like a bolt of lightning hit me right between the eyes. This is such a surprise! I never went fishing before except for catching tiny fish in a stream in back of Uncle Frank's big house in New Jersey.

"I want to reassure your mom that I will take care of you. If she says its okay we have to pack some food and leave for Sheepshead Bay at three o'clock in the morning. Don't worry about the gear; I can borrow the fishing poles, hooks, sinkers and whatever else we need from my older brother. I will pay for the subway ride and the fee for the party fishing boat."

I'm standing in the kitchen looking at them with my mouth open for at least two minutes. I'm wondering if my mother, who hardly speaks any English, knows what Roger is talking about. But it dawned on me that my sister who is playing her records in the other room must have translated Roger's request to my mom.

All this time I'm standing there thinking: I can see my mom out of the corner of my eyes smiling and bobbing her head up and down. I say to myself "Wow! I think that Roger sold my mom on this idea of me going fishing tomorrow." Just at this moment, my sister comes into to the kitchen smiling and laughing happily. I know my sister; I don't think that she is all excited about me going fishing with Roger. I don't know what but something else is going on. I scratch my head and say, "Roger, thanks, for thinking about me but I don't know if I can do this fishing thing."

Haha! "Pepino, it's not such a big deal; we take the D train to Sheepshead Bay, get on a party boat, they set us up on the rail of the boat, they will even put the bait on the hooks for us, we drop the lines into the water and then we wait for the fish to bite,"

"Okay, by looking at my mother I think that she's okay with it too!"

We agree that he will knock on my door at three in the morning for our walk to the Smith and 9th Street subway station for our trip to Sheepsheads Bay. As Roger leaves our apartment my sister is dancing all around me saying:

"I've got a surprise. You'll never guess what it is."

"Okay, okay, stop dancing, you're getting me dizzy! What in the Hell are you talking about?"

She stands still with a big smile on her face.

"We have a telephone! Yeah, we HAVE a telephone in our apartment! Now we can call or get calls anytime day or night. We don't have to wait for Defonte's Sandwich Shop to be open for us to use their public telephone. What do you think about that?"

HOLY SHIT! I'm going on a fishing trip, my sister is out of her mind about our new telephone, and what's next? I just came home to have dinner, listen to some radio stories, and go to bed. But I get to thinking that this fishing trip with Roger couldn't come at a better time. We will be alone and can talk one-on-one about his new inventions, and I can feel him out on the treasure map and pirate game. My sister grabs my arm and pulls me into our living room, dining room, and my part-time bedroom combination to show me our new telephone that I will hardly use since most of my friends don't have one. Anyway, my sister picks up the phone and pretends that she talking to her girlfriend Frances, who doesn't have a telephone either. She puts the phone to my ear so I could hear the dial tone!

WHOOPEE DOOOO!!!

That is exciting, so I guess it will turn out to be a good thing because everyone will have a telephone, television, portable radio and who knows what else in the future. I'm going to bed early and while I'm lying here in bed I can't get much sleep. I keep thinking about the fishing trip, the party boat, the sharp hooks, and the stinky fish, that's if we catch any. I feel like I closed my eyes one minute and before I know it, I hear Roger banging on our front door. I have everything ready, so I jump into my clothes, pick up my lunch bag from the kitchen table and opened the door for Roger.

Leaving the building, the deserted street is very quiet. No one is outside sitting on stoops or crossing streets and all the cars are parked. We are now at Smith and 9th Street and take the escalator way up to the top where we get on the D train to Coney Island. Roger warns me to be careful with my fishing pole because of the overhead fans in the subway car. He tells me that some of his friends weren't so lucky: their poles got caught up in the fan and were completely destroyed. I am so tired that I fall asleep on the train ride to Sheepshead Bay. Sound asleep, I feel Roger shaking me awake. We put our stuff together while getting off the train and walk to a little diner near the station to get two egg sandwiches for breakfast. Boy, did that egg sandwich taste good!

We are walking to the seaport to find a party fishing boat. Walking along the pier a bunch of captains are calling out for us to join them on their boat. Roger picks captain Bill's boat, we are aboard and within ten minutes shove out to sea. It isn't too crowded and looks to me like there are maybe ten people on board. The first mate, Sandy, settles us in our spot and gives us a rundown on how to handle our fishing pole without hooking one of the fishermen next to us. The water is calm at this hour and it's turning out to be a beautiful day. We both catch about twelve porgies, a couple of flounders and I catch the biggest fish of all, a monster black fish that must weigh fourteen pounds! The amazing thing is that the blackfish never took my bait hook into his mouth. Somehow I feel something pulling on my line so I pull up on my fishing pole as hard as I can. Wow, I HOOKED IT! Holy shit, the pull from the fish trying to get away is killing me. I can hardly hold onto my fishing pole. I need all ninety pounds of me to hold on as tight as I can to keep the fishing pole from going into the water. Everyone on the boat is cheering me on: "Hold on kid, hold on, hold on!" I think the fishing pole is bending too far that it is going to snap in two! I'm fighting this battle for about fifteen minutes and the first mate, Sandy, stands next to me with his gaff, a long pole with a big hook at the end. It can reach into the water from the deck of the boat. All of a sudden I'm hearing everybody on the boat cheering like crazy because the big blackfish is close to the surface. At this point, Sandy is able to reach down and hook the fish with his big gaffe, and lift him on board. Sandy suddenly holds up the monster fish to show me and the other fishermen on board the size of this sucker. I see this thing and I'm thinking I am going to pass out it's so HUGE! The funny part is that I hooked this monster blackfish on its tail. The captain and the first mate congratulate me on my big catch. They've seen bigger fish caught over the years, but they never did see a monster blackfish pulled up by its tail by a little kid. I guess they'll be telling this fish story to the other captains and mates at the marinas all over Sheepshead Bay because it's unbelievable.

Everyone is happy for me because the monster black fish is the biggest fish caught so far this day and to boot, I won the fish pool! We give the big blackfish to the first-mate as a thank you and I give the money from the fish pool to Roger. He is able to pay for everything that day and we have twenty dollars left over. That's ten bucks each, not a bad day for a ninety-pound kid's first Sheepshead Bay outing! Sandy cleans our fish for us and we are taking off again to find the subway for our ride home. We are on the train and I can't help thinking about my first day trip to Coney Island last summer with my sister. That day the train was packed with beachgoers. The only way we got a seat on our way home was because we sat next to fishermen going home from Sheepshead Bay with their catch. They smell pretty bad because of the fish they are carrying, so no one wants to sit next to them. We are so tired we don't care that we smell bad. Now I'm thinking that Roger and I are the smelly fishermen, I'm wondering if anyone will sit next to us on our trip home. Who cares? I won't notice because I fall asleep again on our trip home.

I walk into our apartment this afternoon with my smelly fish and my mother runs to me and hugs my smelly body. I think she is relieved that I made it home alive.

After my big hug, she takes my bounty and starts to cook our family a fresh fish dinner. I smell so bad that I take off my clothes and sit in the laundry tub, washing up. I clean up and put on shorts and a T-shirt and I sit out on our fire escape to rest a while. As I'm looking down at the street I see Prospector Frank waving up at me to come down. I am tired but I wave back and leave my apartment to meet him on the street.

"Where were you all day? I came over this morning to find you but your mom said that you weren't home. Do you have any news about Roger working with us on the new Pirate Game? I wanted to tell you that I checked the vacant lot near my house and found a bunch of shiny silver rocks we can use for our Treasure Chest. Then I built a lean-to just in case we want to camp out tonight. Come with me so I can show you what I put together for us."

Frank is talking so fast that I have to stop him.

"Whoa! I wasn't around because I went fishing with Roger at three o'clock this morning. I didn't get a chance to tell Roger our plans for the Pirate Game. I'll come with you to see what you put together in your vacant lot but I can't stay because I just want to have dinner and go to bed, I'm wiped out."

We walk to Huntington Street, and I see Prospector Frank did a good job! He put together a shit load of silver rocks and he made a weird looking lean-to for us to sleep in. I think to myself "fat chance that I'll sleep in this piece of shit" but I don't say anything to Frank. I finally am home, I eat a great fish dinner and go to bed early.

Chapter 66
AAA Crossing Guard-Mining For Silver

If you went to an elementary school in Brooklyn in the 1940's and 50's, chances are you walked there. The school was usually located in your neighborhood on a busy street a few blocks from your home. Crossing from all directions streamed the pupils that attended your school.

Traffic was a problem since the Police Department of NYC didn't always provide traffic controls in the many neighborhoods. This meant that schools faced the monumental problems of keeping the students safe to and from their buildings, as there were few if any school buses for most children who attended either public or parochial schools.

To deal with this issue, schools nominated responsible students, usually 7th or 8th graders to wear a white belt that crossed their chest and circled around their waist, with a silver or metallic AAA (Automobile Association of America) badge worn over their hearts attached to their belt. These students were entrusted with the management of allowing their schoolmates to safely cross the streets. Raising their young hands, they advised the flow of cars, trucks, and buses, as the students faithfully crossed under the watchful guidance of their schoolmate!

AAA Official Crossing Guard Badge

My mother is calling for me to wake up and get ready for school. I can't believe that its morning! I'm still wiped-out from our fishing trip to Sheepshead Bay yesterday. I'm now dragging myself out of bed, washing my face and dressing. I sit at the kitchen table sipping a hot cup of espresso coffee with milk and three lumps of sugar. Wow, is this coffee strong! It took only a few minutes for me to get a jolt of energy. I grab my books and head out to PS 27, only a block away. Lining up with my class, someone smacks me in the head!

Turning around I see Prospector Frank standing right behind me.

"What the Hell was that all about?"

"It's just me to remind you that we have to start working on the rocks I put together for our Treasure Chest Game. I hope you didn't forget to meet me after school this afternoon."

"Okay, okay, cut the shit, you don't have to smack me, I'll meet you at the vacant lot like we planned."

The school bell rings and like soldiers, we all march to our classrooms.

Pepino Working, Directing Children To Safe Crossing

It's after attendance and Miss Kent is reading our lesson. We have three groups, the smart kids don't need many directions, but I'm in the last reading group and I'm still working on the Dick and Jane reading books from last year. Even though I'm not the brightest star in our class I think Miss Kent likes me and she is trying very hard to get me to read at the higher reading level. But I don't know what it is, I just don't see the printed words the way the smarter kids do. As I sit here struggling to read my Dick and Jane book, Miss Kent walks over to my desk.

"Pepino, please come with me out to the hall so I can talk to you about something."

HOLY SHIT!!! I'm in trouble! I know I'm not doing well keeping up with the rest of the class so this is it, they're going to put me BACK into a lower grade! My parents are going to kill me. Standing in the hallway she closes the classroom door, looking at me with her beautiful smile.

"Pepino, I can see that you're having a hard time with your

classroom work, but I also know that you are trying as hard as you can. I have an idea that may help you. Timmy McCarty transferred to another school and he was our AAA crossing guard for a couple of months. So, I put your name in as his replacement. It won't be easy, you have to take a safety course, but I think that you will do a great job! The junior safety patrol was designed to be a student role model program. With the increase of cars in the streets there were concerns for student safety when crossing the streets walking home from school. A Motor Club in Chicago started a School Safety Patrol program around 1920 and many schools around the country started the same program. A policeman named Sergeant Frank Hetznecker who lived in St. Paul, Minnesota made Sam Brown belts that buckle around the waist and shoulder so the drivers would notice them as crossing guards. Later the American Automobile Association, in the 1930's made AAA badges for the school crossing guards. Once you complete a safety course you will also receive a belt and badge.

You probably noticed the guards around the school wearing a white safety belt around their waist and over their shoulder with an AAA badge on it. The school crossing guard can only direct children in crossing the streets, they are not allowed to stop or direct traffic. We came out in the hall now to talk about it because I don't want the kids in our class to know what I am proposing to you until you agree. So, what do you say, do you want the job or not?"

I just stand there looking at her like she is from outer space. She wants *me* to be a school cop? Is she really talking to *me*? I finally closed my mouth and whisper "Yes" I think my eyes were starting to tear up a little. Putting her arm around my shoulder.

"Okay, Lets' go back into the classroom. We'll talk more about it later."

We are walking back into the room and the whole class is looking at me as if they heard every word that was said to me, out in the hallway by Miss Kent. I'm doing my best to keep a straight face as I sit down and pick up my Dick and Jane reading book again. I never thought that I could be a crossing guard because the kids who are picked for the job are the best students in the school. I'm not one of the school's better students but Miss Kent must believe in me and I'll do my best not to let her down. The school day flew by and before I know it, the three-o'clock bell is ringing and I am on my way home!

Bursting into our apartment I tell my mother as best as I can in Italian about my new job. I don't think she understands the gist of it. But she knows it is good news because of the big smile on my face. I'll have to wait for my sister to come home to help me explain what a school crossing guard is all about and a what big deal it is!

Now that I'm all hyped up about the trust Miss Kent has in me, I'll rush over to meet Prospector Frank to help him break and grind the rocks he collected for the glowing silver flakes. I walked over to the vacant lot on Huntington Street and I see Frank, Pecker, and Mike Tomato busy at work. They have hammers and they are pounding away at the pile of rocks in front of them.

Some of the chunks of Silver rocks that break off look really good, gleaming when the sunlight hits them. I always love the look of silver dust and flakes the best. The shine is unbelievable because they look like real silver. We work our tails off and we put aside about fifteen pounds of these gems for our Treasure Chest. We are now sitting around covered with silver dust and broken rocks at our feet, and Prospector Frank's mother has shown up with an ice cold six pack of Pepsi bottles.

She is giving each of us a bottle of Pepsi and walking away without saying anything about how dirty we look. She always lets the boys be boys without the yelling and fussing that some of our mothers would put us through.

So, we build a campfire right next to the lean-to Frank built for our campsite. Mike Tomato brought about two dozen potatoes that his grandfather Mr. Pauli gave him. We throw the potatoes into the fire and are talking about all the neighborhood fights, and the Halloween games we are planning. I don't want to tell my friends that I'm soon to be a school crossing guard. I want to wait for the AAA badge and belt to be in my hands first; otherwise, they will never believe me.

It is dusk now and it is getting cool but the campfire is nice and warm. The glow of the fire is making me sleepy, and I hear Mike Tomato.

"They're done!"

The Potatoes in the campfire are nice and black. Mike is taking a stick and rolling the potatoes out of the fire to cool them off. I pick up a potato while it is still hot and I am bouncing it around from one hand to the other. I'll brake my potato in half with my hands and sprinkle some of Frank's mother's salt and pepper on it. It smells so good, and I'm putting small pieces of the potato in my mouth.

I'm doing my best not to eat any of the burnt black stuff around the potato but it's getting on my fingers and lips and I am shoving it into my mouth. I see the rest of the guys trying to eat the hot potato the same way and it now dawns on me how funny we look with all the black stuff around our mouths. We are all looking at each other and laughing at the same time. We can't stop laughing for what must be almost twenty minutes! We now start throwing the leftover potatoes at each other, laughing and throwing for another half hour before we calm down.

"That's it, I'm going home!"

Chapter 67

Pirate Treasure Chest-Old Fedora Cap

I am walking home from our camp on Huntington Street lugging a box full of silver rocks and silver dust for our pirate treasure chest. I am dirty from the rock breaking and the burnt potato fight at the campfire. Since I'm climbing the stairs of my apartment building, I'll

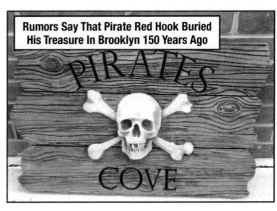

Rumors Say That Pirate Red Hook Buried His Treasure In Brooklyn 150 Years Ago

take the silver treasure box up to Roger's landing and I'll put it near his back door.

I'm walking back down to my apartment hoping that my mother is out running errands so she doesn't see me messed up with the silver dust and potato charcoal stains on my face and clothes. I walk in the door and my luck runs out. There she is sitting at the kitchen table with my sister shucking a big batch of fresh peas for dinner. She is giving me that: "I'm going to kill you look" as I pass her by on my way to the laundry sink to clean up. She doesn't say a word. While I'm getting washed my sister informs me:

Let's Put Rocks That Look Like Silver & Make A Treasure Chest Like Pirate Red Hook Buried in Brooklyn

"Pepino, Mom is telling me that you got an award from your teacher but she doesn't know exactly what the award was all about."

"Yeah, I told mom that my teacher put my name in to be an AAA safety patrol monitor.

I have to take a safety class first. I should get my AAA badge and white belt by the end of the week!"

My sister starts laughing.

"You're lucky Mom didn't smack you around with the wooden spoon when you walked in looking like shit! She didn't kill you because Mom is so happy about your award. I'll tell Mom more about it so she understands that you now will be leaving early and coming home late from school because you will be crossing the little kids coming and going home. Congratulations! Miss Kent must really like and trust you to do a good job."

Wow! This AAA patrol must be a big deal for my sister to congratulate me! I don't think that my mother understands a word of what my sister is saying, she just smiles and moves her head up and down.

Dinner will not be ready for another hour. I'm finished washing up and putting on some clean clothes and go upstairs to talk to Roger. Picking up the box with the silver rocks I lug it up to his apartment. As usual, he is in the back bedroom as I can see him working on the carpet gun cannon. He's slicing an old bike tire that now looks like a large rubber band.

"Hey, Pepino, I think I've got it! This bike tire will launch an eight by eight-inch carpet from our new cannon!"

"Whoa, that's GREAT! I can't wait to set up another war game!"

Roger has stopped talking as I put the box of silver rocks on his workbench.

"Here, we smashed these rocks for our Pirate Red Hook treasure chest game. Everybody thinks that his treasure is still buried somewhere in Red Hook Brooklyn. What do you think?"

"I say it's BULLSHIT, but I love the way these rocks look and glow just like real silver. How in Hell did you get your hands on these Mica stones? They're not easy to find in Brooklyn!"

I have this funny look on my face and think Roger thinks that I can't tell the difference from Mica or any other rocks in the vacant lots around our neighborhood. I'll tell him all about Prospector Frank who put together all the Mica stones for us to smash for the silver. I mention to Roger about my AAA Safety Patrol Badge as he puts his arm around my shoulder and is telling me that it is a great honor to be selected to be a school crossing guard. Wow! Everyone I tell about Pepino getting the AAA badge makes such a big deal about it. I feel like an important muckity-muck. I never felt this way before! I leave Roger the Professor so he can work on our hand-made carpet shooting cannon and the silver treasure chest.

I am back at my apartment, after dinner, doing my homework, and plan to head out to find my friends. All of a sudden I'm hearing a knock on our apartment door! Roger is standing in the hallway holding a small wooden chest. I can't believe what I'm looking at. It's Roger showing me the silver treasure chest for our pirate game.

"Roger, how did you make it so fast?"

"It was easy; you and Prospector Frank did all the heavy lifting. I've had the chest in my room for weeks so when you left I just assembled the silver rocks into the wooden chest and wham, it's done! It came out so good that I just had to come down to show you!"

Standing here in the doorway with my mouth open, I don't know what to say.

"Thank you. I guess now we can work on the rules for the pirate game."

Still standing in front of me holding the chest out in his two hands, with this big grin on his face, I can tell that he is proud of the silver chest he made. We agree to meet again this weekend to work on the rules for the game. He is turning around and walking back upstairs, holding his new creation. Closing the door I will get ready to leave.

Now I'm ready to tell my friends or anybody who will listen to me all about my big deal AAA crossing guard badge.

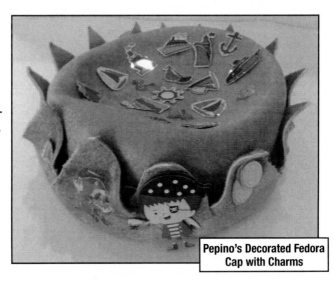

Pepino's Decorated Fedora Cap with Charms

Walking up to Columbia Street to call Jimmy Pizza, as I am getting close to his building I see Jimmy sitting on his stoop cutting a hat with a pair of scissors.

"Hey, Jimmy, why are you cutting that old hat?"

"My uncle Tony 'the Book', told me to take his old hats and cut them to make a funky kid cap and decorate it for myself. My Uncle called his old hats Fedoras. So that's why I'm sitting here cutting this shit. He just gave me a rough idea of how to cut his old Fedora then flip it inside out but I don't know what the Hell I'm doing. Here, take this old Fedora and see what you can make out of it."

Hum, this sounds like a good project for me. I can make a new hat that will make me stand out when I'm crossing the little kids to and from school. Taking one of the old Fedoras, Jimmy gives me an extra scissor he has laying on the stoop. I sit next to him and start cutting off the rim of the old hat just like Jimmy is doing.

While we are cutting the old Fedoras, I'm telling Jimmy Pizza all about my AAA badge.

"No shit!"

It takes us about a half-hour of cutting and shaping to make a cap with the base of the cap cut into a shark tooth design. We flip the rim like a sailor's cap with the shark tooth points facing up. Putting the caps on our heads, I'm thinking that we look like two friggin' cool kids.

"Now comes the hard part!"

He is opening a cigar box sitting next to him that is full of old buttons that his mother gave him, are every color of the rainbow and they are all different sizes mixed in the box. The box has three or four sewing needles and two spools of thread. Jimmy takes a needle, threading black thread into the eye of the needle, and starts sewing a bright red button onto the outer rim of his cap.

Following his lead, I'm sewing a yellow button on my cap. We are finished sewing, putting the caps on our heads and giving ourselves two thumbs up.

"Hey, Pepino, my Mom told me that we can get different charms like; boats, fish, birds, dogs, soldiers or whatever comes out of the gumball machine at the candy store. We can sew these charms on the dome of our Fedora caps. This way each of us will have our own custom cap design."

"Yeah, that's right! Nobody can put together the same bottoms and charms and duplicate our cap designs. My Fedora cap will then be a one and only!"

We are thinking of ourselves as some sort of artist or something because the caps really look good! Putting the decorated cap on my head I'll walk around the block to show off my new Jughead cap to my friends. As I am walking I can imagine myself wearing my white belt, AAA badge pinned on it and my new hat when crossing little kids from PS 27. I like the picture I created in my head.

Chapter 68

Chutes & Ladders-Bruno's Harley-Car Tire Game

Last night I was so excited about my crossing guard badge and my new Fedora hat that I didn't get much sleep. I'm rushed to school so early this morning that I'm the first student in the schoolyard ready to line up for class! A lot of my classmates are making fun of me and my decorated Fedora cap I'm wearing. I don't care what they say, they're just jealous of how cool I look. My new cap separates me from the rest of the heard of idiots on the line with me. I have to start thinking of myself as a leader now and not worry about all the bull-shit insults they're throwing at me. I know that I will do my best to make Miss Kent proud of me.

I'm having a good day in class today. Everything is improving; my math and reading assignments seemed to be a lot easier! Miss Kent gave me a hall pass so I could go to the safety course at 2 PM. I don't know why but I feel special. I pass the safety course and they give me my belt with the AAA badge pinned on it. It's beautiful! I keep looking at it again and again with this big, proud smile on my face.

Its after school and a senior crossing guard is standing next to me on the street corner showing me the ropes.

I have the moves down pat, and you know what, I still can't believe it: the little kids listen to me! I get home about three-thirty all dressed up with my white belt, AAA badge and decorated Fedora cap. I walk into our apartment and my mother is taking one look at me and is crying and hugging me so hard that I can't breathe. After ten minutes of this she is finally calming down. Turning towards the stove, she is plucking a hotdog out of the boiling water, puts it in a bun and is giving it to me. It is like she is giving me a reward for a job well done. I eat the hotdog, kiss my Mom and now I'll go upstairs to show Roger the Professor my uniform. I find Roger is sitting at his cluttered bench as usual.

"Holy shit, is that you Pepino? You look so different. It must be your white belt, AAA badge and that kooky hat you're wearing! You look like a symbol of authority. I'll tell you what; you better wipe that smile off your face and take off all that stuff you're wearing before you go back on the street to hook up with your friends. Don't ever forget that you live in Red Hook Brooklyn, one of the toughest neighborhoods in the City. If you go outside with your uniform and wearing your new hat along with that happy smile on your face, you can bet your ass that the neighborhood bullies will grab you and kick the shit out of you."

I didn't even think about how happy I look, but Roger is right. You can't go around the neighborhood looking happy and all because the neighborhood bullies will wipe that smile right off my face. I stop smiling and I take off my new hat thinking about the beating I could face if Roger didn't wake me up and remind the real world I live in. I'm now taking a deep breath.

"Thanks Roger for bringing me down to Earth. I'm glad you told me what you did. I'll go downstairs and change before I go out to find my friends. Roger, I just want you to know, that when you came downstairs yesterday my head was full of the crossing guard stuff. When you showed me the assembled silver treasure chest, I was surprised that you finished it so fast and I was so happy to see how good it looks. I don't even remember if I told you how great it looked. So now that I'm back on Earth, Roger, thank you for doing such a great job."

"HAHA! Don't get all mushy on me, after all, I only saved your skinny little ass!"

Roger is so good to me. He's like my big brother. Not only does he make all the stuff for our kid games, he will try to protect me from the bullies and shit heads that will kick my ass just for fun. I am following Roger's advice. I head downstairs to take off my uniform and will go out to look for Pecker, Mike Tomato and Reno the Greek to make plans for our weekend. Leaving my apartment building turning the corner I see Joanie waving at me from her stoop. Sometimes I think that Joanie sits there waiting for me to come by. Even though she's a lot younger than me I really don't mind because she's a good friend. Sometimes she thinks I'm like a big brother to her. She forces her father Bruno to take me with them to different places in his Hot-Rod. I'll walk over to her to say hello and sit next to her as she shows me her new board game: Chutes and Ladders.

"Come on, play this game with me. Come ooon, pleeease!"

"Listen, Joanie, you know that I hate to play these stupid board games. I don't like learning all the new rules of the new board games and I'm not good at playing stupid games."

"NOW LISTEN, each player gets a charm or chip that will move on the board after you throw the die. The die has numbers one to six. You roll the die and when it stops you look at the face of the die that shows a number. That number tells you how many moves you have to make in these boxes. If you roll a three you make three moves. Okay, we first roll the die to see who will go first. Whoever gets the higher number goes first. Here you can use this horse charm and I'll use this red chip. I win the first roll so I go first. We start the game from the number one box. You win the game if you get to the last box on top of the board first. Here we go, I rolled a six, now I count out six boxes and I go again because the rules say if you roll a six you keep going until you roll a lower number. Are you following me so far? Okay, you have to follow this trail and if you land on a box at the bottom of a ladder you can climb the ladder to the top but if you land on the box that has the top of the ladder in it you have to go down the ladder. This game will have a lot of ups and downs but remember you have to keep trying to move into the top box to win."

WOW! I can't remember all this shit! We have played three games so far, and I always find the ladder that makes me climb down and Joanie always finds the ladder for her to climb up, so she kicked my ass in all three games we have played. As I am now trying to leave, I hear a loud roar and I look over into the street. I see Joanie's killer dad, Bruno, with a new Harley Davidson motorcycle. Wow, it's a beauty! I love all of Bruno's toys, and now he's got a motorcycle! He must be rich. I'm so afraid of Joanie's father, I'll force myself to walk over to him and tell him how great his new Harley looks. He is even smiling at me! I turn and walk up the block to 'Chickies' grocery store to find my friends. I look up the block and see a bunch of guys rolling old white wall car tires. As I go to the corner I see Pecker is standing there holding one of these tires next to him.

"Hey, Pecker, what the Hell are you guys doing with these old tires?"

"Yeah, we made up a new game! Reno found a load of old car tires in a vacant lot. It looks like somebody dumped about thirty old tires in the middle of the lot last night. So, we took ten tires and made up a game. The first game is like war. We choose sides and then go to different ends of the street and start charging at each other by rolling the tires at the enemy as fast as we can.

Sometimes we hit each other with the rolling tires but most of the time the tires just bounce off each other. Nobody wins the game we're just laughing and having fun with all the action. Then it dawned on Reno the Greek that a small guy like him can squeeze himself into one of the big old tires and that I could roll the tire with Reno in it down the hill. What a trip!"

I look at Pecker like he's crazy. Leave it up to my friends to take the bunch of old tires and use them to kill each other. So, I'm sitting here watching them roll and bang tires into each other and every now and then I see Reno come by going head over heels in the middle of the tire he climbed into. I'll go to the grocery store and get myself an ice-cold coke and a bag of chips and sit on the curb and watch the action.

I sit here for what seems like a half hour and give up the ghost because I'm getting bored. I head home and walk into our apartment and I'm surprised to see my father sitting there at the kitchen window smoking a Lucky Strike. He seems to be staring into space, looking into the distance that is not there. He looks so depressed he seems near tears. I am worried about him, but I won't let him know that. Too bad his ship hasn't come in so that he can land a steady job. He's so happy when he's working. Meanwhile, my sister, Isabella,

Pecker Rolling His Old
Whitewall Car Tire

and my Mom are walking in holding four large shopping bags loaded with white ribbons. Isabella turns to me.

"We have to talk".

She is pulling me by the arm into the next room with a serious face.

"Listen, Dad can't keep up, he can't earn enough money for his part-time day job. There isn't enough steady work for him and we're sinking fast. So, we're taking in some work to do in our apartment. These shopping bags have four hundred bra straps in them. Me and mom figure, if all of us pitch in, we could get as much as $40.00 when we complete the job in about three or four weeks. We have to put metal clips on each bra strap, sew them, cut them and then reassemble them so they can slide. The contractor says we will get paid about one penny for each Bra strap. Just so ya know you may not see your friends much until we finish this job."

Whoa, I can't believe what she's telling me.

Chapter 69

WWII Binoculars-Potato Man-Street Hockey

Yesterday was a long day with a lot of ups and downs. I haven't seen Nunzio in a while so I'm going over to his apartment to call on him this morning.

Knocking on his door he is opening it and inviting me in, leading me into the kitchen, as he finishes eating his breakfast sandwich. We are both sitting at the table and he is holding up his ham and egg sandwich to chomp on it like a beaver chomping a big tree branch. Well, I figure Nunzio isn't going to talk much with all that bread, ham and eggs in his mouth so I'll tell him all about my AAA badge, silver treasure chest and Pecker's stupid whitewall tire game. I don't say anything to him about the bra straps my mom does as piece work that we have to assemble to make some extra money. Poor Dad, if he knew he would be furious at Mom! He would feel like someone stole his manhood, yet I'm kind of embarrassed about the whole thing. Looking at Nunzio I can see his eyes widening as he is chewing away and listening to my stories. Every now and then he is grunting: "Uh-huh, uh-huh," Nunzio is finished now and

Uncle Benny's WWII Binoculars

drinks a big glass of milk to wash it all down. Slurping his glass of milk, he is leaning over with his arms on the kitchen table.

"Holy shit, you're one busy little guy. Well, I've got some news for you too!

My Uncle Benny came over last week and gave me a pair of his old binoculars be brought back from the war. The binoculars are the neatest thing; when you look into them you can see anything you point them at, up close. I mean if somebody is walking two blocks away you can see the buttons on their shirt. If you open your back window, look through them at the building across the yard, you can see some of the women getting ready for bed! When ya know, I take a peek at these girls taking their clothes off my face gets all red."

"Nunzio, you're a freaking Peeping Tom. If somebody sees you looking into their window, they will come over here and beat the Hell out of you. Then when your parents find out what you're doing you will get another beating. What in Hell are you thinking, you will never get away with it! So, stop doing it right now or I will spill the beans on you, got it!"

Nunzio looks down at the table with his sorry face, he's not a bad kid, he's just not too bright about things and I'm just trying to protect him.

High Point Lookout for Skull Island Pirate Treasure

"Okay, okay, I won't do it anymore.

I feel guilty about looking into people's windows because I know that I would be upset if I found out that somebody was peeping at my Mom when she's getting ready for bed."

"I've got an idea, let's go over to the Brooklyn Battery Tunnel construction site and find a mound of dirt and rock that we can climb. Then we can take turns looking through the binoculars and pretend that we are explorers trying to find our way out of the wilderness. This could be part of our silver treasure chest pirate game. These binoculars will come in handy in finding the clues on the Skull Island treasure map."

We leave Nunzio's apartment and suddenly find this vacant lot close to the construction site filled with rocks piled about twenty feet high. It is perfect for our lookout. Nunzio gives me his binoculars and a notepad. I climb to the top of the mound and sit down, looking through the binoculars. Wow, what a view! I can see everything from three or four blocks away, up close! I'm sitting here for about ten minutes and imagine that I am checking the Skull Island map for clues to the pirate silver treasure chest. I can't wait to tell Roger the Professor about my ideas. Calling down to Nunzio, I tell him that's it's his turn to climb up to the lookout.Nunzio Superman is looking through the binoculars with his Superman X-ray vision and yelling down to me that the Potato Man is two blocks away pushing his cart in this direction. I'm thinking to myself how in Hell can the Superman be hungry after eating that huge breakfast sandwich only an hour ago! After all, he's such a big guy, that's why we call him Superman. He is climbing down from the mound of rocks yelling:

"Hurry up! Let's get a couple of baked potatoes and go to Coffey Park to eat them! It's a nice day; we can enjoy eating the potatoes on the grass. Come on, let's go!"

Taking off and running with the binoculars in one hand and the notepad in the other, it's funny to see Nunzio, a fat ass of a guy, running like he's trying to catch a trolley! I'm running right behind him catching up to the Potato Man. Nunzio is such a big guy and I'm a peewee compared to him that we must look like Mutt and Jeff. I don't know why the potatoes cooking on the Potatoes' Man's cart smell so good, but they do. Nunzio pulls out twenty cents and buys two large potatoes, one for each of us. The Potato Man wraps each hot potato in a newspaper. They are so hot I can't hold mine for too long, I put my potato down on a stoop nearby to cool it off a little so I can handle it.

On our way to Coffey Park, we'll stop at DeFonte's sandwich shop to buy two Manhattan Special sodas. At Coffey Park we found this shady spot under a big maple tree, sitting in the grass while eating our potatoes. Boy, you wouldn't think that a hot potato with a Manhattan Special Soda would taste so good, but it does!

We are finished eating and lying there in the cool grass, looking up at the sky day-

Potato Man's Hot Potato And Manhattan Special Are Great Together

dreaming, as we are dozing off for what must be a half-hour and I didn't realize it!

"Okay, that's it, I'm not going to sleep here all day. Let's go find some of the guys on Hicks Street and see what they're doing."

It not easy, but we are managing to get up and walk slowly back home. As we turn the corner on Nelson Street we can see and hear the guys are playing street hockey. I love to play street

I Love Street Hockey With Lots Of Fast Action

hockey. I am running up to them and shouting that I'm going home to get my skates and hockey stick and Nunzio does the same. I'm running up the two flights of stairs to my apartment, huffing, and puffing and as I walk in, nobody is home. I'm looking under my sister's bed and find my roller skates and an old walking cane that I use as a hockey stick. Running back downstairs, out the front door, I hook up with my friends. Finding six guys playing hockey, I am thinking: Great! With Nunzio, we now have four guys on each side. Two old soda crates are set up as goals on either side of the street. Mike Tomato wins the toss and picks me to play on his side. Reno the Greek doesn't mind because he gets Nunzio Superman, who is almost twice my size. It starting to rain a little as this game is starting, but that is okay because the rain will help me skate around Nunzio who can't move as fast as I can. A bunch of girls are standing on the sidewalk watching us play. We use a solid handball as a hockey puck. There's always a lot of action in hitting the puck and each other as we race towards the goal. Some kids like to play street hockey with an old guy standing using his watch to time the two periods but we play for points.

The team that gets ten points in the goal first wins the game. My old cane is not the best hockey stick but my speed makes up for it. I get banged up pretty good and my arms and knees are bleeding.

I don't feel the pain from my cuts and bruises because I'm hot. I score six points out of ten and we win the game! It is like a championship game for the block and the girls are cheering me on. They are going crazy, yelling and screaming when I score the winning goal!

We are taking a couple of victory laps and sit down on the curb to talk about how great we are at kicking Reno the Greek's team's ass. As we are finishing patting ourselves on the back we plan to go into 'Chickie's' grocery store to buy chips and sodas so we can eat and dry off before we go home. Chickie gives me a towel and band-aids for my wounds because she knows that my mother would be very upset if I go home bleeding. I don't care much because I love to play street hockey.

Chapter 70

Billboard-Pretzel-Wizard Of Oz-Zoot Suit

One of the more iconic symbols of Americana comes from the early 1940's. The Zoot suit took America by storm, a style was re-interpreted in a bold new way! As you will learn later in this story, it got its roots from the influx of the Mexican's who took up the slack of missing American boys fighting the war. But it was not only the Latinos who donned the high-waist, wide-legged, close-cuffed, trousers with a long coated wide lapels and padded shoulders!

Reaching Harlem, Chicago, and Detroit the African American community had a profound influence on Italian Americans, Filipino Americans, and Irish Americans in particular that adopted this fad. Unfortunately, anti-Mexican riots in Los Angeles during the war led to the now historical 'Zoot Suit Riots.'

original radio broadcasts

Inner Sanctum

I Love To Listen To Horror & Suspense Radio Programs

I put my trusty cane hockey stick and skates under my sister's bed again. I ate my dinner and now sitting by the radio listening to my favorite radio programs. *Suspense* is one of my favorite programs because it always scares the shit out of me. Tonight they scheduled the *Pit and the Pendulum* by Edgar Allen Poe. So I'm sitting here in the dark with my ear next to the radio and my eyes closed. Whooo! They tell the story as if the ghosts are talking to you! I feel like I'm in the story waiting for the Ghouls to pounce on me and eat me alive! Sometimes I have nightmares about these radio stories but I don't care, I love that creepy feeling I get when I sit there in the dark by the radio being drawn deeper and deeper into the spooky story. As I sit there my sister puts her hand on my shoulder and I almost jump out of my friggen' skin.

"Pepino, CALM DOWN! it's only ME! Sorry, I scared you, but I just wanted to tell you that my girlfriend Frances and I are going to Manhattan tomorrow. I want you to come with us to see a movie in a big theater; we plan to see the Wizard of Oz. I was told that it's a great movie and I would like you to see it with us. Okay?"

I am still shaking because she snuck up on me like one of the ghosts in the Suspense radio story.

"Yeah, I would love to go to New York City, I've never been to a big theater before."

Broadway & 42nd Street Camel Smoke Billboard

"Good, we'll make a day out of it."

I am still shaking a little as I sit back down to listen to the rest of the Suspense story. I'll pull out my cot now and start thinking about our trip for tomorrow.

My friend Henry Black Face told me about this movie after he went to see it with his parents about a month ago. He told me it's a great story about a girl named Dorothy and her dog Toto, who is sucked up by a tornado in Kansas to a strange Munchkin land way up in the sky. When she gets there she does her best to find her way back home on the yellow brick road. Then she meets a scarecrow, a tin-man, and a lion along the way and they all try to help Dorothy find her way home. They tell Dorothy that she has to find the Wizard of Oz and that they are looking to find the Wizard of Oz too. They all need

Pretzel Vendor on Broadway Selling Hot Pretzels

help; the lion says that he needs courage; the tin man wants a heart so he can love and the scarecrow needs a brain so he can solve math problems. They all walk together on the yellow brick road singing songs. They do their best to help each other fight the green wicked witch, the flying monkeys and all sorts of other dangers. According to Henry, the movie has many wonderful songs and all sorts of action in it.

I am so tired from all that playing of street hockey that it doesn't take long for me to soon fall into a deep sleep.

I'm up early this morning and rushing to get dressed for my first trip to Manhattan with my sister Isabella and her best friend Frances. I'm putting on long pants and a clean shirt and sitting in the kitchen waiting for my sister to wake up. It isn't a long wait, as I hear my sister say:

"Pepino! Adiamo! Come on let's go."

Meeting Frances in front of our building we all are walking together to the Carroll Street subway station on Second Place and Smith Street. We get there in twenty minutes and walk downstairs to the train platform. This is a real adventure for me to go and see a movie in the big city. We have arrived at the Forty-Second Street station in Manhattan in forty minutes. We will walk up the stairs to the street and stand on the corner of Forty-Second and Broadway. It's Sunday and I see crowds of people, all dressed up strolling and looking up at the buildings. Last time we were here for the Columbus Day Parade it didn't seem this crazy.

I am a little scared to be in the hustle and bustle of so many people around me so I stand as close as possible to my sister for protection. As we are walking a couple of blocks, I see a huge billboard sign. The billboard must be three-stories high, advertising Camel cigarettes. It has a picture of a man on it smoking a Camel cigarette and blowing rings of smoke out of a hole in his mouth. It is unbelievable to see a billboard three stories high blowing smoke, and I can't take my eyes off the billboard. I walk holding my sister's hand and twist my neck looking at the billboard because it is the neatest thing I've ever seen in my whole life! My sister keeps on pulling me toward the big movie theater on Forty-Fourth Street. I am getting hungry so I nudged my sister and ask her if we could get a snack.

"Okay, I see a pretzel vendor on the corner. How about one of those big hot pretzels? I think all that dough and salt will hold you for a little while."

I'm hungry and in agreement as we walk over to get one. The pretzel is gigantic, hot and smells so good. I start to eat it but I can't finish it because it is too big for a pee-wee kid my size so I give my sister Isabella and her friend Frances some of it to eat.

We've reached the theater, buying our tickets and walking in. Wow! The theater is so big and fancy with plush carpets and shiny polished brass all over the place! It looks so much better than our dinky little Happy Hour Theater back in our neighborhood. The snack stand is huge and don't ask me why their popcorn smells better too. We are sitting in clean soft seats to watch the *Wizard of Oz* movie. My seat is so comfortable I can sleep in it. What a great movie! Henry is right, it has everything; it's a great adventure story, with good guys, bad guys, songs and a big surprise when Dorothy finds the Wizard of Oz at the end. I love the action and the color of the movie is so much better than any theater I've been to in Brooklyn. At the end of the movie, Dorothy, the Tin-Man, the Scarecrow and the Lion get what they want. It has such a happy ending. We are leaving the theater with a happy and positive feeling going through my body. I keep humming the songs and acting like the flying monkeys, dancing and jumping up and down. I must look funny because my sister and Frances cannot stop laughing at me.

Zoot Suit Guy Going to The Latin Quarter In Manhattan

We are walking up Broadway and have found a Horn and Hardart to eat a late lunch. I have a chicken potpie to eat from out of one of their little windows. It is so good! I never had a chicken pot pie before. My sister Isabella and her girlfriend Frances eat pork and beans and I don't think that their lunch smells as good as mine. After lunch, we do some window-shopping. I can't understand how my sister can shop through a store's window when all the stores are closed on

Sunday. I find out later that window-shopping means that you don't need any money to look at all the fancy stuff on display in the store windows. I guess that makes sense to some girls. I thought it was just a big waste of time. I am bored out of my mind with all this window-shopping. I snap out of it as I see a couple of young guys walking around all dressed up with bright colored suits, chains, two-tone shoes, wide brim hats with feathers, as they look like Peacocks.

"Who are these clowns? Why are they dressed up that way? Where are they going?"

My sister Isabella and Frances crack up laughing at me!

"Those guys are wearing Zoot suits, and they are probably going to the Latin Quarter to hang out, listen to the music, and if they get lucky they may meet some pretty girls."

Looking at her with a squished face, like what the Hell, are you talking about? My sister is getting the message.

"The Zoot Fashion started in California during the war when a lot of people from South America and Mexico came to the U.S. to help us in the war effort. They replaced many of our young men who enlisted to fight the war. Many of the Latin men who came here to work dressed up in Zoot suits when they got off from work to party and have some fun. The Americans thought that the Zoot suits made them look funny. So when the Navy ships were in port and the sailors got R and R leave they would bump into these Latinpartygoers, and it was like oil and water because the Navy sailors got drunk, made fun of the Zoot suit guys and all Hell would break loose. It was so bad that riots broke out and the police had their hands full in trying to keep them apart. After the war when things calmed down, many young American men started wearing the Zoot suits themselves. To tell you the truth it was many young Italian-American men who liked the Zoot suits. I'm sure that there is more to the story but that's all I know."

So I'll ask my sister:

"Do any of the young guys in our neighborhood wear Zoot suits?" She looks at me and answers:

"I don't think so. First, the Bullies in our neighborhood would make fun of them and then kick them in their ass. A young guy in Red Hook Brooklyn doesn't have the guts to walk around looking like a peacock."

Hum... I wonder if these Zoot suit guys really stand out dressed like that. Maybe it's to get the girls to notice them. If the girls like them to dress up like a peacock well, that's all that matters. We are heading to the subway station to take the train back to Brooklyn.

Chapter 71

Spam-Puzzle Game-Candy Cigar-Kerchief Wars

It's hard to get out of my mind the sights, sounds, and fun I had with my sister Isabella and her girlfriend Frances in Manhattan yesterday. I finally got to see what the big city is all about, the crowds of different people from all over

There is Nothing Better Than Spam And Eggs For Breakfast

the world looking for fun and adventure, the skyscrapers and quick pace that Red Hook never has. The foods, huge movie houses, live theaters, fancy stores and there is something for everybody: even a kid like me! I can't wait to go back to

You Can Eat Spam For Breakfast, Lunch Or Dinner

Manhattan with my friends. The crowds of people rushing around with blank looks on their faces are probably thinking about where they're going or what kind of food they will eat. I guess we look the same to each other.

I'm going out this morning excited, looking for my friends to tell them all about my adventures in Manhattan and the crazy looking peacock guys walking around in their cool Zoot suits. They will never believe me! Yet, I can't seem to find anyone around right now!

I know it is kinda early so I'll just have to ring somebody's doorbell. I'll check Nunzio's house, he's always up early. I'm ringing

Nunzio's doorbell and his mother is opening the door and tells me that I'll find him in the kitchen. Ah! There he is, sitting at the kitchen table eating breakfast again!

"Hey, Nunzio, sorry to bother you while you're eating but I gotta tell ya: my sister and her girlfriend Frances took me to Manhattan yesterday, you're not going to believe what that was like!"

Nunzio is looking at me half interested.

"Okay, I don't want to stop eating my Spam and eggs because they don't taste as good when they're cold, sit down at the table with me and tell me all about it."

"We went into Manhattan early yesterday by subway, got off on 42nd Street and Broadway. It seems like we walked for miles watching all these strange people rushing around the streets there."

I tell him about the billboard sign of a man smoking a Camel cigarette with a smoke ring coming out of his mouth.

"Yes, you heard me; he was making actual smoke rings. Unbelievable, isn't it?"

I'm talking and talking about the movie house, the *Wizard of Oz* movie, the pretzel man and the giant pretzel I ate, my chicken pot pie, window shopping, and the weirdest thing of all: the guys in Zoot suits! I can barely catch my breath.

"Wait a minute, what in the Hell is Spam?"

Looking up at me with a little egg dripping down his chin he says:

"You NEVER ate Spam!? It's different from ham and I love it. My mother calls it, "Spiced ham" because the taste is different from regular ham. It's chopped up ham with other stuff in it, but I don't know what the other stuff is. I think that my mother likes the idea that she is saving money because Spam costs a lot less than real Ham and it doesn't go bad. I like to eat it in the morning with sunny-side-up eggs because I can swish the Spam around in the egg yolk before I eat it. For lunch, I put Spam in between two slices of bread with a little mustard and sometimes my mother cooks Spam with beans for dinner. The best thing about Spam is that it comes in a can and it lasts forever until you open the can, so we always have a couple of cans in our pantry.

Here, taste it."

Nunzio puts some Spam on a clean fork and reaches out so I can try a bite of it.

I'm stretching my body over the table towards him with my mouth open and he is putting a piece of Spam into my mouth. Nunzio smiles and says:

"Good, isn't it?"

"Holy shit, you're right, I like the taste of this Spam! I'm going to tell my mother to get some of this spiced ham for dinner and she can save money too. I don't know if she will ever by food in a can."

At the same time, I'm telling him how much I love the taste of Spam I'm thinking of my mother. She never buys food in a can. Everything she cooks has to be homemade. One day I saw a can of Chef Boyardee Ravioli in a can at Defonte's. I love Ravioli, so I bought it. When I took it home my mother laughed at me! But I opened the can anyway and put the Ravioli in a saucepan to heat up. While it was heating up in the sauce it didn't smell that good. I took one bite of the Ravioli and threw them in the trash because it tasted so bad. The Ravioli in the can doesn't even come close to my mother's homemade ravioli.

Nunzio is finishing his Spam and eggs while getting up from the kitchen table and announces:

"I want to show you something!"

Walking into his bedroom, it dawns on me that Nunzio hasn't heard a thing I said about my trip to Manhattan. He was too freaking busy eating his Spam and eggs to listen to me! To tell you the truth, now, I'm really pissed off. He comes back into the kitchen with a big smile on his face and says:

"Here, look at this mini puzzle my dad gave me. You jumble these numbers and then you slide them back in order as fast as you can. It's a game and here's how you play it. Let's say we get six of our friends together, we all stand in a circle. I jumble the numbers and give the puzzle to Reno the Greek, he has one minute to put the numbers back in order. If he makes it in time, he stays in the circle, then Reno jumbles the puzzle and hands it to Mike Tomato. Let's say Mike doesn't do it in one minute, he

Candy Bubble Gum Cigars For
The Puzzle Game Winners

then has to drop out of the circle and wait for the next game to start.

Because he's out Mike has to hand the puzzle back to Reno to jumble the numbers and then Reno can hand the puzzle to Jimmy Pizza who is the next guy in the circle. The thing is that the player always controls the puzzle and the last player in the circle after everyone else drops out is the winner of that game. Then everybody forms a new circle and starts a new game. What we do before the first puzzle game starts is we all put in a nickel each in the pot to buy a pack of bubble gun cigars. The winner of each game gets a bubble gum cigar as his reward before we start the next game. What do you think?"

"It sounds like a fun game to play indoors on a rainy day. But you know what? I'm pissed off at you for not hearing anything I said about my trip to Manhattan yesterday. I feel like telling you to shove your puzzle game up your ass."

"I know, I know, when it comes to food I block everything out of my mind. It's like I'm in a trance, I don't see or hear anything while I'm eating. I just can't help myself. You know what; now that I finished eating I will give you my full attention. I'm sorry, I really want to hear what you have to say. Now that you know about my eating habit, please wait until I'm finished eating before you tell me anything, otherwise you're just pissing in the wind."

Nunzio is one of my best friends and I can never hold a grudge against him. Making up we are walking over to 'Chickie's' grocery store to hook up with our friends. We see Jimmy Pizza, Mike Tomato with Blackface Henry running away from Joey Hook Nose's beautiful sisters, Donna and Ginger. I met the teenage girls about two months ago when Roger took me over to their house to buy abroken down old bike from Joey Hook Nose. His sisters are so beautiful, with their green eyes, blond hair pushed back into a ponytails and their hot dynamite looking bodies stuffed into their tight white sweaters and blue jeans. They look much older than sixteen and seventeen. Anyone would think that they were in their twenties. Why in Hell are they running after my stupid friends? All of a sudden Jimmy Pizza is running by me throwing this rag!

"Here, grab this and run like Hell."

Catching this colorful silk rag, I am running as Ginger is coming after me yelling:

"Give me my freaking kerchief back, you asshole!"

I'll keep running up Hicks Street, I'm too fast for her but she isn't giving up! She is chasing after me as fast as she can. All of a sudden I see Reno the Greek running full speed coming towards me in the opposite direction with his hand out, yelling:

"Pass it over, pass it over, come on, come on."

Tossing it to him he grabs it like we are in a relay race. Good thing he is taking the kerchief because I am running out of steam. Stopping to take a rest I see Donna who catches up to Mike Tomato and grabs him by the hair, pulling it as hard as she can. Mike is screaming from the pain but the stupid idiot won't let go of her kerchief! After a minute or two he finally throws the kerchief at her and is running for his life again!

Reno the Greek is running by me once more and throws Ginger's kerchief at me and I take off because I don't want Ginger to grab my hair and rip it out of my head the way Donna did to Mike Tomato. The girls are really pissed so I throw the kerchief over my head and it flies right into Ginger's face. I won't stop to look at her, I'll just run as fast as I can. I stop running after a half block, turn and see the girls holding their kerchiefs and bending over with one hand on each knee, trying to catch their breath. The guys come up to me and I suggest breathlessly:

"Let's... let's get the Hell out of here fast. When the girls catch their breath, they will come after us and kick our ass!"

I know that we are no match for two pissed-off teenage girls in a fight. We walk to Columbia Street to Defonte's Sandwich Shop and buy a couple of bags of potato chips and the new lemon soda called 7-Up to wash it down. We are all sitting together on the curb.

"Where the Hell were you when the girls were chasing us Nunzio?"

"Are you kidding? When I saw those crazy girls with fire in their eyes chasing you guys I found a quiet spot away from the action to watch the Kerchief War and I laughed my ass off! The best part was when Donna caught up with Mike Tomato and tried to rip the hair out of his head! Sorry, Mike, but it was funny watching you scream and yell in pain when she grabbed you by your hair. But the best part was seeing you hold on to the kerchief while Donna was dragging you around the street by your hair. Why didn't you just let go or throw the kerchief at her?"

Nobody is saying a word, as we all look at Mike Tomato wearing a stupid look on his face and we are all laughing at the same time. This is it, we can't stop laughing, and even Mike is cracking up.

Chapter 72

Brownie Camera-Coke Machine-Ice Cone

Frances & Pepino Picture From
Her New Brownie Camera

The kerchief war we had with the girls was really something. It was fun for most of us but it wasn't that much fun for Mike Tomato when Donna caught up to him. Donna was crazy mad when she grabbed Mike's hair and pulled it as hard as she could. She was trying to get Mike to let go of her kerchief. But the idiot kept holding on to it as Donna dragged him in the street. It was funny to look at but painful for Mike. I think Mike learned his lesson. If you steal a kerchief from a teenage girl run like Hell but don't get caught. If she does catch up to you and grabs your hair, throw the kerchief as far as you can and as fast as you can, because, if you don't let it go, she will beat the crap out of you. I'll go home leaving the guys sitting on the curb giving Mike Tomato all kinds of shit. As I'm on my way home I see little Diane, Roger the Professor's sister playing Hopscotch with her friend Judy. Diane is a cute kid and sometimes I play Teatime with her and her dolls.

There is no way my friends can find out that I play Teatime with a little girl because if they do, they will never let me forget that I play sissy tea games with little girls. My friends will laugh me off the block, but I like Diane and I play with her when she gives me a cute smile and a: "Pretty please?" Whenever Roger sees me play Diane's little fantasy game in their apartment, he laughs at me too. But, he likes his baby sister so he doesn't give me too much grief. As I pass Diane and her friend Judy she yells out to me:

"Hey, Pepino, can you play Teatime with me and Judy today?"

I'll put my head down and make believe that I don't hear her as I walk away as fast as I can. I am so hungry walking up to my apartment I think I'll have lunch. I would like to have a Spam sandwich but we didn't have any Spam and I don't think that my mother will ever buy spiced ham in a can. So, I'll make myself a tomato and olive oil sandwich for lunch and sit out on our fire escape to eat it. It's a nice cool day and it feels good to sit out here looking at all the people doing stuff down on the street below. I finished my lunch now and I'll be going out and buying myself a treat in the candy store down the block.

Suddenly, my sister Isabella pokes her head out the window.

"Hey, Pepino, Dad needs you to go to the unemployment office with him because they're having trouble understanding his

broken English. His unemployment insurance is running out. Dad doesn't want me to go with him because I'm a girl, he would rather have you translate for him."

Holy shit, another job! I'm working my ass off assembling bra straps at night for extra money and now this.

"Okay I'll go with him".

I'm kinda thirsty, it will be great to buy a soda so I can wash down the sandwich I had for lunch. As I walk into the candy store I greet Mr. Giuseppe.

"Pepino, I haven't seen you for a while. Where have you been?"

Frances New Brownie Camera Takes My Picture

I don't want to give him a long story or even talk about it.

"Around".

"What kind of candy are you looking for?"

"I don't know yet, but I would like to buy a soda first."

"Okay, you can get a Coke out our new soda machine at the end of the candy counter."

What the hell is a soda machine? Walking to the end of the counter I can see a huge red metal box that looks like a refrigerator with big painted letters that say: "Coke a Cola." It has a window so you can see the bottles of Coke in it. Taking a close look at the machine I'm finding a coin slot that looks like a public telephone with printing on it that says: "*Insert coin here.*" I'll put a quarter in the slot and press a button. I hear all kinds loud rumbling and banging sounds. WOW! There's a big boom in the opening where it says:

"*Take your soda out.*" I'll take my soda out of the machine that is ice-cold and use the cap opener attached to the machine to open my bottle of Coke. Wow! What will they ever think of next?

I'll go back to the counter, I have a question for Mr. Giuseppe.

"Mr. Giuseppe, when did you get the new Coke machine?"

"We got it three or four months ago. I like the new machine because I don't have to do a thing. The Coke Company installed it, and then the Coke truck comes by every week to collect the money in the machine. The truck driver replaces the bottles missing and locks it, giving me my share of the money he took out of the change box and leaves. Isn't that neat? You should come by more often, who knows what's next!"

"Big deal."

I'll go sit on the stoop next door to eat my candy and finish my Coke. I see my sister's girlfriend, Frances is walking by with Mary Jane. Frances is calling out to me:

"Hey, Pepino, we came around to find your sister, Isabella, do you know where she is? I want to show her my new Brownie Camera."

"No, not really, but tell me, what's a Brownie Camera?"

"See this black box I'm holding? You look through this little hole here and when you see a person you press this button and snap a picture of that person!"

"Really? You can take my picture with that black box?"

"Yeah, come over here and stand next to me. I'll give the camera to Mary Jane so she can take our picture."

Jumping off the stoop I stand next to Frances. Mary Jane is holding the black box in front of her face and orders: "Smile" making a click sound with the camera. I slide over to Mary Jane.

"Let me see the camera?"

Putting the black box in front of my face the way she does! I look through the little hole.

"Where's the picture you took? I don't see it."

Well, both Frances and Mary Jane crack up laughing. It takes them a couple of minutes to stop laughing as I stand there waiting for an answer. Frances rubs the tears off her cheeks.

"Silly, you have to wait for me to develop the film inside the camera before you can see your picture. It takes about a week for the Drug Store to develop the film and that's when you will see the pictures."

I don't understand anything she is saying and I don't want to look too stupid.

"That's great, I can't wait to see the pictures."

I walk away but I can still hear them laughing at me. I'm now standing on the corner of Hicks Street and I see Pecker and Jimmy Pizza buying a couple of ice cones from the ice cone man's little push cart.

I like to watch the ice cone man making his treats. He buys a big block of ice; scraping the ice with a special hand-held ice scraper. After the ice scraper collects the ice chips he tilts the scraper and puts the ice chips into a paper cup. Then you choose the flavor syrup you like on your ice chips. That the hardest part for me, do I want cherry or orange, or peach, or coconut, vanilla, or any of the twelve other flavors lined up next to his block of ice. My mouth is watering for an ice cone but I am out of money buying a soda and treats in the candy store. Walking up to Pecker and Jimmy Pizza, we all are sitting on the curb together. As they are eating their ice cones, I will tell them all about the Brownie camera and the new soda machine at the candy store. I have decided to ask them if they are all ready for

Ice Cone Man Makes A Cool Treat With Shaved Ice

Halloween because it's only two days away! I think that Halloween is the best holiday of the season. There are a bunch of games we play with the girls before it gets dark. We get treats to eat, but the best part about Halloween is the sock wars and pranks after dark.

Jimmy Pizza tells me that Mike Tomato put aside a load of rotten tomatoes, bananas, and oranges he collected from his grandfather's wagon. Yesterday Mr. Pauli gave Mike a Bunch of potato sacks for us to make spooky Halloween costumes. We laugh as we think about the pranks we pulled last year and we're hoping that we can top them this year. We'll just have to wait and see.

Chapter 73
Halloween Bingo-Apple Dunk-Ouija Board

I've been waiting months for Halloween and finally, the big day is here! I'm so happy that Halloween falls on a Saturday this year, this way school doesn't get in the way of our fun and games. We have a whole day to play games and then our gang will dress up like ghosts or vampires and go 'Trick or Treat' around the neighbohood. All my friends are looking forward to Halloween. It's the only time we can be bad without getting into too much trouble with our parents. The real fun starts late at night when it gets dark and we play pranks on the neighbors who've busted our balls all year long. We will get crazy and have chalk, flour socks, rotten fruit, eggs and vegetable wars. It's still kind of early so I'll wait a while before I ring Joanie's doorbell to see if they're ready to play some Halloween games. Every year Joanie's, Mom, Mrs. Tina, sets up Halloween games and treats for the neighborhood kids. Mrs. Tina is so nice and I hope and pray that Joanie's Dad is not home this year.

If I'm lucky her Dad will be out breaking somebody's legs. Mr. Bruno scares me to death, with his muscles popping out all over the place showing off his killer tattoos. I can't wait, so I'm leaving my apartment and walking over to Joanie's house across the street to get there about eleven AM. I'll walk over to her front door and ring her doorbell, I hear footsteps behind the door, as it opens, Joanie greets me.

"Pepino, you're early, nobody is here yet!"

Now I'm hearing Mrs. Tina yell out:

"DON'T LET HIM GO! Pepino can help us decorate the room for the Halloween games."

So, Joanie is stepping aside and letting me in. As I enter the room I see all kinds of Halloween stuff stacked on the dining room table. Mrs. Tina puts me to work: first, I have to blow up a bunch of orange and black balloons, then climb up the ladder to tape the black and orange paper streamers all-around the room close to the ceiling. I am finished with the streamers and will climb the ladder again to tape the orange and black balloons close to the streamers that I just taped near the ceiling. I am looking down from the ladder and I see Joanie's Mom is putting

Halloween tablecloths on the dining room table.

She is spreading out about ten Bingo cards with a photo of a pumpkin in the center. Next, to each card, she is putting a small bowl of candy corn. I guess the candy corn is there so we can mark the numbers called on our Bingo card when Joanie calls out the Bingo numbers.

Mrs. Tina is now coming out of the kitchen with a big tray of homemade Halloween butter cookies and placing the tray in the center of the table. Wow, these cookies look and smell so good; I can't wait to eat a few. She is also adding two large pumpkins with carved out Jack-o-Lantern faces on each side of the cookie tray. I'll climb down from the ladder and step back to look at the room. The Halloween decorations look beautiful; Mrs. Tina really knows how to make the room come together for a Halloween party. Everything is in place and the doorbell is starting to ring over and over again. Now we have six girls and four boys in the house looking for a place to sit. Joanie is yelling out:

"Okay, sit down, we're going to play Bingo first! I will call out the numbers. Whoever gets Bingo first wins the game and they can take a Halloween butter cookie from the plate, then we will start a new game."

Looking around the table I see Joanie, Jennie, and Frances with her big brown eyes and beautiful long brown hair pulled back into a ponytail, but I don't know the other three girls. The guys I know, Jimmy Pizza, Mike Tomato and creepy Six Finger Ricardo Lopez.

I didn't think Ricardo is friendly with Joanie. He only lives a few doors away from her on the same side of the block. The only thing I can think of is that their Mom's may be friends and that's why he's here. He still gives me the creeps. I'm glad that he's sitting on the other side of the table. But now I'm stuck having to look at him with his creepy six fingers. To boot, his sister Maria Headlights Lopez painted his face with two extra eyes underneath his real eyes with her black makeup brush. Okay, okay, don't freak out, it's Halloween you're supposed to look weird and he does. I'll just have to look at my Bingo card instead of staring at Ricardo.

We have played Bingo for almost two hours and I've won five cookies! Boy, the homemade butter cookies are so good!

Mrs.Tina is entering the dining room.

"Okay, we're all set to play the second game. Follow me into the kitchen where I set up the apple-dunking game."

We are following her into the Kitchen and see a big laundry washbasin filled with water with a bunch of red apples floating around, set up on the kitchen floor.

"If you don't know the rules I'll tell you. You all pick a card from this deck of playing cards to see who goes first, second, third and so on. Then the first player kneels beside the washbasin and tries to bite an Apple and pull it out of the basin. Each Apple has a prize in it, you can win a dime, win a quarter or if you're really lucky you can win a fifty-cent piece. Don't be afraid to dunk your heads into the basin. I have a bunch of towels here to dry you if you get wet. Are you ready?"

Frances is pulling first-place and now I have second place. I'm worried that I will have to dunk my head after creepy Six Finger Ricardo with all his spits floating around in the water! That would be so disgusting. I would probably throw up if that ever happens.

Lucky me! Frances will dunk first and I don't care if it's her spits floating in the water because I can't take my eyes off of her. It is fun trying to fish out apples floating around in the basin. We are laughing at each other seeing ourselves sticking our heads, bobbing, and squirming deep in the water trying to snag an apple. We all look ridiculous that we can't stop laughing.

We are drying up and Mrs. Tina ushers us back into the dining room where she closes the blinds on the windows and the room gets dark, very dark. She is lighting some candles and is putting them in the Jack-o-Lanterns that are on each side of the Ouija board. It is making the room look spooky. The dining room table is clear except for the wooden board in the middle with a desk lamp shining so it will glow. It looks so spooky with the two large Jack-o-Lanterns glowing on each side of it. Mrs. Tina is explaining that the Ouija board is a game that lets us ask the ghosts in the room questions. She explains that this game started in China thousands of years ago so that the Chinese people could talk to their ancestors. Holy Smoke, now I'm really scared. Ghosts! What the Hell is this she is talking about?

"Joanie and Frances will go first because they played this game before. Now we all have to be very quiet otherwise the ghosts will not come to the table to talk to us." says Mrs. Tina.

Is she serious about this ghost stuff?

Now I'm shaking in my sneakers and I feel like I have to pee. Frances and Joanie are putting their hands together on this triangle piece of wood on the Ouija board so that it can slide to the printed "Yes" or "No" on the board. Mrs. Tina informs us that the alphabet is also printed on the board just in case the Ghosts want to spell out a word or two. We haven't even started and this game is freaking me out.

Everybody is real quiet as Joanie whispers:

"Is anybody here?"

The triangle piece of wood suddenly is starting to move slowly, then faster with Joanie and France's fingers on it! This can't be real! They just want to scare us. Now the wooden triangle is going crazy, moving faster and faster in a circle and shoots over to the printed "Yes" on the board! Everybody is moving back from the table at the same time and whispering: "Whoa!" Now, we're all scared shitless. Frances is asking:

"What is your name?"

The piece of wood is going crazy again spinning and spinning spelling out "Bill".

Who the Hell, is Bill?

We are now playing this spooky game for an hour or more. It seems that Bill is Joanie's uncle who died and told her that he was okay and not to worry because it's wonderful where he is now!

BULLSHIT!

Mrs. Tina Gave Each Of Us A Candy Apple To Take Home

I don't believe a word of it. But I can tell that most of the kids are looking scared out of their minds
because their eyes are opened so wide that it looks like their eyeballs are going to pop right out of their heads!

Now it is my turn, I'll put my fingers on the wooden triangle to ask the ghost a question. I have to do so with creepy Six Finger Ricardo. The stupid thing goes around and around and again it is like we have no control, and spells out:

"Look out for the Dead Horse!"

What in Hell is the ghost trying to tell us? I am glad that the Ouija game is ending because Mrs. Tina is giving us chocolate treats and apple cider to drink. It is late afternoon and as the Halloween party ends, Mrs. Tina gives each of us a candy apple to take home. She is such a nice lady and she is so much fun to be with. Now we all are going home to dress up in our home-made Halloween costumes and parade around the neighborhood for treats and later when it gets dark all the weirdoes will finally come out.

I get home and find my Mother sitting at the kitchen table softly crying by herself.

"Momma che cosa a fatto? (Mom, what happened?)"

She is telling me that Dad cannot get anymore unemployment insurance, The extra money for bra strap work is over and my Dad's part time work is down to one day a week. She goes on to say that she is at the end of her rope, she can't continue to borrow money from Uncle Frank, our friends and neighbors. She's desperate but can't tell Dad that she has to wire a request for money to Dad's Uncle in Rome. If Dad finds out he will be very, very upset. She asks me to go with her to the Travel Office which is a combination, bank, wire service, document notary and other services. I tell her not to worry that I will do anything she asks.

A Place Called Brooklyn-Red Hook Stories

THE SERMON OF THE BUTTONS

It is Sunday morning, bright and sunny and I am getting dressed for church. Dad was still in bed and it was time to leave for church. "Pepino, go get some money from your father for the collection."

I wake up Dad and tell him: Mommy said, give me some money for church." (I didn't have to say please when Mom ordered it) Slowly he opens his eyes and rolls over and grabs his pants from the side chair next to the bed, reaches in and gives me 2 shiny newly minted nickels.

As I head toward the kitchen from the bedroom, I pass Mom's sewing basket, and an idea hits me. For a nickel, I could buy a bottle of Pepsi, and for another nickel, I could buy a package of 5 or 6 small powdered donuts. If given powdered donuts, you could get me to do anything, say anything or lie about anything! Yes, powdered donuts were my addiction!

So quietly I go into Mom's sewing box where she kept her buttons and reasoned that if I took 2 shiny metal buttons, I could confuse Mom when they came to collect money, then afterward, I could celebrate with a Pepsi and donuts! I couldn't believe my genius had taken me so far!

The Visitation Church was a beautiful church, with marble floors and columns, stained glass windows and a large tower that sat over the back entrance. There were additional altars with many statues gracing the side aisles.

Being a large church, with a school, and about 5 priests, the ushers always dressed to the nines, and when collecting, had these long handles collection baskets made of what looked like wicker.

Mom and I sat, she in deep meditation and prayer, and me deep into whether or not I could scale the grotto wall behind the main altar. Suddenly I noticed the ushers with the collection baskets and reached for my first button. As the basket slid under my nose, I slipped in the first of the shiny buttons. Mom deposited her money, and went back into her prayers (probably for my soul) and said nothing.

Ah, my plan was working!!!

Donuts for sure!

The second collection comes, and like the first, I slip in the other shiny metal button, Mom deposits her money, and once again goes into deep pray-filled pleading for my wicked soul. Oh! The joy of deep quiet celebration, knowing there were donuts soon in the horizon, glory is to God!

Mass is over and as we walk home I start to talk to Mom, but she is not answering me. I figured her maternal instincts for survival have kicked in. This goes on for a few blocks, nothing being said by Mom. We climb the steps to our second-floor apartment when I announce to Mom that I am going downstairs for a while. (Donuts on my mind)

Suddenly, I feel this grip on my shoulder and the words: "Embarrass me in church?" Whack, dragging me into the apartment. "How dare you embarrass me in the church of all places?" Whack, whack, and whack. If nothing else at this critical moment, she was certainly hitting the target!

This went on all the rest of Sunday morning, every time she saw me, "Embarrass me in church?" Whack, and more whacks. Dad kept a low profile; he didn't want to get in the way of her fury, no need to interrupt. That whole morning and early afternoon, I started to pray out of self-preservation and rescue, hoping for company to show up immediately, if not sooner.

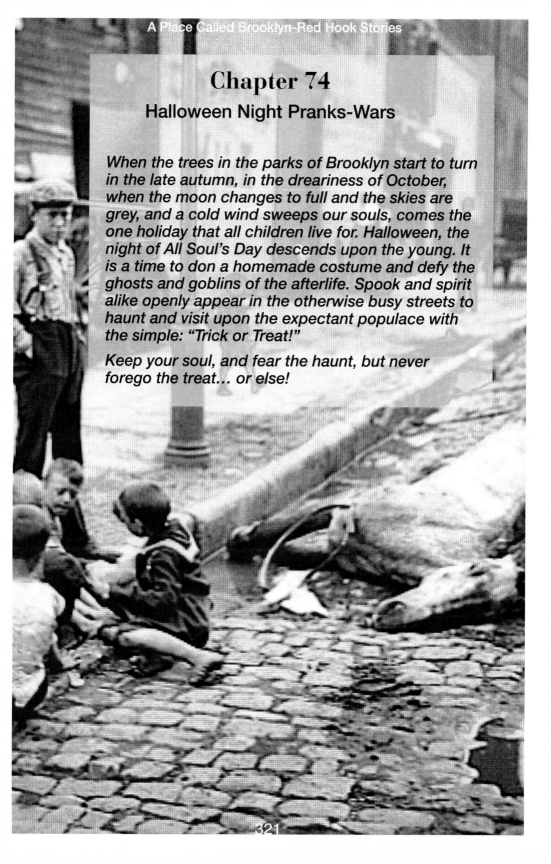

Chapter 74
Halloween Night Pranks-Wars

When the trees in the parks of Brooklyn start to turn in the late autumn, in the dreariness of October, when the moon changes to full and the skies are grey, and a cold wind sweeps our souls, comes the one holiday that all children live for. Halloween, the night of All Soul's Day descends upon the young. It is a time to don a homemade costume and defy the ghosts and goblins of the afterlife. Spook and spirit alike openly appear in the otherwise busy streets to haunt and visit upon the expectant populace with the simple: "Trick or Treat!"

Keep your soul, and fear the haunt, but never forego the treat... or else!

Uncle Bill's Ghost Tells Pepino On The Ouija Board To Look Out For The Dead Horse

We are leaving Joanie's house and I notice a bunch of kids sitting on a curb on Columbia Street looking at something. Curious, we are all walking over to see what is going on. Looking into the street we can't believe our eyes, I almost pooped my pants. We all stand there with our mouths open because we see a dead horse lying in the street. How could Joanie's dead Uncle Bill know that there's a dead horse on Columbia Street! Did Mrs. Tina play a trick on us? It can't be because I had my hand on the Ouija pointer that was spelling out the dead horse message. Could it be that creepy Six Finger Ricardo was in on it? Maybe the Chinese people who invented the Ouija Board thousands of years ago knew really how to talk to the dead. Really, really, talk to the dead? I see the dead horse but I still can't believe my own eyes. I feel like my whole world is now upside down. This is such a creepy feeling! The Hell with it, we have to get ready for trick or treat and I'm not going to think about this weird crap right now.

I'll tell my friends that I'm going home to get into my Halloween costume, and I'll meet them on Hick Street in about a half hour. I am leaving them all staring at the dead horse lying in the street.

Now that I'm at my apartment, I will tell my sister Isabel about the Ouija Board. I'm telling her about Uncle Bill and the dead horse in the street message.

"Get out, I heard about those Ouija Board stories but I don't believe them to be real!"

"Hey, I was there on the Ouija Board when Uncle Bill sent the

Neighborhood Kids Ready To Go Trick Or Treating

message about the dead horse and when I left the Halloween

party there it is, I see the dead horse lying in the street. What in the Hell do you make of that?"

"Bullshit, somebody played a whopper of a trick on you kids."

I knew she wouldn't believe me so I'll drop it. I'll get dressed, get my chalk and flour sock and go out to find my friends.

I'm on Hicks Street and I see a small group of my friends with some little kids dressed up in homemade Halloween costumes. Our little parade of trick or treat kids is starting up and down the block collecting candy, fruit, nickels, and dimes from some of their neighbors. We have to warn the little guys to be careful about eating some of the fruit or cookies they get.

"Do not eat that stuff right away because some of the people on the block are mean and they will put stuff in your goodies that can hurt you. Make sure your parents check your goodies for BB's, Razors, dirt, pepper or anything else that doesn't look right!"

It's too bad that some people can be so cruel by trying to hurt a bunch of little kids who are out just to have some fun on Halloween. Sometimes the teenagers can be cruel too. They play Halloween pranks on their neighbors that are dangerous. Then the neighbors try to get back at them. One trick they play is to hand out candy apples, then they sneak in their batch of beautiful Candied Apples, with rotten onions candied in bright red to look like the real thing. When a teenager takes a big bite out of what they think is a candied apple, they get a mouth full of an onion that tastes like rotten eggs. Mrs. Folly is not a happy person, to begin with. My mother told me that Mrs. Folly's husband died at an early age and she has been bitter ever since that happened. She keeps to herself and doesn't have any woman friends.

My Mother once pointed her finger at me and said in Italian:

"Listen, you have to respect any adult even if they're mean to you. That's the rule if you disrespect anyone for any reason and I hear about it, you will have to deal with the wooden spoon. Got that?"

Sometimes it is really hard to obey my Mother's rules. Mrs. Folly is still pissed at the neighborhood kids who shot a Spalding ball through her open window when they were playing stoopball last summer. The ball bounced all over her apartment and knocked over her prized porcelain lamp that broke into a thousand pieces.

So, Halloween is perfect for her to take revenge against the teenagers that broke her beautiful lamp many months ago. Mrs. Folly gets back at the kids with the rotten onion candy apple look alike, then the teenagers take revenge at Mrs. Folly by throwing eggs at her clean windows. There is no winner because the fight of who gets the upper hand never ends.

It is 10:00 PM and the trick or treat kids are off the block and at home checking all the goodies they collected. The teenagers and the want-to-be teenagers, nine to twelve years old, come out to play tricks and fight each other just for fun.

I see Roger the Professor walking down the block with a brown paper bag and a can of lighter fluid in his hand. His face is covered with black charcoal, wearing his sister Maria's bright red lipstick on his lips and wearing a black wool cap pushed down over his ears.

"Hey, Roger what the Hell are you up to? Are you supposed to be a ghost or something with all that black charcoal on your ugly face?"

He is laughing, his white teeth looking brighter than ever against his black face.

"Yeah, do you like my Halloween coal miner costume? About this brown paper bag, I went to Coffey Park today with a little bucket and I picked up as much fresh dog poop as I could find and I put it in this bag. Now I'm going to Mrs. Folly's house to put this bag full of dog shit on her stoop close to her front door. Then I soak the brown paper bag with this lighter fluid, strike a match, light the bag and ring her doorbell five or six times, then I run like hell. I won't run too far away, I'll just run a safe distance and find a hiding place behind some garbage cans. This way I watch Mrs. Folly stomp the burning bag when she tries to put the fire out. If my plan works, she will have dog crap all over her feet and legs. What do you think? Do you want to watch the action?"

I'll find a safe spot about six doors away so I can watch Roger do his evil deed. Sure, enough everything Roger said went as planned. All of a sudden I see flames shooting up on Mrs. Folly's stoop and fat Roger running towards me yelling:

"GET DOWN, GET DOWN!"

It takes Mrs. Folly only a couple of seconds to open the front door and start stomping on the paper bag as hard as she can with her feet. She does a good job in putting out the fire. Then we hear a loud, very loud scream.

"Ahaaaaa, what is this, SHIIIIIT??? It's all over my shoes!!! I'm going to get the son of a bitch who did this and I'll kill you, YOU LITTLE BASTARD, YOU!"

As she stomps the fire out she sits down on the stoop with two hands on her face and she keeps on saying in a low voice:

On Halloween, The Girls Love To Mark The Boys With Chalk

"I'm going to get the bastard, I'm going to get the bastard!"

Roger and I are sliding down as far as we can behind the garbage cans laughing. We are laughing so hard that tears are flowing down our cheeks.

Hearing Mrs. Folly crying and sobbing and sobbing, it is like she can't stop. I look at Roger with his coal miner costume and black face and say:

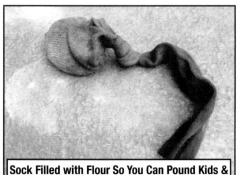

Sock Filled with Flour So You Can Pound Kids & Cover Them In White Flour. Spooky…

"Roger, I don't like Mrs. Folly but that was a mean trick you played on her.

That poor lady is falling apart. Now I have to go to confession and apologize to God for not stopping you and for laughing at Mrs. Folly. When I confess my sins to Father Ryan I think he will order me to say fifty 'Hail

Mary's' and fifty 'Our Father's' and then he will kick me around the block for being so mean."

"Pepino, don't be such a Pussy; it's only a Halloween prank."

"Oh Yeah, if this prank was pulled on your mother I don't think you would be laughing. You would search for the bastard who did it and then you would kick his ass."

We watch Mrs. Folly get up, turn and walk back into her house still crying. Okay, that wasn't as much fun as I thought it would be. I'll leave Roger who is still crouched down behind the garbage cans and look for my friends. It is almost midnight and I hook up with my friends Pecker, Reno the Greek, Nunzio Superman, Blackface Henry, Jimmy Pizza, Mike Tomato, Prospector Frank and a bunch of other kids I don't know. Their clothes are all marked up with color chalk, mostly from the girls who chased the boys and marked them for fun. This happens every Halloween and I think the boys like the idea of the girls running after them.

The girls marked them up good this year because most of the guys are wearing all kinds of crazy colors. Now we have to choose sides for our Halloween war games. We have our flour socks ready and the rotten tomatoes, fruit, and potatoes that Mike Tomato saved from his grandfather's vegetable wagon.

Now it starts, and we are whipping each other with socks filled with flour, and that really hurts and we are starting to look like ghosts with all that white powder flying all over the place. The rotten tomatoes and potatoes are flying everywhere! It is a great battle and it doesn't matter whose team you're on because we just hit anyone who is close to us.

The war is finally over and we all smell like rotten fish looking like a bunch of Zombies. Our faces, clothes, arms, sneakers, and hair are covered with white flour mixed in with rotten produce all over our bodies, what a sight! We are sitting on the curb looking and laughing at each other. It is a perfect Halloween holiday and now we can look forward to cold weather, snow, and Christmas…

Chapter 75

PS 27 Supply Room-Rope Flying Game

Vicks Vapo Rub Is My Mothers Cure-All Medicine

This year's Halloween wars are the best ever. I got home at midnight with all this crap on me and my mother can't believe it's me walking in the door. She has that 'What the Hell did you do!' look on her face. The white flour is all over me mixed in with eggs, rotten tomatoes and vegetables. I smell pretty bad too from the battle sweat and rotten produce stuck to my body. Mom isn't saying a word, she just points to the laundry basin. That is a signal for me to wash off all that stuff stuck with me. I'll keep quiet for fear that she may go for the wooden spoon and give me a few more, black and blues. But I don't care, I had so much fun banging my friends with the flour sock and smashing rotten produce in their faces! It is all worth it!

After I take off my clothes I'll sit in the tub to let the water splash all over me. My mother doesn't like the cleanup job I am doing so she jumps into action with a bar of Octagon Soap in her hand. My mother is scrubbing my head so hard

Apartment Laundry & Bath Tub

I think my hair is going to fall out! She now thinks I am clean enough and is picking up my dirty clothes and dumping them in the trash. Now that I am cleaned up I'll put on a new pair of underwear and get ready for bed. I am so sleepy but I don't feel good. It is like I am coming down with a cold. My Mom picks up on the signs and comes towards me with a jar of Vicks Vapo Rub, her cure-all for the sniffles. She rubs a big wad of Vicks on my chest and puts some in my nose. Boy does this stuff smell!

Today is Sunday and I still feel sick so I 'm not going out. I'll spend the whole day listening to the radio and reading comic books. I miss not going out to meet my friends and trade Halloween war stories with them. I am still so sick that I put more Vicks Vapo Rub on my chest, hoping that this sick feeling will go away.

This morning is Monday morning, my energy is back and the sniffles are gone! My mother is right. The Vicks Vapo Rub did the trick! I don't know what's in it but its great stuff. So, I'll get dressed and go to school. I'm lining up in the schoolyard and run into Jimmy Pizza. He is smiling at me.

"Weren't the Halloween War Games something else? I can't get over all the crap we threw at each other. My body is so black and blue from getting beat up with those flour socks. I hurt so bad that I think that some of the guys must have put rocks or chalk in their flour sock. After we stopped beating each other we must have looked like shit. I don't care because I had a great time."

I couldn't agree more. We are laughing out of control because we are thinking how ridiculous we looked when the war games were over. We are doubled over when our assistant principal Mr. Houzer walks over and points his big fat finger and tells us to:

"Shut up or else."

We stand up and stop laughing because Mr. Houzer, who is over six-feet tall and must weigh 300 pounds, wouldn't think twice about giving us a smack or two in the head if we don't listen to him. The bell is ringing and we follow our classmates into the classroom. I'm at my desk and see Miss Kent is waving at me to come over to her. Getting up close to her she is whispering that she has a new monitor assignment for me and that she will explain everything after our lesson this morning. I say 'okay', and she goes to the blackboard, picking up a piece of chalk and starting to write our new lesson. Thanks to Miss Kent, I feel so good about myself. It all happened after she got me the Triple-A crossing guard assignment two months ago. Now I feel like somebody and my schoolwork is much better. I can't wait to hear what she wants me to do next.

It is lunchtime and Miss Kent is calling me up to the front of the classroom and asking me to follow her into the hallway. She is telling me more about my new assignment.

"Pepino, do you know where the school supply room is?"

Teacher Requested Library
Paste From The Supply Room

"Yes, it's down the basement some-where past the lunchroom."

"That's right! Your new assignment is in the school supply room. Go there and report to Miss Alana who runs the supply room for an hour during everyone's lunch period. Every day each teacher sends notes down to Miss Alana asking for chalk, pencils, erasers, glue, writing paper and a bunch of other stuff. Your job is to put together what the teachers need and deliver it to their classrooms as fast as possible. Do you understand what I'm asking you to do?"

"Yes, but what do I do about eating lunch."

"Well as you're going back and forth to the supply room you will pass through the lunch room. After you make a couple of trips, stop in the lunchroom and ask to see the head lunch matron, Mrs. Wells. Tell her that I sent you and ask her to give you a sandwich, milk, and cookies for your lunch break. Since you're working for the school you don't have to pay anything for your lunch. But you have to eat as fast as you can because you have to hustle back to the stock room to deliver more orders. Is that okay with you?"

I don't want to look too excited.

"Yes, I would be happy to help out whenever I can. Thank you for thinking of me."

I'll leave Miss Kent in the hallway and run as fast as I can to the supply room down in the basement. I have only an hour to de-liver the supplies, eat lunch and get back to my classroom for our afternoon lessons. I'm there but don't know why for some reason I like the way the supply room smells. It makes me feel so special to work with the teachers and I get a free lunch to boot. I Love You Miss Kent. Before I know it, the school bell is ringing and it is time for me to report to my crossing guard as-signment.

I cross the little kids for about fifteen minutes and head home.

I am walking home on Columbia Street, and at the corner near Defonte's Sandwich Shoppe. Looking across the street I can see Joanie and Jenny playing with a rope tied to a lamppost. It must be a new game because I've never seen them do this before. The rope is about fifteen feet long and it's tied about halfway up the lampost. Joanie is holding the end of the rope with both hands as tight as she can and standing far away from the lamppost as possible. I don't think that they're playing jump rope because Joanie is holding so tight that the rope is straight out like a clothesline. She is taking off and running as fast as she can from the lamppost. She reaches a top speed and is leaping into the air, and the force of her speed is launching her six feet into the air and now she is flying around and around while she's holding onto the rope. Wow, she's a lot stronger than I thought she is, she's actually flying. Joanie and Jenny can't stop laughing as they are taking turns flying like a bird.

I'm watching them and I can't help thinking about when the Superman movie starts and they yell out "Is it a bird? Is it a plane?

Joanie & Jenny Playing The Flying Rope Game

No, it's Superman or maybe I should say Supergirl!" Joanie and Jenny flying around the lamppost and now run out of energy. They stopped because they are out of breath and sitting down on Joanie's stoop to rest.

"Wow, I can't believe you are flying so high! I think you look like Supergirl! Who told you about this game? Do you tie the rope yourself or does somebody help you?"

Joanie is looking up at me and catching her breath.

"My Dad told me about this game. He took a long rope and tied it about halfway up the lamppost for me. Then he showed me how to run and fly like Dorothy in the *Wizard of Oz* movie. It was his idea of how to do it but he warned me to be careful because I could get some bad rope burns on my hands playing this game. That's why Jenny and I called it quits. My hands are killing me!"

"I give you and Jenny a lot of credit. I don't think that I could fly that high the way you did." Joanie is smiling at me.

"Thanks, I'm glad you stopped by because I was going to call you. My Dad gave me a new card game called Old Maid and I was going to ask you to play this new game with me today. But I can't play cards now because these rope burns on my hands hurt so bad. I know you don't like to play games but just think about it."

"Sure, I'll give it a shot when your hands are feeling better, I'll see you later!"

I've decided to go home and do my homework.

As I'm walking into our apartment my Mom says "Venia con me alle banco". So, I follow my mother to the International Banco Italiano on the corner of Union & Columbia Streets. Walking into the place I can't believe my eyes. The place is big, very big. There are tellers in the back section and up front I see rows and rows of fancy desks with men dressed beautifully in suits and ties. There are large photos of passenger ships mounted on every wall. The sound of six teletypes are pounding away with women collecting and sending messages. All the women I notice, working here have very small desks with type-writers and telephones mounted on them. There's all kinds of action going on around me, sounds of telephones ringing and people yelling back and forth trying to get attention. Wow, this is it, when I grow up this is the type of work I want to do. As it turns out, my mother doesn't need me here to translate her request because most if not all the people work here speak three or four languages. She is done and we walk home together.

Chapter 76

Thanksgiving Food-Old Maid-Juke Box

It's the third week of November and Halloween seems so long ago. Now everyone is looking forward to the Thanksgiving Holiday. All the Kids love this holiday because they have four days in a row off from school. The adults love this holiday too because of all the food they get to eat and spending time with all their family and friends for a big celebration. Thanksgiving is almost a week away and our mothers are working hard putting all the special food together for the holiday. I got home from school the other day I found the hallway in our building full of tomato crates lined up on our staircase with barely enough room to walk by. I counted forty crates loaded with fresh Plum Tomatoes.

I squeezed by the crates and walking up the stairs to my apartment I could smell the aroma of tomato sauce and basil cooking. At my door, I see my mother and her lady-friends peeling and crushing tomatoes as fast as they can. There are pots of boiling tomato sauce on every burner of our gas

Forty Crates Of Plum Tomatoes Stacked Up In The Hallway

stove. Some of the ladies were scooping up the hot tomato sauce and putting it into glass Ball canning jars and empty 16oz. soda bottles that look alike for storage. The ladies were sealing the jars with a glass lid and rubber gasket. They also filled bottles with sauce using a funnel. They sat me at a little table because my job was to cap the bottles that they are filling with tomato sauce. As the filled bottles were coming to me I put crown metal caps on the mouths of the bottles, putting the bottles under a capper and pressed down on the handle as hard as I could. The downward pressure from the capper forced the metal crown cap to crimp and seal around the opening of the glass bottles.

I put the sealed jars the ladies filled with tomato sauce and the bottles I sealed into an old wooden Pepsi soda crate on the floor next to me. I did this again and again until the wooden crate was filled and ready to be stored in the wine cellar.

I love the smell of tomato sauce. When there was a break in the action, I usually took a piece of Italian bread and dipped it into the hot fresh tomato sauce cooking on the stove. Wow, does that taste good! But there wasn't much time to dip and eat because another batch of jars full of tomato sauce were ready to be capped. This assembly line went on and on for hours until all the crates were gone from the hallway and we cooked and sealed the hundreds of jars of tomato sauce that are now in the

Fresh Tomato Sauce, Canned In Ball Jars for Storage

wine cellar for storage. It was hard work but this way our families will have homemade tomato sauce and homemade pasta they can cook for the holiday or anytime they need it.

When all the wooden crates were out of the way, the ladies cleaned the kitchen and all the dirty pots and pans. My mother told me to sweep the hallway and the staircase and clean up all the wood chips that have broken off from the wooden tomato crates. She handed me a bucket full of soapy hot water, brush and mop to scrub the staircase and mop the hallway. It's a dirty job but my mother wanted to make sure that the hallway was clean for the other tenants who live in our building. After scrubbing each step and mopping the hallway clean my sister Isabella pulled me aside and talked to me in a whisper: "Good news, Dad's Uncle Tomaso Monteleone, sent money to Mom's account at the International Banco Italiano. You can't repeat what I'm about to tell you, I mean it, you can never tell anyone especially Dad. Mom asked Doctoro Monteleone for three hundred dollars which will help Mom pay part of the five hundred in debts we owe and leave us a little money for the Christmas holidays until Dad gets on his feet. You know what, he sent Mom two thousand dollars instead with a message saying. "This gift is for the Love of my family". What a man he is. He always is and always will be MY hero! I love him so much. I'll tell you more about him later.

"My head is spinning from what my sister just said. My parents never had so much money at one time. One way or another I think my Dad will know what my Mom did, but I don't think he will ask her any questions about where the money came from. I finally sat by the radio in the dark and listened to the creepy stories broadcast of *Mystery Theater*. I don't know why I do this because some of the *Mystery Theater* stories scare the shit out of me. I'm scared out of my mind, so I will get into my cot, put the blanket over my head and try to fall asleep.

Today, home from school I notice the clean soapy smell in the hallway from my scrubbing each step and mopping the hallway. Walking into our apartment I see the ladies back at work making pasta. I have to be careful where I put my school books down because every surface in our apartment is covered with drying pasta. There's pasta drying on our chairs, trunk, beds, it's everywhere! I can't believe that these women can mix flour with water, knead the dough, roll it out and form little pasta caps with a butter knife that they call 'Orecchiette' in Italian meaning:

"Earlobes." I have to get out of here before I make a mistake and smash some of the little pasta caps that are drying all over the place. If I do smash some of these little caps, the ladies will smash me, for sure.

Making Little Cap Pasta By Hand & Set To Dry

I'll put my books underneath my mother's bed and go downstairs to see whom I can find. Walking out of the building I'm remembering now that Joanie wants me to play her new, Old

Maid card game with her. So, I'll walk across the street and knock on her door. Her mother Tina is opening the door so I'll ask her if Joanie is home.

"Hi Pepino, yes, Joanie is home, she's in the dining room finishing her homework. Come in, come in."

"Hi Joanie, I came over to see if you want to play that new Old Maid card game you told me about? My apartment is full of drying pasta and I can't do any homework until the ladies are finished drying and packing the pasta in paper bags for storage. That can take another hour or two. I hope you don't mind my coming over."

"No, don't be silly, I finished my homework and it would be great to show you how to play Old Maid."

I'm sitting at the table across from Joanie as she is taking out a deck of cards called Old Maid explaining how to play the game.

"Okay, the whole purpose of the game is not to get stuck holding the Old Maid card at the end of the game. Because if you do get stuck, you lose, then we start a new game. It's better to play this game with three or four kids but it's okay to play with two people. I will deal out all fifty-one cards of the deck. I will get twenty-five cards and you will get twenty-six cards. Now we will look at our hands and try to match up as many pairs as we can and lay them down in front of us face up. Okay, now I have to pick a card from your hand. Don't show me your cards.

After I pick a card from your hand I will match it to one of the cards I'm holding to make a pair and put it down in front of me. You do the same when it's your turn. Since you started out with twenty-six cards I know that you're holding the Old Maid card. If by chance I pick the Old Maid card out of your hand I will put it in my hand and shuffle my cards so that you don't see where I put it. Because when it's your turn to pick a card I will try to give the Old Maid card back to you. After we pair up all the cards one of us will get stuck holding the Old Maid card and that means you lose the game! Then it's your turn to shuffle all the cards and deal them out as I did. Do you have any questions?"

"No"

We are to playing the game. I think Joanie has x-ray vision

because she has won every one of the six games we played. I give up and leave her to find my friends. Walking up to Columbia Street I see Jimmy Pizza sitting in front of his father's pizza parlor, bar, and restaurant.

"Hey, Jimmy, What's up? Everybody is at my house canning tomato sauce and now they're making pasta for the Thanksgiving Holiday. I just had to get out of there. What's new with you?"

He is laughing.

"Yeah, it's like the entire neighborhood has gone crazy making food for the holiday. My mother and her friends are making these little mini meatballs for the chicken soup that everybody loves to eat around Thanksgiving. They're making all kinds of cookies too. Our kitchen is like a disaster hit it. If I didn't leave they would put me to work and that's why I'm sitting out here."

He is getting up and turning while waving at me to follow him into his father's pizza parlor.

"Come with me, I want to show you my father's new Juke Box."

"What the Hell is a Juke Box?"

"You'll see, just come back here with me."

We are walking by the tables and chairs towards the back of the restaurant and I'm seeing this beautiful thing about the size of a refrigerator all lit up with colorful lights. Jimmy is walking up to it while turning and facing me.

"This is a Juke Box! Look into it and you will see sixty records all lined up. Here is a list of all the songs you can play next to these buttons. You put a nickel into this coin slot, you find the song you want to play on the list and push the button next to it and like magic, the machine pulls the record you selected and plays that song for you. Isn't that neat?"

I'm leaving the restaurant shaking my head.

"Holy shit what, WILL they think of next?"

Chapter 77
Thanksgiving-Parade-Pee Wee-Kite Flying

"Uncle Tomaso is a genius, he is so smart that he was sponsored at sixteen-years-old to attend a University in Rome. Over the years he earned three degrees, in Science, Math, and Literature. He became a professor at the University, he also made investments that grew and grew. The last big project he completed was to build the first Macy style department store in Rome, called CIM, with escalators. Everything he touched turned to gold, but he never forgot where he came from. He also paid for my education in Italy before we left for America. I can go on and on about his accomplishments but the most important part of the story is that he is always there to help his family in a crisis. That is why we can be very thankful this Thanksgiving. God Bless Uncle Tomaso."

Finally, Thanksgiving Day is here. Mom got me up very early this morning because she wants to get my cot out of our living room so that she can set up a dining area for the big Thanksgiving celebration. My sister tells me we will have twenty people coming to our apartment for a sit-down dinner. I am looking around the room and can see that it's going to be a tight fit to get all these people around our dining room table. I'm telling my sister that it's impossible to get all these people to fit around our table.

"Don't be silly, our neighbors will bring a couple of folding tables and extra chairs. All the kids will eat at the kid's table in the kitchen. We will manage to get everyone in here somehow."

I'm starting to laugh thinking...

"Yeah, bullshit, I can't see how they're going to pull this off."

"The Thanksgiving feast won't start until late this afternoon so you have to get out of our way. Just go and hang out with some of your friends until we're ready to eat."

Black Jack Licorice Gum Is Hard To Find

"OKAY! OKAY! I'm going. Don't push me."

Even though it is early I hate to leave because our apartment smells so good from all the cooking and baking. Thanks to Uncle Tomaso, I've never seen so much food. I'll put on my jacket and take a hike.

As I'm going over to call Jimmy Pizza I find he is sitting on his stoop. I think he is sitting in the cold because his mother must have thrown him out, too!

"Hey, Jimmy, what's up?"

"I'm sitting out here because there's too much cooking going on in our apartment. My father told me not to go too far because

Thanksgiving Is Not Just About Eating Turkey

he's baking twelve big turkeys in our pizza oven and when they're done I have to help him deliver the turkeys to our neighbors. He told me that they should be done in about another five to six hours, so I have to sit here freezing my ass off until he calls me. Here, have a piece of gum. It'll help you warm up a little."

"Thanks, I love the taste of licorice in Black Jack Gum. Where did you get it? It's not that easy to find it in our Candy Store, they always run out of it so fast."

Jimmy opens his mouth and I can see and smell the black licorice gum he is chewing.

"You're not going to believe it; I got six packs when I went Trick or Treating with the kids on Halloween. I only have two packs left and when I run out I'll have to go hunting for more."

"Wow, that's great! it's a lot better than the shit candy I got on Halloween. Your father won't be looking for hours, let's go over to Mike Tomato's house to kill some time."

Jimmy gets up from the stoop and we are walking to Hicks Street to find Mike. We get to 'Chickie's' grocery store and find Mike sitting in the back room listening to the radio with his brother Vinnie. At least it is warm in here. Mike sees us coming in and says:

"Hey guys, come over here, we're listening to the broadcast of the Macy's Thanksgiving Day Parade in Manhattan. My Mom saved the Daily News newspaper with all the photos of last year's parade, look at these pictures of the crowds and floats! I wish we could go see it on Thanksgiving. It sounds like all the kids are having a great time. At least we can listen to the crowds cheering and the bands marching and playing their music on the radio here. But I still wish we were there."

We are all sitting in the little kitchen in the back of the store listening to the radio announcer tell us what is going on and he's describing all the different floats that are going by. He is so good at it that I can picture what the floats look like in my head. I always remember people talking about the big Thanksgiving Day Parade in Manhattan but I never heard it broadcast live on the radio. It's a treat to be here with Mike Tomato listening to the radio broadcast of the parade, it's so exciting! We are all sitting around the radio, without saying a word, and it's been over an hour. I never thought that Thanksgiving could be so much fun until now.

The parade is coming to an end, we are all pulling back from the radio and Jimmy Pizza observes:

"Last week my sister took me to the Clinton Theater to see the Babes in Toyland movie. Have any of you guys seen it yet?"

Nobody is saying a word.

"It's a really fun movie to watch. The story is about Santa's, six-foot tall toy soldiers fighting the boggymen in Toyland. Laurel and Hardy are so funny, and I think that one of the best parts of the movie was seeing Laurel whack his pee wee with a stick. It reminded me when we didn't have a ball to play stickball with last summer. One of the guys came up with the idea of shaving two points on an eight-inch long stick. Then, putting the stick on the ground and hitting one of the points with a longer stick so that the eight-inch stick would fly up into the air. The batter has to hit the little stick as hard as he can towards the guys playing in the field. If one of the players catches the little stick it's his turn to be the batter. If nobody catches the stick, one of the players can field the little stick, pick it up, and slide it on the asphalt to the bat on the ground that was put there by the batter. When the little stick hits the bat and flies into the air the batter has to try to catch it. If he doesn't catch it, the player who threw the little stick at the bat will now get a turn to be the batter. It's like playing stickball without a ball. I couldn't

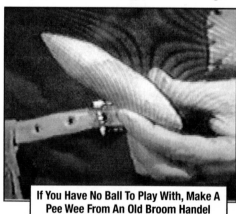

If You Have No Ball To Play With, Make A Pee Wee From An Old Broom Handel

believe it when I was watching the March of The Wooden Soldiers movie and I see Laurel hitting his pee wee the same way.
All I can say is you should go see this movie, it's a blast!"

We are about to break up and leave 'Chickies' grocery store and
Nunzio Superman has arrived with something in his hand.
"Hey, Nunzio, you just missed a broadcast of Macy's
Thanksgiving Day Parade. What the Hell are you holding?"

"My Mom and Dad threw me out of the house and said here, go
fly a kite for a couple of hours. So here I am with this kite in my
hand and I don't have any idea of how to put it together. Does
anybody here know how to assemble this thing?"

Vinnie jumps up.

"Yeah, I do. I had one about a year ago. Let me have it, it's not
that hard to assemble."

Nunzio is giving Vinnie the kite as we are all sitting around the
kitchen table watching Vinnie assemble Nunzio's new kite.
Vinnie finishes and is holding it up so we all can look at it. It's
beautiful; it's printed with a picture of Superman on the front of it
with a long white tail at the bottom.

"Let me have it, let me have it!"

Nunzio is taking the kite away from Vinnie.

"How do I make this thing fly?"

"HA! It's not that easy! Let's go outside and I'll show you how."

Standing outside the store Vinnie instructs us.

"First you hold the Kite as high as you can in one hand and the
string reel in the other hand. Then you run as fast as you can.
You let go of the kite and roll out the string from the reel slowly
while you're still running, that's when the wind will launch your
kite. The more you keep feeding the rope, the higher the kite will
fly. You have to be careful because flying a kite in the street is
dangerous. For one thing, a car or a truck can hit you. The
problem is that you're looking at the kite and you're not looking
at where you're going. The second and most important danger
are those electric lines up there because the kite can get hung
up on one of those lines. That's when you can say goodbye to
your kite. If you keep pulling on the rope to release your kite you

341

pull down a power line and get electrocuted. That's when you can say goodbye, World!"

Nunzio is looking at Vinnie with this dumb look on his face. I think that Nunzio is not ready to run and launch his kite after hearing the goodbye World warning.

"The best place to fly this kite is in Coffey Park because your kite may get hung up in a tree but you don't have to worry about getting hit by a car or truck and the power lines."

It doesn't look like Nunzio is ready to run out into the street to fly a kite! He's deciding to go home to store his assembled kite for a launch on another day. Jimmy Pizza is leaving to help his father deliver the cooked turkeys, and I will go home too because I'm ready to stuff my face with all the good food at our Thanksgiving Day feast!

I'm home and its' still kind of early, with my sister Isabella sitting in the kitchen alone.

"Hey, Sis, it's so quiet here, where's Mom?"

"Can you believe it, she went to Marietta's house to pick up a bunch of home-made Ravioli and Dad went along with her. I think we'll be eating leftovers all week long. Sit with me and I'll tell you about Dad's Uncle Tomaso Monteleone who lives in Rome. Tomaso is our grandmother, Isabella's, (who lives in Mola De Bari,) brother. It's a long story but I'll shorten it because Mom and Dad could return at any moment.

Uncle Tomaso is a genius, he is so smart that he was sponsored at sixteen-years-old to attend a University in Rome. Over the years he earned three degrees, in Science, Math, and Literature. He became a professor at the University, he also made investments that grew and grew. The last big project he completed was to build the first Macy style department store in Rome, called CIM, with escalators. Everything he touched turned to gold, but he never forgot where he came from. He also paid for my education in Italy before we left for America. I can go on and on about his accomplishments but the most important part of the story is that he is always there to help his family in a crisis. That is why we can be very thankful this Thanksgiving. God Bless Uncle Tomaso."

Chapter 78

Blizzard of '48-Selling Trees-Snow Fights

It's a week before Christmas and all the kids in our neighborhood are excited about the holiday. We're sitting in our classroom doing our best to keep up with our lessons but everyone is day-dreaming about the greatest holiday of the year. We can't wait to see all the colorful lights, decorations, Christmas trees and most of all the gifts.

Monster Blizzard Dumps Over Two Feet Of Snow On Brooklyn

We are back to our classroom after lunch-break and I notice that something strange is going on. Miss Kent and the other teachers are in the hallway for a long time talking. I don't know what's going on but it can't be good. Miss Kent has come back into the room with a weird look on her face. She's sitting down at her desk now and isn't saying anything. She just looks at the class and waits. All the students are mumbling to each other trying to figure out what the Hell is going on. All of a sudden Mr. Houzer, the assistant principal sticks his fat head into our door-way and says to Miss Kent:

"Okay, It's a go!"

Suddenly, she gets up from her desk and saying:

"Attention please, we are going to have an early dismissal today. We didn't plan for it but we just got word that there is a monster snow blizzard heading our way. Please put on your coats, gather all your belongings and line up."

Now there's a loud commotion in the classroom. Everyone is talking at the same time. A lot of the kids are scared. Some kids can't believe that we getting out early. The rest of the class is just screaming and yelling because they're so happy that we are going to have a snow blizzard. At this point, Miss Kent is doing her best to control the class so that we will have an orderly dis-missal. As we are lining up, I take a look out the classroom window and see snowflakes falling. "Wow! This thing is starting already!" I'm getting my stuff together and getting in line with the rest of the class.

Exiting the main entrance, I can feel the cold wind on my face and the snow blowing around like crazy. I'm putting my head down and plowing through the snow on my way home. The cold wind is pushing me back and making it very hard to walk. It is taking fifteen minutes for me to get to my apartment building when it normally takes me only five minutes.

The wind is so strong I can barely open the front door to my building. I've managed to finally step inside and I'm stomping my feet while taking off my coat to get all the snow off. I'm in our apartment and my sister and my Mom are having coffee at the kitchen table. They both have a big smile on their face.

Roger Waiting For Delivery Of Eighty Trees To Sell

"Okay, what's so funny?"

My sister chimes in and says,

"Well, Mom and I are just sitting here having a little celebration because our prayers have been answered. First, we had so much help from Uncle Frank, our friends, and neighbors when Dad was out of work. Second, was the generous money gift Uncle Tomaso set to bail us out of a desperate situation. Now we just got news that Dad's ship came in and his contractor guaranteed Dad a minimum of four months of work on this job. We are so thankful because we know that none of this would have been possible without God's help. Our family is truly Blessed."

I didn't know what to say, I'm just looking at them crying. I'm trying to calm down and my sister is saying,

"Wow, good thing they let you out early from school! It looks like this snowstorm is going to break records! But just in case we need some extra food, here are two dollars, go down to Nicks and buy two quarts of milk and some American bread so we have something to hold us over."

I take the money, put on my coat, and I go downstairs to

DeFonte's to buy milk and bread. As I go out our building's entrance, the wind and snow are hitting me like somebody is throwing sand in my face. Nick's door is only ten feet away and it is taking me forever to get to it! Walking into the store I can see that almost all the milk and bread is gone. I will manage to get one quart of milk and two loaves of Italian bread. I drop off the milk and bread in our apartment and go upstairs to find Roger the Professor.

I find Roger in his bedroom/laboratory/workshop, looking out his window. As I walk in Roger is excited.

"Do you believe this shit? I'm waiting for a delivery of eighty Christmas trees from a farm in upstate New York and this snowstorm will screw up my timing. It's only two weeks till Christmas. I have to get the tree delivery, make a stand to hold them up for display and sell all of them by Christmas Eve. Who the hell ordered this blizzard to come now?"

"OH! You're selling Christmas trees? You never told me! Can I help you sell them? How much money can I make?"

"HAHA! Okay, I can use the help. I'll give you a dollar for every tree you sell. Do you agree?"

"Hell yeah, if I sell twenty trees that's twenty bucks in my own pocket, right?"

"You're pretty good at math, yes, that will come out to twenty dollars. But don't spend the money so fast: you haven't sold a tree yet! You haven't spent six to eight hours at night in the freezing cold trying to sell these trees and when you do, you may just give up and quit."

"Hey! I'm strong, I can do it! I can do it! Please, give me a shot. Twenty bucks is a lot of money to me!"

"Okay big head, you're in, but you better not screw me and quit, when it gets tough out there."

Shaking hands, Roger is telling me that he will call me when the Christmas trees are delivered.

Now I'm thinking of all the money I'm going to make selling trees with Roger when it gets dark, plus the money I'll make shoveling snow for my neighbors in the daylight before I report to Roger's tree stand for work.

I am home now and watching the falling snow and listening to the wind howling from my apartment window. It is supposed to snow all night and tomorrow too. Wow! I've never seen so much snow on the ground; it has to be at least two feet or more by now!

I wake up from a deep sleep and realize there's no school today because of all the snow yesterday and today. So, I'm

Pepino is Shoveling Snow To Make Extra Money

going down to our cellar to find an old shovel I can use to clean off the sidewalks on my block for the neighbors who are willing to pay me a little cash. Two of our neighbors say that they will give me two dollars each to move the snow from their sidewalk into the street. I agree and go to work. It is taking me an hour to do a little square. I'm not moving the snow fast enough and it will take me all day to do these sidewalks for two bucks each. I think that my neighbors put one over on me. So, I'll ring their doorbells and tell them there's no way I will shovel two and a half feet of snow off their sidewalks for two bucks. They look out at the snow and agree to double the money and we have a deal! It's still hard work but that's eight bucks for a half day's work, not bad!

I am cleaning the snow off the sidewalk and the sun is coming out so I'm going to stop shoveling to rest. Looking up the block I can see a bunch of my friends shoveling like crazy too. Even though all these kids are out here looking to make extra money, I think we will be shoveling snow for the next two or three days. No one I talk to has ever seen so much snow on the streets at one time. The adults tell me that this storm is one for the ages. I hope I can keep it up and make money from shoveling this shit and be strong enough to sell trees with Roger. The snowstorm is so bad that our school closed for three days and they don't plan to reopen until after the weekend. This is great because I'm thinking that now I have five days to make a ton of money just before Christmas. I have been shoveling snow for two days and I am giving up. My little body cannot keep up and I am running out of steam.

I am now walking home and turning the corner onto Columbia Street and I see my sister cleaning off a parked car!

"Hey, Sis, why are you cleaning the snow off that car?"

"This is my boyfriend's car!"
"You have a boyfriend? When did this happen?"

Pepino's Sister Is Cleaning Off Her New Boyfriend's Car

"It's a long story. Frances introduced me to this cute guy named Johnny and we became friends. Please don't you go telling Mom. Okay?"

"Holy shit, I can't believe it, my sister has a boyfriend!"

Roger seems to appear out of nowhere and he is telling me to meet him on Saturday in front of the food market on Union Street to sell Christmas trees. This will give me a day to rest up before I meet him. I count my money; I got a total of eighteen dollars for shoveling this crap for two days. That's a lot of money for a nine-year-old kid to make but I hope that it doesn't snow like this for another hundred years or more.

It's Saturday and I meet Roger and we sell ten trees. Roger sold seven trees and I sold three. Roger is a better salesman than I am. He can throw the bullshit better than anyone I know. The problem for me is that when an adult picks out a tree and I give a price, the customer says: "No, no, much too high!" and that's when I freeze. Roger sees that, and comes over and closes the deal. So, he makes the sale and doesn't pay me a buck. I think I'm going to be working for him for next to nothing. Crap, I never learn, he always does that to me. I'm locked in now and I will see it through. I don't think I'll see the twenty bucks I thought I could make when I made this deal with Roger.

It's Monday and school has reopened. After school, it will be time to play in the snow with my friends before I report to Roger to sell trees. We are having some great snowball fights; the sleigh rides are great too! My favorite snow ride is the car tire tube ride down the steps. We tied two ropes on either end of the

347

tire so that we could hold on to it. If you're not careful you can fall off and break your neck. Once you start flying down the steps there's no stopping. You sit on the air-filled tire tube and bounce and fly down the steps without knowing where you are going to land. Wow, what a ride!

It may take weeks for this snow to melt away. The adults and teenagers are getting into the fun too, now! They are building snow igloos that look like castles the little kids can play in. Some women like to build snowmen and dress them up in old clothes. It's a winter wonderland and everyone is out enjoying the fun, except for the teenagers who build a fort and load it with snow-balls. When a trolley, truck or car comes by their fort, they all bombard it with snowballs. They're always looking for trouble and you know what, sometimes they find it. When they piss off a truck driver he gets out of the truck to chase after the teenagers who hit him. If he catches one of them he kicks and smacks the Hell out of him. But they never learn because they just keep doing the same stupid thing over and over again!

Chapter 79
Christmas Eve-Wish Book-Fish Feast

If your family hails from certain parts of Italy, as an Italian American, you understand the most important and cherished day of the year is Christmas Eve. It is a day despite Christmas Day, carries all the memories, joys, and traditions, traditions that are steep in culture and religion. It is a day to avoid meats and instead, feast on the sea, the delights that so many Italian Americans crave. It is the day of the seven hills of Rome, thus the seven fishes? Maybe.

It is only one day, waited for 364 days a year. It is Christmas Eve, that special time that defines who Italian Americans are and where they originate. It is the day that is spent laughing, eating and drinking wine, and enjoying the company of family and friends. But most of all it is a time to celebrate life.

It seems to be most magical when entering Mom's or Nana's kitchen, smelling the fish sauce made from lobster or crab, the different fish dishes assembled, and all the contributions the guest may bring. Family commitments sometimes take one or two of them away, but funny how in spite of that, they seem to be present! The table set is waiting for not the diners, but the spir-ited revelers, the joy of La Famiglia! Glasses and bottles like Christmas lights on a tree, decorate the table!

Someday, this tradition may die away for many. No longer for whatever reason, will it be celebrated as it once was but the memories will linger on?

Sears Wish Book Is A Beautiful Way To Dream About The Toys You Want

The Blizzard of '48 has stopped Brooklyn in its tracks, literally closing the 9th Street subway station! Schools and churches are closed now for days. No trolleys, cars or trucks can move either. School is finally reopened and kids can-not stop talking about the snowstorm. We trade war stories about the snowball fights we had and the extra money we made shoveling snow. Our parents and teachers tell us that we may never see a blizzard like this one as long as we live!

A lot of snow melted but it didn't make a dent in all the snow we shoveled into the streets. Coffey Park looks untouched because there was no reason to move the snow there. When I walk there to see what is going on I see that somebody made a snowman sitting on the park bench. The darn thing looks real. It is hard to get around but I think that everybody had a great time. Roger the Professor set up the Christmas tree stand on Union Street and we are working our asses off for ten days now, selling these trees night after night in the freezing cold weather.

The Snow Blizzard Of 48 Was So Bad Cars, Trucks, & Trolleys Could Not Move For Days

I'm not making twenty bucks like I thought I would, selling trees but I do pretty well anyway. I make a total of twelve bucks. I am a little-pissed off because I feel that Roger screwed me out of at least five bucks! With all the money I made shoveling snow plus the twelve bucks Roger gave me it's still a good payday for me.

Christmas Eve is a couple of days away and we are just about finished selling all the Christmas trees. There are three trees left on the stand when Roger comes up to me and says:

"Hey, Pepino, Thanks for not bailing out. It was tough work standing out here in the cold and snow every night selling these trees but you didn't quit on me. You did a great job and I want you to take one of these trees home with you tonight for Christmas."

I stand there looking at him for several minutes. I am frozen and it isn't because of the freezing cold.

"Thanks, Roger, my Mom would love to have one of these beautiful trees for Christmas. She's not going to believe it when she sees me walk in the door tonight dragging this beautiful tree into our apartment. She is going to be blown away. Thanks Roger for this gift, I'll never forget it."

"Ha! Cut the crap shithead. Don't get all mushy on me and you better not cry either. Merry Christmas."

He is right because I am about to cry. I start walking home with my beautiful Christmas tree. I cannot believe that Roger is being so nice to me! It's not like him; he's always trying to screw me over, what the Hell got into him? Maybe his brain is frozen and when he wakes up tomorrow he'll come to his senses. I'm so happy about the crazy thing he did. I don't care what made him do it. I'll drag the Christmas tree up to our apartment on the second floor, and knock on my door so that somebody can open it for me.

As she is opening the door my sister is remarking:

"Why are you knocking? Can't you just open the door?"

That's when she gets a good look at the tree.

"Wow, where did you get this thing? It's beautiful!"

She finally opens the door all the way so I can drag the tree into our dining room. The dining room is the biggest room in our apartment. It's the only place that we can set up a Christmas tree. My mother isn't home from shopping yet, but boy will she be surprised. I hope that my Mom is as happy about the tree as my sister is.

"Wow, Pepino, this is some tree! I'm so happy that we have a Christmas tree this year! I'll help you decorate it. I'll buy some lights and tinsel from the Five and Dime store today. You know that Christmas is a couple of days away, so I brought home a Sears Wish Book for you. This way you can look at and wish for some of the toys that you want Santa to bring you this Christmas. Watch out, it's heavy!"

I take the Sears book from her. Wow, it's about the size of a telephone book. The cover of the book has a color photo of Santa; I think that in this picture, Santa is supposed to be writing a list of kids who were good or bad this year. It's like when our parents tell us if we're bad, Santa is bringing us coal this year, so we better be good! Ha, more bullshit!

Inside The Sears Wish Book, I Found A Perfect Photo Of A Christmas House

Opening the book, I turn to the toy section and I see a page of a beautiful color photo showing a perfect Christmas tree in a room with toys sitting in a bookcase. My guess is that this photo was taken in a house where rich people live because in our old neighborhood in Brooklyn nobody has a room that looks like this. This wish book has got to have a thousand pages in it. I love it; this book has everything in it for adults and kids to wish for. But this Santa thing my sister is talking about is bullshit. The only Santa I know is my mother and father. I don't think that they have enough money to buy me anything I pick out and put on my Sears wish list.

But it's fun to look at all the toys and stuff that Sears has in this book. At least I can dream about getting some of this stuff for Christmas. Thanking my sister for the book I help her set up our tree into a corner of our dining room. My sister has gone out to purchase a couple of light sets and a box of tinsel. We put the lights and some tinsel on the tree, and realize that it needs some more decorations on it!

I remember now that Roger gave me about fifty labels to mark the price on each tree that we were selling. I stuffed the extra labels in my pocket. I tell my sister that I have I bunch of labels that we can color with crayons and put on the tree to give it more color. We do that and ya know, now that we are finished, it looks beautiful!

In the next couple of days, I have to help my mother get ready for Christmas Eve. Most of the fun we have together is during Christmas Eve. You can't eat meat on Christmas Eve so my mom and her friends cook all kinds of fish and calzones stuffed with different types of cheese. Then they make a ton of cookies and they buy wonderful pastries for dessert. The adults drink homemade wine, Italian cordials, and espresso. Then we go to midnight mass at Saint Stephen's Church and eat again when we come home. We play bingo or cards for pennies, laugh, eat, drink and have fun for most of the night. A lot of the kids fall asleep, but the adults keep going as long as they can. It's like they don't want the celebration to ever end. It's the best time of the year for our family and friends. The only thing I don't like is when I go shopping with my mother for the stinky fish. We go to the fish market on Union Street to look for clams, squid, octopus, oysters, sea urchins, shrimp, and live lobsters and sometimes she even buys live eels. All the fish is very expensive. My Mom and her friends save up all year long to buy the most expensive fish for Christmas Eve. They even spend hours cleaning and preparing the fish we eat either raw or cook it in a bunch of different ways.

I don't eat everything they make for Christmas Eve dinner. For one thing, the eels give me the creeps. When I look at them is a tank filled with water they slither all over the place like snakes. I hate snakes and I don't have the courage to eat one. My family and a lot of their friends like to eat eel fried up in a batter but they still look like snakes to me, yuck.

When I talk to my friends about the different fish we eat they think I'm crazy. They say:

"Yeah, shithead, you can't eat eel but then you eat raw sea urchin."

They're right because most people can't bring themselves to eat a raw slimy orange-pink sea urchin. I like the ocean flavor of the sea urchin with lemon on it. Most of my friends like the four-inch cut pieces of fried eel better because it tastes like chicken. It doesn't matter because when we sneak a drink of homemade wine with our fish dinner everything tastes the same. All of a sudden I hear f ootsteps in the hallway. My sister calls out to me from the kitchen.

"I think I hear Mom coming up the steps. Let's be quiet and surprise her when she comes in."

"Okay!"

We are both sitting down at our kitchen table as Mom is walking in the door loaded down with three shopping bags of food for the Christmas holiday. She is lifting the bags as high as she can and plopping them down on the kitchen table. She looks at my sister then turns and looks at me. She knows that something's up be-cause I never sit in the kitchen with my sister unless we're having a family dinner. At this point, my sister and I crack up laughing and my mother joins in too. She looks a little confused because she has no idea what we're laughing about. We get up from the table at the same time and hug my mother and we start to push her into the dining room. She's still laughing until she spots the decorated Christmas tree with the lights glowing. We're still holding her as she is sitting down but she never takes her eyes off the beautiful Christmas tree, lit up and decorated with colorful labels. Her face is now almost solemn, her eyes fixed as she tightens her grip on us. The three of us sit together in the same chair looking at the tree. My mother starts to cry tears of joy while she is rocking us, entwined in disbelief and joy. I am so happy that our surprise made our mother happy too!

Chapter 80

Christmas Day-New Year-Tree Bonfires

It's 7:00 AM and today is Christmas Day! I will see what gifts Santa (Hahaha) put under the tree for me. I was up so late last night celebrating Christmas Eve I can't keep my eyes open this morning. I can't remember anything after I got home from midnight Mass. I must have fallen asleep because all I can remember is the noise in the background of people laughing, yelling and just having fun. Santa must have come to our house to put presents under the tree while I was sound asleep, funny how I don't remember seeing or hearing him.

I think I'm the only one awake this morning! That's good news. This way I can check all the presents and try to figure out which ones are from my Sears wish booklist. The rule in our house is that we can't open any gifts until everyone is awake. So, I'll just have to use my X-ray vision to see through the Christmas wrapping paper to know what's in the

Pepino Is Waiting For His Family To Wake Up So He Can Open His Gifts

package. If that doesn't work I go to plan "B", feeling the box and shaking it a little. Oh well, I'm doing everything I can and still don't know what's in the gift boxes.

It's not easy being the first one awake; I'll just have to wait for everyone to wake up. I can help to move things along by making a little noise, too. Nothing is working for me so I'm going to sit on the floor looking at our beautiful Christmas tree and wait and wait some more.

It's now after nine in the morning and I think I hear my mother moving. She is walking out of the bedroom, giving me a smile and walking into the kitchen to make coffee. I'm thinking to myself:

"Ma, come on Ma, I can't wait any longer. You're taking forever to make coffee!"

I see my sister and father coming into the room. Sitting on chairs next to me, they are waiting for my mother to join us. Its nine-thirty and I'm ready to jump out of my skin if we don't open our gifts soon. Mom comes out of the kitchen, NOW everyone's here! My sister is assigned the job of reading the names on each gift and passing them out. I got four gift boxes and it's taking me all of three minutes to open them. I'm not looking at anyone else because I'm not interested in what they got for Christmas. Now I sit back to see how I did this year. Let's see; a chemistry set, a View-Master, an erector set and the greatest prize of all… a set of Lionel Trains! Wow! I must have been really good this year; it looks like I didn't make Santa's shit list.

My Mom and Dad are looking at me this whole time, smiling, seeing how happy I am with all my gifts. Getting up, and hugging and kissing them I know how hard it is for them to put the money together for these expensive gifts they bought me for Christmas. I'll put aside the chemistry set and the erector set because I will need Roger the Professor to help me and teach me how to use them. I know how to use the View-Master and will put it aside too. Now I can work on assembling the greatest prize of all, my new Lionel Train set. It is taking me well over an hour to read the instructions to put the train tracks around our beautiful Christmas tree. Everything is now hooked up and I place the train engine and four cars on the train tracks. I give it power and there it goes, chugging along around the Christmas tree! I got to be the happiest kid in the world seeing the train running and hearing its whistleblowing. It's not just the stuff I got for Christmas that's making me happy; it's' knowing how much my family loves me. What a feeling! Mom is back in the kitchen once again to make another meal for friends coming over for dinner this afternoon. At this point I realize that all the food and gifts would not have been possible if our rich Uncle Tomaso Monteleone in Rome didn't come to our rescue this year. My sister Isabella is right, he is our hero. We can never thank him enough for his loving support for our family.

My sister is helping Mom clean and prepare the Chestnuts. Cutting a 'cross' on each chestnut top, I ask her why she does that.

"Pepino, each cross is from when I worried about you this year!"

Mom is putting meat into the oven and she starts frying her wine dough balls for dessert. I love her dough balls that she calls Struffoli. After she fries them and they cool off, she melts sugar with butter and pours it all over the Struffoli, then she puts honey and rainbow sprinkles on them. They not only look good, they taste great and it's hard to stop eating them. Next thing I know Roger the Professor is standing over me looking at the stuff I just got!

"Wow! You did good this year. You are one lucky kid!"

Before I can say anything, he adds:

"Yeah, yeah, don't worry, I'll work with you on the erector set and the chemistry set. I see that you put those extra price labels to good use in decorating the Christmas tree. I was wondering where they all went."

He wishes my parents a Merry Christmas and leaves. With all the shit Roger gives me I can't get mad at him because he's like a big brother to me. I'll stop playing with my train set so I can get dressed to go out to see how my friends made out for Christmas.

I Love My Mom's Fried Dough Balls Or Struffoli As They Are Called In Italian. You Can't Stop Eating Them

The neighborhood is like a ghost town, all the stores are closed for the holiday and the kids must be all indoors playing with their new stuff.

I'll go visit Jimmy Pizza since his family is coming over to my house later for Christmas dinner. I'll walk over to his building and knock on his door.

No one is answering! I'll knock again, this time harder. I'm hearing people moving around in his apartment. The door is opening a crack and it's Rosie, Jimmy's Mom, she looks at me surprised.

"Huh! Pepino, what time is it? We're just getting up. Please wait out in the hall for a few minutes for us to get dressed. Okay?"

She shuts the door and I'm thinking to myself:

"Whoa, I didn't think that anybody would be sleeping this late!"

A couple of minutes have passed and now the door opens again and this time its Jimmy who says:

"What the HELL, are you doing here? How late is it? Okay... you're here, come in, come in."

I am sitting near the Christmas tree with Jimmy. His little brother Tommy just stands there on his scooter looking up at the tree. The poor kid doesn't know what to make of all the gifts that are under the tree. Jimmy is calling out to him:

"Hey, Tommy, look at what Santa brought you!"

Jimmy's Little Brother Tommy Just Stands There Looking At The Tree

It's not taking long for him to get the message. Now everyone in Jimmy's family is coming in and starting to tear the Christmas paper off the presents. Jimmy got a new pair of roller skates, a record player and the greatest prize of all; he got a Red Ryder BB Gun!!!

Jimmy is out of his mind seeing a BB gun. He never thought he could ever get one for Christmas. Whoa, I think I got great gifts, but a BB gun, how can you top that? We'll talk for a while and I'll wish his parents a Merry Christmas and go home.

I'm home and my mom and sister are cooking up a storm. Everybody is starting to come over and the dinner table is already full of food. Wow! Everything looks so good. It's such a happy time of the year! Merry Christmas!

It's been a few days since Christmas and we are now playing with our new toys. Roger helps me put together a crane with my erector set. Roger is so smart; I'm learning a lot of things from him. School is out but our time off is melting away. There is still a lot of snow on the ground from the Great Blizzard of '48 and our gang is enjoying every minute of it.

Since it is after Christmas, some people are starting to put their Christmas trees out on the sidewalk. We'll collect the dry trees and pile them in the vacant lot on Columbia Street. We're hoping to get fifty trees together for the big New Year celebration. We don't have much time because the New Year celebration is here at midnight tonight! Our gang is combing the neighborhood to find as many trees as possible. We're all

Brooklyn Christmas Tree Bonfire New Year Celebration

excited because at midnight we get our noisemakers, pots, and pans together and stand ready to make as much noise as we can. We're all waiting and listening for the radio announcer to yell out "HAPPY NEW YEAR!" and everybody; adults, kids, grandparents, friends and whomever to start screaming and celebrating the New Year.

"WELCOME 1949!"

We've been banging away for fifteen minutes or more now. Someone is giving us the signal to form a circle around the big pile of dried up trees we put in the vacant lot on Columbia Street. Suddenly the countdown is beginning:

"FIVE... FOUR... THREE... TWO... ONE!"

A man is running over and is putting a torch into the base of the trees and you can hear a big whoosh and a firestorm explosion! The trees are so dry and burning so fast that it's going to be over in about ten seconds. WOW! What a sight! There is nothing like this. You get a rush of energy from just looking at it.

Another year has gone by and Pepino is growing up so much he feels and looks older.

THE END!

Shakespeare once wrote that 'All the World's a stage', and so a young boy must perform acts in his life while learning on that stage. Forging his own tools, in his own way he paves the road leading to discovery and experience. A young man grows from those acts, challenges, and experiences that stay with him along the way, as well as those imposed upon him. In the end, the man reflects upon all he learned and faced in each act of his life, spent only on that same stage.

Love, Pepino

EPILOGUE

It is in the genetic makeup of each of us to seek out an education, apart from the structured world of schools and "schooling".

Pepino got his formal education on the streets of Brooklyn, among his peers and from more fundamentally his family and heritage. In the course of just 6 months, he learned that life beyond the confines of his apartment was most important to him. What makes the World tick? Who matters in our lives and when does it matter? Is there a God?

It is the wise, hopeful, and respectful cultivation of learning on the streets of Red Hook, undertaken in the belief that all should have a chance to share in the life that Pepino got his education from, one that guided him through the rigidity of school and church. It involved all of life's lessons, the good and bad, the realization that as the World can shatter around us we can still seek out the answers to the truths that occupy our hearts and minds.

In six short months of life at the age of 9, Pepino made new friends, experienced success learned the lessons of dedication and hard work and more importantly, that work was more than labor, it was an identity.

And what does it teach us as readers? That life holds all the ugliness and sadness without discrimination for a young child, yet life does glorify and reward. His Dad's loss of work and his Mom's sacrifice to feed her children, his parent's need to translate from the inferiority complex visited upon immigrants who didn't speak the language, all made his fabric woven, his threads each a moment in his life that woven together is Pepino, well educated and schooled.

A PLACE CALLED BROOKLYN is more than a story of a young boy, it is a historic reference to life in 1948, a glimpse into life that today still stands relevant to America's immigrants seeking their place in America.

A Place Called Brooklyn-Red Hook Stories

Photo Credits

Back Cover - from Explore Brooklyn Neighborhood site (explorebk.com)

Chapter 1 - Three men standing, Cornacchiulo Family Photo, Dock Workers, Public Domain Photo

Chapter 2 - Mom calling out at window, Public Domain
- Cargo Hook, Public Domain

Chapter 3 - Hot DogVender, Amazon/Artnet

Chapter 4 - Fire Escape, Cooling Off, Old NY Photos

Chapter 6 - Defonte's Sandwich Shop, Cornacchiulo Family Photo

Chapter 7- Penny Jar Game, Cornacchiulo Family Photo
- Pea Shooter Supplies, Cornacchiulo Family Photo

Chapter 8 - Pitching Pennies Game, Cornacchiulo Family Photo

Chapter 9 - Roof Top Pigeon Coop, Public Domain

Chapter 10 - DeNobili Cigars Photos, Cornacchiulo Family Photo

Chapter 11 - PS 27 School, Cornacchiulo Family Photo
- Watermelon - Cornacchiulo Family Photo

Chapter 12 - Kids Licking Ice, Retro Snapshots
- Johnny Pump Water Spout, 1971 DailyMail.com

Chapter 13 - Kids Playing Buck-Buck, Arthur Leipzig (Flo Peters Gallery)

Chapter 14 - Fireworks Show, Public Domain Photo
- Baseball Card Bubble Gum, Public Domain Photo

Chapter 15 - Egg Cream Soda, Public Domain Photo

Chapter 16 - The Lone Ranger, Wikipedia

Chapter 17 - Carpet Gun, Cornacchiulo Family Photo

Chapter 18 - Hopscotch Game, Saint Ann's Well Road photo-1970
- Carpet Rifle Shooter, Cornacchiulo family photo

Chapter 19 - Red & Black Army Flags, Cornacchiulo Family Photo

Chapter 20 - Charlotte Russe, Public Domain- Lost Foods of NYC

Chapter 21 - Vintage Roller Skate, Cornacchiulo Family Photo

Chapter 22 - Homemade Street Scooter, Cornacchiulo Family Photo

Chapter 23 - High Bouncer Ball, Cornacchiulo Family Photo
- Brooklyn Stoop, Cornacchiulo Family Photo

Chapter 24 - Coney Island Postcard, Amazon
- Coney Island Subway, NYC Subway Museum Archives
- Smith & 9th Street Sign, Cornacchiulo Family Photo

Chapter 25 -
- Street Stickball Game, NYC Parks & Recreation Photo

- Jacks Game, Cornacchiulo Family Photo

Chapter 26 - Radio Stories, Public Domain Photo - Wooden Tops, Cornacchiulo family photo

Chapter 27 - Sugar Wax Juice Bottles, Cornacchiulo Family Photo - Candy Store, Public Domain Photo

Chapter 29 - Coffey Park, Cornacchiulo Family Photo
- Coffey Park Swings, Public Domain Photo

Chapter 30 - Danny Defonte, Cornacchiulo Family Photo
- Defonte's Sandwich Shop, Cornacchiulo Family Photo - Children Playing Marbles, WorldGallery.co.uk.

Chapter 31 - Manhattan Special and Sandwiches, Public Domain Photo

Chapter 32 - Borden Frostick, Public Domain Photo.

Chapter 33 - Matinee Clinton Theater, Public Domain Photo
- Good & Plenty Candy, Cornacchiulo Family Photo

Chapter 34 - Mola DeBari Festival Photo, Molesi Club Web Site

Chapter 35 - Open Air Market, Public Domain Photo
- Live Market, Public Domain Photo

Chapter 37 - Visitation Church, Cornacchiulo Family Photo
- WW I Soldier Statue, Cornacchiulo Family Photo

Chapter 38 - Saint Stephens Church, Public Domain Photo
- Flattened Pennies, Cornacchiulo Family Photo

Chapter 39 - Girls Jump Rope, Source Art.com.

Chapter 40 - Hand Made GoCart, Source Artpictures.com

Chapter 41 - Mock Motor Bike, Cornacchiulo Family Photo

Chapter 42, Old Baby Carriage, Del Broccolo Family Photo.
- Chess Set, Cornacchiulo Family Photo

Chapter 43 - St. Stephens Church, Public Domain Photo
- Handball, Public Domain Photo
- Street Festival Music Procession, - Mola Di Bari Brooklyn Street Procession, Molesi Club Web Site

Chapter 44 -
- Visitation Church, Cornacchiulo Family Photo Zepole Dough Balls, Public Domain Photo.

Chapter 46 - Merry Go Round, Public Domain Photo
- Church with Fireworks, DelGraphics photo

Chapter 47 - Pepino & Sister, Cornacchiulo Family Photo
- PS 27 Grammar School, Cornacchiulo Family Photo
- Bamboo Finger Locks, Public Domain Photo

Chapter 48 - Ebbets Field Photo, Amazon

- Daisy BB BB Gun, Cornacchiulo Family Photo
- Jackie Robinson Photo, Amazon

Chapter 49 - Kid Eating Chicken Feet, Public Domain Photo
- Dr. Watson & Sherlock Illustration, Public Domain Photo.

Chapter 50 - Pimple Ball & High Bounce Cornacchiulo Family Photo
- Finger Rubber Pistol, Cornacchiulo Family Photo
- Battery Tunnel Construction, Public Domain Photo

Chapter 51 - Prospect Park Entrance, Amazon
- Balsa Wood Airplane, Cornacchiulo Family Photo

Chapter 52 - Monkey Photo, Public Domain Photo
- String Game, Public Domain Photo
- Wine Press, Cornacchiulo Family Photo Italian Men Playing Bocce Ball, City of N.Y. Parks & Recreation.

Chapter 53 - Italian Grappa Bottle, Cornacchiulo Family Photo
- 78rpm Records & Record Player, Public Domain Photo

Chapter 54 - Hershey Chocolate Bar, Cornacchiulo Family Photo
- King of the Mountain Photo, Helen Levitt.

Chapter 55 - Francesco Photo, Cornacchiulo Family Photo

Chapter 56 - Telephone Both, Public Domain Photo
- Good & Plenty Box, Cornacchiulo Family Photo
- Christopher Columbus, Public Domain Photo

Chapter 57 - Smith 9th Street, Cornacchiulo Family Photo
- Coney Island D Subway, NYCSubway.org
- Black Plague Drawing, Public Domain Photo

Chapter 58 - Immigrants, Public Domain Photo
- Sister Mary Catherine, Public Domain Photo

Chapter 59 - Horn & Hardart, View Master, Public Domain Photo

Chapter 60 - Nunzio New Television, Public Domain Photo
- Rocket Take Off, Public Domain Photo
- Brooklyn Bread, Cornacchiulo Family Photo

Chapter 61 - Shoes on a Wire, Wikipedia
- Little Girls, Public Domain Photo

Chapter 62 - Zip Gun Material, Cornacchiulo Family Photo - Drive-In Movie Speaker, Public Domain Photo - Drive-In Movie, Public Domain Photo

Chapter 63 - Typha (Punks) Plant, Public Domaine Photo
- Woolworth Store, Public Domain Photo

footnote: Many public domain photos listed were rarefied on Google

Many of the photos used in this book are for illustrative purposes only, depicting a fair representation of events, times, and places. Many photos represent true representations of people, places and things as they were.

A PLACE CALLED
BROOKLYN

Brooklyn is a land of many things: imagination, creativity, and leadership. Over the years the Brooklyn neighborhoods have yielded impressive personalities that grew up in the streets and later became famous or near famous. It boasts such luminaries as Peggy Noonan, Vince Lombardi, and Mel Brooks. It knows no bound and crosses them all, in the areas of medicine and science, sports, art and literature and of course music. This list below is not complete as there are too many notable people to mention that hail from this great borough in this relatively small space. Brooklyn, above all a people place.

Woody Allen (born 1935) – film director, actor and screenwriter (Midwood)

Harriet Beecher Stowe

Joseph Bologna (1934–2017) – actor

Barbara Boxer (born 1940) – politician; U.S. Senator from California (since 1993)

Mel Brooks (born 1926) – actor, comedian, film director, film producer and screenwriter (Williamsburg)

Steve Buscemi (born 1957) – actor, film director and screenwriter

Tony Danza (born 1951) – actor

John D'Aquino (born 1958) – actor

John Henry Davis (1921-1984) U.S. weightlifter 6 time world champion and 2 time Olympic gold medalist

Larry David (born 1947) – writer, producer, actor, and comedian (Sheepshead Bay

Dom DeLuise (1933–2009) – comedian and actor

Richard Dreyfuss (born 1947) – actor

Jimmy Durante (1893–1980) – actor and comedian

Edie Falco (born 1963) –actress]

Lou Ferrigno (born 1951) – former bodybuilder, actor (Midwood)

Harvey Fierstein (born 1954) – actor and playwright (Bensonhurst)[38]

Bobby Fischer (1943–2008) – champion chess player (Flatbush)

Rudy Giuliani (born 1944) – former United States Attorney, former Mayor of New York; 2008 Republican presidential candidate

Jackie Gleason (1916–1987) – actor and comedian (Bushwick/ Bedford–Stuyvesant)

Louis Gossett, Jr. (born 1936) – Oscar-winning actor (Sheepshead Bay)

Arlo Guthrie (born 1947) – singer (Coney Island)

Buddy Hackett (1924–2003) – actor and comedian (Williamsburg)

Marvin Hamlisch (1944–2012) – Oscar-winning composer of film scores (Midwood)

Anne Hathaway (born 1982) – Oscar-winning actress

Susan Hayward (1917–1975) – Oscar-winning actress (Flatbush)

Rita Hayworth (1918–1987) – actress

Curly Howard (Jerome Lester Horwitz; 1903–1952) – comedian; member of The Three Stooges (Brownsville)

Moe Howard (Moses Harry Horwitz; 1897–1975) – comedian; leader of The Three Stooges (Brownsville)

Shemp Howard (Samuel Horwitz; 1895–1955) – comedian; member of The Three Stooges (Brownsville)

Jimmy Kimmel (born 1967) – comedian and television talk-show host

Bernard King (born 1956) – NBA Hall Of Famer (Fort Greene)

Carole King (born 1942) – singer-songwriter (Madison)

Larry King (born 1933) – television talk-show host and interviewer

Marvin Kitman (born 1929) – television critic, humorist, and author

Steve Lawrence (born 1935) – singer and actor

Vince Lombardi (1913–1970) – Pro Football Hall of Fame coach (Sheepshead Bay)

Sid Luckman (1916–1998) – NFL quarterback and Pro Football Hall of Fame

Norman Mailer (1923–2007) – author and playwright

Barry Manilow (born 1943) – singer-songwriter (Williamsburg)

Robert Merrill (1917–2004) – opera singer

Arthur Miller (1915–2005) – Pulitzer Prize-winning

Mary Tyler Moore (1936–2017) – actor

Eddie Murphy (born 1961) – actor and comedian

Peggy Noonan (born 1950) – author, columnist

Rhea Perlman (born 1948) – actress

Suzanne Pleshette (1937–2008) – actress (Brooklyn Heights

Buddy Rich (1917–1987) – drummer and big-band leader

Adam Richman – actor; host of reality-television series Man vs. Food

Joan Rivers (1933–2014) – comedian

Phil Rizzuto (1917–2007) – Major League Baseball player and broadcaster

Chris Rock (born 1965) – actor and comedian (Bedford–Stuyvesant)

Mickey Rooney (1920–2014) – five-time Oscar-nominated actor

Mike Rosen (born 1944) – radio talk show host and newspaper columnist

Carl Sagan (1934–1996) – scientist, author, educator (Bensonhurst)

Bernie Sanders (born 1941) – Independent U.S. Senator from Vermont (Madison)

Adam Sandler (born 1966) – actor and comedian

Chuck Schumer (born 1950) – U.S. Senator from New York (Flatbush)

Neil Sedaka (born 1939) – singer-songwriter

Erich Segal (1937–2010) – author Academy Award-nominated screen writer, and educator (Midwood)

Jerry Seinfeld (born 1954) – actor and comedian (Borough Park)

Bugsy Siegel (1906–1947) – gangster

Beverly Sills (1929–2007) – opera singer

Phil Silvers (1911–1985) – actor and comedian

Paul Sorvino (born 1939) – actor

Connie Stevens (born 1938) – actress and singer

Patrick Stewart - Actor

Jerry Stiller (born 1927) – actor, father of Ben Stiller

Marisa Tomei (born 1964) – Oscar-winning actress

Joe Torre (born 1940) – Major League Baseball player, New York Yankees and Los Angeles Dodgers manager, Hall of Fame (Marine Park)

John Turturro (born 1957) – actor and director

Nicholas Turturro (born 1962) – actor

Mike Tyson (born 1966) – heavyweight boxing champion

Eli Wallach (1915–2014) – actor

Walt Whitman (1819–1892) – poet, best known for Leaves of Grass; journalist and Brooklyn Eagle editor; essayist and humanist

Shelley Winters (1920–2006) – Oscar-winning actress

Henny Youngman (1906–1998) – comedian